PRAISE FOR EARLENE FOWLER'S
Benni Harper Mysteries

Arkansas Traveler

"*Arkansas Traveler* is truly multilayered. From the smell of hot sweet-potato biscuits, the autumn colors of the black gum trees, and the soulful hymns at the Foreign Missions Pie Auction, each vivid detail brings the South to life. There's much humor (the gossip is free at Beulah's Beauty Barn & Elvis Emporium) and food abounds (think moist and chewy pecan pie, thick with nuts). The author also serves up some unforgettable lines like, 'He's a walking advertisement for the benefit of vasectomies.' Always good, Fowler's writing improves with each book. Her plot here is lean and strong [and] her main characters continue to evolve in fresh, realistic ways."   —*Ventura County Star*

Seven Sisters

"Engrossing . . . a compelling story of families torn apart by divided loyalties."   —*Publishers Weekly*

"A resonant story of complex patterns and hard-earned grace."
—Jo-Ann Mapson, author of
The Wilder Sisters and *Hank & Chloe*

"May be the best of the series. . . . The emphasis on skeletons in a California family's closet echoes Ross Macdonald, while the tone and feel of the novel will remind readers of Nevada Barr."   —*Booklist*

continued . . .

ARKANSAS TRAVELER

EARLENE FOWLER

BERKLEY PRIME CRIME, NEW YORK

THE BERKLEY PUBLISHING GROUP
Published by the Penguin Group
Penguin Group (USA) Inc.
375 Hudson Street, New York, New York 10014, USA
Penguin Group (Canada), 90 Eglinton Avenue East, Suite 700, Toronto, Ontario M4P 2Y3, Canada
(a division of Pearson Penguin Canada Inc.)
Penguin Books Ltd., 80 Strand, London WC2R 0RL, England
Penguin Group Ireland, 25 St. Stephen's Green, Dublin 2, Ireland (a division of Penguin Books Ltd.)
Penguin Group (Australia), 250 Camberwell Road, Camberwell, Victoria 3124, Australia
(a division of Pearson Australia Group Pty. Ltd.)
Penguin Books India Pvt. Ltd., 11 Community Centre, Panchsheel Park, New Delhi—110 017, India
Penguin Group (NZ), 67 Apollo Drive, Mairangi Bay, Auckland 1311, New Zealand
(a division of Pearson New Zealand Ltd.)
Penguin Books (South Africa) (Pty.) Ltd., 24 Sturdee Avenue, Rosebank, Johannesburg 2196,
South Africa

Penguin Books Ltd., Registered Offices: 80 Strand, London WC2R 0RL, England

ARKANSAS TRAVELER

A Berkley Prime Crime Book / published by arrangement with the author

PRINTING HISTORY
Berkley Prime Crime hardcover edition / April 2001
Berkley Prime Crime mass-market edition / April 2002

ISBN: 978-0-425-18428-8

BERKLEY® PRIME CRIME
Berkley Prime Crime Books are published by The Berkley Publishing Group,
a division of Penguin Group (USA) Inc.,
375 Hudson Street, New York, New York 10014.
The name BERKLEY PRIME CRIME and the BERKLEY PRIME CRIME design
are trademarks belonging to Penguin Group (USA) Inc.

PRINTED IN THE UNITED STATES OF AMERICA

18 17 16 15 14 13 12 11 10 9

For Judith Palais,
Whose editorial talents
are only outweighed by her matchless
grace and kindness

and

For Deborah Schneider,
whose agenting abilities and steady good sense
are a balm and help to many

To both of you I offer
my deepest respect and affection

Many people helped me during the course of writing this book. My sincere thanks to each of them:

To you, O Lord, I lift up my soul; in you I trust, O my God. —Psalm 25:1–2

To Clare Bazley, Veronica Carrillo, Tina Davis, Karen Gray, Jo Ellen Heil, Christine Hill, Jo-Ann Mapson, Pam Munns;

And always, a huge hug of gratitude to my husband, Allen—my best friend, the love of my life, forever and ever, amen.

Not much is known about the Arkansas Traveler quilt pattern. It is a fairly old pattern, most likely dated by quilt historians through its name. "Arkansas Traveler" was a popular folk song and skit whose origin has been traced back to the middle of the nineteenth century. It is usually credited to Colonel Sanford "Sandy" Faulkner, a Little Rock plantation owner who claimed the tale was inspired by a real conversation with an Arkansas backwoodsman. The Arkansas Traveler quilt pattern is actually more than one pattern—one is a spool-like design, the other is a four-pointed star made of diamonds. The patterns have also been called Secret Drawer, Travel Star, Spools, and Cowboy Star.

1

THE BIG-CHESTED man sitting at the crowded Waffle House counter wearing the red plastic hog-head hat grinned and winked at Elvia. Her full lips, painted an eerily similar shade of crimson, shot him a frown worthy of Queen Victoria. He chuckled and whispered something to his friend, who wore not only a hog hat, but a red-and-gray sweatshirt stating, BEWARE, I HAVE HOG MANIA.

"I've had enough," Elvia said, pulling her beige cashmere cardigan closer around her. "You can take me home now."

I laughed and eagerly perused the sticky plastic menu. It had been way too long since I'd eaten a gut-busting Waffle House breakfast. When we pulled out of Little Rock's airport parking lot, my first glimpse of the towering black-and-yellow Waffle House sign caused me to cajole my friend into the restaurant's pure plastic interior. Waffle House restaurants were a Southern staple, something of a cross between a Denny's and a donut shop. I loved their unadorned, stick-to-your-ribs, grease-is-good workingman's food. Truth be told, there were cold mornings fixing fence in San Celina when

I'd trade my best broke-in Justin boots for a mess of their hash browns.

"We just landed an hour ago," I said. "Give Arkansas at least twenty-four hours before you hightail it for the hills."

"Benni, we are sitting in a restaurant, the term loosely applying, being gawked at by grown men wearing plastic pig faces on their heads. Need I say more?" She grabbed a napkin from the dispenser and irritably scrubbed at a dried egg spot on the table. "I can't believe I agreed to come with you."

"Elvia, it's October. Hog hats are a fashion statement this time of year. No one looks twice at anyone wearing one. It's football season, and they're probably still high from yesterday's triumph over 'Bama."

"What's a bama?"

"University of Alabama. The Arkansas Razorbacks kicked their Crimson Tide butts 27 to 6. The tide is ebbin', and I can't wait to lord it over Amanda." I stirred my coffee, licked my dented spoon, then pointed it at her. "Even the most sophisticated Little Rock executives wear their hog hats with pride." I didn't dare let on that her beloved Emory, of the Perry Ellis suits and Hugo Boss ties, my own dear cousin who we were about to see in the next few hours, had a deluxe, custom-made hog hat that he treasured and wore to games and football parties without an ounce of embarrassment. The eyes lit up and glowed red when he pressed a hidden button. He was the envy of all his equally fanatic Razorback friends. "Besides, you said you wanted to see Emory on his home turf before your relationship went any further. Razorback football is a *muy grande* part of his turf. But I promise it's not the *only* thing. You'll love Sugartree." I gave her a reassuring smile.

She rolled her dark brown eyes, not believing me a moment.

"Then you love Emory. That should cover a multitude of fashion sins."

Her stiff expression softened, corroborating my words. It had only been in the last month that she'd finally been able to admit she was in love with my fifth cousin, who was more like a brother to me. The day she admitted she cared for him, that their relationship had "possibilities," he burst into my office at the Josiah Sinclair Folk Art museum, where I worked as curator, and danced me around the room singing "Goin' to the Chapel . . ."

Emory had been in love with Elvia for twenty-four years, since the summer he was eleven and I was twelve. He had come to visit my family on our ranch outside San Celina on the Central Coast of California to heal from his mother's recent death. Twenty-three years later, he'd moved back out West specifically to woo and win her hand in marriage. After a year of persistence, it looked like he was finally in the homestretch. Though she didn't know it, the first month he came to San Celina he'd bought a two-carat, emerald-cut, platinum-set, blue diamond engagement ring. At thirty-six, I was finally going to be a matron of honor in my best friend's wedding. If everything went as planned, that is.

"I can't believe I let you talk me into this," she repeated, smiling this time. "But it does feel as if he's been gone for weeks, not days." For Elvia, that was as close as she was going to get to a confession of undying love and devotion to a man.

Emory had come to Sugartree three days earlier to help our great-aunt Garnet, Uncle WW, and his daddy, Boone Littleton, get ready for Sugartree Baptist Church's Homecoming festivities. Besides experiencing the beautiful state of Arkansas for the first time, Elvia was going to her first church homecoming, which is basically like a huge family reunion. Every person who's ever been a member of the church (including those who left under less than stellar circumstances . . . homecomings were supposed to be a time of all-encompassing and retroactive forgiveness) comes back and catches up with those who stayed. Homecomings usually took place about once every ten years, and this year was a particularly special one since it was celebrating the hundredth anniversary of the church.

"He's called me four times a day since he left," Elvia said, trying unsuccessfully to hide her pleased expression. Ideas for silly bridal shower games started swirling around my head.

"Men in love, they're something else." I sighed, remembering that intense time when you first discover you're in love. Gabriel Ortiz, my own very sexy, blue-eyed second husband, could still inspire that longing in me, even after two years together.

Our waitress, a Waffle House classic in black pants and maroon apron with a wide cheerful smile and champagne-blond hair sprayed as stiff as our plastic menus, sidled up to our table.

"What'll it be, girls?" she asked, gazing curiously at Elvia. There was no doubt Elvia was going to stand out in a state where the two major cultural groups were African-American and Anglo. Drop-your-jaw gorgeous and elegant as a *Town and Country* fashion ad in her cashmere sweater set and black wool pants, she was also the only dark brown skin in the cafe. From my trips as a child, I knew there were not an overwhelming number of Hispanics in Arkansas, and those who lived here tended to keep to themselves. Not for the first time did I wonder how the primarily white and black population of Sugartree was going to react to my best friend.

We gave the waitress our orders, and she yelled out, "Double order—scattered, smothered, covered, chunked, topped, diced, and peppered. And one piece of toast." She gave Elvia another curious look. "Hon, are you sure you don't want anything else? Why, that little ole piece of bread wouldn't make a maggot fat."

Elvia's upper lip twitched in horror at the woman's graphic word picture. "Thank you, no. The toast will be fine. Butter on the side, please. What type of herbal teas do you carry?"

I snickered behind my plastic menu.

The waitress's mouth twisted in a crooked smile. "I'm sorry, ma'am, all's we have is Lipton."

Elvia gave a small sigh. "All right, then, please just bring me some fresh-squeezed orange juice, low pulp. Thank you."

"Excuse me?" the waitress said, her pencil frozen over her order pad. "Is she serious?"

"As a funeral," I said, giving her an apologetic grin. "Just bring her the Lipton. And an extra plate, please. We'll share my hash browns."

"Over my dead body," Elvia said when the waitress was out of earshot. "And what was all that she yelled about your potatoes?"

"Scattered means hash browns. Smothered is onions, covered is cheese, chunked is ham, topped is chili, diced is tomatoes, and peppered is jalapeño peppers. I ordered the peppers in honor of your Mexican heritage." I grinned at her.

She grimaced back. "Do they come with a side of Tagamet? The toast will be fine."

"Emory loves Waffle Houses."

She glanced around the brown-and-orange decor, shifting uncomfortably in the molded plastic bench seat. Metal ashtrays sat proudly on every table. Practical round globe lights dangled over every booth. The air inside was so cold condensation rolled down the windows in long decorative drips in an effort to combat the often still-muggy Arkansas mid-October weather. It was standing-room-only at the counter this late-afternoon hour with men sporting watermelon-sized stomachs, gimme caps jammed on their heads advertising everything from Ozark's Best hog feed to Wal-Mart to Bubba Paul's Pulled Pork BBQ to Napa Auto Parts.

"Then let's hope they never covet the California market," she said.

Just as I'd almost finished my double order of hash browns, even convincing Elvia to take a bite or two ("You make me eat *menudo* every year," I reminded her), the hog hat men stopped briefly at our table.

"Woo Pig Soieee!" The man in the sweatshirt gave the official Razorback call. "Here you go, ladies." He tossed a red-and-white lapel button on our table.

"Go, Hogs," I replied with a smile. He touched the rim of his hog hat and dipped his head.

Elvia picked up the button, frowning at the backs of the laughing men. It said, "Hogs Smell Good."

"*¡Ay!*" She closed her eyes for a second. "I want to go home."

"It's going to be fine," I said, taking the button from her hand and pinning it on my T-shirt. "You're going to have a ball."

"*¡Ay!*" she moaned, then crossed herself and muttered a quick Hail Mary.

2

WE CLIMBED BACK into my rented Ford Explorer and started driving north. Sugartree, a small town of about five thousand or so, was an hour north of Little Rock. Late-afternoon shadows clung to the pine and black gum trees that lined the highway. Always the first trees to signal fall, the black gum leaves had already started turning a glossy deep carmine. I rolled down my window and inhaled a deep breath. It had been ten years since I'd been back to Arkansas. That trip I was twenty-six and married to Jack Harper, my childhood sweetheart and late first husband. Though the memory of driving on this road with him wasn't as painful as it might have been if I didn't have Gabe in my life, the smell of the piney woods did cause a twinge of sadness as I remembered the three weeks Jack and I had spent here. I mentally nudged that feeling away and recalled instead my earlier summers here with Dove. Some of my best childhood memories involved Sugartree, including my first kiss behind the Dairy Queen when I was twelve years old. I pressed down on the accelerator in my eagerness to see Sugartree again.

"When did Gabe say he could get away?" Elvia asked, looking pointedly at the speedometer. I eased up on the gas pedal.

"He has a meeting tomorrow with his department heads, then he's taking Scout out to the ranch and catching a ride with a friend down to L.A. He's going to spend Monday night there, then fly in Tuesday."

"When's your father coming?"

"Oh, I forgot to tell you, he's not. Arturo's the only person he trusts to watch the ranch, and he had to drive down to Mexico because his mama's sick. Daddy said it didn't matter, that he didn't have any great desire to see Arkansas again. Personally, I think he's relieved. There's a lot of memories of my mother in Sugartree." My mother died of breast cancer thirty years ago when I was six years old, and my father had never remarried, instead pouring his whole life into our cattle ranch outside San Celina. I'd been raised by him and his mother, my gramma Dove, who'd moved out from Arkansas right before my mother died.

"How long has Dove been here?"

"She and Isaac drove out about a week and a half ago. I got another frantic phone call from her last night. She and Aunt Garnet started squabbling the first day she arrived and haven't stopped. Apparently there's a ruckus going on with Sugartree Baptist Church because of talk about a merger with another church. Some people aren't happy about it. But, according to Dove, attendance has dropped drastically in the last few years with young people moving down to Little Rock or leaving Arkansas altogether. The only financial hope Sugartree Baptist has is joining with another church. The other Baptist church is also having attendance problems and is losing the lease on their building. It's going to be razed to build a motel and cafe. And, surprise, surprise—Aunt Garnet and Dove view the merger quite differently. Dove is a lifetime member, so she gets a vote, which irritates some people, specifically her sister."

"So what's the problem? Sounds like a merger is the perfect solution."

I glanced over at her. "You don't know Baptists. They are the most fiercely independent people there are. Not to mention hardheaded. Changing a Baptist's mind once it's set is like whittling steel." I gave a half-hearted laugh. "I can say that 'cause I grew up one. But that's not the real problem."

"What is?"

"To put it plain and simple, the church down the road is African-American, and that doesn't sit well with a lot of old-timers in both churches."

Her sculpted eyebrows came together in a small scowl. "Oh, come on, Benni. This is the nineties."

"And this is the South. Some white people are still annoyed they lost the Civil War or, as some of them call it, the War of Northern Aggression."

"So I imagine Cinco de Mayo is not a holiday they celebrate with great enthusiasm." Only someone who knew her as well as I did would hear the almost imperceptible catch in her voice.

I reached over and squeezed her hand. "Don't worry, *mi amiga*. Anyone who treats you with *any* disrespect will have Emory and me to contend with. And you know how creatively evil he and I can be when we put our heads together."

She pushed a strand of smooth black hair behind her ear. "I'm not worried." The apprehensive glint in her eyes said otherwise.

A flood of love and protectiveness for my friend welled up inside me. I so wanted things to work out between her and my cousin. I knew that the differences in their backgrounds were a very real obstacle, just as it was and still is for Gabe and me, but I also truly believed that love was greater than any differences, greater than any prejudice. I refused not to believe it.

"Wait'll you meet Emory's daddy," I said. "He's a character and a half. It's good you like chicken."

Boone Littleton, Emory's daddy, owned Boone's Good Eatin' Chicken, a smoked chicken and turkey business that had had its ups and downs through the years, but in the last year or so had boomed, causing the company stock to soar in value. Emory's stock and the shares he inherited from his mother were now worth a fortune. His father's chicken was famous all over Arkansas, Tennessee, and Mississippi. Even though I'd just gorged on Waffle House cuisine, my mouth watered in anticipation of one of his smoked chicken dinners with baked beans, coleslaw, corn bread, and one of his chocolate fried pies for dessert. I couldn't wait to drop by the tiny original restaurant in Sugartree.

Though she knew Emory was financially well off, I wondered if Elvia had any idea how prominent his family was in Arkansas. Glancing over at her worried expression, I thought it might be better if she didn't know. Though my friend loved nice things, she was a daughter of working-class people and therefore had almost an automatic distrust of the rich.

We pulled off the highway onto a smaller country road, passing a sign that said: SUGARTREE 5 MILES. Next to me, Elvia straightened in her seat, clasping her manicured hands tightly in her lap. I knew better than to try to comfort her again, that it would only make her more nervous, so I turned on the radio and started singing along with Dale Watson, a country singer who never received airplay in California, his music being too "country." He was obviously more appreciated by DJs in Arkansas.

"Almost there," I said, when we came to the Sugartree city limits sign. Then I literally squealed out loud and pulled a sharp left into a parking lot, causing Elvia to grab the dashboard.

"What is it?" she cried.

After parking, I turned off the ignition and pointed up

at the red-and-white grocery store sign with the Porky Pig-like cartoon character wearing a jauntily tilted military-style cap. "Piggly Wiggly," I said, resting my arms on top of the steering wheel.

Elvia groaned. "Even their grocery stores have pigs on them."

"Blue Bunny and Yarnell's ice cream," I said gleefully. "Delta Gold syrup. White Lily flour. Aunt Nellie's corn relish. Martha White cornmeal. Crowder peas! Eight flavors of grits. Eight! You can't get *that* in California."

"Eight?" she repeated, her voice weak, staring at the smiling pig on the brown bag of groceries of a passing woman.

"Emory loves the Redeye gravy and Country Ham flavor. Don't worry, they're instant. They'll be easy to fix."

My soliloquy to Ozark foods was interrupted by knocking on the car window. After seeing who it was, I squealed again and threw open the car door. "Duck? Duck Wakefield! Is that really you?"

"Benni Harper! I heard a vicious rumor you were sneakin' into town. Welcome home, Curly Top."

I jumped out and hugged the tall, rangy, fortyish man tanned a rich tawny brown. His laugh brought back the memory of muggy Arkansas summer nights filled with the scent of sweet honeysuckle, freshly mowed grass, and the taste of half-melted Dairy Queen chocolate sundaes.

"You haven't changed a bit," he said, holding me by the shoulders and looking me up and down.

"A compliment I don't believe, Duck Wakefield, but thanks anyway."

"You still eating that crappy food?"

"My blood cholesterol is 150, thank you very much. So there." I turned and motioned Elvia out of the car.

"High cholesterol's not the only reason people have heart attacks," he said, shaking a finger at me.

"You and Gabe are going to get along great," I said,

laughing. When Elvia came around the car, I said, "Elvia, this is the famous Dr. Duncan Wakefield the Third, cardiologist supreme, who, to his old swimming hole buddies like me and Emory, is referred to simply as Duck."

"That's Dr. Duck to you," he replied. He held out a sturdy hand to Elvia. "Ms. Aragon, your virtues and beauty have been widely praised by my childhood friend, the esteemed Emory Littleton. I can see he didn't exaggerate the beauty part, and I can only assume your other virtues are also not a product of his often grandiose Southern hyperbole." A white perfect smile softened his craggy features. Though not as conventionally handsome as my cousin, Duck never had any trouble getting girls with his lean outdoorsman looks and quick wit. Not to mention he was an outrageous flirt.

"Thank you," Elvia said, her normally haughty expression melting slightly under his smile. "But we all know how enthusiastic Emory can be."

"In this case," Duck said, his face solemn but his hazel eyes twinkling, "his enthusiasm was more than justified. It was required."

Elvia actually gave a small giggle. My mouth dropped open in shock. A giggle hadn't passed through those lips since the sixth grade.

I groaned out loud. "Okay, Duck, let's not pour more molasses than we need in the beans here." Secretly I was thankful he'd set my nervous friend at ease. "Have you seen Emory today?"

"For a little while this afternoon. Amen talked him into goin' with her to evening church services at Zion Baptist. He's hopin' to help her convince some of the unenthusiastic voters there that merging with the white folks' church isn't necessarily selling out to the Man."

"If anyone could convince the holdouts, it would be Emory and Amen."

"Amen?" Elvia asked.

Duck and I looked at each other and laughed.

"I guess I should have given her a rundown on the town's cast of characters on the flight out here," I said.

"*That* would have taken a flight to Australia," he replied.

"Amen Tolliver is another old friend," I told Elvia. "Emory, Duck, Amen, and I were called the Fearsome Four by our families 'cause of all the trouble we got into. Miss DeLora, Amen's grandmother, was Uncle Boone's live-in housekeeper from the time Emory's mama died when he was eleven. She practically raised Emory. Amen lived in Little Rock with her mama, but used to stay the summers with Miss DeLora." I turned back to Duck. "How is Miss DeLora? She's got to be in her eighties now."

"Boone finally talked her into retiring when she fell and cracked a femur bone trying to carry a load of laundry downstairs. She absolutely refused to allow him to send the laundry out. She's livin' about a mile outside town in that old hunting cabin of Boone's out on Mayhaw Lake. She always loved that cabin. He had the whole place rebuilt, then deeded it over to her. You know he thinks the world of Miss DeLora, would give her anything. She's still makin' quilts, I hear. Had some kind of group from Harvard or Princeton—one of those eastern schools—come film a documentary about her and what they called her African-American art quilts. You know Miss DeLora, though. She doesn't take to such fancy talk. Told them she just made blankets out of scraps, pure and simple. That J. C. Penney did, too, and sold them a heck of a lot cheaper, especially if you had a coupon. Amen said she had a grand time putting those Northerners on. She made them eat collard greens and fatback. Said some of them, the vegetarians, I guess, turned almost the color of the greens, but they choked it down so as not to insult her. They forgave her when she served them up some of her Lemon Chess pie and told them her story about cooking dinner for Mrs. Roosevelt."

"Eleanor Roosevelt?" Elvia asked.

"The one and only. Get Curly Top to tell you the story. It's a semisecret legend around here."

"She doesn't sound like she's changed one bit," I said, smiling.

"Feisty as ever and all for the churches merging. She said it's about time Christians became a little more color-blind. To quote her, ain't no soul she ever heard of got a color. Dove's been out to see her a couple of times already, I heard."

"They always did get on good," I said.

"Two peas of a pod," he agreed. "Amen's dyin' to see you. You'd best call her as soon as you get to Garnet's."

"I know it's probably obvious to you here," Elvia said, "but how does a person get a name like Amen?"

Duck and I both laughed.

"She's the last of ten children," I said. "So when she was born her mother said . . ."

"Amen," Elvia filled in, laughing, too. "I get it. My mother can relate." Elvia was the oldest of seven children and the only girl.

Duck glanced at his watch. "Well, I was supposed to just be running into the Pig real quick to get some milk, eggs, and cereal. Tiffany Anne's stayin' with me tonight, and we've already eaten Egg McMuffins two days in a row, so I thought I'd feed her at least one decent breakfast before I drop her off at school tomorrow." He glanced over at Elvia. "Tiffany Anne's my twelve-year-old daughter. She stays with me every other weekend."

"Dove told me about you and Gwenette breaking up," I said. "I'm real sorry."

He shrugged. "Happens. She left me for a podiatrist." A self-mocking grin appeared. "Lordy mama, talk about your humbling experience. A *podiatrist*."

"You medical snob," I said. "Feet need doctors, too."

"Well, I should've seen it coming when she was down

to Dillard's in Little Rock every week buyin' new shoes."

"At least he'll be having to pay for them now."

He leaned down and kissed my cheek. "That is my greatest revenge. Gwenette could spend a thousand dollars a month on shoes. See you tomorrow evening. Boone and Emory's havin' a fund-raising dinner for Amen."

"That's right. Aunt Garnet said she was running for mayor. But I haven't seen any signs."

His rugged face turned dark. "That's been a problem. Every time we put 'em out, someone messes with them. I'm afraid it's going to get uglier before the election next month."

"Didn't she pretty much expect that?" I turned and explained to Elvia. "She's the first black and the first woman to challenge Sugartree's highest political office."

"She sure did bite off a big chunk to chew," Duck said.

"Who's she running against?"

"Grady Hunter."

"Oh, geeze, that is a big bite. He's white, rich, and from an old Sugartree family," I said for Elvia's benefit. "Think she has a chance?" I asked Duck.

He gave a big sigh and shook his head. "Between you 'n' me and the Piggly Wiggly sign, I doubt it. But you know Amen, she's bound and determined to give it a shot."

"Good for her," Elvia said. "Wish I had a vote."

"Well, we can go to the dinner, contribute money and our moral support," I said. "That's something."

"It surely is," Duck said. "Better run. Nice meetin' you, Ms. Aragon."

"Elvia," she said, smiling. "And it was a pleasure meeting you, too, Dr. Wakefield."

"Just call me Duck," he said.

"Or Quack, as he has also been known to be called," I said.

"Kiss my grits, Curly Top," he said and waved goodbye as he hurried toward the store.

"He seems nice and intelligent," Elvia said when we climbed back into the Explorer.

"A few of us po' white folk around here actually is ed-ju-cated and right open-minded at times," I said in my best imitation of a bad Southern accent.

"Point taken, *amiga*. I'll try to keep an open mind. Just no more Waffle House breakfasts."

"At least not today," I said.

3

I CIRCLED THE town square once, giving Elvia a taste of downtown Sugartree, not in a great hurry to get to Aunt Garnet's house. It was past six o'clock, and I knew most likely everyone would still be at evening church service.

The red brick Blevins County courthouse squatted in the middle of the town as it had since 1839, surrounded by thick leafy blackjack oaks, hickory trees, and bright yellow sugar maples. Its white trim and gothic columns gave it a look of old-fashioned gentility and sturdy righteousness. A place where Atticus Finch could have comfortably practiced law. Out front a small sign in the shape of an open book said: IN 1849, TWO YEARS AFTER THE CREATION OF BLEVINS COUNTY, THE SITE OF THE TOWN OF SUGARTREE WAS LAID OFF AS THE PERMANENT SEAT OF JUSTICE OF THE COUNTY. Next to it, a sober gray granite war memorial listed the Blevins County men and women who'd made the "supreme sacrifice" in the service of their country. I knew one of the men listed under the Vietnam War dead—Clive Phillips. He taught Emory and me to scissor-kick and float like a dead man in the "guppy" swimming class at the community pool when we were six and seven years old.

Most of the businesses were closed now, but I pointed out some of the places Emory and I had hung out as kids— such as Hawley's Drug Store where we bought grape Nehis and cherry Cokes at the soda fountain and fetched Goody's headache powders for Aunt Garnet. Mr. Hawley let us read the comic books for free as long as our hands were clean. I wondered if he still owned it.

"Headache powders?" Elvia said.

"We don't have them out West. At least I've never seen them. It's a running argument between Dove and Garnet about which is better, Goody's or BC."

"They're actually powder?"

"In little packs of folded paper. You put them in water or on your tongue. It's amazing. Gets rid of your headache like that." I snapped my fingers.

She shook her head as we passed the Razorback Feed 'n' Seed store and Dandy's Five & Dime. A display of Hula-Hoops and trick-or-treat costumes dominated the dime store's hazy front window. "It's as if we've gone back in time thirty years."

"A good part of my allowance supported that five and dime store," I said. "There's Beulah's Beauty Barn and Elvis Emporium!" I pointed to a small brown natural stone building catty-corner to Billings' Beans-N-Biscuit Cafe, known to locals as the 3B Cafe. A banner in Beulah's window said in bright pink letters: WELCOME HOME, SUGAR-TREE BAPTIST FAMILY MEMBERS (20% DISCOUNT ON WASH AND SET WITH OUT-OF-STATE LICENSE).

"B seems to be a popular letter here," she commented.

"We'll be spending an afternoon at Beulah's one day this week."

She jerked her head around to stare at me, her mouth gaping slightly. "I don't think so." She touched her shoulder-length black hair in a subconscious protective gesture.

"Not to have our hair done," I said, laughing at her hor-rified expression. "To catch up on what's really going on in town. Garnet and her friends have standing appoint-ments. Some of them for forty years. Beulah's a hoot. She knows more of this town's secrets than all the Baptist, Methodist, Pentecostal, and Catholic ministers put together. And if you get her on the right day, she'll give you a tidbit that you can dine out on for a month. Besides, you can't miss her Elvis boutique. She's in the Elvis Century Club."

"The what?"

"The Elvis Century Club. To belong you have to have visited Graceland at least one hundred times. She has proof, too. Receipts and pictures from every visit. Her scrapbook is on display in the boutique."

"Sounds . . . lovely," Elvia said, still holding her hair.

After promising her a walking tour tomorrow, we drove the three blocks from the town square to Aunt Garnet's two-story farm-style house. Tall, bushy sweet gum trees clasped leafy hands over our heads as we drove slowly over the bumpy streets. When I pulled into the long driveway, I saw someone rise up from the porch swing and move out from the shadows of the house's deep veranda. I smiled and waved at Isaac, my gramma's—as she liked to put it—gentleman friend. Behind him stood my uncle William Wi-ley, better known as Uncle WW. He was Garnet's quiet but quick-witted husband, who'd recently retired from his fifty-year plumbing business and was now, according to Dove, driving Aunt Garnet crazy "fixin'" things around the house.

"I married him for better or worse," she complained to Dove a few months back, "but not for lunch."

"Hey, Isaac, how's the South been treating you?" I called, stepping out of the car.

He came down the steps and caught me up in a massive hug. With his six-foot-four-inch body it was like being squeezed by a big ole bear, if the bear had hair the color of White Lily flour pulled back in a long braid down his back. I was sure that Isaac Lyons, world-renowned photographer, five-time married man of the world and founder and president of the Dove Ramsey fan club, had sent a great many of Dove's old friends in Sugartree into a gossiping tizzy. I would have given two inches of fresh-grown hair to have been a fly on the wall of Beulah's *last* Saturday morning.

"I love the South," he said, letting my feet touch ground again and going over and hugging Elvia in a more restrained way. "Almost as much as I love your gramma."

"Why aren't you two in church?" I asked. "I can't believe the girls let you or your wicked souls out of it."

"I reckon Isaac had one of them migraine headaches all you city folk seem to favor so much," Uncle WW said, coming down the steps. I went over and hugged him, his grizzled face giving a pipe smoker's half-smile. His scent of vanilla pipe tobacco and Ivory soap made me feel like a little girl again.

"You don't get migraines," I accused a grinning Isaac. Then I looked back at Uncle WW. "And what's your excuse?"

"I reckon he needed a sympathetic friend to fetch him water for his medication," he said, his face sober as a state trooper's, his pale blue eyes twinkling.

"You are bad boys," I said, wagging a finger at them. "God's gonna smite you good for lying."

"I didn't lie to Dove," Isaac said. "Only Garnet. Do I get partial credit?"

"That's between you and the Lord," I said, laughing.

After helping us unload our suitcases, we all settled down on the front porch with the requisite Southern drink, iced tea.

"Garnet's got a big spread fixed for y'all," Uncle WW said. "But you know how she likes to do things herself, so we'd best be waitin' till church is over and she can dish it up."

"That's okay," I said. "We ate as soon as we got off the plane."

Elvia glanced at me and rolled her eyes.

"Had yourself a Waffle House feast, did you?" Uncle WW said, winking at Elvia. "This girl's plumb crazy for Waffle House." He circled his temple with a forefinger.

"So I gathered," Elvia said, smiling in spite of herself.

"Just so you know, not all of us here are that nuts over the place. I prefer McDonald's or Shoney's myself."

She laughed, and I finally relaxed, leaning my head back against the padded back of the porch swing I shared with Isaac. Elvia took a place next to Uncle WW on one of the four cane-seat pine rockers. My family would make her feel at home, I was sure of it.

By the time Dove and Garnet drove up an hour later in Garnet's huge green Buick sedan, we'd already heard about every squabble they'd been in during the last week and about Uncle WW's fountain garden in the backyard.

"It's best to see it in the daytime," he said. "I've been talking with a buddy of mine about hooking up some lights so's we can enjoy it at night, but Garnet's done closed the purse strings." The amount of money he'd been spending on decorative fountains since he'd retired a year ago had been a source of much-discussed conflict between him and my great-aunt.

"Honeybun, Elvia!" Dove cried, coming up the stairs and pulling me to her in a hug. "How was the airplane ride, girls? Are you hungry?"

"Just fine," I said. "We got here about an hour or so ago. I ate at a Waffle House the minute we landed, but I could eat again."

"A Waffle House? Lord, then Elvia must be starved," she said, letting go of me and hugging her.

"Just a little," Elvia said.

I crossed the porch to greet my aunt. "Hey, Aunt Garnet, how are you?" When I hugged her, her scent brought back memories, too. Jean Naté cologne and a slight whiff of lavender talcum powder always made me think of my austere and proper great-aunt. Taller than her older sister Dove's five-foot, one inch by three much-touted inches, she was the opposite of Dove in every way you could imagine except one. Her family was her life, and she was truly glad to have us here.

"Benni, dear, you're finally looking well," she said, touching my cheek with her thin, cool hand. "You've been at the top of my prayer list for the last couple of years."

"Thanks," I said, wondering if I should take that as a loving gesture or an admonishment. Trouble had seemed to dog me since I'd lost my first husband, Jack, in a car accident almost three years ago. But joy had found me, too, and he was due to arrive day after tomorrow. "Uncle WW says you've fixed us some supper."

"Yes, yes, come in out of the evening air," she said, pulling her short lacy jacket close around her. "It feels like we're to have an early fall."

After a "light supper" of baked chicken and dressing, three-bean salad, corn bread, homemade pickles, fresh tomatoes, lime Jell-O with pineapple chunks, and tangy-sweet coleslaw, we retired to the living room with pieces of her sour-cream coconut cake. I was contemplating a second piece and being teased by Isaac and Uncle WW that I was going to explode, when Emory arrived.

"Hey, y'all," he said, bursting through the door. Amen and a young, good-looking black man trailed behind him. Emory immediately crossed the room and pulled Elvia out of her chair. "Excuse me while I kiss my girl." And he did, right there on the lips, in front of everyone. Being home gave my cousin a boldness that disconcerted even the unflappable Elvia.

"Emory," she murmured, pulling away, though, I noted,

not too quickly. Her brown cheeks flushed pink.

Everyone couldn't help laughing at the goofy grin on Emory's face.

"I do believe that boy's besotted," Uncle WW drawled.

"Hey, Amen," I said, going over to my old friend. "It's been way too long." We hugged, then held hands and unabashedly inspected each other. She was thinner than the last time I'd seen her ten years ago and more grown-up-looking than I ever thought possible. Her hair was short and clipped close to her head in an elegant style, and her black eyes were highlighted with a professional-looking makeup job. Her neatly arched eyebrows gave her face an optimistic, slightly questioning look. She wore khaki slacks, a tan silk shirt, and a tailored houndstooth jacket.

"You look like a million bucks!" I said.

"Girlfriend, these days that better be before taxes, or it ain't a compliment," she said, her smile a sparkling ivory against dark coffee skin. "You don't look a bit different than when you were twenty-six. I'd kill for your secret, Benni Harper."

"Good living and a pure heart."

"Lord have mercy, now I *know* that's a lie." She looked me up and down in the same way Duck had. "Emory, when are we going to get this girl out of those nasty ole jeans permanently and into some nice wool gabardine?"

No one laughed louder at that unlikely thought than Elvia.

Amen turned and grabbed the young man's hand. "You remember my nephew, Quinton, don't you?"

"Is this little Quinton?" I exclaimed, looking up at the smooth-skinned young man wearing a shy smile. He'd grown into a long-limbed, handsome man with crisp black hair and skin the color of dark, cooked caramel. He wore a conservative sports jacket and a pale blue dress shirt. A small diamond stud sparkled in one ear.

"Not so little anymore," Amen said. "Quinton's attend-

ing the University of Arkansas at Little Rock. He's major-
ing in law and he's also my campaign manager."

I couldn't believe this was her nephew who ten years
ago spent an afternoon with me, Emory, and Jack shooting
baskets for quarters down at the high school. By the end
of the match, he'd collected five bucks from each of us.
"Shoot, you were twelve the last time I saw you," I said,
standing on tiptoe to hug him. "I was taller than you."

"And I could still beat you at basketball," he said, smiling down at me. "Nice seeing you again."

"Now," Amen said, strolling across the wide living
room. "I got to take me a gander at the woman who put
that silly grin on Emory's face." She stood in front of Elvia.
"It's Elvia, right? I'm Amen Harriet Tolliver, in case no
one thought to mention me before. Girl, you are as beautiful
as he claimed, which doesn't surprise me one little bit, and
I bet you're as smart as he says, too, but I know you can't
have a lick of sense or you wouldn't be havin' anything to
do with the likes of him." She jerked a thumb at a still-
grinning Emory.

Elvia stood there for a moment, not certain how to react.
My friend was actually an incredibly shy person, and I
knew all this attention was killing her inside. Elvia stuck
out her small hand. "Nice to meet . . ."

"Oh, go on," Amen said, brushing her hand away and
pulling her into a hug. "I was just teasin' you. You're family as far as I'm concerned. You've done turned this boy's
head into mush, and believe me, that's not as easy to do as
it looks. He doesn't treat you right, you just give me a call.
I'll set him straight and if I'm not there, you just call my
grandma, Miss DeLora True. She'll take a hickory switch
to him."

"And not for the first time," Emory said, laughing.

After more hugging and exclamations and more coconut
cake, the older folks decided to call it a night while Emory,

Elvia, Amen, Quinton, and I chose to sit out on the front porch.

"I've missed the smells here," I said, leaning back in one of the pine rocking chairs. Out in the yard, crickets and frogs competed in a dueling chorus of sound. "And the sounds. I miss katydids."

"You should come visit more," Amen said. "I can't believe it's been ten years."

"Me either," I replied. "But you know how time can get away from you. When Jack and I had the ranch, it seemed like we never were caught up on work, then there was the accident, and well, my life really got complicated for a while."

"Jack," she said with a sigh. "Lordy, what a sweetheart he was. I bet all this brings back some memories."

I nodded. "It does, but I'm okay. I still miss him, but . . ." I let my voice trail off.

"But, as you said, your life got complicated. And when *is* Mr. Complicated due to arrive?" Amen said, matching her rocking to mine.

"I pick him up in Little Rock day after tomorrow."

"Rumor has it he's one *very* fine-looking man."

"He suits me."

She leaned forward and slapped her thigh, giving a hearty laugh. "Spoken like a true Western woman. Few words, fewer details. We need to get you back here more often so all the Southern don't leak out. Girl, you've done forgotten how to gossip. I want to know *more*. Do his kisses make you frowzy-headed?"

"He does all right," I said, tossing an ice cube at her, which she expertly dodged. "I want to hear about your new career. You aren't giving up nursing for politics, are you?" In her last Christmas card, she'd told me she was head surgical nurse at a hospital in the neighboring town of Bozwell where Emory had once worked on the newspaper and where for a short time, before Amen was married, I knew

she and Emory had dated, though I wasn't going to tell
Elvia. In fact, there were very few women our age in this
town Emory *hadn't* dated, another fact I was going to keep
to myself.

"As much as I'd love to throw myself into this campaign
full-time, I've still got to bring home the bacon. I've got
an always hungry seventeen-year-old son to support." Her
husband had died of a heart attack a couple of years before
Jack died.

"So what grade is Lawrence now?"

"A senior, if you can believe it. I can't myself, to tell
you the truth."

"Pictures," I demanded.

She pulled out her wallet and passed me a couple of
prom pictures of her son. He was big and strong-looking
with her late husband's round, gentle face.

"What a cutie," I said, passing them to Elvia.

Amen grinned with pleased embarrassment. "I think so.
But then, I might be prejudiced. He's a lot like his daddy—
a big ole baby, really."

"A big ole two-hundred-thirty-pound baby who's bein'
sought after by no less than six major universities for football scholarships," Emory said.

"He gets straight As, too," she said. "He wants to be a
doctor. A pediatrician. He just loves little kids."

"Good for him," I said. "So are you still at Bozwell
General?"

She shook her head no. "I'm working as a visiting hos-
pice nurse now. It gives me a more flexible schedule."

"That must be difficult," Elvia said. "Working with patients who are dying."

Amen tilted her head and looked thoughtful, her dark
eyes lost in the evening shadows. "Sometimes it is, but it
can also be uplifting, believe it or not. Some folks' faith in
God at such a frightening time inspires me and helps me
keep my own life in perspective."

"So, what made you decide to run for mayor?" I asked.

"She was sick of the old white boy network running this town like they own it," Quinton said, sitting forward on one of the wicker porch chairs, almost tipping over in his eagerness. "This town needs to step into the twenty-first century, and Amen's going to help it do that."

Her gentle laughter echoed across the porch. She laid an affectionate hand on her nephew's forearm. "As you can see, my supporters have great faith in me. I just wanted to get more involved. When we started a quilt guild here in Sugartree, we began making quilts for the police officers to carry in their cars to give to kids who were being removed from abusive situations. That led into donating money from opportunity quilts to a women's shelter, then we helped raise money for a new addition to the shelter, and before I knew it, we started a food bank and ride service for the elderly to get them to the medical care they needed and . . ."

"And this town would be a heap better off if she won," Emory said. "Quinton's right about the old white boy network. They're only concerned with letting developers turn Sugartree into a fancy retirement community and tourist town. All the while there's kids livin' here who still only eat one meal a day because that's all their parents can afford."

"Emory, why don't you give my speech for me tomorrow night?" Amen said, winking at me.

He leaned back in the wicker loveseat he shared with Elvia and put his arm around her. "Nah, you'll say it better than I ever could. Just got off on a tangent."

"Sweet boy, tangents like that we need more of," she said, glancing at her watch, then standing up. "Shoot, I hate to break this up, but I have an early call tomorrow."

"We're walking over to my house," Emory said, taking Elvia's hand. "Daddy should be home by now. He's dying to meet Elvia."

Elvia tried not to look panicked. I leaned close and whispered in her ear. "Don't worry, Uncle Boone's a good guy. We'll talk up in the room later."

She nodded silently.

Amen, Quinton, and I walked out to the road and watched them stroll hand-in-hand down the dark street around the corner to Emory's house.

"What a classy lady," Amen said. "I'm real proud for Emory. It's about time he settled down and started himself a family."

"Well, it hasn't quite got that far yet, but we're hoping," I said, leaning against the fender of her restored 1965 red Mustang. "Neat car."

"My one indulgence," she said. "Lawrence thinks he's getting it for a graduation present." She chuckled. "He thinks wrong."

"How's things on the campaign trail, really?"

She crossed her arms over her chest and shrugged one shoulder. "Up and down. I don't have to tell you it's not easy. There's lots of folks who'd be happier seein' me in their kitchen scrubbing their floors or serving drinks at their cocktail parties instead of tryin' to sit behind that walnut mayor's desk."

I nodded. Though the South had come a long way in race relations in the last thirty years, like the rest of the country it still had a ways to go. "Any especially bad incidents?"

"Nothing we can't handle," Quinton said, his rich baritone voice tinged with anger. "Just a bunch of stupid redneck honkies trying to scare us off."

"Quinton," Amen said, her voice kind but reprimanding. "Please remember that Benni is . . ."

"A whiteneck honky who is much more diligent at using sunscreen these days considering the rapidly rising rates of skin cancer," I finished, laughing, trying to ease the tension.

They joined in the laughter, though Quinton's still sounded bitter.

"Seriously," I said. "I heard from Duck that people have been messing with your signs. What have they been doing?"

"You've seen Duck already?" she said.

"In the parking lot of the Pig. He was going in to get some decent breakfast foods for his daughter so she wouldn't have to lie to Gwenette about eating every breakfast at McDonald's."

She raised her eyebrows at Gwenette's name. "She's comin' to the homecoming festivities, I heard."

"Too bad," I said, not even trying to hide my feelings from Amen. She knew me too well for that. Then I immediately felt guilty. "Oh, geeze, that's not very nice. Dove and Miss DeLora would whup me upside the head if they heard me. Church homecomings should be about forgiveness and coming together in mutual agreement and support."

"We'll come together in mutual agreement and support. You agree to support me when I push her in front of a speeding freight train."

We giggled like we were ten years old again. Gwenette Ann Wakefield was one of those Southern belles you couldn't help but hate. The kind who always made the homecoming court, never sweated but "glowed," who the girls always made fun of but secretly envied, and the boys lusted after from the first flip of her big pouffy blond hair. The year she became first runner-up for Miss Arkansas, her head became almost as big as her hair.

Quinton shook his head, his face a little annoyed. "It's not funny, Aunt Amen. She's a huge part of Grady Hunter's support, and lots of people read her magazine."

"She's got a magazine?" I asked.

Amen rolled her eyes. "It's called *Sugartree Today*. A kind of look-at-me-don't-you-wish-you-had-my-life thing. She and her friends and their numerous vacations, pastimes, and pseudocharities are her favorite topics. Believe it or not, she does carry some influence in town. You know how the South loves and worships beauty queens, even runner-ups."

"Anyone who has half a brain knows you'd be a great mayor," I said.

"Then let's hope that particular constituency is registered to vote."

"We can hope and pray. See you tomorrow?" I asked. "We haven't really been able to catch up, and I want you to get to know Elvia better. You'll really like her."

"I'm sure you're right. How about a chocolate fried pie break at Boone's at two o'clock? My treat."

"Then I wouldn't miss it. Take care now."

"The same to you, girl." She hugged me one last time, her strong fingers pressing into my back. "It's so good to see you. Welcome home, Benni Harper."

It was only as I was waving good-bye that it occurred to me that she hadn't ever told me what those redneck honkies were doing to scare her. I shivered involuntarily, a goose running over my grave, as her parting words echoed in my mind.

Welcome home, Benni Harper.

4

AN HOUR LATER, from the guest bedroom downstairs where I was staying, I heard the front door creak open. I gave Elvia fifteen minutes then went upstairs, trying to avoid the squeaky warped spots on the hardwood floors, the places my cousin Rita said made it hard to sneak in after curfew. I tapped softly on her door.

"Come in," she said in a low voice.

She was given the room I always stayed in as a child. It was decorated with the odds and ends of treasured family antiques too memory-filled to sell, but not quite matching any of Aunt Garnet's Early American Ethan Allen decor. A gold-framed picture of their only grandchild, my cousin Rita, sat on the five-drawer bird's-eye maple bureau. An old Sugartree Hornets football banner hung above one twin bed; over the other was a picture of Jesus surrounded by laughing children of all nationalities and colors.

Elvia sat cross-legged in red satiny pajamas under the Jesus picture, her black hair tied back with a matching ribbon. Her face was bare of makeup, giving it a wan but delicately vulnerable look. I joined her on the bed, mimicking her position, our knees touching.

She pointed to the framed picture of my cousin Rita on the maple bureau. "Will I have to share this room with her?" She tried not to look alarmed. My wild-child, rodeo-cowboy-loving cousin and Elvia had not taken to each other, to put it mildly.

"Don't worry, she's not coming. She's back with Skeeter, believe it or not, and there's some big rodeo in Montana he's riding in."

Relief softened her features.

"How was the meeting with Boone?" I asked.

She plucked at the sleeve of my flannel pajamas. "Where in the world did you find these?" she asked. My light blue pajamas were covered with bucking broncos and wild-eyed cowboys.

"Gabe bought them for me. He saw them in a boutique down in Santa Barbara when he was at a police chief's seminar a few months ago."

"That man can read you like a book."

"Yeah, well he also bought me something from Victoria's Secret, too, and the deal was I didn't get the pajamas unless I agreed to wear the . . . Well, let's just say I didn't bring it with me to Arkansas."

She gave a soft laugh. "Marriage blackmail. Is that what I have to look forward to?"

I raised my eyebrows at her, my heart hopeful. "You tell me."

She shook her head. "Emory's father was very sweet to me. I see where Emory learned his manners."

"Uncle Boone, Aunt Garnet, and Miss DeLora. He didn't have a chance."

"I didn't realize his house was right behind this one."

I nodded. "It was real fun when we were kids. You can see his bedroom window from our window here. We used to send Morse code messages with flashlights. Meet me in the tree house was our favorite. We spent a lot of time up in that old oak tree."

"He showed me the tree house. Quite impressive."

"Did you go up in it?"

"No, he tried to convince me to climb the rope ladder, but I told him I'd wait until the elevator was put in."

"Spoken like a true diva," I said, bumping her knee with mine. "What'd you think of his house? Aren't the pillars a hoot? I think Emory's mama had a thing for *Gone With the Wind*."

The Littleton house had always been one of the town's showplaces. One of the largest houses in town, it was made of fawn-colored brick and had a deep hardwood front porch supported by four white pillars. The double front doors, carved with dogwood blossoms and doves, were designed by an artist in Charleston, and the first glimpse of the huge entryway never failed to take my breath away. Two intricately carved cherry wood staircases, which carried through the dogwood and dove theme, wound their way from Italian marble floors to the second floor where there were six bedroom suites, five bathrooms, and a huge master bedroom suite with a separate sitting room.

Her face was troubled. "It's . . . bigger than I expected."

"My exact words to Gabe on our wedding night," I said, grinning.

"Oh, you," she said, grabbing a pillow from behind her and smacking me with it. I wrestled it from her before she could strike again. "I'm serious. Just how much . . ." She stopped. "No, never mind. I don't want to know."

I hugged the captured pillow to my chest. "All you need to know is Emory loves you. And that you're going to live happily ever after."

The troubled light in her eyes didn't ease. "Do you really believe that, Benni? Happily ever after? Do you think that's possible for anyone?"

I thought about her question for a moment. "No, I guess not. I mean, ever after, that part I do believe. The happily comes and goes. So I think we can live ever after with someone we love, sometimes happily, sometimes not so happily, but certainly ever after." But even as I said the words, I knew even they didn't ring true. I didn't live ever after with Jack. Sometimes people left you. Sometimes they just left.

"Those were some of the most convoluted sentences I've ever heard put together," she said, but smiled, her tension easing a little.

"Relax," I said, patting her knee. "As Aunt Garnet would say, just take a deep breath and think of Arkansas."

She shook her head at my silly remark and leaned back against the maple headboard. "So, this Amen. She and Emory dated, didn't they?"

I bit my lip, trying to keep a poker face. "Why would you think that?"

Her confident laugh eased my worry. These people wouldn't intimidate her for long. "Benni, you look like one of my brothers when Mama catches them sneaking a smoke out in the garage. I'm not blind and I'm not naive. I know Emory dated a lot of women before me."

"It wasn't serious between him and Amen. Just a summer fling. Kind of like me and Duck."

"You and Duck!"

"Well, they were a bit older when they dated. . . . Nineteen or twenty, I think. Actually, me and Duck never really dated. He just gave me my first kiss when I was twelve. Behind the Sugartree Dairy Queen, if you must know the gory details."

She poked my flannel-covered knee with a red nail. "Why, you little sneak. Was he a good kisser?"

I giggled and pushed her hand away. "I thought he was, but what did I know? He was an older man. All of fourteen years old. And for the record, Emory paid him five bucks to perform the deed. Duck was really popular even then. In reality, he'd never have looked twice at a tomboy like me."

"Did you know Emory paid for it?"

"Not until long after I was married to Jack. Emory's always haranguing me about paying him back."

"I feel so out of place," she said, suddenly serious again.

I reached over and took her hand. "Emory loves you. When someone loves you, you're never out of place."

Her dark eyes studied me. "Truth time. Could you ever, in your wildest imagination, see me living here?"

That stopped me. Elvia living in Sugartree was beyond my comprehension. "No, but visiting once a year wouldn't be so bad, would it?"

"If that's all it was. What if after we're married he decides he can't live away from the South? He grew up here. This is his home. The business he will inherit is here. You see how relaxed he is, how happy. He just came to California for me, but can you see him living in San Celina permanently? Raising children there? It's not like you and Gabe. Gabe had lived away from his hometown for twenty years before he met you."

I realized she was right and that I'd never thought of it that way. I loved having Emory live in San Celina and selfishly and self-centeredly assumed that if he married Elvia, he'd just stay there the rest of his life. But Elvia was right. He'd spent his whole life in the South. I'd never even considered the fact that he might want to live and raise his children there.

"Have you two talked about it?" I asked.

"No," she said, sighing. "We haven't gotten into details like that." She waved her hand irritably. "Who knows, this might be a moot point. It probably won't even work out with us. Why should he be any different than any of the others?"

I didn't answer. Her love life had always been a touchy subject between us, especially since that disastrous affair she'd had with a sabbatical replacement professor when we were seniors in college. I'd hated him, thought he was just out to use her and told her so. It was the only time in our relationship when we went for three months without speaking. I turned out to be right, a fact that didn't give me any satisfaction because of the pain it put her through. No man had captured her heart since. Until now.

"Where are you sleeping?" she asked.

"Downstairs in the magnolia room."

"The magnolia room?"

I unfolded my legs and stood up, shaking the right one, which had gone to sleep. "You'll have to come see it tomorrow. It's called the magnolia room because of Great-Great Gramma Neeta's bed. It's got magnolias carved all over the foot and headboard. Me and Gabe are staying there 'cause we're the most newlywed in the family. It's tradition."

She pulled the bed pillow close to her chest and ran her fingers over the pillowcase's colorful embroidered flowers. "He doesn't arrive until Tuesday?"

"Right." I looked at her, waiting for something else. Then her unspoken request dawned on me. "You know, it's kinda lonely down there. Do you mind if I sleep up here with you until he comes?"

Gratitude flashed across her face. "If you promise not to snore."

"Hit me with a pillow if I do," I said, crawling in the other twin bed.

"Count on it, *amiga*," she replied and turned out the light.

IT TOOK ME a few minutes at breakfast to realize an incident of earthshaking proportions had happened before I got up.

Dove and Aunt Garnet bustled around the oval walnut dining table, setting down more food than we could eat in a month of Sundays.

"Where's Elvia?" Dove asked.

"She'll be down directly but she doesn't eat much breakfast."

"She can have a biscuit or two," Dove said, setting down a plate of fluffy white cathead biscuits. Steam curled off their golden tops.

I inhaled deeply and sighed. "Don't worry, I'll eat her share."

"Hope you're hungry," Aunt Garnet said, moving around Dove and setting down a blue Fiestaware plate of identical biscuits.

"Wow, you two must have been up since five o'clock baking," I said, sitting down next to Isaac.

"I was," Aunt Garnet said, her voice sweet as the pitcher of sorghum she sat next to my plate. "*Someone* needs to feed this hungry household a decent breakfast."

Dove made a growly sound deep in her throat.

"Could you pass the grits?" I asked Isaac. The panicked look on his face surprised me. He glanced at Dove, then Garnet. Both of them smiled at him with the innocent, deadly grins of water moccasins ready to bite.

Something wasn't right.

"Which ones?" Uncle WW said cheerfully.

"The plain ones," I said, reaching for the butter dish.

"I mean, which plain ones?"

That's when I really looked at the table. It was full of food all right. Double everything. Double platters of fried ham. Double plates of biscuits. Double bowls of grits. Double pitchers of juice. Double dishes of scrambled eggs. Even double plates of butter.

"What's going on here?" I asked.

"Blackberry jam, Benni, dear?" Aunt Garnet said, her thin rice-powdered face smiling at me. She set a blue cutglass dish of dark preserves in front of me. I started to scoop some out when it was whisked out from under my spoon and replaced with a pink dish of red preserves.

"You don't like blackberry, you like raspberry," Dove said. "I brought these from home."

I sat there with my spoon in midair. "Will someone please tell me what's going on?"

Aunt Garnet's head lifted, and she sniffed the air like a hunting dog scenting squirrel. "Oh, dear, my cinnamon rolls are burning." She dashed into the kitchen.

Dove smiled and continued to rearrange the food on the table, pushing some dishes aside and others toward me, Isaac, and Uncle WW.

Aunt Garnet came back out a few seconds later holding a pan of rolls that were black and crispy on top. "Who fiddled with the temperature on the oven?" she demanded.

Isaac glanced nervously at Dove, who continued to smile and rearrange the dishes. Uncle WW just kept dishing out food from whatever bowl or platter was closest to him.

"*Someone* is in deep need of spiritual readjustment," Aunt Garnet said.

"Grits, anyone?" Dove said.

When they both retired to the kitchen, a pointedly silent kitchen, I quickly asked, "Okay, boys, what happened between last night and this morning?" I'd already figured out a food war of some type was going on.

"They're just squabbling," Uncle WW said, unperturbed. But then, he'd been living around these sisters for over fifty years.

Isaac, normally as unflappable as an owl, looked ready to bolt. "It started with some kind of argument about pecan pie last night," he said. "It happened when you kids were out on the porch. Something about whether you pour the filling over the pecans or mix the pecans in the filling. When we came down this morning, they were both working in the kitchen making duplicate everything."

"Oh, no," I moaned. "Not the pecan pie debate. The last time they got into it about that, they didn't speak for six months."

" 'Fraid so," Uncle WW said. "Then it'll move into what's better, Yarnell's ice cream or Blue Bunny, Goody's versus BC headache powders, Martha White flour versus White Lily, California chicken versus Arkansas chicken. I'm thinkin' we should just have ourselves a foot race out front and declare a winner once and for all."

I giggled, the mental picture of Dove in her round-toed leather boots and Wrangler jeans running against Aunt Garnet in her Stride Rite pumps and flowered housedress too rich this early in the morning. "We could sell tickets, take bets. I'd take Garnet on a fifty-yard-dash 'cause she's got longer legs, but Dove's a better bet for endurance. We'll have to discuss the length of the race."

"I'm flexible," Uncle WW said, grinning.

"Have they always, um, competed so . . . enthusiastically?" Isaac said, his smile a little shaky.

Uncle WW and I almost choked on our biscuits, laughing.

"I'm sorry," I said, touching Isaac's forearm, then wiping away the tears running down my face. "I just forget that you don't really know Dove that well. She and Garnet have been like a couple of competing bird dogs since Aunt Garnet had the nerve to get herself born and knock Dove out of her cherished only-child spot. The best thing to do is go along and eat up while you can. These feuds can take weird turns sometimes, and they get caught up competing in something else other than cooking. As Daddy always told me, better put a biscuit in your pocket for later."

"Thank the good Lord for cafes," Uncle WW said.

I took a cup of coffee with cream and a hot biscuit upstairs to Elvia who was finishing her eye makeup.

"You look great," I said.

"Thanks." She took the coffee and sipped it. "Sit down and let me do your hair. It'll relax me."

As she combed and separated sections of my hair, I told her about the latest feud between Dove and Garnet.

"How in the world are they going to live in the same house all week and go to all these church functions while fighting?" she said, French braiding my curly, reddish-blond hair with speedy expertise. "Doesn't it embarrass them to pick at each other in front of everyone?"

"Everyone in town knows the Mosely girls are always trying to one-up each other. It's kind of a town pastime, watching them compete. People would be disappointed if there wasn't a competition. Me and Uncle WW are thinking about making book on who'll triumph."

"Does either of them ever actually win?"

"We don't think so. I imagine they'll do this until one of them dies."

"Then they'll probably be sorry they spent their whole lives fighting."

"I doubt it. The one who dies first will most likely sit up on a cloud and flaunt the fact that she got to see heaven first."

When my hair was done, we decided to use the back stairs to sneak past the feuding sisters. When we came out of the screened back porch we were confronted with Uncle WW's fountains gurgling in all their glory.

"Wow," I said.

"I wonder how much water goes through these in a day," Elvia said.

"Let's walk through them and go see Emory." I pointed to the back of the fountain-covered half-acre yard to the gate connecting Emory's backyard with my aunt and uncle's. We started walking toward the back fence on the gravel pathways that Uncle WW had fashioned. There were small concrete benches set among the fountains and the hundreds of flowers, shrubs, and even edible sections—I saw remnants of pole beans, onions, tomatoes, and carrots.

There had to be at least fifty fountains, all spouting water in some different way—water came out of swans' beaks and trolls' buckets and frogs' mouths and tree stumps.

There were koala bears, eucalyptus trees, raccoons, and dolphins. I counted three different clam shell fountains, a California forty-niner who held a gold pan with the water flowing into a slush box, four elephants, a pod of whales, two roadrunners, and a ceramic dog holding a ceramic hose in its mouth. A gray stone book fountain sat on a pedestal in the middle of the garden, water bubbling around the book, on which was written, "All our visitors bring happiness—some by coming, others by going."

As we walked deeper into the fountain garden, the sound of rushing water became louder and louder.

We pushed gratefully through the wooden back gate. The whooshing sound of the fountains receded as we walked the pathway through the quiet, English-style garden toward the back patio.

"You know," I said, "a few fountains are soothing, but that sounded like Niagara Falls. Not to mention that suddenly I have a strong urge to pee."

When we walked under the tree house in the towering oak tree next to the flagstone patio, something wet hit the top of my head. I instinctively reached up to feel what it was, then received a stream of water full in the face.

"You cut that out, Emory Delano Littleton!" I yelled up at him. He squirted me again with his long-range water rifle.

I grabbed the rope ladder and scrambled up it, dodging blasts of water. "I'm going to get you," I said, sticking my head through the opening in the tree house floor.

"Why, good morning, Miz Albenia," he said, blowing at his firearm's plastic barrel. "Lookin' a bit damp this morning. Reckon it's goin' to be a right muggy day here in Sugartree." He called out to Elvia, "I'll be down in a minute, darlin'."

"No hurry," she called back. "You two kids play in your tree house as long as you like."

"You freak of nature," I said, sitting down next to him

on the plush red carpeting and stretching out my legs. I leaned over and dried my face on the sleeve of his white polo shirt. "Wow, the tree house hasn't changed one bit."

The one advantage to having a rich cousin is you got to play with all his expensive toys, including the tree house his dad had had designed by a prize-winning architect from Atlanta. With a row of built-in bookshelves, three windows with shutters, and a tile roof with a skylight, it was big enough to host a party for six people. Emory joked that if he could move it to New York City he could rent it for three thousand a month.

Below us we heard Elvia talking to someone. Her delighted laugh floated upwards to our perch in the tree. We scrambled up and stuck our heads out the window overlooking the patio. She and Miss DeLora had apparently introduced themselves and were in the process of having a swell ole time.

"You're in big trouble now, buddy boy," I said. "Miss DeLora's gonna tell her the down and dirty truth about you, and she'll be on the next plane back to San Celina."

Miss DeLora, wearing a starched, yellow calico dress and white straw sun hat, sat across from Elvia at the glass patio table, talking in that smooth, alto voice that had soothed Emory, Amen, and me to sleep more times than I can remember. It had a sweet airiness that made you think of wind in the piney treetops and small chittery bush animals. That voice read me *To Kill a Mockingbird* for the first time, and I've never forgotten it.

"Stop right there!" Emory yelled. "I'm coming down."

"Don't you hurry yourself, little man," Miss DeLora said, waving a wrinkled brown hand, not even looking up. "Me and your young lady's going to have ourselves a nice cup of peppermint tea while you two monkey-children swing in the treetops."

We sat back down on the red carpet, our backs against the tree house's oak paneling.

"You're right, sweetcakes," Emory moaned. "I'm a goner."

"If you'd been a better kid, then Miss DeLora wouldn't have so many tales to tell."

"You're one to talk. When old Brother Cooke visits Sugartree Baptist, he still talks about the time you put red dye in the baptismal pool behind the pulpit. Washed in the blood, my eye."

"I didn't think that up, Duck did! I just executed it because I was the smallest one and could fit in the pastor's study window."

He laughed. "You almost *got* executed for it."

"You little slime ball. You and Duck got away before they could catch you. You know, I've never ratted on you two, but I still could."

"You can rat on *us* when you pay *me* back the five bucks you owe me for getting Duck to teach you how to kiss. Better yet, maybe Gabe should pay me. He's reaping the benefits."

"Suck a rotten goose egg," I said, reaching over and hugging him. "Gosh, it's good to be back, isn't it?"

"It sure is. Like some ole Kansas girl said, there surely is no place like home."

"I heard the meeting with Boone went good."

He nodded. "Daddy likes her a lot. But you know Daddy, he's never met a stranger, and he's liked all the girls I've brought home."

"Does he know this one's different?"

Emory studied me with his bright green eyes, crinkled in an almost smile. "Is she different?"

I smacked him in the chest. "Don't mess with me, cousin, or I swear I'll punch those green bedroom eyes of yours clean into the next county. Elvia's my best friend."

"I thought I was your best friend. Fickle, fickle."

"My best *girlfriend*. And I don't want her hurt." I tucked

my arm through his. "And I don't want you hurt either. How do you think it's going, really?"

He shrugged, trying to be nonchalant, though I could see the apprehension in his face. "Only time will tell, I suppose."

"What're you up to today?" I asked, changing the subject.

"I have a ton of stuff to do to get ready for Amen's fund-raiser barbecue tonight. I wanted to spend the day with Elvia, but Daddy's been so busy at the plant he left most of the arrangements up to me."

"Anything I can do to help?"

"Just keep Elvia from being too bored today. After tonight I can spend the rest of the week with her. It's lousy timing, I know, but I feel like I owe this to Amen."

"Elvia will understand. Man, I hope Amen wins."

"Me, too, sweetcakes, but some people are real upset about her running, and she's also part of the group who started this church merger idea, so there's that hostility to contend with, too. Lots of people in this town are still mentally livin' in the days before Martin Luther King Jr. made his 'I Have a Dream' speech, and they want to keep it that way."

"I'm glad she's got you and Boone rooting for her."

"Such help as it is. There's a mess of folks in Sugartree who don't put much stock in what me or Daddy have to say either."

"But they put lots of stock in the success of your smoked chicken. Green is the only color most folks aren't prejudiced against."

"That's a mouthful, cousin." He stood up and held out his hand. "Let's go see what damage Miss DeLora has wrought upon my sterling character."

Elvia and Miss DeLora were laughing at something when Emory and I walked up and took a seat.

"What's so funny?" he asked, giving Miss DeLora a

pained look. "Lordy, you're not telling her about my bed-wetting days, are you? Miss DeLora, I'm tryin' to *win* this one, not chase her away."

"You just settle down," Miss DeLora said, her rich espresso-colored face lighting up with affection for Emory. "We wasn't even discussin' you." She turned back to Elvia, took her hand, and patted it. "Oh, he's always been a heap too involved with his own self, but I reckon you can wean that out of him, though Lord knows I've tried and not had one tablespoon of success."

"Benni, stop her," he moaned. "She's cuttin' me off at the knees here."

"It's so great seeing you again, Miss DeLora," I said, ignoring him. "You're looking wonderful. I saw Amen last night, and she looks great, too."

"I am proud as punch of that girl," she said, beaming. "She's the smartest one of the bunch."

"Miss DeLora was telling me about her herb garden," Elvia said.

"Y'all have to come out and see my place," Miss DeLora said. "If the Lord Jesus brought down heaven to earth, I swear this'd be what it looked like. Why, Boone practically turned that little cabin into a mansion."

"And there isn't no one who deserves it more'n you for puttin' up with us Littleton men for so long," Emory said, bending down to kiss Miss DeLora's cheek. "Ladies, I wish I could sit and chat, but I've got a zillion details to see to before the fund-raiser tonight." He went over and kissed Elvia quickly on the mouth. "I'll leave you in Benni's capable hands. She'll give you a tour of our town. Tomorrow I'll take you around and correct all the lies she told you."

"Eat dirt, Beauregard," I said.

"You'll regret those words, my dear Priscilla," he said in a thick Southern drawl. He stood in front of the French doors and clasped a hand over his heart dramatically.

"When they find my broken and maggot-filled body in a shallow Yankee grave."

"I'll name our firstborn after you, Beau, honey," I answered to his retreating back. "Even if'n he wurn't yours."

"Beauregard and Priscilla?" Elvia said.

"An old game we used to play when we were kids," I said. "We used to dress up in old clothes and act out skits. The attic in this house is unbelievable, trunks and trunks of old clothes. Some of them go back to the Civil War."

"And they always left it in a mess," Miss DeLora said. "A couple of little brats, they were."

"Ah, Miss DeLora, haven't we made up for our misspent youths now that we're grown?"

"Hmph," she said. "Ain't enough time on this ole earth to make up for the mischief y'all used to get into. Y'all lucky I didn't sweep you out with the fireplace ashes and leave you for the trashman."

I grinned at Elvia. "Deep inside she knows we were good kids."

"Only when you was takin' naps," she said. "Why, my Amen was a good girl until she hooked up with the likes of you and Emory and that doctor fella."

I laughed and didn't say anything. She obviously still didn't know that half the time our escapades were thought up by her own darling Amen who had an imaginative mind and a bucketful of nerve from early on.

"So, are you ready for a tour of the town?" I asked Elvia.

"Ready as I'll ever be."

I gave Miss DeLora a quick hug. "See you tonight."

We wound our way back through the fountain garden and headed downtown. While we circled the town square, I gave a running commentary about each place of business, its past and present owners, its place in Emory's personal history. Sugartree looked entirely different this bright Monday morning with people shopping, bustling in and out of the courthouse for various official reasons, and baggyjeaned kids loitering on their way to school. Elvia and I stopped in at a half-dozen places where I introduced her and stayed to shoot the bull with people who'd known me since I was a girl. Of course, I couldn't resist taking her to Beulah's Beauty Barn and Elvis Emporium.

The pink-and-aqua shop with its old-fashioned bonnet hair dryers and faded pictures of Arkansas beauty queens going back to the fifties hadn't changed one iota since the last time I'd seen it ten years ago. The colorful Elvis shrine next to the cash register still reigned supreme. In front of his gold-framed picture was a gallon pickle jar where the hand-printed sign said: "MONEYS COLLECTED GO TO LOCAL CHILDREN'S CHARITIES BECAUSE ELVIS LOVED KIDS."

Beulah herself didn't look one minute older, though I knew she had to be in her late sixties. Her brick-red dancing curls, black eyeliner, and sky blue eye shadow were as classic as she was. She greeted me with a rib-crushing hug the minute she spotted me.

"Benni Louise, it's been a crow's year since I've seen you." She felt my hair. "And you need a good conditioning."

"I'll make an appointment," I said. "We're just visiting today." I introduced her to Elvia.

"Now there's some healthy hair," she said, reaching out and feeling a lock of Elvia's hair. "Good cut, too."

"Thank you," Elvia said.

Beulah turned back to the woman in her chair. "We've got years to catch up on, Benni," she said, teasing the woman's short taffy-colored hair. "You make sure and drop back by."

"You know I will," I said.

"Where y'all going now?" she asked. She gazed down at the woman's roots. "Hon, these roots can last one more week and that's it."

"I know, Beulah," the woman said. "I'm waiting for my egg money to come in."

"Better tell them chickens to lay a little faster," she said, giving a big hoot of a laugh.

"We're going to stop by the 3B," I said. "Say hey to John Luther."

"He'll be real proud to see you," she said. "See you at the quiltin' on Tuesday?"

"Probably," I said, though I had no idea what she was talking about. "It's probably a quilting bee up at the church," I told Elvia as we walked the block to Billings' Bean-N-Biscuit.

"John Luther Billings is another kid we used to hang out with," I continued. "But he lived out of town on a farm, so we only saw him on Saturdays and Sundays. He used to be able to burp the whole National Anthem."

"Impressive," Elvia murmured.

I laughed. "It was when we were ten."

A cattle bell attached to the front door announced our entrance.

A pretty young blond girl in her late teens carried three plates of eggs, grits, and bacon to some men in overalls sitting at one of the ten booths that lined each side of the narrow cafe. The air smelled of butter and coffee and maple syrup.

"Hotcakes are comin'," she told the men. She gave us a shy smile. "Y'all can sit anywhere you like."

"Thanks, but we're just here to say hey to John Luther. Is he around?"

She gestured toward the double doors at the end of the aisle. "Daddy's cooking today. Leon's home with the flu."

In the kitchen, John Luther had his back to us and was flipping two rows of pancakes.

"Hey, Johnny, make sure all the bubbles have popped," I said.

He swung around, and a huge smile lit up his broad, hound dog face. "Benni Harper, you little twit. Come over here and hug my neck."

After quick introductions, he continued to flip the hot-cakes while I filled him in on the last ten years.

"I heard about Jack," he said, his golden brown eyes drooping slightly. "Sure am sorry."

"Thank you," I said.

"Heard you got hitched again, though. Did he come with you?"

"He'll be here tomorrow. He's . . ." But before I could tell him more, his daughter burst into the kitchen, her face white and terrified.

"Daddy," she cried, her voice trembling. "He's out front again!"

John threw down the metal spatula. It hit the concrete floor with a loud clang, splattering batter. He pushed through the swinging doors and strode down the cafe's short aisle. I followed him, wondering what the ruckus was about. The three men eating breakfast stopped talking and watched him head for the front door.

"Be cool now, J L," one called.

"Cool, my ass," he replied.

Except for his daughter, who seemed to have disappeared, we all flocked to the window to see what was going on.

He walked over to the passenger side of a bright green jacked-up Chevy pickup with a Confederate flag in the back window. Painted on the truck's door in fancy script were the words WHITE IS BEAUTIFUL. John started jabbing an angry finger at the young, blond man looking down at him. The man was handsome but had a spoiled, sullen expression on his face. A cigarette dangled from his thick lips. We could hear the timbre of John's shouting voice, but the lack of a good muffler caused the truck's engine to drown out his exact words. The man laughed, his face contorting in a mocking sneer.

John Luther shook a fist at the man. With a screech the truck took off, leaving John in a cloud of black exhaust smoke. He stood there breathing heavily, his fist still held up in the air.

I opened the door and joined him on the sidewalk. There was no way we could pretend something hadn't happened, so I decided to just jump right in and ask about it.

"Is everything okay?" I asked.

He turned to look at me, his eyes cold and angry, then just as quickly changed back to easygoing John Luther. "Fine," he said, waving a hand in dismissal. "I'm sorry you had to see that. Just a little problem we've been having with one of the local boys harassing Tara." He glanced over at the cafe where the three men and Elvia had wisely moved away from the window.

"My gosh, the last time I saw Tara she was seven years old. Time sure has flown."

"Tell me about it." He gave another angry glance down the street though the truck was long gone.

"Excuse me for being nosy, but who was that hassling her? An old boyfriend?" I felt sorry for young girls these days. Dating was certainly different now than it was when I was in my teens. So many relationships included violence, and it seemed it was starting at younger and younger ages.

"Not by a long shot. Just some joker she dated once. He . . ." John Luther stopped. "I don't really want to go into it. He's just one of those jerks who can't believe someone would say no to him. But then, what do you expect? He's a Hunter."

"As in Grady Hunter, the mayor?"

"The one and only. That's his son, Toby. A walking advertisement for the benefit of vasectomies, if you ask me." He wiped his hands on his stained white apron. "Well, the show's over for today." He gave me a wry smile. "Welcome home, Benni Harper."

I scratched the side of my neck, not certain if I should smile back. "You're not the first person to say that to me."

"I'd better get back inside and start preparations for

lunch. Come back when there's not so much turmoil, and I'll make you and your friend a real Arkansas stick-to-your-ribs breakfast feast."

"You got it, John Luther."

Elvia questioned me as we walked down the street. "What was that all about?"

"Something between his daughter, Tara, and that boy who is apparently Grady Hunter's son."

She shook her head. "Grady Hunter? Refresh my memory, *amiga*."

"He's the incumbent mayor and Amen's rival. He owns half the town and is a very respected deacon at Sugartree Baptist. He's also, from what Dove told me, the head of the group that's against the churches merging."

"Looks like his son is every minority's nightmare," she said.

"Like father, like son, I guess. There's a lot of good and decent people in this town, but some real jerks, too. Like everywhere, I guess."

We spent another hour or so walking around the town, but by lunchtime I grew tired of greeting old acquaintances, and we decided to retreat to Aunt Garnet's cool and comfortable front porch.

"We'll do the infamous Dairy Queen and Dandy's Five and Dime another day," I promised.

Back at Aunt Garnet's we found an empty house.

"Everyone must be out doing their part to get ready for the coming festivities," I said, bringing in the jar of sun tea sitting in the front yard. In the kitchen, there was a note from Dove . . . and Garnet.

"Sandwiches in the refrigerator, girls," Dove's note said. "I made your favorite tuna salad. Here's a list of the week's activities." Her neat, blunt printing listed each day's agenda.

Aunt Garnet's note said, "Benni and Elvia—sandwiches in the refrigerator. I made your favorite chicken salad.

Here's a list of the week's events." A duplicate list of the church and town doings was written in Garnet's pretty, cursive handwriting.

"The battle continues," I said, holding up the notes. "Guess we'd better eat some of both and peruse these lists."

Elvia smiled while opening a cupboard to look for plates. "Reminds me of Mama and her sisters when they make tortillas. Always mine is softer than yours, mine never falls apart, yours are too hard or too moist, they taste like cardboard. Tía Maria always accuses Tía Josefina of using old lard."

We took our sandwiches and iced tea out on the porch. After eating, we lay back in the padded wicker lounges, drowsily discussing the week's activities.

"There's Amen's fund-raising dinner tonight," I said, reading the lists. "Then there's a quilting bee at the church in the morning. I think they're working on a quilt to give to Brother Cooke, our old preacher. I pick up Gabe at three in Little Rock. Then it's dinner at Garnet's. Wednesday night there's a gospel sing, pie social, and auction at the church with the combined Sugartree and Zion choirs. It's going to be something to watch a bunch of uptight white folks and spirit-filled black folks try to harmonize on gospel tunes." I scanned the list. "There's a lot going on. They're even having a day at the old Sugartree pioneer cemetery cleaning off graves. That's on Friday. Saturday morning's the kids' carnival, and Saturday afternoon the Ping-Pong ball drop. Saturday night is the progressive dinner. Sunday is the big day, of course. The preacher does his best to save as many souls as he can, and then there's all-day singing and dinner on the grounds."

"What's a Ping-Pong ball drop?"

"That's a new one on me. Some kind of game, I guess."

"Hope I brought the right clothes for everything," Elvia fretted.

"You'll look perfect. You always do."

She leaned her head back and closed her eyes. "I don't care if I look perfect, I just want . . ." She didn't finish her sentence, but I knew what she was thinking. She just wanted to fit in. To not embarrass Emory. To make him proud of her. And to not lose herself in the process.

"You are my best friend. You will always be perfect to me."

Without opening her eyes, she waved her hand, dismissing my words, but her lips gave a small smile.

AT A QUARTER to two, I woke Elvia from her nap. "We're supposed to meet Amen at Boone's at two." We walked the four blocks to Boone's Good Eatin' Chicken Cafe. It sat next to the offices of the town's weekly paper, the *Sugartree Independent Gazette*. A poster supporting Grady Hunter was posted in the *Gazette*'s window. A poster with Amen's image and the words IT'S TIME FOR A CHANGE was taped in Boone's window. Amen had beat us and was sitting in a back corner booth with a cup of coffee and papers spread all over the table.

"I bought your pies already," she said, pointing to a white bag on the table. "They're fresh out of the oven." She shifted some papers to make room for us. Above her on the plain pine walls a hand-painted sign declared: LISTEN UP. BARBECUE IS A NOUN, NOT A VERB.

"I'll get us some drinks," Elvia said, walking over to the counter.

"How's it going?" I asked, pulling out one of the turnoverlike chocolate-filled pies. It was still warm in the middle.

"Pretty good," Amen said. "I'm going over some of the town's old budgets in preparation for the debate Grady and I are planning."

"You'll wipe up the floor with him," I said confidently. She laughed, shaking her head. "Your support is flatter-

ing, but you haven't met Grady. Trust me, he's a formi-
dable opponent."

When Elvia came back with a couple of Cokes, we settled into small talk and old stories about our childhood
escapades, the emphasis on Emory, for Elvia's amusement.

After a convoluted story about a skunk, a squirrel, and
Emory's disastrous attempt to learn wildlife tracking in the
Boy Scouts, we had her in tears laughing. "I'm not sure if
you're doing much to convince me why we should have a
relationship," she said, wiping the mascara from under her
eyes with a napkin.

"What's the joke, ladies?" We looked up at a distinguished-
looking man in his mid-forties with silvery hair and a pleasant, even-featured face. His dark blue eyes took us all in,
but honed in on Amen.

"Grady," she said, holding his gaze for a moment. I
swore I could feel an electrical charge between them. "Nice
to see you. I'm just chatting with an old friend of mine.
Benni and Elvia, this is our mayor, Grady Hunter."

"Benni? As in Benni Harper?" he said, shaking my hand.
"It's a real pleasure to meet you. Boone's been so excited
about you and Emory coming back home. You and your
wonderful grandmother, Dove, are staying with Garnet and
WW, right?"

"Guilty as charged," I said. "This is my friend, Elvia
Aragon. She's visiting with me also."

He shook her hand and murmured greetings. A few seconds later, his face registered recognition. "Elvia Aragon.
You're the lovely lady Emory's been writing home about
for the last year. You've made quite an impression on our
Emory."

Elvia smiled but didn't answer.

He turned back to Amen. "All ready for our debate?"
His smile seemed genuinely concerned.

"You know I am, Grady. I'm going to beat the pants off
you."

He gave a chuckle and moved his head slowly back and forth to encompass all of us in his smiling radius. "She probably will. But if I have to be bested, I'd rather it be by Amen than anyone else on earth." His words actually sounded sincere.

"Grady Hunter, you are full of it," Amen said, grinning. "Now go away so we can plan strategy."

"Just came by to get my daily fried pie," he said. He bowed slightly at the waist. "Ladies, so nice to meet you. I imagine we'll cross paths again this week."

"Same here," I replied.

After he left, I turned to Amen and said, "He's certainly a smooth one. Was any of that for real, or was it part of his political *schtick*?"

She stared thoughtfully over at the front window where we could see him stopping in front of Boone's to talk to three elderly ladies holding plastic shopping bags. In seconds, he had the ladies laughing. "No, believe it or not, it isn't. He's not a bad person, just a little too self-centered and a little less socially progressive than this town needs. Frankly, like most rich white folks, he has no reason to want change. But he will listen, which is more than you can say for a lot of them." She turned back to look at us. "To tell you the truth, if I wasn't running I might have voted for him myself."

AT ELVIA'S INSISTENCE, we were back at Aunt Garnet's and getting ready around four o'clock, even though the party wasn't for two hours. My clothing choice was easy with my one pair of nice black dress pants and a long-sleeve butterscotch-colored silk cowboy shirt. Add my black Tony Lama boots, a pair of tiger's-eye and silver earrings, and some hastily added mascara and blush, and that was my beauty routine. The whole process took about fifteen minutes. It took Elvia that long just to put her hair up in a twisted elegant hairdo using some kind of complicated hair paraphernalia.

Dove, Aunt Garnet, and the men came home from shopping in Little Rock when Elvia was trying on her second outfit.

"We're fixin' to leave. Y'all comin' soon?" Dove called through the door a half-hour later. Elvia was pulling on her fourth outfit. I stepped out into the hallway, closing the door gently behind me.

"She's still trying to decide what to wear." I gave my gramma the once over. "Cool outfit, Dove."

"You like it?" She twirled around in her scoop-necked black and gold lacy dress that had a definite gypsy flavor. It showed off the milky white skin on her chest and the tiniest bit of cleavage. "When I was tryin' it on at Dillard's, Garnet whispered to WW in that screechy voice of hers that I look like a harlot." She beamed, enjoying the image.

"Shame on you," I scolded. "You're a guest in her house. You shouldn't be doing things just to annoy her. That's what you'd tell me."

"Honeybun." She leaned over and kissed my cheek. "Mind your own dang business."

I rolled my eyes. "Yeah, yeah, do as I say, not as I do."

I went back into the room where Elvia was considering a plain off-white Anne Klein jacket and slacks with a copper-colored shell blouse. When she started critically dissecting what was wrong with the jacket, I pulled her arm and said, "We gotta go. All the good food's gonna be picked over."

"Is that all anyone ever thinks of around here?" she asked, her voice petulant. "What their next meal is going to be?" She was nervous, so I didn't take her snappish reply personally.

"What *else* is there to do in Sugartree?" I asked.

By the time we arrived at Emory's house at six o'clock, it was already teeming with people. We'd walked around the corner and entered through the front door even though it would have been easier to sneak in through the backyard.

"I'm not walking through the brambles in this suit," Elvia said. "It cost me four hundred dollars. I don't want to snag it."

"Okay, whatever you want." I didn't point out that the pathways through both Aunt Garnet's backyard and Emory's were wide and clear and bramble-free. I suspected our journey had more to do with the psychological aspect of coming in the front door rather than the back.

Upon seeing us, Emory immediately swept her into the crook of his arm, and her face started to relax. "Excuse me, cousin," he said. "But I got to show off my girl."

"Feel free," I said. "Where's the chow?"

"She never changes, does she?" he said to Elvia.

"Hey, I'm sublimating my other natural urges. Gabe doesn't arrive until tomorrow."

"And not a moment too soon, sweetcakes," he said. "Those pants fit you nicely now, but one more pulled pork sandwich and you're going to be straining something besides your credibility."

"Get lost," I said.

"Just remember the food's not free at this shindig. We'll be hitting you up for donations to Amen's campaign fund."

I stuck out my tongue. "I already gave her a check this afternoon so I can eat with impunity."

"Lord save us all, she's been reading the dictionary again."

After he led Elvia away, I wandered through the house, nodding and speaking briefly to people I knew, ending up on the back patio where we'd visited with Miss DeLora this morning. The catering company had done an incredible decorating job. Red, white, and blue party lights in the shapes of flags were strung around the patio. Round tables, placed strategically around the freshly mowed half-acre garden and lawn, were covered in white tablecloths with red, white, and blue flower arrangements. In the center of each was a small poster of Amen surrounded by a group of schoolchildren. I spotted Amen from a distance, over by the koi pond, where she stood talking to a group of men in gray suits, her face serious and intense. I caught her eye and gave her a thumbs-up. She gave me a quick nod and smile, then turned her attention back to the businessmen.

I filled my plate with pulled pork barbecue, baked beans, hot biscuits, and coleslaw and headed for a small table under the tree house. Political functions always made me feel awkward and a bit nervous. As I ate my dinner and watched the activity around me, I wondered if there was a way I could manage to sneak up into the tree house without anyone noticing. The vantage point from there would be perfect, and I wouldn't have to make strained small talk with anyone.

"They'd definitely notice a woman climbing a rope ladder trying to escape," Duck said, walking toward me carrying a filled plate.

I laughed and gestured to the empty chair next to me. "How'd you know what I was thinking?"

"You've glanced at the ladder longingly about four or five times in the last five minutes," he said, spreading a white linen napkin over his slacks.

"And what are you doing watching me?" I said.

He glanced up at the tree house. "I wasn't watching you. I was also looking with great longing at that ladder. You were in my line of vision."

"You hate these things, too?"

"With a passion. I never was one for politics but I want to support Amen. She's right in that this town needs some changes. I'm just not sure there's many other people who agree."

"There seems to be a lot of people here tonight."

He shrugged and dug into his coleslaw. "Emory and Boone have lots of people who owe them, both financially and politically, so they want to stay on their good side. How many people who *say* they're going to vote for Amen and how many actually do is an entirely different thing." He paused and took a sip of tea. "No one's run against Grady Hunter the last two terms. She doesn't really believe she's going to win, but that's just between you and me. She wants to exude confidence to her constituency."

"Somehow I can't imagine Amen not getting what Amen wants."

He shook his head and dabbed at the corners of his mouth with his napkin. "It takes more than want to change a whole society's view. But it has to start somewhere."

"What about the problems you alluded to before, with the signs?"

He leaned closer to me. "She's not that worried about it but she's gotten a couple of threats."

"Like what?"

"Stealing her signs off people's lawns or spray paintin' them with graffiti. Phone calls to her campaign headquarters saying they're gonna burn her house down. They made allusions to that man who was drug behind the truck by those white supremacists a while back."

I shivered involuntarily. "That's pretty scary stuff. I hope she's being extra careful."

"As careful as I can convince her to be," he said, his voice tart and irritated. "But you know Amen, she's not afraid of anything. Not for herself, anyway. She does worry about her son, but I've talked to Lawrence, and he makes sure to never be alone. At six-foot-four and two hundred thirty pounds and a bunch of friends not much smaller, not many are going to mess with him."

I folded my napkin neatly and placed it on my empty plate. "Amen never was a cowardly kid, so I guess that hasn't changed. Has anyone reported the incidents to the police?"

He shook his head no. "She won't let us. Said that's just playin' into their hands."

"She really should. It would help build the case in the event something does happen. It would give the district attorney more physical evidence to work with."

He laughed. "You sound like a cop."

I returned his laugh. "No, just married to one. And you're going to meet him tomorrow."

"I can't wait. Does he know about our wicked past?"

"No, but I plan on milking it for all it's worth, so exaggerate, okay? Say it's the best kiss you've ever had. That you've never, ever forgotten it."

He gave me a teasing wink. "And who says that would be an exaggeration?"

"Very good, Dr. Duck. Keep it up." I stood up, picking up my plate. "I think I'll take this to the kitchen, then try and find Uncle Boone. I haven't gotten to say hello to him yet."

"Okay, see you later."

In the kitchen, where the catering staff was busy filling more platters with hors d'oeuvres, I dropped off my plate, contemplated a deviled egg, then resisted and wandered back into the crowded foyer. Many of the people here were strangers to me, and I was feeling a little disoriented. I climbed the stairs and used one of the bathrooms, taking my time to primp and enjoy the relative quiet. When I was through, still not ready to face the roaring crowds, I headed down a long familiar corridor to the narrow stairway leading to the attic.

The slant-roofed room was quiet and cool, the voices below transformed into a soft murmur that filtered through the open door. Nostalgia, sweet as honeysuckle, surrounded me as I picked my way around the trunks, satiny wingback chairs, and a dusty brocade love seat. I opened a trunk and picked up the scratchy lace wedding dress laying on top. The pungent scent of mothballs took me back to the long warm summer afternoons Emory and I had spent up here, trying on clothes and discussing the mysteries of life in the profoundly comic way only ten- and eleven-year-olds can.

"When do you think you'll get married?" I'd asked him one time. It was the summer before his mother died. I was trying on this same wedding dress, ancient even then, pulling it on over my shorts and tank top. The strong musty smell coming off the layers of netting caused me to sneeze violently. Sun filtered through the lacy open curtains covering the round attic window.

"I dunno," he said, slipping on a double-breasted forties-style jacket and brandishing a wood-handled buck knife I was sure his daddy didn't know was up here. "Maybe never. Girls stink up a place."

"We do not!" I said, putting my hands on my hips.

He dropped his arm, letting the knife dangle at his side. I couldn't see his hand in the long jacket sleeve, only the blade of the knife. It was spooky. A ray of light from the attic window caught the steel blade, causing it to glitter. With his free hand he pushed his perpetually sliding eyeglasses up his freckled nose. "I don't mean you. You don't wear that smelly stuff. I mean girls like Gwenette."

"Yeah, she does stink," I agreed. "She's always spraying something on herself. But there's probably lots of girls besides me who don't stink. You could always marry one of them. And Dove and your mama and Aunt Garnet stink, but in a good way."

He considered that for a moment, then said, "You're probably right. Maybe when I'm fifty, then. Like after I go to college and stuff. After I go to New York and become a famous writer."

I nodded. "Fifty seems about right. That's probably when I'll get married, too. I'm going to marry a lion tamer and travel with the circus."

He put on a stained sailor cap, his thin, pale face thoughtful. "I can see that. Will you get me free tickets?"

"Sure, front row. For you and all your famous writer friends." I twirled around in the full-skirted dress until I collapsed on the floor in a dizzy heap.

"Hey, sweetcakes, what're you doing hidin' up here?" Emory's adult voice brought me back to the present.

He stood in the doorway of the attic, his hands deep in his pants pockets, his straight, silky blond hair flopping across his forehead in that rakish way that had always driven women crazy with desire.

"Just remembering old times," I said, letting the dress fall out of my hands back into the trunk. "How's the fund-raiser going?"

"Great, great." He walked into the room and stood next to me, staring down at the open trunk. "Amen's given her speech already, and I think even convinced a few people that votin' for her wouldn't be a bad idea. It's an uphill battle, but she's more than capable of climbing it."

"Duck told me about the threats. They scare me."

"Yeah, me, too. But she's got lots of people watching out for her. Quinton's staying with her and her son through the election. He's got some of his college buddies travelin' with her when he can't. We try not to let her be alone, though she fights us like a wild cat on it."

"Amen in politics," I said, shaking my head. "You know, the longer I think about it, the more sense it makes."

"My feeling exactly."

"How're you and Elvia . . ." I started.

He held up a hand, and I stopped talking.

"Listen," he said, his expression alarmed.

The sound of angry voices was loud enough to filter through the closed attic window. We rushed over to the window and pushed it open.

In front of the house, a small crowd had gathered on the wide front lawn. On the street a bright green, jacked-up truck idled, its loud muffler already familiar to me. Another car, an older, primer-gray Chevy Camaro, sat behind it.

Boone, his arms crossed over his chest, talked to someone in the truck.

"I bet it's Grady Hunter's son, Toby," I said. "I saw him in that same truck at the 3B Cafe this morning."

"That little pissant," Emory said. "He's going to give Daddy another heart attack." He turned and ran out of the attic with me close behind. Out front, we pushed through the small crowd of curious people to reach Boone. Toby Hunter's face held the same mocking sneer as this afternoon. Quinton Tolliver stood behind Boone wearing a look that could only be described as lethal. Inside the two vehicles, I quickly counted seven young men.

"Now, get on out of here," Boone was saying. "We don't want any trouble."

"Daddy, what's going on?" Emory said, coming up behind his father. Emory was at least five inches taller than Boone, but shared his wiry, quick frame. Boone wasn't a big man, but according to family stories, he'd whipped men twice his weight when he got riled, which wasn't very often. Besides his blond good looks, Emory had inherited his father's low-key, easygoing personality. But you didn't want to make them mad. Ever. Because they believed in fighting until someone hit the ground unconscious or dead, and with a Southern man's crazy arrogance, it never occurred to them that the person on the ground could be them.

"I reckon this here is a public street," Toby said. Next to him, hidden in the shadows of the truck, his friends laughed.

"Toby," Emory said, his voice easy but steel-edged, "just beat it. You've had your fun, now go on home and tell your daddy that you successfully harassed his opponent and caused a scene."

"I said I reckon this is a public street," he repeated, ignoring Emory.

Boone started toward the truck, one fist raised, but Emory caught his dad's shoulder and stopped him. "Remember what the doctor said. You're not supposed to be gettin' riled up."

"That boy needs to be taught a lesson," Boone said. "And if'n his daddy isn't gonna teach him manners, I reckon it's up to me."

"Daddy, just let me handle it," Emory said, pushing in front of Boone.

Emory walked up to the truck. "Now, Toby, I don't want to have to call the police, but . . ."

"You stupid asshole, my daddy owns the police in this town," Toby said.

I saw Emory tense and one hand close into a fist.

A thin, powerful voice came out of the crowd. "Toby Maxwell Hunter, I done wiped your little white butt as a baby, and you're actin' about the same age as when I did it." Miss DeLora, dressed in a pale blue chiffon dress, pushed in front of Emory. "Now you get on outta here and leave folks be. We ain't doin' nothin' to hurt you and yours, so y'all got no business here."

"Looky there," Toby said to the driver of the truck. "Emory's wet nurse is standin' up for him. Ain't that sweet as can be."

"Miss DeLora, I can handle this," Emory said, gently trying to pull her back.

Amen had pushed her way through the crowd and stood beside her grandma. "Emory's right, Grandma. Let's go back into the house."

Miss DeLora jerked away from both of them and moved closer to the truck. "Now, get. I mean it, get on home." She waved her hands at him as if he were a pesky cat.

"Ain't no black mammy gonna tell me what to do," he drawled. Then, with a high-pitched laugh, he hacked and spit tobacco juice, spraying the front of her dress. She gasped in surprise, falling back into Amen's arms. Amen's face exploded into a mixture of anger, horror, and disgust.

At the same time Emory and Quinton bounded forward

and grappled for the door handle of the truck. Before they could get it open, the driver took off, the Camaro behind it. Quinton ran after the vehicles for half a block, yelling curses. Emory, breathing heavy, stood out in the street watching the truck and car screech around the corner.

A group of ladies had gathered around Miss DeLora, making sympathetic noises and giving advice on the best method to remove tobacco stains. Amen gripped her grandmother's shoulders as if she'd float away if she let go.

"Now, now," Miss DeLora said, trying to calm everyone down. "Y'all don't fret on me. I'm fine. The boy's just actin' like the fool his daddy and mama raised him to be. All's I need is some club soda to blot this stain with."

After a long emotional hug, Amen let her grandmother be led away by the group of ladies and walked over to me. "If I had a gun I'd have killed him," she said, the tone of her voice removing any doubt to her sincerity.

"I would have handed you the ammunition. What a little pig."

"Don't insult the porcine family," she said grimly. She glanced over at Emory, who had his arm around his dad while they walked over to Quinton, who was still standing in the middle of the street, staring after the truck. "I'd better go see if Quinton's okay."

"Let Emory and Boone talk to him," I said. "I think it's kind of a guy thing."

Her face went stiff with rage. "Guy thing, my eye! It's a race thing, and you know it."

I stepped back, embarrassed and shocked. "I know that, Amen," I finally said. "I meant that sometimes guys can calm each other down easier. Just like women are sometimes better at comforting each other."

She touched a trembling hand to her face, covering it for a moment. Her face was contrite when she brought her hand down. "I'm sorry, Benni. I didn't mean to snap at you. Seeing that little punk diss my grandma like that just froze me inside. You go for a long while, and it doesn't happen, and you're lulled into this sense of anonymity, of safety. Then all it takes is one remark, and you remember there are people out there who'd kill you just because of the pigment of your skin."

"I'm sorry," I said, tentatively touching her arm. "I wish . . ."

She hastily brushed away the tears in her eyes. "I know. Miss DeLora would be the first to tell me to grow up, accept the fact that change takes time. She's probably bothered less by this than Quinton and me."

"I doubt that, but she's like my gramma, has seen too much to be surprised." I looked around at the small knots of people still milling around, talking about the incident. "Speaking of Dove, I wonder where she is."

"Probably in the backyard. This all happened so fast, I bet most of the people here didn't realize anything was going on out front."

"You're probably right. I think I'll go look for her and fill her in. She'll want to go fuss over Miss DeLora. Not that your gramma needs it." I looked intently in my friend's shiny eyes. "Are you going to be okay?"

She nodded, straightening her spine, the unflappable Amen back in charge. "I'll be fine. I think I'll go see to Grandma then try to talk my nephew out of ambushing Toby and his gang, try to convince him we'd be better off fighting with laws than fists."

"Except you're going to have to do some fancy lying to convince him of that, 'cause you're itching to punch someone silly right now, right?"

She grimaced. "You know me too well. I sometimes do wonder if I bit off more than I can chew with this campaign."

"Of course you didn't. There's a reason your mama named you after Harriet Tubman, the *only* woman in U.S.

military history to plan and execute an attack on enemy forces."

That made her smile. "Where did you learn about Harriet Tubman?"

"Where else? My own revolutionary gramma. When she saw that my history books in high school only allotted one paragraph to Harriet Tubman, she made me do a ten-page report on her, then mailed copies to the superintendent of the San Celina school district and every member of the school board. The next year, they spent a whole week on black history and have ever since."

"Dove's a kick in the pants," Amen said, laughing. "Guess it's good she wasn't out here. I'm not sure we could have controlled both of them."

"And I'm not sure we should have. A day with Miss DeLora and Dove is just what that snotty-faced boy needs."

Her face turned serious. "I'm afraid it's too late for that. He's a menace, and Grady's doing nothing to control him."

"Then it's time to go to the police," I said.

"Except what he said about the police in this town is true. Grady Hunter does own them." Before I could answer, she said, "I'll see you later."

"Later," I repeated and watched her walk toward the house.

"How's Amen doing?" Emory asked, coming up beside me.

"She's angry, of course, but in control. How's Quinton?"

Boone, his white hair glowing bluish under the street lights, walked with Quinton toward the house, talking low and urgently to him.

"He and Daddy get on good so he'll listen to what he has to say. Hard to believe a bunch of little jackasses like Toby Hunter and his gang of white-trash rejects could cause so much hullabaloo." His voice was hard and flat.

I glanced back down the dark empty street. A cool evening breeze blew through, rustling the tops of the red maple trees, its eerie sound causing me to shiver under my thin silk shirt. Emory slipped his arm around my shoulders and hugged me to him.

"Don't worry, sweetcakes, we've got things under control. Amen's going to be safe."

"I hope so," I said, not feeling as confident as he about that fact.

While Emory went to look for Elvia, I found Dove, Isaac, Aunt Garnet, and Uncle WW out on the back patio discussing the incident.

"I was afraid something like this would happen," Aunt Garnet said, her voice fretful. "There's bound to be more problems if the churches merge. Sugartree's not ready for this. Why can't folks just leave things be?"

Uncle WW just shook his head, his unlit pipe dangling on his lips. I didn't know if that meant he agreed or disagreed with her.

"I can't believe the words comin' out my own sister's mouth," Dove said to Isaac. "They purely shame me."

Aunt Garnet replied to Isaac, "I can't believe my sister thinks she has the right to come into our town, the town she hasn't lived in for nigh on *thirty years*, and think she has the right to an opinion about how we run things." She pulled her pocketbook close to her chest. "It's all happening too fast. You can't make people change that fast."

Dove said to Isaac, who was getting a distinctly alarmed look on his face, "I can't believe my sister is talking like she hasn't got a Christian bone in her body."

"I can't believe *my sister* is so ignorant about what it's like to live in the real world, not someplace crazy like California," Aunt Garnet shot back to Isaac.

"I can't believe *my sister* . . ."

"Isaac," I jumped in. "I want to show you something in front that I was hoping you'd take pictures of while you were here."

"Certainly, çertainly," he said, his expression grateful.

"Ladies, please excuse me. I'll be right back."

With a grinning Uncle WW watching us, Isaac and I walked through the house to the front yard.

"Thank you," he said, leaning against one of the white pillars. "I owe you one." We silently watched people move toward their cars and trucks. Talk of the incident with Toby Hunter had spread through the party and had been like a splash of cold well water on the festive mood. "I don't know if those two will last out the week without killing each other."

I leaned against the opposite pillar. "They'll be fine. The best thing to do is ignore them. That's what the rest of us do."

"I'll try," he said, his voice uncertain.

I laughed. "Isaac Lyons, you've been all over the world, taken photographs in wars and famines, of popes and queens, not to mention Hell's Angels and gang bangers. For cryin' out loud, you've been married five times. Are you telling me a couple of elderly Southern ladies have you running scared?"

He looked down at me, his face perfectly serious. "You bet your pecan pralines, kid."

"I know this is a dumb question, but did you bring your cameras?" I asked.

"Always. Promised Dove I'd take pictures of the home-coming."

"I was thinking . . ."

"Of me taking pictures of Amen and her campaign for mayor? Already thought of it. Actually took some casual shots earlier this evening, when she first arrived. It might make an interesting feature somewhere."

"I figured that even if she can't win, maybe the record-ing of her efforts, if they were seen by enough people, would at least make people think."

He leaned over and ruffled my hair. "You and I are on

the same wavelength. I'll talk to Amen tomorrow and see if she'll give me full access."

"I can't imagine why she wouldn't."

That night, after we'd all gone back to Garnet's and everyone was tucked into bed, Elvia and I discussed the incident. The moon shone in through the thin window shade, and I could make out my friend's form lying on the twin bed across from me.

"Dove and Aunt Garnet almost got into a fistfight about this incident with Toby Hunter." I told her about their hot words to each other.

Over in the other bed, she silently listened, then said, "Well, your Aunt Garnet's got a point."

"What?" I said, sitting up. "You can't be serious! She's totally against this church merger. Tell me how Christian that is!"

"Benni, it's not that I agree with her feelings. It's just that, in a way, I understand what she's saying. Mama has this saying, *No es lo mismo hablar de toros que estar en el redondel*. Roughly translated it means talking about bulls is not the same as facing them in the ring. Dove—and you know I love her like my second mother—doesn't live here and hasn't for a long time. It's easy for someone outside of a community to come in and tell you how things should be, then leave you with the consequences. Your aunt's right. You can't change people that fast."

"But you have to start somewhere," I said.

"Yes," she said, her voice floating softly across the room. "But you have to let people choose that themselves. Isn't that the whole idea of freedom in our country? Shouldn't freedom encompass staying the same if that's what you want to do?"

I thought about what she said for a moment. "You're not saying that people should stay bigoted like that Toby creature, are you?"

"Of course not," she said, her voice patient. "But think

about it. Dove and Garnet were literally raised in the same house, by the same parents, with the same culture, skin color, and religion, and *they* can't get along longer than three minutes. And people are expecting a black and a white church to blend into some kind of cohesive whole? I'm not defending your aunt's views. I don't even agree with them. It's just that some people, some really good, decent people, don't necessarily want to make a grandstand effort. Some people challenge things in little ways every day of their lives. That doesn't make them bad or less brave."

I didn't answer right away. Was she talking about herself? About her and Emory? "Why does it all have to be so hard?" I finally said.

"I don't know, *amiga*. I honestly don't know."

"Well, I hope that little jerk Toby gets what's coming to him. The picture of him spitting on Miss DeLora is something that my brain will never forget. Believe me, if ever I've felt murderous thoughts in my heart, it was at that moment."

And, we found out the next morning, I wasn't the only one.

5

� the chapter number are three decorative four-pointed star motifs✳

THE NEXT DAY, when I stumbled downstairs in my pajamas looking for breakfast, the dining table was bare. The feud had obviously been moved from food into other areas. I was searching the kitchen cupboards for coffee filters when Uncle WW came in through the side door.

"Third shelf to the left of the stove," he said. "Got some doughnuts here." He sat a couple of white bags down on the white tile counter.

"You're an angel," I said, opening one and pulling out a fresh maple bar. I took a generous bite and let the sweet warmth coat my mouth. "Where are the girls?" I opened the coffee canister and started measuring out coffee.

"Guess there's to be a quiltin' bee," he said. "They're up to the church gettin' ready for that, I reckon." He glanced up at the pink plastic daisy clock on the wall. The time read seven-forty-five. "Most of us round here get up before noon."

"Hey, I'm on vacation," I said.

The phone rang, and he picked it up at the same time Elvia wandered into the kitchen. She was dressed already, looking fresh and crisp in a pair of wheat-colored jeans and a white cotton T-shirt. Her hair was pulled back in a dark shiny bun.

"No double breakfast this morning," I said, pointing to the bags of doughnuts. "The competition has moved on. Uncle WW's provided sustenance, though. There's a creme-filled in there, I think."

She nodded, not answering, and walked over to the coffeemaker to wait for the pot to fill. We both poured a cup of coffee and were sitting at the breakfast nook in the corner of the kitchen when Uncle WW, his face sober as a judge's, hung up the phone.

"The manure's goin' to hit the fan now," he said.

"What's wrong?" I asked, licking a flake of icing off my finger.

"Toby Hunter's dead."

I looked up at him, shocked. "Dead? Like in a car accident?" With the way he pealed away from Emory's house last night, it wouldn't have surprised me.

"Nope, he was beat to death. Found his body out on one of the side roads near Mayhaw Lake. Right next to his truck."

"Madre de dios," Elvia said softly.

"Who was that on the phone?" I asked, looking down at my half-eaten doughnut, my appetite gone.

"Your aunt Garnet. They just heard at the church. Brother Woodward was comin' back to the parsonage as they were opening the fellowship hall. He said it happened real early this morning."

"Poor Grady," I said.

"Especially after losin' his wife so young and all. He's had it tough, that's a fact," Uncle WW said.

"When did his wife die?" I vaguely remembered her from church, a slender, freckled woman who sang a weak soprano in the choir.

"Oh, 'bout eight years ago now. Had cancer. Took a

long time to pass on, poor soul. 'Bout tore Grady to pieces. And Toby was her pride and joy. Probably good she's not here to see how he turned out. Though she never could see what a little hooligan he always was." Uncle WW's face turned pink. "Don't mean to be speaking ill of the dead."

"Well, the truth is the truth," I said. "Did Brother Woodward say they had any idea who could have done it?"

"Not that they're sayin'," he replied, his bushy eyebrows raising slightly.

"There's lots of people who probably had a grudge against that boy," I said.

Uncle WW shrugged. "Guess we have to wait and see."

Emory came over while I was upstairs changing. He and Elvia were on the porch swing, their heads close together, when I came outside.

"No spooning in broad daylight," I said. "You'll scare the horses."

"Hey, Benni Lou," Emory said. "What's up for today?"

"For me, the quilting bee, I guess. I don't pick up Gabe until three o'clock and I promised I'd lend a hand getting the opportunity quilt finished. I think they're also working on something for Brother Cooke and his wife."

"Think he's forgiven you yet for your baptismal water fiasco?" Emory said, his eyes twinkling.

"I can still rat on you," I said, sitting down in a wicker porch chair. "It's not too late for Brother Cooke to kill you."

We instantly sobered at my choice of words. "Yikes," I said. "Speaking of that, I take it you heard."

Emory nodded. "Grady called Daddy early this morning, right after he found out. You know they've been buddies from way back, even though Daddy's supporting Amen's run for mayor. He was sobbin' and apologizin' for what Toby did last night and swearin' he was going to get whoever did that to his son." Emory pulled Elvia a little closer.

"He was talking out of his mind, and Daddy knew that. Just let him ramble."

"Did he tell Boone what happened? All Uncle WW knew was Toby got beat to death out by Mayhaw Lake."

"Guess he was hit in the back of the head a number of times with some kind of blunt object. They're thinking a hunk of wood, though they didn't find anything at the scene with his blood on it. Most likely the killer took it with him. The back of his head was pretty messed up from what they say. Guess they caught him walking away, and *they* was some kind of mad."

"That certainly enlarges the suspect pool, doesn't it?"

"No doubt."

We sat silent for a moment, contemplating the possibilities.

"Well," I finally said, glancing at my watch, "it's almost eight-thirty. I'd better get on over to the church before the hens start clucking about the lazy habits of Californians."

Emory laughed. "Sweetcakes, your lazy nature's probably done already been pecked to death hours ago. No doubt they've moved on to more scintillating subjects like your many forays into crime back in San Celina or whether you'll actually wear a dress to church this Sunday or not."

"Eat Arkansas clay. Where are you two headed?"

"I'm going to drive Elvia into Little Rock," Emory said. "Show her the university, some of the other sights."

"Don't forget the old mill," I said.

"What old mill?" Elvia asked.

"The opening scene of *Gone with the Wind* was filmed in North Little Rock at this old mill. It's pretty cool. The house on *Designing Women*, that TV show you liked so much, is in Little Rock, too."

"And a few museums of note," Emory said dryly. "We do have some culture here in Arkansas."

"Take her to Corky's," I said, then turned to my friend.

"It's the best barbecue in Arkansas even if it did originate in Memphis."

"Go do some stitchin'," Emory said. "Leave Elvia's Southern education to me."

I walked the four blocks to Sugartree Baptist Church, enjoying the cool, early-morning fall air and the brilliant colors of the changing leaves. In San Celina, fall was more brown and gray with a few touches of gold. I'd forgotten how bold nature's colors could be. I cut through the middle of the busy town square where business was going on as usual at the red brick courthouse. Looking at the surface of this small town, you'd never know a brutal murder had occurred last night.

Grady Hunter's campaign office was closed, the shade drawn down over the glass-front door. I wondered how the death of his son would affect his run for mayor. I felt a little guilty for not feeling more remorse about Toby Hunter's murder, but both encounters I had with him yesterday had not given me any reason to think that the world wouldn't be a better place without him. Grady seemed like a nice man, and I trusted Amen's opinion of him, but I couldn't understand how someone like that could produce such an obvious sociopath as Toby. I passed by the Beauty Barn and was tempted to stick my head in to hear what the ladies had to say about the crime. Plenty, I was sure, but I could do that later.

The freshly mown lawn of the church was still soaked with dew, turning the bottoms of my Wranglers soggy and limp. In honor of homecoming, the parking lot separating the sanctuary and the fellowship hall had a fresh coat of asphalt and new white lines. Half the spaces were filled with the sparkling clean old Buicks and Chevys of the church's quilting ladies.

Next to the pastor's office, under the very window of my infamous entry into Sugartree Baptist prankhood fame, Frank Lovelis, the church's longtime janitor and handyman, was trimming bushes with handheld clippers. Frank had worked for and attended the church for as long as my memory extended. He wore the same gray work pants and shirt that I'd always remembered him wearing. A short, broad-chested man with rough walnut-brown skin and coarse features, he had sad brown eyes and a low, hesitant voice. He didn't talk much, but if you were polite to him, he'd pull a cellophane-wrapped butterscotch candy from his pocket and hand it wordlessly to you, the white around his dark eyes sometimes growing watery and red.

"Hello, Mr. Lovelis," I said, stopping for a moment. "How are you?"

"Fine, Miss Benni," he said, his head nodding in small, uncontrollable jerks. He always addressed everyone by Miss, Mrs., or Mr. and their first name. Whenever I heard a preacher talk about the definition of the word *humble*, Mr. Lovelis always came to mind.

"You remember me?" I said, smiling.

"Yes," he said. "Mr. Emory talks of you all the time. I remember you, yes."

I looked over at the fellowship hall. "I'm braving the dragon's lair this morning."

He gave a jerky nod. "Yes, miss, they're a'talkin' away."

"The grounds look marvelous," I said.

"Thank you, miss." He glanced back to his bushes, a not-so-subtle indication that he wanted to get back to work.

"Well, you have a nice day," I said.

"Yes, miss, you, too." He reached into one of his pockets, pulled out a butterscotch candy, and held it out, his eyes studying the ground at my feet.

"Thank you, Mr. Lovelis," I said, taking the candy. For a second his calloused fingers touched mine. "I'll see you around."

"Yes, miss," he said and turned back to his bush.

Inside the large, airy hall, all the partitions that normally separated the room for Sunday school classes were folded back, and twenty or so ladies were gathered in equal numbers around two large quilt frames, fingers moving in and out as fast as their tongues were flying.

"It's about time you got here, Benni," said a rosy-cheeked woman with a dark curly cap of hair. She came out of the attached kitchen carrying a glass pitcher of lemonade. "How long has it been since we've seen each other? Ten, twelve years? You haven't gained an ounce. I hate you." She smiled, showing pretty white teeth that appeared brighter because of her red lipstick.

"Leave it to her to get here in time for the coffee break," Dove called from over at one of the quilts. I turned and stuck my tongue out at her, sending the ladies around her to clucking. Beulah, the youngest woman sitting around the quilt, gave a great hoot. I waved at her and grinned.

"I tried to teach her respect," Dove said. "Just never took. Slid right off her like she was covered with bacon grease."

The other ladies murmured in agreement, throwing in comments about their own ill-behaved children and grandchildren.

"She's always treated *me* with respect," Aunt Garnet said from over at the other quilt. "Guess that says something about a person, don't you think? We're treated how we're expected to be treated."

The room went silent. I froze, looking at her then Dove. This was not good. And, dang it, it involved me.

"Come in the kitchen and help me with the goodies," the dark-haired lady whispered in my ear. "They'll settle down once they get some sugar in them."

Back in the kitchen as I helped her take the lids off Tupperware cake holders and unwrap foil-covered brownies and cupcakes, she said, "You don't remember me, do you?"

I folded a piece of tinfoil and gave her a long look. Finally a light went on in my head. "Shirley Hazard, is that you?"

"It's Shirley Hazard Arnett now," she said, laughing gaily. "Better save yourself a piece of whatever you want, 'cause I know these ladies. They are worse than a plague of locusts. This'll be gone in a half-hour, tops."

Shirley was another girl who had often joined our little gang of children. She lived down the street from Emory. Her father, Dr. Hazard, had been the local dentist. She used to sneak us the plastic giveaway toys he bought for his young patients. I remember all of us fighting one summer over a ring that flipped open to reveal a place for secret messages.

"Arnett? Did you marry Howard Arnett? You always despised him." Howard was the mortician's son, a skinny, anemic-looking boy a year younger than us. He would never come up in the tree house because he was afraid of heights. Shirley used to taunt him from the window of the tree house.

She pulled a knife out of a drawer and with practiced ease fixed the smashed side of a coconut layer cake. "Yes, but he turned out to be real cute once he grew up, filled out, took off his braces, and got contacts."

"I heard you moved away to someplace. . . . Wasn't it Atlanta or something?"

"Birmingham, Alabama, actually. Howard opened up an auto repair shop there. He works on foreign cars. Mercedes is his specialty."

"So he didn't go into his father's business?"

"No, his brother, Alex, did. We moved back to Sugartree about three years ago, and Howard opened up a shop in Little Rock. After my daddy died, Mama was lonely, and since I'm an only child . . ." She left the obvious unsaid.

"Does Howard's daddy still own the mortuary?"

"Yes, but Alex does most of the work these days. With a couple of assistants, of course." She leaned closer, her voice dropping. "It's also the official county morgue, seein'

as we don't often need one here in Sugartree. You heard
about Toby Hunter?"

I nodded, trying to think of something appropriate to
say. "He was so young."

"It's always sad when someone young dies, but I heard
that boy was a trial for Grady from the time his hormones
kicked in at twelve. I guess losin' his mama when he was
so young probably didn't help, but, honestly, we've all had
our sad times. Isn't no reason to turn mean on folks."

"All I heard was he was beat to death."

"That's what they're sayin'. They brought him in early
this morning when I was over there doing some paperwork." She looked at the coconut cake critically, gave it
one last swipe, then moved on to a chocolate sheet cake
whose top layer of icing had stuck to the lid of the cake
carrier. "I work at the mortuary part-time when I'm not up
here at the church." She smiled at me, holding the icing-
covered knife in front of her. "I teach the senior ladies'
Sunday school class, am in charge of the nursery, and was
just elected president of the Women's Missionary Union.
And I have two kids in high school."

"Wow, you do have a plateful," I said appreciatively.
"Do they have any idea who might have killed him?" I
couldn't help asking.

She shrugged and went back to scraping icing off the
plastic lid and transferring it to the cake. "He was an ornery
kid. Liked to drink too much and carry on. Been arrested
more than a few times for driving drunk and doing things
like putting cherry bombs in the mailboxes over in the
black part of town. Heard rumors about him breaking into
a few houses and stealing stuff, but if he did, it was hushed
up. I don't have to tell you Grady Hunter's pretty important
in town, has all manner of influential friends here and in
Little Rock. Guess he should have spent less time with
them and more watching his son." She shook her head in
disapproval. "I heard the police talking outside my office.

I guess they dragged his best friend, Eddie Johnston, out of bed to see what he knew. He said last time he saw Toby he was heading home after they'd had a burger at the Dairy Queen. Of course, how much of that is true remains to be seen. They could've just as easily and more'n likely been drinking beer at some roadhouse. Might've been a fight between him and Eddie or one of his other white trash friends, but there's lots of people in this town who bear a grudge against Toby Hunter."

"Like who?" I asked.

She shook her head, her ivory cheeks blushing pink. "Oh, I've said too much already. Howard's always sayin' I'm worse than a mockingbird."

"How's Grady taking it?" I asked, arranging some German chocolate cookie bars on a platter.

"Haven't heard, but I imagine he's real torn up, his only child and all. And the unexpectedness of it." Her eyes widened slightly in curiosity. "But I guess you'd know about that. Heard about Jack when we were in Alabama. You doin' okay?"

"Fine," I said, wiping my fingers on a pink paper napkin. "It is hard when someone you love dies unexpectedly. You never . . ." I thought for a moment, searching for the right words. "You never quite stop believing they'll walk through the door and life will pick up where you left off."

Her smile was mischievous. "Guess that might cause a little excitement in your life now if *that* happened."

I laughed. "Yes, it definitely would. I'm going to pick up Gabe this afternoon."

"Your aunt Garnet thinks the moon and stars of him. Talks about him all the time, what a handsome, well-mannered man he is."

"He can be charming. Elderly ladies are his specialty."

She nodded out toward the fellowship hall where the talking had risen at least three decibels. I hoped I wasn't the subject. "Then he ought to do fine this week."

"No doubt," I said.

We carried the cakes, pies, and cookies out to the big room and arranged them on the long paper-covered tables. The ladies, most of them Dove and Garnet's age, made a last few stitches, then gradually, still talking, meandered over to the ladened table.

"The coffee's almost done, ladies," Shirley said, pointing to the fifty-cup stainless steel coffeemaker. "Hot water's in the kitchen if you want tea. Let's say the blessing, and then you can tear into it."

After the fastest blessing in church history, the ladies crowded around the table. I smiled and chatted with them as I laid out plastic spoons, pink paper napkins, sugar cubes, and powdered cream.

"How come you don't have no babies?" Mrs. Ryan, the organist said, her voice sharp enough to cut five-year-old fruitcake. Though she was completely deaf at ninety-two, she still played the organ for every Sunday service, wedding, and funeral at Sugartree Baptist. Today her platinum wig sat slightly askew on her dried-apple doll head.

I shrugged at the inevitable question and said, "Just not blessed yet, Mrs. Ryan."

"You work outside the home?" Mrs. Versie Pitts, the head deacon's wife asked. She was a mere sixty-two, a bit young for this group, and stout and solid as a tree stump. She was best known for her kind heart and her tendency to hiccup when she was nervous. She taught me and Emory three years in a row in Vacation Bible School when we were eleven, twelve, and thirteen. She spent a lot of time hiccuping.

"I work as a curator for a folk art museum," I said. "It's supposed to be part-time, but you know how that goes."

She leaned over the table and said in a loud whisper, "Quit that job right now. Too much mental stimulation freezes up the uterus, and then the baby can't stick. Trust me, hon." She patted my hand and took three lemon bars.

"Yes, ma'am," I said, resisting the urge to roll my eyes. "Have you mentioned this theory to Duck Wakefield? I'm sure he has some doctor friends who'd love to study on it."

She waved a plump hand at me, then added a chocolate-covered homemade doughnut to her plate. "Oh, those doctors think they know everything. I'm telling you, my granddaughter, Clarice, quit workin' at the bank down to Little Rock and *kaboom*, it was not but three months later she was expectin' twins."

"Kaboom, huh?" I said.

"Just like that." She snapped her fingers.

"Thanks, I'll keep it in mind."

Beulah, who'd been standing behind Mrs. Pitts for the whole exchange, rolled her eyes. "There's one for your diary," she said, taking an oatmeal cookie.

I watched Mrs. Pitts walk away, a bit irritated at her nerve and yet oddly amused, too. I knew she wasn't a mean person and would give her last nickel to help someone in need. I remember as a child her telling us stories of taking people into their home who were just passing through Sugartree on their wanderings to find something. She'd give them a hot meal and wash their clothes or find them new ones in the missionary barrel. She and her husband, Joe, were the ones years ago who'd taken in Frank Lovelis when he was found wandering drunk in the streets of Sugartree. They got him the job as church janitor, and he'd lived in their garage apartment ever since. As kids, we'd never heard what his story had been, where he'd come from, how he'd ended up in Sugartree. It was a great source of speculation and tall tales among us in the late evenings spent up in Emory's tree house.

"What was that old busybody telling you?" Dove asked, coming up behind the table and standing next to me.

"How to unfreeze my uterus so babies will stick," I said. "Too much mental stimulation. That's my problem."

"Land's sakes, Versie Pitts is as good and honest as they come, but sometimes that woman can be a chicken salad sandwich minus the chicken."

I smiled. "It'll give me something to amuse Gabe with when I see him this afternoon."

"When is my boy due in?" Dove asked, surveying the spread and choosing a piece of red velvet cake. She stage-whispered to me, "Melba Rae Satterfield made this. Make a note. She's got the cleanest kitchen in town."

"Duly noted. And three o'clock." I leaned closer to her. "Uncle WW told us about Toby this morning. How's everyone taking it?"

Her pale eyes grew watery. "That poor man. We took some food over to Grady's house before we got here. His housekeeper said he wasn't even there, was down at the police station. Lord, that is the hardest thing for a parent to experience, havin' one of their children pass on before they do."

"I met Grady Hunter yesterday. He seemed pretty nice."

She nodded and looked down at the piece of cake in her hand. "He is, from what Garnet says."

When a couple of women walked over to greet her, I took a molasses cookie and wandered over to study the quilts in progress. Walking across the long fellowship room was like time-traveling back into my childhood. The walls reflected the different Sunday school classes with primary grades' hand-colored pictures of Noah's Ark and some interestingly conceived purple and blue zebras and red elephants to the Bible verse memory contests of the older children (at the top of everyone's list and still a perennial favorite—John 11:35—"Jesus wept") to the teenagers' brightly colored "What Would Jesus Do?" posters.

The quilts, though they wouldn't win any awards in today's quilt world with its emphasis on original design and nontraditional patterns, were also timeless favorites. One was a signature quilt, obviously meant for the former pastor, Brother Cooke and his wife. It was a nine-patch set-on point using fall colors in a mixture of solid color fabric and conversation prints of pumpkins, maple leaves, and tiny acorns. The colors were soothing to the eye with its blend of topaz, crimson, rust, coffee brown, and tan. Touches of orange, an unexpected and often misused color, gave it interesting spots of color and kept it from being boring. These ladies might not know all the avant-garde designs, but they knew the colors of their land, and their stitching was something younger quilters could and should admire.

I leaned over it, holding my cookie away so it wouldn't scatter crumbs. In the middle of every other square was an embroidered name. In the quilt's center, a topaz square, larger than the others, stated in cursive stitching that I recognized as Aunt Garnet's handwriting: "Honoring Brother Edwin Cooke and his wife, Martha—A Good Name Is More Desirable Than Great Riches."

"Huh," Dove said behind me. "That's 'cause they're feelin' guilty for how little they paid him over the years. Garnet and WW used to have to stand on their heads and whistle Dixie backwards to get the church to vote them even the tiniest raise. She said those poor folks weren't paid enough to choke a gnat. Garnet might be a lot of things, but she ain't cheap."

"Why, Dove Ramsey," I said, turning to face her. "I can't believe you're actually saying something nice about Aunt Garnet."

Her face went rigid, then she narrowed one pale blue eye at me. "That's between you and me, missy. I mean it, I'll wear you out if you tell Garnet I said that."

I held up my hands. "Your secret's safe with me. Far be it for me to spread gossip that actually says something nice about someone."

"You've got a smart mouth," she said, smacking my shoulder.

"Wow," I said, going over to the other quilt, the one

they were auctioning off this Sunday afternoon to raise money to help cover the expenses of the possible church merger. It was a Crown of Thorns, a difficult pattern that reminded me a lot of Double Wedding Ring. The background was off-white with the circles of the crown made of red, brown, gold, and off-white. It was bordered in gold fabric, and the stitching on it had to be sixteen or seventeen stitches to the inch, each one as even and neat as if one person had stitched the whole quilt. It was obvious this group of women had quilted together for many, many years.

"These are beautiful," I said to Aunt Garnet when she walked up next to us. She and Dove eyed each other but didn't speak.

"Yes, well, the signature quilt for Brother Cooke was a last minute thing," she said. "Actually we made them a presentation quilt before they left a few years ago that was much prettier. It was an appliquéd album quilt with scenes from the Bible. My square showed Paul and the burning bush."

Dove opened her mouth to correct her, but I grabbed her arm and pulled her away before she could.

"I'll see you tonight, Aunt Garnet," I said. "Gabe will be with me."

She beamed at his name. "He's such a dear man. You are so lucky he married you. Especially at your age."

I bit my tongue and smiled at her. "Yes, ma'am, I am."

"That's what you get," Dove said when I safely settled her over by the refreshment table. "Why are you bein' on her side anyway when she makes nasty remarks like that? Paul and the burning bush! Wonder what Moses would have to say about that?"

"So she's a little confused. I'm just trying to keep the peace. You know, blessed are the peacemakers 'cause they'll inherit the earth, not that that's such a good deal these days."

"The peacemakers will be called sons of God," Dove said, correcting me. "So that lets you out."

"I'm sure the Lord meant for it to be gender-inclusive. Anyway, just be good for two seconds, okay?" I pointed to the wall that held the high school student's poster. "Ask yourself—what would Jesus do?"

"He'd've thrown up His hands in despair years ago." She set her bottom lip. "The Lord has no use for someone that stubborn."

"The oak calling the ironwood tree a hardhead," I said.

"Go get your husband and leave me be," she answered.

Even with a lot of puttering around back at Garnet's house and a leisurely drive to Little Rock, I was still an hour early for Gabe's plane. I tried to concentrate on a discarded copy of the *Arkansas Democrat-Gazette*, but my mind flitted back to Shirley Arnett's words about lots of people in this town bearing a grudge against Toby Hunter. I was surprised that it wasn't talked about or at least mentioned this morning at the quilting bee, but then again, maybe it had been before I arrived. If Sugartree Baptist was anything like our church back home, then the seniors, the quiet bedrock of the church, knew more than the young people about what was going on with folks. I definitely had to park myself in Beulah's Beauty Barn one of the next few mornings and see what some of the town's gossip queens were saying about Toby's murder.

When Gabe walked through the Delta airline gate, I wiggled my way through the crowd toward him.

"*Querida!*" His strong arms closed around me and lifted me up. I buried my face in the crook of his neck, a sense of peace coming over me when I inhaled his musky male scent. It still amazed me how much this man could cause my heart to jump, even after almost two years of marriage. "I missed you like crazy," he whispered in my ear.

"Me, too, Sergeant Friday," I said, using my now affectionate but originally derisive nickname for him.

He let my feet touch the ground, and after a quick kiss we started toward the baggage claim area.

"Don't you have any carry-ons?" I asked, linking my arm in his.

"Had a *Time* magazine, but I left it on the plane."

I shook my head in amazement, wanting to ask him what he'd do if he got a headache or needed a tissue or a snack. But I didn't. My husband is a remarkably handsome man, part Hispanic, part Anglo with deep-set gray-blue eyes, a still-flat stomach, and long, muscled runner's legs. His thick black hair and mustache had only just recently been sprinkled by the silver age fairy, which only added to his appeal. I had no doubt that if his attractive brown brow had wrinkled even slightly with the signs of a headache or hunger, there would have been at least three women with supplies ready. And he would have made them feel like the most wonderful and kind-hearted ladies on earth for helping a poor, suffering man in need.

Then again, he also could be an unbelievably arrogant, patriarchal know-it-all who always, with no regard for *anyone* else, used all the hot water while taking a shower in our tiny house.

And he could make me laugh like no one else ever had.

"So," he said as we waited for his bag, "what's happened in Sugartree in the last two days? Did I miss anything exciting?"

"Not much," I said, keeping my face nonchalant.

He stared at my face a moment, then groaned. "You found another body, didn't you?"

6

"I RESENT YOU assuming I'm involved with it," I repeated, watching him throw his bag in the back of the Explorer and shut the door.

"You've said that three times already," he said patiently.

"I wasn't anywhere near the body! You're always assuming . . ."

He pushed me against the back of the car, his pelvis holding me captive, and took my face in his big, sure hands. "Let me kiss my wife before we get into it, okay?" When his lips touched mine, I couldn't resist, and we kissed until an elderly man walked by and cleared his throat. Next to him, a gray-haired lady wearing a green cloth coat with a fake fur collar stared openly.

"Sorry," Gabe said, winking at the lady, "but my sister and I haven't seen each other in a very long time."

The lady gasped and pulled at the now-smiling man's arm, hurrying him along.

"That was real funny," I said, climbing in the Explorer, laughing in spite of myself.

"Just trying to get into the swim of things. They probably didn't think it was strange at all. Actually, don't you think they looked a bit alike? I bet their family tree hasn't forked too many times in the last few generations."

"*That's* even less funny, Friday. Promise me, no cousin-marryin'-cousin jokes. I've got more'n enough to worry about with the squabbling sisters without wonderin' about you gettin' lynched because you're pokin' fun at Southern folks."

He fiddled with the electronic gadgets in the Explorer, fitting the seat to his legs and adjusting the mirrors. "You've only been here two days, and your accent's getting as thick as molasses. I find it extremely sexy."

I showed him my fist. "Just watch it, okay?"

He leaned over and kissed it, then grinned at me. "You know I'll have half the ladies in town charmed before dinner and the rest by dessert."

"That's supper here, you arrogant, Midwestern son-of-a-sodbuster. Dinner's done and gone already."

"Duly noted, sweetheart." He rested his hand on my thigh. "Two days apart is too long."

I put my hand over his, pressing it into my leg. "Likewise." We smiled at each other. "How did Scout react when you left him at the ranch? Does he miss me?"

"Are you kidding? When I left, your dad was asking him if he wanted bacon or sausage with his scrambled eggs. Your puppy's not even going to know your name in a week."

I smacked his thigh. "That's not funny."

"So," he said, his face turning into its sober, chief-of-police expression. "Tell me about this homicide."

In the hour's drive to Sugartree, I filled him in on who was who, what had happened last night at the fund-raising dinner, and what Shirley Arnett had told me this morning at church.

"A detective hasn't talked to any of you?" he asked, slowing down as we came to the center of town. Activity was winding down for the day since it was almost five o'clock. Half the parking spaces surrounding the red brick courthouse were empty. A couple of men in conservative Brooks Brothers–style suits talked and laughed in front of the courthouse's double glass doors. "That's odd. Then again, it's probably a very small department."

"Haven't talked to anyone yet," I said, glancing at Amen's campaign office as we drove by. It was dark and empty. Five doors down, at Grady Hunter's, the lights were on, and people moved about inside. "Turn right here." I wanted to show him Emory's house, so he could form a mental picture of last night's events.

"Just how much money does your cousin have?" he said when he saw the house, a surprised expression on his face.

"A lot, and believe it or not, that's making it harder for Elvia to commit to him, not easier."

"I believe it," he said, taking one last glance in the rear-view mirror as we turned the corner to drive up my aunt's street. "Marrying someone of a different culture is hard enough. Marrying out of your economic class is often an impossible hurdle to overcome."

"That's ridiculous," I said, turning to face him, straining against my safety belt. "Are you telling me that you're going to feel different about Emory simply because he has a little money?"

"That mansion tells me he has more than a little money."

"So what if he does? That doesn't change who he is."

"No, but to pretend like it doesn't matter is being naive."

It was a hard thing for me to consider when it came to my cousin. I always knew he was wealthy, but somehow it never seemed to matter. Maybe it's because I saw him through times when Uncle Boone's business hadn't been doing very well, and Emory had remained the same generous, caring person.

"It shouldn't matter," I insisted.

He didn't answer me, knowing that there wasn't much

further we could get with this line of conversation.

"Is Aunt Garnet anxious to see me?" he said, his voice teasing.

"She can't wait, and you know it. I'm telling you, though, you'd better walk softly the next week or so. She and Dove are on the warpath, and they might be taking hostages."

"As long as I'm fed Garnet's angel food cake and Dove's fried okra, I'll be a happy prisoner of war."

"There's a good chance you might have missed the cooking competition. They've moved on to bigger and better battles."

But they surprised me and managed to put a meal on the table in honor of Gabe. There weren't duplicate foods, but there was essentially two meals with each of them fixing their best dishes. He was in Arkansas hog heaven.

At dinner Emory told us that a detective had finally dropped by to question him and Boone. The young man had caught them just when Elvia and he were arriving home from Little Rock. Boone wasn't home, so the detective said he'd try to find him at his office.

"What'd he ask you?" I said, buttering one of Aunt Garnet's cracklin' corn bread muffins, holding up my hand before Dove could speak. "Pass the sweet potato biscuits, please." Dove's face relaxed into a smile. If this kept up, we'd have to start our own Weight Watchers chapter.

"Just what I saw and heard. Wanted to know if Toby actually threatened anyone."

"I can't believe I missed the whole thing," Elvia said.

"It happened pretty fast," I said. "Did the detective give you any idea who they suspected?"

Emory took a sip of iced tea. "I think he was fishin' to see if Quinton, John, or I had threatened Toby. He seemed especially interested in Quinton."

"I hope they don't try to pin it on Quinton just because

he's black," I said, voicing out loud what all of us had been thinking.

"Me, too, sweetcakes," Emory said. "But it wouldn't be the first time in Southern history, believe me."

We were sitting on the front porch in gastric misery, watching the sun hover around the tops of the pine and hickory trees, when Dove and Garnet appeared on the porch carrying their respective black leather purses.

"I'm off to stuff envelopes for Amen," Dove said, leaning down to kiss Isaac on the cheek.

"I'm off to stuff envelopes for Grady," Garnet said, glaring at her sister's back.

"Oh, Lordy, I'm just stuffed," Uncle WW said, patting his small pot belly and causing the rest of us to laugh.

It wasn't fifteen minutes later that an undistinguished white Ford sedan drove up and a young man in his early twenties stepped out. He was wearing a subtle plaid sports jacket, conservative gray pants, and black loafers. His brown hair had been freshly cut, revealing a white line around his tanned neck that we could see from the porch. As he was walking up the drive toward us, his shoe caught on something, causing him to do that little catch-yourself dance to keep from falling. His round, choir-boy face was red as a pomegranate when he righted himself and continued toward us.

"That's the detective who talked to us this afternoon," Emory said, standing up to greet him. "Billy Brackman."

Gabe chuckled softly next to me. "Make sure and ask for his Junior G-man badge." I frowned and shook my head at him to behave himself.

"Nice seein' you again, Mr. Littleton," the young man said when he reached the bottom step.

"Billy, I told you Mr. Littleton's my father. Just call me Emory."

Billy cleared his throat, his face still flushed. "Yes, sir, uh, Emory." He glanced around at the rest of us and said,

"I hate to bother y'all on this fine evening, but I'm lookin' for a . . ." He double-checked the small wire-ring notebook in his hands. ". . . a Mrs. Albenia Harper."

"That's me," I said, standing up.

"Uh, Mrs. Harper, if you've got a few minutes to spare, I'd sure appreciate you talkin' to me about the events surrounding the altercation at Mr. Boone Littleton's house last evening."

"Sure," I said, walking across the porch toward him. "Where would you like to talk?"

He pointed out toward his car. "Why don't we just walk out there where we won't disturb these fine people. It won't be but a few minutes of your time, I promise."

"No problem," I said.

Out by his car, he fumbled through his notebook, still trying to regain his composure. He looked up at me and said, "Please bear with me, ma'am. I have the questions I need to ask here somewhere."

"My husband's a police officer," I said, trying to break the ice. "He was the dark-haired man sitting next to me."

"Is that right?" He glanced over at Gabe. "Where at?"

"Right now he's chief of police in San Celina, California. That's a college town about five hours north of Los Angeles. But he worked for the LAPD for twenty years in undercover narcotics and homicide."

His eyes widened as he tried not to look impressed. "Really?"

"When we met, I was throwing rocks at a police car. I was a suspect in a murder."

He stared at me a moment, then laughed. "You're shittin' me." His face turned red again. "I'm sorry, ma'am. That was a real unprofessional thing to say."

I laughed. "No, I'm not kidding you, Detective Brackman. But I didn't do it, I swear, and he married me three months later." I leaned closer to him and whispered, "They were very small rocks, and I was really, really stressed."

He grinned, his shoulders relaxing a little under his jacket. "I'd surely like to hear *that* whole story sometime." He glanced over at Gabe again. "LAPD, huh? Cool." He shoved the notebook in his pocket and said, "Shoot, forget this. How 'bout I just ask you what happened?"

He listened intently without interrupting when I told him everything I saw and heard from the time I was in the attic until Toby Hunter and his friends drove away.

When I finished, he waited a moment before commenting. A cool evening breeze kicked up some leaves, causing them to stick to our legs. I reached down and brushed them away.

"So," he said. "I don't reckon you recall anyone makin' any threats."

"No, not to speak of." Amen's remark about killing him if she had a gun wasn't something I was going to give this detective. Amen would no more kill than I would.

He looked at me a long moment, waiting.

"No," I repeated, wanting to kick myself for giving him something to even consider. You'd think after being married to a cop I'd have learned to answer simply yes, no, and I don't recall.

He scratched behind one ear. "I heard Quinton Tolliver was pretty upset."

"Wouldn't you be if someone spit on your grandmother?"

"Did you hear him make any threatening remarks?"

"No. Do they have any suspects? I'm sure a guy like that had all sorts of marginal friends."

His young face was genial but unrevealing. "Ma'am, I appreciate your cooperation. You and your family have a good evening now."

Rats, he was obviously experienced enough to sidestep nosy questions. I smiled and said, "Thank you, Detective."

Back on the porch, Emory was teasing Elvia, trying to

get her to admit that pulled pork barbecue was better than carnitas.

"It's okay," she said, smiling. "It's just kind of bland, don't you think?"

"Bland! How can you say that?"

"Maybe with a few jalapeño peppers . . ."

He made some exaggerated gagging sounds.

"Okay, you two," I said, going over and sitting on my husband's lap. "It'll be pork barbecue on Mondays and carnitas on Tuesdays. Does that solve your problem?"

"What did the detective ask you?" Gabe said, nuzzling my neck.

"Just wanted me to give my story, which I did in twenty-five words or less. I asked him if there were any suspects, and he very smoothly wished me a good evening."

"Good for him," Gabe said.

"Look, am I the only person here worried that this might somehow hurt Amen and her family?"

"We're all worried," Emory said. "But let's not speculate too much until we have more information."

"You're sounding less and less like a journalist every day," I said.

"Thank goodness for that," Gabe commented.

"Hey, now," Emory said. "Let's not disparage the good profession of journalism too much. The people do have a right to know . . ."

Before it could turn into another spirited debate between them about journalistic ethics, I said to Gabe, "The detective seemed very impressed with your LAPD credentials." With my thumb I smoothed down a couple of rogue hairs on Gabe's thick mustache.

"Well, I am an impressive sort of guy," he said.

I gave the end of his mustache a solid tug.

"Ow!" he said.

"Quit being so arrogant. At the risk of Garnet's wrath,

let's walk down to Amen's headquarters and see if we can help."

"How about me and Elvia meeting you at the Dairy Queen in about an hour?" Emory said. "I have a few more places I want to show Elvia."

"Be careful," I told my friend. "He's going to take you to all the make-out spots."

"Why do they get to make out and we have to stuff envelopes?" Gabe protested.

"Because we're an old married couple. Besides, I want you to meet Amen."

Isaac and Uncle WW, unwilling to incur the bad favor of either sister, chose to stay on the porch and watch the sun dip below the pine tree horizon.

In Amen's small two-room office next to Beulah's, there were half a dozen people doing as many different tasks—making phone calls, stuffing and addressing envelopes, running copies, typing address labels.

"Hey, kids," Dove said from behind a table near the window. A stack of white envelopes and pink fliers sat in neat piles in front of her.

Amen was in the small office in back typing on a laptop computer. She looked up and smiled at my greeting. "Hey, y'all here to help? Grab a bunch of envelopes and start stuffing."

"If that's what you need us to do," I said.

Amen shook her head no. "No, just testing you. We're almost done for tonight. We're running out of fliers so we'll be closing up shop in a half-hour or so." Her eyes flitted back to her computer screen. "Except for me. I'm working on a speech for tomorrow morning's Rotary Club meeting. Any excuse to take a break, though, is more than welcome."

She stood up and walked over to Gabe, holding out her hand. "I'm Amen Tolliver. You must be Benni's very significant other."

"Oh, I'm sorry," I said. "Yep, this is the one and only Gabriel Ortiz."

"Nice to meet you," he said, shaking her hand, his manner friendly but, I could tell, wary. "Benni speaks highly of you."

They studied each other intently. I felt a small tension between them that perplexed me.

"Same here," Amen said. "Benni's done bragged up and down the town about you. It's good we finally meet."

"I didn't brag that much," I said, elbowing her. "He's very conceited. Don't make it worse."

She smiled and spread her arm out, presenting the little room. "So, what do you think of my battle headquarters?"

"Very impressive," I said, gazing around the dark-paneled room covered with various posters touting her political abilities and admonishments to vote with your conscience, not your pocketbook. "You're in a room surrounded by posters dedicated to your favorite person. Heaven on earth."

She crumpled up a small flier and threw it at me. I ducked and let it fall to the floor. "Ha, you've lost your arm, Amen Tolliver. Good thing you went into politics and not sports."

"She's a hard pill to swallow sometimes, isn't she, Mr. Ortiz?" she said, her dark eyes challenging.

"Nothing I can't handle," Gabe said, his voice neutral.

"Yes, sirree, a hard pill indeed," she said, looking first at him, then at me, her left eyebrow raised slightly. I knew that look. Amen had it whenever she encountered someone who particularly annoyed her. I gave her a puzzled look, which she ignored. What *was* going on between these two?

Luckily Duck picked that moment to walk in.

"Curly Top!" he said. "Wondered when I'd run into you again."

At the sound of Duck's affectionate nickname, Gabe's face stiffened with territorial jealousy.

"Duncan Wakefield," Duck said, striding over to Gabe with an open hand. "But call me Duck. Everyone does. You must be Gabe. Great to meet you. Curly Top and I go way back, share some particularly special moments, but I'm sure she's told you all that."

"Actually she hasn't," Gabe said, shooting me an irritated glance.

"I was going to," I said, giving him my most winning smile.

Duck laughed. "Whatever she tells you, only believe half of it."

"I'll keep that in mind," Gabe said, his eyes informing me we'd talk about this later.

Duck went over to Amen and gave her a quick hug. "How's it goin', Mayor Tolliver?"

"You optimist, you," she said, her eyes shining with appreciation for his support. Then they grew troubled. "Have you seen Quinton today?"

"We had breakfast in Little Rock this morning. Didn't he tell you?"

"No, I haven't seen him all day and I'm worried. Especially after what happened to Toby Hunter last night."

"He came to the city to sign up for some law seminar. Said he was going to drop by and see some friends and wouldn't be home until late. I told him to call you and let you know."

She shook her head and sighed. "He's worse than Lawrence. I don't want him being anywhere he can't be accounted for. Toby's gang of rejects are probably driving around lookin' to pay back."

"He'll be fine," Duck said, resting a hand on her shoulder.

The fear in Amen's face was something I'd never seen in her. "I hope so."

His hand still on her shoulder, he said, "There were a couple more tonight. I have them in my truck."

Her eyes darted over to a pile of signs sitting next to her desk, covered with a white tarp. They'd obviously been in people's yards already. The posts were stained black with damp soil. Her chin went up. "Later, Duck."

"What're those?" Gabe asked, going over to the pile of yard signs.

"Leave those alone!" she said.

He threw the tarp back, revealing posters of her face covered with the spray-painted words "No nigger mayor" and thick wide swastikas.

I felt my stomach lurch in disgust. Gabe's face flushed with anger, his jaw hardening.

Amen grabbed the tarp from his hands and threw it back over the posters. "You don't take orders very well, do you, Mr. Ortiz?"

"Have you reported these to the police?" he asked.

"Right, like they're going to worry too much about it, especially now with Toby Hunter getting himself killed."

"Amen, you know he's right," Duck said, giving Gabe an apologetic look. "I've been trying to get her to report these for a week, but she refuses."

"What good would it do except stir up more animosity and cause bad publicity for me?" she asked. "There's lots of people on the fence about who to vote for, but if they think that electing me mayor would cause some kind of race war in the town, I wouldn't have a chance. Can't you see that?"

"You could be hurt," Duck said, his voice weary from an obviously much-repeated plea.

"Amen," Gabe said, his face softening slightly, "the police can't do anything if they don't know about it."

She went back to her computer, hit some buttons, and stared at the screen for a moment before answering Gabe. "I know that, but I'm telling you, the whole police force in this town is made up of white men, many of whom owe their jobs to the very people who don't want me in office.

How much time do you really think they'd put into finding out who did this? Especially now, with the mayor's son dead." She closed the lid of her laptop and looked up at us, her face grim. "Besides, after last night, we pretty much know who's behind it, don't we?"

7

"I DON'T THINK she meant Grady Hunter," I said to Gabe a few minutes later as we walked toward the Dairy Queen. The streets were nearly empty though it was only a little past eight o'clock. It was something I'd forgotten—how early the sidewalks rolled up in these small Southern towns.

"Why not? That's who I'd guess was behind it."

"For one thing, I met him, and he didn't seem the kind of man who'd put his son up to something like that."

"Are you saying you trust a politician?" Gabe's laugh was cynical.

"No, but I trust Amen. She really respects him. She told me and Elvia yesterday that she doesn't think he's been a bad mayor, just one who's behind the times. She says his biggest problem is he just has no impetus to change."

"Most rich white people don't."

His bitter words startled me. Not knowing quite how to answer, I changed the subject. "So, what did you think of Amen?"

He gave it some thought, then said, "She's a brave woman."

"That's a given. But what did you think of her personally?" Without a doubt, there'd been tension between them, and I wanted to know why.

"She seems nice."

Okay, he was forcing me to just flat out ask. "*Mi esposo querido,* I know when someone annoys you. What was it between you and Amen?"

He laughed and kept walking, not looking at me. "You have the worst Spanish accent I've ever heard. I told you, she seems nice."

I grabbed his arm, stopping him. "Can the bullcrap, Chief. What *is* it?"

He shrugged, trying not to show his irritation. "Okay, she's just . . . I don't know, not entirely . . ." His blue-gray eyes bore into mine. "Sweetheart, that woman is hiding something."

"Hiding something? That's ridiculous."

"Fine. You want to know what I think, then you tell me it's ridiculous. *That's* why I didn't want to say anything."

"I'm sorry, I don't mean you're ridiculous. I just can't imagine what Amen would have to hide. I've known her almost my whole life. She and Emory are practically siblings. If she had anything to hide, don't you think he'd know about it?"

He tilted his head. "Maybe he does."

"And not tell me? I'll jerk him through a knot if that's true."

"At any rate, I am impressed with her guts. I respect the fact that she won't let those bigots run her off."

"I hope she'll be okay," I said.

Gabe interlaced his fingers through mine. "I hope so, too, *querida.*" He brought my hand up to his lips and kissed it. "Not to change the subject, but what's the story behind you and, what was his name, Quack?"

I pulled my hand out of his and smacked him on the shoulder. "That's Duck. Dr. Duck Wakefield actually."

He did his best to keep his face neutral, but I could tell he was impressed. "He's a doctor?"

"A cardiologist, so you'd best be nice to him in case you have a heart attack while you're in Arkansas."

He snickered. "A doctor named Quack."

"*Duck,* and quit making fun of him."

"So, how are you and this Dr. Donald Duck connected in the past? And as long as I'm asking questions, why does he call you Curly Top?"

I held out a strand of my very curly hair. "The answer to the second question is obvious, don't you think? And the answer to the first, if you must know, is he gave me my first kiss. Behind that very Dairy Queen up there."

He glanced to where I pointed. A block away, the Dairy Queen was a bright beacon on an unusually dark street. Two or three obviously teenager-owned cars and pickups were parked in the shadows of the large lot. I could see Uncle Boone's tan Cadillac parked in a front space. The car was empty, so Emory and Elvia must be waiting for us inside.

"Is that right?" he said, grinning. "And how old were you exactly?"

"Twelve. But he was fourteen so he was experienced." I walked slightly ahead of him. "Most memorable kiss I ever had."

His hand closed on my upper arm, turning me around. "Is that right?" he said. "Guess we'll just have to take steps to remedy that." Before he could, I jerked out of his grasp and started running.

"You gotta catch me first!" I yelled over my shoulder. "Loser buys the ice cream!"

Even with my head start, he beat me to the Dairy Queen's front door by two lengths, then caught me up in his arms and twirled me around. We were giggling and out of breath, poking and grabbing at each other like two kids, when Emory and Elvia walked through the glass doors.

"Y'all better stop actin' like a couple of hooligans, or I'm going to have to call the law," Emory said.

Elvia watched our shenanigans with an indulgent, relaxed smile. Her face was softer and calmer than I'd seen it in the last few days. It was definitely the face of a woman who'd been thoroughly and expertly kissed for a long period of time.

"Better fix your lipstick," I whispered to her as we walked inside the Dairy Queen. "It's looking a little mussed."

Her face turned pink, and she swatted at me, missing me by a mere inch.

At my insistence, we took our ice cream outside to eat. "I want to hear the frogs," I said.

"She's actin' like they don't have frogs in California," Emory said, carrying his banana split and Elvia's vanilla malt over to the redwood tables.

"I'm telling you, they sound different here," I said.

"Where's the men's room in this place?" Gabe asked, after setting my Moon Pie sundae and his strawberry shake on the table.

"Out back," I said. "Make a note of the wall next to the service door. It was in that very spot history was made twenty-four years ago."

Emory held out his hand. "For which you still owe me five bucks."

"Shut your mouth," I said, jerking my head over at my husband. "He thinks it was voluntary."

Gabe's face lit up. "You mean Emory had to pay this Dr. Quack to kiss you?"

"Thanks a lot, cousin," I said. "Wait'll I get your girl alone. I'm going to tell her about the summer you decided to paint your—"

"Stop right there," Emory broke in, his face red. "She doesn't need to know about *that*."

"His what?" Elvia said, her eyes bright with curiosity.

"Hold that story," Gabe said, laughing, "until I get back."

Emory and I were still teasing back and forth when the primer-gray Camaro drove up and backed into a spot next to our table. A large Confederate flag in the rear window hid the backseat occupants. The muffler, in need of some work, drowned out our words.

"Excuse me while I pick my ears up off the table," Emory joked.

Three young men stepped out of the car, all wearing T-shirts, jeans, and short, military-style haircuts. Two dangled cigarettes from their lips; the third wore a black parachute-cloth jacket with white letters stating, "White Is Might."

When they glanced over at us, my heart started beating faster. I looked at my cousin to see if he recognized the vehicle. It was the same one following Toby's truck last night.

Emory's shoulders tightened under his pale gold golf shirt. "Stay cool, ladies," he said, turning his attention to his banana split. "Just eat your ice cream."

We did as he said, trying to make casual conversation. I kept my eyes on Emory, resisting the urge to stare them down. I knew, like mean dogs, it would likely set them off. As they walked behind Emory and Elvia, the one in the jacket reached over and flipped a strand of Elvia's dark hair.

"Ain't that sweet. Mr. Emory Littleton takin' his little Mexican housekeeper out for a night on the town."

In one swift movement, Emory stood up and swung his fist around, catching the speaker in the jaw.

"Asshole!" the man yelled, the blow knocking him back-ward. He lunged at Emory, and they grappled awkwardly.

Elvia sat stunned in her seat, her eyes frantic.

I stood up, planning to run for Gabe, when another of the men jumped Emory's back. Instinct overcame good sense, and I scrambled over the table, knocking my sundae onto the ground.

"Go get Gabe!" I yelled to Elvia.

I jumped on the second guy's back, pounding his right ear with my fist.

"Hey! Stop it, you little . . ." he yelled, trying to beat me off with one hand.

"Leave my cousin alone!" I screamed in his ear.

"Benni, get outta here!" Emory yelled.

"Let him go!" I kept pounding on his head and trying to dodge his blows. Behind us, the third guy gave a high-pitched hyena laugh.

With a grunt, the guy I clung to gave a great heave and threw me off his back. I hit the concrete curb with the side of my hip. For a moment, hot pain seared through my upper leg, and a shower of stars sparkled across my line of vision.

At the sound of heavy breathing, I looked up and glimpsed the shiny blade of a buck knife. Thick beads of sweat dotted the man's angry, red face.

He grabbed my forearm and squeezed it until I squawked in pain. "Here's a little permanent reminder to stay away from grown men's fights." Elvia screamed as I struggled to pull my arm away from the blade.

From somewhere came an almost animal roar. Gabe brought a fist down on the man's wrist. The knife clattered to the concrete, and in seconds Gabe had him pulled off me and in a choke hold.

Hearing his friend's strangled protests, the first guy backed away from Emory and stared, his chest heaving. Gabe's face was cold as a river rock as he tightened his arm around the man's neck.

"Gabe," I rasped out, unable to call out any louder.

The man's face started to turn dark red.

At that moment, a blue-and-white Sugartree police car squealed into the parking lot, followed in seconds by another. Two young patrol officers jumped out and drew their guns, pointing them directly at Gabe.

"Let him go, now!" one yelled. His voice gave a soprano squeak on the word "go." His short, spiky blond hair glistened under the bright Dairy Queen lights.

"Gabe!" I screamed and jumped up. "They have guns!"

"Now, Officers," Emory said, moving toward them, his hands held up. "Don't overreact here . . ."

"Stay right there, sir!" yelled the other officer, a barrel-chested brunette with a similar spiky haircut. He trained his gun on Emory. "Don't take another step."

Emory froze in his tracks.

The squeaky-voiced officer moved a step closer to Gabe, who didn't seem aware of his presence. "Let go!" the officer yelled again, lowering his voice one octave. "Now."

"Gabe!" I screamed again. "Please!"

Gabe turned his head and looked right into the face of the young officers. His expression caused the officer's gun to tremble slightly. My stomach tightened, and white-cold fear enveloped my whole body. Black edges start to close in around my eyes. I shook my head, willing the faintness back.

"Gabe," I said, trying to keep my voice calm. "Let him go."

His head turned toward my voice, then he slowly loosened his hold on the man, letting him tumble to the ground, gasping.

"Down on your knees," the blond officer commanded Gabe, his trembling gun still trained on him.

Without saying a word, Gabe knelt down.

"Hands behind your head," the young officer commanded.

Gabe did what the officer said, his face like granite. A sob caught at the back of my throat as I watched him being treated in such a humiliating way. I couldn't let these men do this to Gabe. I started toward them, but Emory caught my arm, holding it in a tight grip.

The blond officer holstered his gun and took out handcuffs. I jerked out of Emory's grasp and started toward them.

"Are you out of your mind?" I said, pointing at the three men behind us. "They were attacking *us*!"

"Stay where you are!" the barrel-chested officer yelled, holding out his hand, his gun now pointed at me.

Emory grabbed my arm again. "Benni," he said softly. "Wait until they put away their guns." Then he said, "Officers, this isn't what it looks. Mr. Ortiz is a police officer . . ."

"Sir," the blond officer said, "please stay out of this." He clamped the steel cuffs around Gabe's wrists. Behind me, one of the punks snickered.

Emory and I turned to glare at him.

"Shut up, you lowlife jerk," I said.

He flipped me the finger.

Gabe's face showed no expression as the officer patted him down, looking for weapons.

"In my left rear pocket is my wallet," Gabe finally said, his voice calm. "My badge is in it."

"Mister," the cop said, his voice thick with sarcasm, "I know my job."

"What about them?" I pointed at the smirking young men who'd started the fight. "They're the ones who caused this! They're the ones . . ."

"Ma'am, please keep your voice down," the barrel-chested cop said, finally putting his gun away. "There's no need to yell."

"The heck there isn't!" I shot back.

"Let me handle this," Emory said low in my ear. He walked over to the officers, who'd just pulled out Gabe's wallet. Under the glaring parking lot lights, I could see a vein throb in Gabe's temple, purplish and taut against his skin.

"Crap, Mike," the blond officer said. "He *is* a cop. Oh, man, he's a chief."

"Are you sure?" the barrel-chested officer replied, his damp face slightly panicked.

At that moment a dark blue Oldsmobile pulled up, and Grady Hunter stepped out. He stared at the scene for a moment, an uncomprehending look on his face.

"Grady, for cryin' out loud, call off the Sugartree Gestapo," Emory snapped. "This is Gabe Ortiz, Benni's husband."

Grady looked at Gabe kneeling on the ground, then at me. "Mike, Dwayne, uncuff Chief Ortiz right now."

"Shit," the blond said under his breath.

He undid the cuffs, and Gabe stood up, ignoring Dwayne's offer of a hand. He walked directly to me and took my arm, inspecting it. "*Querida,* are you all right?"

There was only a slight bruising where the man had grabbed my arm. Gabe ran gentle fingers over the swelling.

"I'm fine," I said, reaching up and touching his jaw. It was still stiff and hard as a block of steel.

After speaking with the officers, Grady Hunter walked over to us.

"Mayor Grady Hunter," he said, holding out his hand to Gabe. "My deepest apologies, Chief Ortiz. Our officers here in Sugartree have been a little jumpy lately. They're young and impetuous. I'm sure you understand."

Gabe took his hand but didn't answer.

I piped up, "How come those officers weren't jumpy enough to aim their guns at that white trash?" I said, pointing to the skinheads who were inching their way toward their car. "They started it. That one pulled a knife on me."

When I looked down at the ground, the knife was gone. And I was willing to bet that it wouldn't be found on any of them. When our attention was on Gabe being handcuffed and searched, they'd most likely ditched it.

"Bobby Lee, Delton, Carl, you boys stay right where you are," Grady said. "I want a word with you." He turned back to us. "Again, I apologize for this misunderstanding . . ."

"Misunderstanding, my ass," Emory said. "Those little peckerwoods started this, and we want to press charges."

The mayor looked at Emory calmly, his politician's face benign. "Who threw the first punch?"

Emory's face turned red. "Now, Grady, they were harassing us."

"I do believe, Emory, maybe the only person who has a viable cause to press charges here is Chief Ortiz or his wife." He turned to Gabe. "Do you want to carry this any further, sir?"

Gabe looked over at the young officers standing next to their cars. Their faces shone with sweat. They couldn't meet his eyes.

He shook his head no. When I started to protest, I felt his hand squeeze my upper arm, so, trusting his judgment, I reluctantly kept quiet.

"My condolences on your son, Mayor Hunter," Gabe said, his voice kind.

A wave of shame came over me. In the commotion I'd completely forgotten that Grady had lost a son early this morning. Whatever Toby's problems, he had still been Grady's child.

Grady nodded. "Thank you, Chief Ortiz. I'll give those boys a good talkin' to, sir. The officers, too. Again, I humbly apologize. This won't happen to you in my town again."

Gabe turned back to me and Emory. "I think our evening is over."

"It is for me," Emory said. He turned to speak to Elvia. It was only then we realized she was gone.

He turned back to us, his eyes bright with panic.

I glanced over at the Dairy Queen. Inside, back in the corner, I could make out a small huddled form. "She's inside."

Emory started toward the building, but I grabbed his arm. "No, let me, Emory."

"I have to go to her, Benni."

"Trust me. Let me talk to her first."

"Okay," he said, unconvinced. "But I'm right behind you."

Gabe and Emory followed me inside the building. We walked across the cold room to where Elvia sat in a booth, staring straight ahead, focusing on some unknown scene. I slid in across from her while Emory and Gabe stood next to the table. When she looked up at me, the fear in her eyes brought a heavy lump to my throat.

"Elvia," I said softly. "We're going to drive home now."

Unshed tears caused her eyes to look blacker in the harsh restaurant lighting. "Home?" she said, her voice curt and low.

"Back to Aunt Garnet's. Everything's okay. See, Gabe's all right." I looked up at him. "Emory's all right." I reached across the table and took her cold hand in mine. "Elvia, everything will be okay. I promise."

"You can't promise something like that."

She was right, and I felt foolish for saying the words, but like all Anglo people who are confronted with overt racism and feel helpless, I wanted to do or say something to convince her that not all of us are as ignorant as those jackasses.

"Hermana, por favor," Gabe said, touching a hand to her shoulder. *"Vamanos a la casa."*

His simple Spanish words seemed to restore some of her confidence.

Emory, unable to contain himself any longer, said in a voice broken with emotion, "Elvia."

She looked up at him, her black eyes staring into his green ones, then slid out of the booth. He pulled her into his arms and started whispering in her ear.

I nodded at Gabe. "Let's wait for them outside."

In the parking lot Grady Hunter was still talking to Toby's three friends over by their car. One of them smirked at us, and for a split second I wished I had a loaded shotgun in my hand.

I slipped my hand into Gabe's. "Let's wait around back so we don't have to look at those pathetic jerks."

"No," Gabe said, staring directly at the young man until he looked down in discomfort. "We'll wait right here in front so they *can* see us."

I squeezed his hand. "Elvia was really scared."

"She had a right to be," Gabe said.

The silence between us was heavy and a little frightening to me. I knew this was a situation I would never truly understand, something Gabe and Elvia shared that I couldn't. I turned his hand over, kissed one wrist, then looked up at him and whispered, "I'm so very sorry, Friday. We should just go back to San Celina tomorrow."

He kissed the top of my head and said, "Sweetheart, if we let this ruin our visit, then they've won twice. Do you understand that?"

"Is that why you wouldn't press charges?"

"Making this situation bigger than it needs to be will only cause problems for your aunt and uncle and Emory's dad. I don't want to do that and I didn't think you would either. They have to live here. Besides, Grady Hunter has enough on his plate right now, don't you think?"

"You are such a good man."

"Just a practical one."

It was past ten o'clock when we got back to my aunt's house and everyone had retired for the night.

"We're going to sit out here on the porch for a while," Emory said.

I leaned over and hugged my friend. "I'm sorry, Elvia."

"Oh, *gringa loca*," she said, hugging me back. "It's not something you could help."

A short time later, Gabe and I were lying in the carved magnolia bed and I was telling him the history behind the bed, trying to make him laugh and erase some of the ugliness of the night's incident.

"So my great-great grandfather, Hezekiah Neebuck Mosely, told my great-great grandmother, Sadie Juanita . . ."

"Just a minute," he said, sitting up, his back against the headboard. The carved magnolia blossoms made a wooden halo around his head. "Your grandfather was named Hezekiah Neebuck?"

"Neebuck is actually short for Nebucanezzar, but he was always called Neebuck."

"Hezekiah Nebucanezzar." He shook his head. "And what's with Sadie Juanita?" he asked. "Juanita?"

"Juanita's always been a popular name in the South. I'm not really sure why. They called her Neeta."

"Let me get this straight. Neebuck and Neeta?"

I poked his bare chest. "Would you let me finish the story before you start making fun of my relative's monikers?"

"Proceed," he said, his eyebrows lifting in amusement.

"The story goes, Grandpa Neebuck begged and begged Grandma Neeta to marry him, but she had her choice of beaus since she was the town doctor's only daughter and was real pretty besides. She was dating seven different men, one for each day of the week. All of them wanted to marry her. Well, Grandpa Neebuck knew he had to do something to stand out from the crowd so he had this cherry wood bed custom-made in New York and sent down by railroad. Sugartree was the last stop on the line back then, and there was just a big tag on the wooden box that said—Hezekiah Mosely, Sugartree, Arkansas. He had it brought to this very house, which his daddy built when he was a boy, and set it up right in the middle of the backyard, causing his neighbors' tongues to wag to no end. When he took her out that night for ice cream, he brought her back here and took her around to the garden. He'd made up the bed with his mama's hand-stitched, double-wedding-ring quilt and her best embroidered pillowcases and sheets, and when Grandma Neeta saw it, he knelt down and said, 'Sadie Juanita, I can't promise you a bed of roses, but I can offer you a right nice bed of magnolias.' They got married three months later and spent every night for the next sixty-two years sleeping in this bed."

"How could she say no?" he said. The smile I'd been angling for came to his face.

"How could she, indeed?" I answered, throwing back the very same quilt and placing my lips on his solid chest. I started kissing him, touching his warm skin with the tip of my tongue. I wanted to make him forget, if only for a little while, what had happened tonight. I wanted to replace it with better memories.

"You know," I said, working down his chest to his firm stomach. His large hand rested on my back, caressing it slowly, up and down. "When I was a little girl, about four or so, I used to be sent in here to take a nap and I'd use each of those ten magnolias for"—my lips traveled lower— "a toehold and I'd climb to the top of the headboard"—his hand tightened on my back—"and then I'd jump off onto this very bed." I kissed the hard jutting of his hipbone. "Then I'd climb back up and do it again and again until my aunt Garnet would come in and catch me, and she'd always say . . ." I nipped him gently, causing a moan to erupt from the back of his throat. "Albenia Louise Ramsey, why are you such a bad little girl?"

"And what did you say?" he asked, his voice deep and husky.

I raised my head up and looked directly into his blue eyes, smoky and dark with desire, and smiled.

"Because it feels *so good*."

Gabe's laughter rang out, and he pulled me up to him, kissing me deeply, and within the hour, without a bit of protest, another honorable Southern woman surrendered herself under Great-Great Grandpa Neebuck's carved cherry wood magnolias.

8

THE NEXT MORNING I was sitting at the vanity wrestling with the tangles in my hair when Gabe came into the room, his hair wet and slicked back.

"Shower's free," he said.

"Guess I'd better get in there quick," I said.

He leaned down and pushed my hair back, kissing the nape of my neck. "Last night was awe-inspiring, Señora. Think your aunt Garnet would sell us that bed?"

"I doubt she'd sell it to me, but she'd probably give it to you if you smiled at her right."

He grinned at me in the mirror.

"Yeah," I said. "Just lay that one on her, and the magnolias are yours."

No breakfast was waiting for us in the kitchen, the competition obviously having moved to greener pastures, so I suggested we walk over to the 3B Cafe for one of John Luther's breakfast specials. The cool air was tinged with the sweet, smoky scent of burning leaves as we meandered across the busy courthouse square to the cafe.

"Just a second," I said when we passed Beulah's Beauty

Barn. "I want to stick my head in here and see if I can get an appointment."

While Gabe waited out in front of Beulah's big picture window, I stepped inside the beauty parlor. It was busy this morning since it was Wednesday, and there were big doings at the church tonight. Aunt Garnet's sister-in-law, Vernell, perched in Beulah's chair, the pink one nearest the window, waxing downright poetic about a new red velvet cake recipe she'd cut out of *Southern Living* magazine this month. The other chair, the baby blue one, was manned by Maybellene, Beulah's daughter, a stout, golden-haired lady who looked to be in her forties. The air was warm and steamy and punctuated every few minutes by laughter. All five hair dryers were full with women reading *National Enquirer* and *People* magazines. Every customer was attired in Beulah's custom-made pink and blue plastic smocks. One drying lady was saying to another, "It was a twenty-mile-an-hour quilt. Looks good when you're drivin' by at twenty miles an hour."

"I seen that quilt," the lady in Maybellene's chair chimed in. "It would take at least sixty miles an hour to make those blocks look decent."

"Hey, y'all," I said, taking a handful of M&M's from the bowl in front of the copper and steel hand-punch cash register. I remember Beulah letting me push down the keys when Aunt Garnet paid for her wash and set. The five-dollar key always stuck.

"Hey, Benni Louise," Beulah said, without missing a beat teasing Vernell's bluish-white hair. "What're you up to today?" She winked at me and nodded her head toward the front window. "And how come you left that handsome fella of yours outside?"

" 'Cause I was afraid he'd take one look at you and purely leave me flat," I said, climbing up on the padded stool behind the counter and hooking my heels on the middle rung. In the glass case rested the same pink and blue glittered combs and brushes that were for sale the last time I was here. I ran my fingers over the register keys.

"You got that right, honey," she said with a watery cackle, starting the back comb on Vernell, who nodded at me in the gilded mirror. "He's a fine hunk of hormones, I'm here to tell you. Is he worth the trouble?"

I turned and contemplated him through the glass. He'd folded his arms across his chest and was staring out at the square. His black hair glistened in the morning sunlight. Turning back to the ladies, I said, "Most times."

"More like bedtime," the lady sitting next to Vernell said, her head half-covered in tiny pink curlers.

"They're handy on trash day, too," Vernell pointed out. She leaned over and sipped from a can of diet RC sitting on Beulah's curler tray. She made a scrunched comical face in the mirror. Laughter rippled through the sweet-smelling, muggy room.

"And when the gutters need cleanin'," another lady said.

"Killin' spiders," Maybellene said around a mouthful of bobby pins. Her hair was so blond and teased so tall and airy it got me to craving a helping of cotton candy. "And snakes."

The whole room of ladies nodded, murmuring a group assent at those necessary tasks.

I glanced back out at Gabe, wondering if he knew he was being discussed. He looked down at his watch and shifted his weight from one leg to the other.

"He's got a real nice butt," Beulah noted. All the women in the vicinity of her voice stretched their necks to look.

"Heavens, don't tell him that," I said. "He's conceited enough for two men and a boy." The women cackled at my remark.

"Ain't they all?" one commented.

I slid down off the wooden stool. "I'd better get going. Just wanted to see if anyone could squeeze me in this morning for a trim."

"I got a free twenty minutes at eleven," Maybellene said. "Just a trim?"

"Yeah, I'm tryin' to grow it out."

"Be here sharp," she warned. "It's a packed day."

"We're just goin' over to the 3B for some breakfast. I'll be here at five till. Promise."

"My scissors are a'tremblin' in anticipation," she replied.

Outside, I linked my arm in Gabe's. "Okay, ready to tie on the feed bag. I made an appointment for a cut at eleven."

His eyebrows shot up. "You're getting your hair cut?"

I squeezed his arm and laughed. "Don't worry, it's just a trim."

Inside the cafe, John Luther was standing behind the register cracking open a roll of quarters. A man with a wrinkled prune face wearing dirt-stained overalls and a white gimme cap that simply said, "Feed," held out an open palm.

"Hey, John Luther," I said. "Brought my boyfriend for some of your famous cheese grits."

He smiled and gave change to the whiskered old man. "See you later, Doyle. I'll be by to pick up that chicken feed this afternoon. Don't you be sellin' it all 'fore I get there."

The man grunted and helped himself to a toothpick.

"Does your husband know you're feedin' your boyfriend breakfast?" John Luther asked, holding out a friendly hand to Gabe. "John Luther Billings. Welcome to Sugartree, Mr. Ortiz."

"Gabe," he said, shaking John Luther's hand.

"Y'all sit anywhere," he gestured to the almost empty room. Breakfast had been long over for most of his customers. "Coffee?"

"You bet," I said. "Lots of cream."

"So," Gabe said, peering at me over his menu. "What are our plans after you get clipped?"

"Just hang out until the gospel sing and pie social tonight."

He set his menu down and said, "I'd like to get some fishing in while we're here."

I took a packet of sugar from a plastic basket shaped like a chicken. Shaking it, I said, "The guns and ammo shop across from Hawley's drugstore should sell temporary fishing licenses. Why don't you check it out while I'm in Beulah's? They probably know some good spots to fish, too. We could go back by Aunt Garnet's, grab some of Uncle WW's fishing gear, buy a pack lunch from Boone's, and catch us some fish."

"Sounds like a plan."

"Here you go," John Luther said, setting two white mugs of steaming coffee in front of us. He placed a tiny metal pitcher of cream next to me. "Y'all know what you want?"

"Blueberry pancakes with an order of hash browns," Gabe said.

"Make it two," I said.

"Easy enough. Grits?"

"Nope," Gabe said.

"Yep," I replied. "Want 'em plain, though. Instead of the hash browns, come to think of it."

John Luther picked up our menus and, with a slight hesitation, cleared his throat and said, "Gabe, heard you grew up in a small town."

Gabe nodded, his eyes studying John's face curiously. "In Kansas. Just outside of Wichita."

He cleared his throat again and said, "Then I know you understand how small-town talk is."

Gabe nodded again, his face turning from curious to wary.

"I heard about what happened at the Dairy Queen last night and I just wanted to apologize on behalf of our town for the shabby treatment you received and assure you that the majority of our fine folks here in Sugartree do not treat visitors with such disrespect." His face turned angry for a moment. "Sure as I'm standing here, those little jerk-offs need to be taught a lesson."

"Thank you," Gabe said. "But there's no need for you to apologize. Arkansas hasn't cornered the market on ignorant human beings. We have our fair share in California. Wasn't the first time that's happened to me. Probably won't be the last."

John Luther's broad face relaxed. "That's real nice of you to be so open-minded. Breakfast is on me."

"That's not necessary," Gabe said.

"Are you kidding?" I piped up. "Mr. Johnny Luther pinch-a-penny-till-it-shrieks hardly ever gives anything away. We're taking him up on it."

John Luther patted the top of my head, something he knew I despised. I slapped at his hand. "Ain't she just the cutest thing when she's bein' obnoxious? Did she ever tell you about the time she broke my arm? I remember it every time the weather changes and it hurts like the dickens."

"Forget my childhood shenanigans," I said. "What about those guys who hassled us last night? What's their story?"

His face grew cold. Spots of angry color dotted his high forehead. "They're part of the group Toby Hunter hung out with. He was kind of the ringleader, so I reckon they're feeling at loose ends. Heard they had some ties to some white supremacist group in Little Rock, but that just might be rumors. They're a bunch of troublemakers, that's a fact. Kids with too much time and money on their hands. A few years on a chain gang cutting kudzu would do 'em a world of good."

"Heard anything about Toby's murder?" I asked, ignoring Gabe's toe nudging my foot under the table.

John Luther shook his head, glancing back toward the kitchen. "Lots of people wanted that boy gone," he said. He looked me straight in the eye. "Including me. But, believe me, someone got there before I did. If it had been me, more'n the back of his head would have been beat in." He tucked our menus under his arm and headed back down the single aisle of the cafe. "Breakfast will be up shortly."

"His broken arm was an accident," I said before Gabe could comment on my questioning John Luther about Toby's death. "It was just as much Emory's fault as mine. We were pretending to be firemen."

"Firemen?"

"We told John Luther to jump from the tree house into a blanket we were holding. We were pretending to rescue him from a burning building. We severely underestimated his weight and our ability to hold on to the blanket."

"Whose cockeyed idea was it?"

I avoided his eyes and concentrated on putting the exact right combination of cream and sugar in my coffee.

He sipped his coffee. "You were lucky his arm was all that broke."

"Yeah, yeah, yeah, I heard that lecture already, *papacita*. Don't let John Luther kid you. He was the envy of every kid in Sugartree. He wore that cast like an Olympic medal all summer. Not to mention it got him out of working the harvest at his daddy's farm, which he hated."

"I see you've never been an easy girl to play with," he said, chuckling. After breakfast I still had fifteen minutes until my hair appointment, so Gabe and I sat on a park bench under a tree in the square, watching the town of Sugartree go about its daily business.

"Okay, now that we're out of your friend's earshot, tell me what his story is with this Toby Hunter." He leaned back in the wood-slatted bench and put his arm around my shoulder. Above us, mockingbirds darted from tree to tree, trilling out songs and warnings to mark their territories.

"It has something to do with Toby and his daughter." I told him about the incident yesterday when Elvia and I were having breakfast there. "It sounded like Toby was stalking her or something."

"That would upset any father."

"I can't imagine John Luther killing someone, though. He's always been the most passive one of our whole gang."

"Threatening a man's daughter could cause even the mildest man to lose control."

"I guess you're right." I lay my head against his shoulder and looked up at the treetops, contemplating the amount of anger I'd seen that one young man inspire in just the last two days. It was a wonder someone hadn't killed him before.

We sat there for a moment, enjoying the hustle and bustle of other people's lives.

"Gabe?" I said.

"Hmmm?"

"Is what you said to John Luther true?"

"About what?"

"That how those cops treated you wasn't the first time something like that's happened to you."

"Yes."

"When? Where?"

"Do you mind if I don't go into details right now? I'll tell you someday, but I just want to enjoy our time here without dredging up old and painful history."

I rested my hand on his thigh, wishing I could change what happened his first night here, wishing I could change the other incidents like it in his past. "I hate them for what they did to you."

"Comes with the territory, *querida*. I learned early in my life that people with white skin can change their clothes and go anywhere in this country and fit in or, at the very least, not stand out." He looked at his arm, still a deep mahogany from his months of surfing with his son, Sam. "But no matter how expensive my clothes are or what kind of car I drive or how much education I have, there are people who will look at this brown skin and make assumptions."

"I'm sorry," I said.

He kissed my temple. "Nothing for you to be sorry for, *niña*. It's just the way life is."

"Well, to quote your very articulate son, it sucks. It sucks big-time."

He threw back his head and laughed. "We are going to have to buy that boy a word-a-day calendar to enrich his limited vocabulary." He glanced at his watch. "You've got exactly two minutes to get to your appointment. After that, I want you to show me the Arkansas you love. I want to stop wasting my time talking about last night and spend it imagining you are a happy little girl busy breaking your friend's arm and dyeing the baptismal tank red."

I bolted upright. "Who told you that? I swear, I'm gonna kill Emory. Worse, I'm gonna rat on him and Duck to Brother Cooke."

He stood up, pulling me with him. "My sources are sacred."

"You've been talking to Dove," I accused. "And don't be so smart. When I tell Brother Cooke you're Catholic and have only been sprinkled, never fully immersed, he's going to open up his full-on, no-holds-barred-you're-going-to-hell-in-a-gilded-handbasket witnessing extravaganza on you. Don't come hiding behind my skirttails when he's dragging you toward the baptistery."

"That's shirttails," he said. "Is the water warm? I might consider it."

"Hey, kids, where y'all headin'?" Amen said, coming down the stairs of the courthouse. She was dressed in a conservative gray suit and carrying a black leather briefcase.

"Wow, you look like a lawyer," I said.

"Bite your tongue, girl." She nodded at Gabe. "Heard about last night. Cleaning up that joke of a police department is one of my first priorities if I'm elected mayor."

"*When* you're elected mayor," I said.

"From your lips to the good Lord's ears," she said. "You okay?" she asked Gabe.

"Fine," he said, his voice cool. "No harm done."

"Right," she said, her smile cynical. "Just another little razor slash to the soul."

He shrugged and didn't answer. I glanced from her to him, again trying to figure out what had caused this instant animosity between them. Was it because she was a politician, not one of Gabe's favorite types of people? Even though he was disgusted by behavior like those young officers showed, he was protective of his profession and balked at any politician who made claims they could tell the police how to run their department better. Or was it what he claimed, that she was hiding something? Another aspect of politicians that Gabe hated, having seen it too much in his law enforcement career.

"How long are you going to be?" Gabe asked me.

"I shouldn't be more than an hour," I said. "How about meeting me at Hawley's drugstore? There's a soda fountain there and magazines to read."

"Sounds fine. See you later." He nodded at Amen. She nodded back.

"Where're you goin', girl?" she asked.

"Over to Beulah's for a trim and hoping to catch a free ride on the gossip train. C'mon, walk me over there."

"Is Gabe all right?" she asked as we crossed the thick grass and waited at the tall curb for three pickups full of camouflage-dressed hunters to drive past. Bumper stickers advertising "Ducks Unlimited" decorated every truck. "What happened to him last night is unforgivable and unacceptable as far as I'm concerned."

"Physically he's fine. I'm sure it upset him, but he won't talk about it. That's how he is. Don't let anyone see what hurts you." We stood in front of Beulah's, and I waved at her through her big window and mouthed, "Just one minute."

Amen shifted her briefcase to her other hand. "Sure broke my heart when I heard about it. Those little jackasses. I wanted to apologize for our town but I could tell he just wanted to let it drop." She hesitated for a moment, then said, "Does he . . . Is it just my imagination . . . or did he and I get off on the wrong foot?" She wouldn't meet my eye, and I knew how hard this was for her to articulate. Amen had always had a lot of pride and would never be the one to come to you first when you'd had a tiff. I guess she'd changed in more ways than I realized in the last few years.

"Oh, Amen, he's just being a cop, you know? They're suspicious of everyone. It's in their DNA, I think."

Her dark eyes scrutinized me. "He's suspicious of me?"

"He's got a crazy notion you're hiding something, and Gabe's a stickler for everything being completely above-board. Which is kind of ironic, if you ask me, for someone who hides so much of his own feelings. I told him he was way off base. What could you possibly have to hide?" I laughed.

She didn't.

As a matter of fact, her face was as serious as a pall-bearer's.

"Amen? He's not right, is he?"

She hesitated, then slowly nodded. "Sorry, Benni."

"What are you hiding?"

Beulah rapped on the window, pointing at her watch and gesturing me inside. I held up an index finger and turned back to Amen. "What is it?"

"Come out to my grandma's cabin around two o'clock. I'll tell you then. It's too complicated to get into now."

"But . . ."

Beulah opened the front door and yelled out, "Quit your jabberin' and get your butt in here, Benni Harper, or we're rafflin' off your appointment."

"Yes, ma'am," I called back. "I'll be right there." I

turned back to Amen. "Okay, two o'clock at Miss De-Lora's."

"Her cabin's out by Mayhaw Lake. Do you remember how to get there?"

I nodded.

"It's changed some since Boone rebuilt the cabin. There's a wishing well in front, but the old hickory tree's still there. My Mustang will be parked in the driveway." She turned and walked away, her dark head held high.

"Oh, Amen," I said to myself. "What have you got yourself into?"

9

BEULAH POINTED OVER to the back room where the pink wash sinks resided. "Get in there and let Crystal Lee wash you so's Maybellene can get you cut. We've got a full house today and don't have time for you to be visitin' the day away."

"Yes, ma'am," I said, slipping my arms through one of Beulah's smocks. Crystal Lee, Maybellene's daughter, appeared to be about seventeen or eighteen years old. She was a short, round-hipped, pretty girl with deep dimples and curly rusty-red hair. Sparkly butterfly clips floated around her big hair.

The washroom was entirely devoted to Elvis's younger years. There were dozens of black-and-white pictures from his Hollywood films. In the background, the soundtrack from *Clambake* played softly.

She smiled at me and said, "I love your hair. Hope you're not letting Mama cut off a real lot." The tiny silver-colored ball piercing her tongue clicked against her front teeth. I was tempted to warn her not to open her mouth in an electrical storm, but, as Dove would no doubt advise me, I kept my own counsel.

"I'm just here for a trim. And some interesting talk."

She tucked a pink towel around my neck. "Oh, we got plenty of that around here," she said, giving a shy giggle. She poured some thin, minty-smelling concoction on my hair and started massaging my scalp. "Hope you don't mind me rubbing your head. It's something Memaw wanted us to start doing to compete with that new salon out by the Wal-Mart. She said we have to compete with service 'cause that's our strong suit, so we're rubbing people's heads now. The older ladies seem to like it."

"It does feel good," I said, leaning my head back over the wash sink and settling into the chair.

"So, how's your visit been so far?" she asked cheerfully, punctuating her words with clicks from her tongue jewelry.

"Pretty good. There's been some rough spots."

"Toby Hunter," she said without hesitation.

"Boy, you must be psychic."

She sighed and massaged my temples. "Not so hard to figure out. It seems like most the time there's trouble in Sugartree, he's involved one ways or another. I've known Toby since we were in the primaries in Sunday school. He was meaner than a badger even then. He used to throw the wooden Noah's ark animals at me when I was four and he was seven. Still got a scar." She pointed to a thin white line above her pink-painted lips.

I lifted my head slightly to look at it. "So, I take it he had a lot of enemies in this town."

"For sure. He got, like, really creepy in high school. Five years ago at Halloween when I was a freshman and he was a senior, he came dressed in a Ku Klux Klan outfit. Claimed he was Casper the Ghost, but the pointed head gave him away. He did it to get people's goats. Worked, too."

She rubbed her strong fingers along the edge of my hairline, pressing deep into my scalp. A rich combination of rosemary and mint engulfed the tiny room, and I was tempted to just lay back and relax. But curiosity had seized me, and I'd found a fountain of information that would rival Uncle WW's backyard extravaganza. And I'd only have her for a few minutes.

"He was sure a jerk at Amen Tolliver's fund-raising party," I said.

"I heard about that! Not that I'm surprised. He's plain lucky someone there didn't take a shotgun to him."

"So," I couldn't resist asking, "who do you think killed him?"

"Oh, shoot, it could've been any of a dozen people. Why, I'd place money on Ricky Don Stevens right off. I've even *heard* him say, more'n once, too, that he'd like to kill Toby Hunter."

"Ricky Don Stevens?" The name didn't ring any bells.

"Tara Billings's boyfriend. He's had a crush on her since he was thirteen. You've probably met him."

"Where?"

"He works over at the Dairy Queen. He was workin' last night when . . . Well, you know what happened."

I was slightly irritated but not surprised that Gabe had already become a subject of gossip. "You mean when the cops illegally harassed my husband."

Her face blushed pink under her frizzy poodle curls. "I think what they did to your husband was awful, but some of the patrol officers are old buddies of Toby's. They all kinda hung out together, to drink beer and hunt." She tilted her head and smiled at me, pink lipstick staining her right front tooth. "I hope your husband's okay. He sure is good-looking."

I smiled back, telling myself to chill out. This young girl didn't have anything to do with those cops or their attitude. "He's fine. And, yeah, he is pretty good-looking for an old fart."

She giggled again. "Right before you came in, Mama said if'n he was hers, she'd lock him in the bedroom and wear the key around her neck. But don't tell her I told you."

"Your secret's safe with me. About this Ricky Don . . ." I was curious about his connection with this and, though I'd never admit it out loud—especially in Gabe's presence—I was trying to come up with suspects other than Quinton. Just in case.

"I saw him this morning at Leon's Donut Shack. He feels real bad 'cause it was him who called the police. There's some cops in Sugartree who are real nice, real fair. You were just unlucky enough to get the assholes." She blushed again. "Pardon my French."

"So, Ricky Don and Tara are an item?" I asked, trying to remember what the boy who served us at the Dairy Queen looked like, but coming up blank.

"Shoot, he's been tryin' to get her to wear a promise ring since they was fourteen. But Tara's always been real independent. Said she wanted to play the field before settlin' down and havin' a passel of babies." She heaved a deep sigh. "Now, me, I'd just love to get married and have me a big ole bunch of babies. But now that I'm out of high school, Mama and Memaw want me to go off to beauty school in Little Rock, get myself some training so I'm not dependin' on some man. Mama and Memaw are real big on not dependin' on men."

"Why would Ricky Don want to kill Toby?" I asked, hoping to verify my suspicions.

She turned on the water, tested the temperature on her arm, then proceeded to wet down my hair. "Well, 'cause of what Toby did to Tara, of course. It really messed her up. I mean, she used to be the happiest girl, and now, I hear tell, she barely leaves the house. Hasn't been to school in three weeks." Crystal Lee *tsked* under her breath, sounding like my aunt Garnet except for the metallic clicking. "I heard her daddy was thinkin' of home schooling her. And it's her senior year, too. What a cryin' shame."

"I saw her at the 3B," I said.

"You know," she said, squirting shampoo on my head,

"I heard her daddy was gonna try and get her to work there a couple days a week. Try to get her back out with people." She started scrubbing my hair with youthful enthusiasm. "Hope it helps."

"Toby came by when I was there," I said, hoping to get her to tell me what he'd done without me out-and-out asking.

"Shoot, that must've made Mr. Billings madder than a wet mud hen."

"He was pretty pissed."

"Mr. Billings just thinks the moon rises and falls on Tara."

I couldn't stand it any longer. "What exactly did Toby do?"

"Well," she said, her voice dropping lower, "he took advantage of her. I mean, she was out drinkin' and carousin' with him, no doubt about that. And she is eighteen, so there was nothin' her daddy could really do to stop her. You know Mr. Lovelis, the janitor at the church? He was going fishing early one morning and found her sitting on the road out near Mayhaw Lake, clean out of her mind. Didn't even know where she was. He took her home to her daddy. Guess she'd been, well, you know, sexually attacked. Except she didn't remember anything. Not a thing." She started rinsing my hair, doing it quickly and expertly. I wouldn't have her to myself much longer.

"Why do they think Toby did it?"

She turned off the water and squeezed the excess water out of my hair. "Sit up, now." She pulled the towel around my neck up and wrapped it around my head, turban-style. "They had a date that night, and according to her, the last thing she remembers is drinking and dancing with him at the Blue Dog Tavern outside of town. Next thing she remembers is sitting alongside that road where Mr. Lovelis found her."

"Was she drugged or something?" I asked.

"They don't really know," she said, taking a sweet-smelling hand towel and patting my wet face. "I heard she was so hysterical she wouldn't let her daddy take her to the hospital."

"Did Toby get arrested?"

"Oh, the cops talked to him. Leastways, they said they did. His daddy's got an awful lot of pull in this town, especially with the police department. Mayor Hunter and Chief Bollwood go way back, belonged to the same fraternity in college. Story goes that Toby claims he and Tara got in a fight, and she left with some other guy. He got three of his buddies to back him up. Thing is, not a one of them could give a good description of this so-called other guy. So there you go. Toby gets away with something again."

She shook her head. "It's a shame, for sure. I hope Tara can go on with her life. She's a real sweet girl."

Out in the main room, Maybellene was sweeping up around her chair while a spirited argument about Beulah's Elvis altar was going into high gear.

"I don't care what Miss Teresa hickory-stick-up-her-butt Sullivan says," Beulah said. "I told her that puttin' a fried peanut butter and banana sandwich in front of Elvis's picture on his birthday ain't any weirder than puttin' flowers on her own mama's grave." She glanced around the room, making sure everyone was listening so the story would get retold right. "You know what she said? That dead people can't eat. You know what I told her? That they don't smell too good, neither."

"Why, Beulah, you done made a double nintendray," the silver-haired lady in her chair said.

"Why, I sure did," she exclaimed, her cackle the loudest of the bunch.

"Crystal Lee scrub you down good?" Maybellene asked me. "She give you the free scalp massage?"

"Yes, ma'am," I said. "It was wonderful. That minty stuff is still tingling my head."

"Well, sister, what is it you need?"

I'd already gotten what I'd come in here for—more information about Toby—so I just said, "Take off about an inch. Kinda trim up the split ends."

"You got it."

As she cut my hair, I listened to the latest gossip about people's trials and tribulations with jealous boyfriends, toddlers unwilling to potty train, fathers who drink too much bourbon, and one lady whose teenage son just revealed to her he wanted to go to clown school.

"Oh, Lord, Dixie," Beulah said. "That means for the rest of your life you'll have to introduce him as my son, the clown."

"It was all those times I let him play with his daddy's shoes when he was a boy," Dixie said, holding a specially designed tulip-shaped plastic shield over her face while Beulah sprayed her hairdo with about half a can of Final Net. "I swear, that boy has a thing for shoes that don't fit his feet."

"I think they call that a fetish," said another lady waiting in one of the hair-drying chairs.

"Nah, that's only if he likes to wear them when he's doing the dirty deed," Maybellene said, using a whisk broom to sweep off the loose hairs on my shoulders. "How's that, Benni? Do you need it blow-dried?"

"Looks great. I'll just let it dry naturally." I slipped a five-dollar tip on her table when she turned her back.

"Before you leave town, you bring that fine-looking man of yours inside here so's we can take a closer look," Beulah said as I paid for my trim. "We need some fresh material in this place."

"Y'all sound like you're doing okay to me," I said, their laughter following me out the door.

The short walk to Hawley's drugstore gave me time to

mull over what I'd learned from Crystal Lee. From that information, there were two more likely suspects than Quinton for Toby's murder. Of course, I didn't want to think that John Luther would kill anyone. Then again, it had obviously been a crime of opportunity, not an elaborate plan. And like Gabe said, even a passive man might go temporarily insane where his daughter was concerned.

Inside Hawley's drugstore, Gabe was sitting at the counter drinking a Coke and reading an *Arkansas Sportsman* magazine. I waved at old Mr. Hawley behind the prescription counter in back. The smell of the cramped drugstore was that nostalgic combination of malty fountain drinks, sweet medicine, and sharp, waxy floor polish. It was a scent you never encountered in today's modern mega-drugstore.

"Do you want something from the fountain?" Mr. Hawley called. "Mrs. Hawley's down to the Piggly Wiggly pickin' up some cold cuts for lunch, but I can come up and mix you something."

"No, thanks," I called back. "I'll just drink some of my husband's. Did you get a fishing license?" I asked Gabe, slipping onto the slick green stool next to him. For old time's sake, I twirled around a few times.

"It's good for a week," he said.

I grabbed his paper cone of hand-mixed soda and took a drink. "Ummm, I forgot how good a perfectly mixed Coke tastes. It looks like our plans for fishing this afternoon have to be changed. At least, mine do. You can still go."

"What's up?"

I admitted he was right about Amen hiding something and how she'd invited us out to Miss DeLora's at two o'clock. "But you don't have to go."

"We only have one car," he pointed out.

"Oh, that's right."

"I'll drive you out there," he said, taking the soda out

of my hands and finishing it. "We can go fishing tomorrow."

"Miss DeLora lives out by Mayhaw Lake. Maybe she has some fishing tackle you can borrow."

"It's not that important. I'm really here just to support you, visit with your family." He folded up the magazine and stuck it under his arm. "Besides, I'm a little curious about what your friend Amen will reveal."

I slid down off the stool. "Ha! You're always telling me I'm the nosy one. Admit it, you're just as nosy as me."

"I was a homicide detective for five years. I have a professional reason to be curious. You, on the other hand, are just a busybody."

I jerked the magazine from under his arm and smacked him across the chest. "You take that back."

"It's the truth," he said, laughing and holding up his hands in defense.

I smacked the palms of his outstretched hands.

He grabbed for the magazine. "You're always hitting me," he said, still laughing. "Why are you always hitting me?"

I danced out of his reach. "Because you deserve it, Friday."

"If y'all are gonna be foolin' around like that, go outside," Mrs. Hawley said, coming in the front door carrying a red and brown Piggly Wiggly bag. Her pink cat's-eye glasses were the same style she'd worn for the last forty years. I wonder if she realized they were back in fashion again.

"Yes, ma'am," I said, smacking Gabe one more time before darting out the door.

Outside, I handed him back the magazine and said, "We'll be catching heck about being thrown out of the drugstore tonight from Aunt Garnet, mark my words."

"You'll be catching heck," he said smugly. "Aunt Garnet *loves* me."

It took us about a half-hour to get the Explorer and drive out to Miss DeLora's. I kept us entertained reading sections of the sports magazine out loud.

"Bagging Trophy Bucks During the Rut," I read. "Tips on Hunting October Squirrels. Which one would you like to hear first?"

"I bought it for the article on bass fishing," he said.

"Oh, sure. Hey, here's something right up your alley. An advertisement for deer scent. Guaranteed with two drops to arouse sexual interest and curiosity in both bucks and does. And look, they've got another lure made from doe urine. Says it's one hundred percent natural doe-in-heat urine collected during the twenty-four-to-thirty-six-hour breeding period. How do you figure they do that?"

"I don't even want to think about it. I just want to go fishing. Nice, asexual fishing. No urine involved."

I hadn't been out to Mayhaw Lake for ten years, but I remembered how to get there without any wrong turns. Things had definitely changed since I'd last seen the lake. At the turnoff, there was a fancy wooden sign advertising LOTS FOR SALE—BUILD TO SUIT.

As we drove around the lake, it became obvious that the modern American's obsession with planned retirement and recreation had come to roost with a vengeance in central Arkansas. This had once been a fairly untouched, local recreation spot where Sugartree citizens and other small-town visitors could fish, picnic, and camp. The far side of the lake, the hardest place to get to, had also been a popular place for teenagers to park, drink beer, and make out. Now it appeared the lots were being sold for vacation cabins. Some of the cabins looked like something straight out of *Architectural Digest*, leading me to believe that it most likely wasn't the average Sugartree resident buying them.

"Looks like Mayhaw Lake is going upscale," I said as we drove along the narrow, two-lane road, looking for Miss DeLora's cabin. I recognized it the moment we saw it. It was a real log cabin, not the manufactured kind.

"That's my uncle Boone's old hunting cabin," I said. Only it had been completely rebuilt from the primitive cabin Boone and his friends used to stay in back in the fifties. The difference between it and the paint-by-number cabins of her neighbors was sheer authenticity. If I remembered correctly, this cabin was well over a hundred years old. Rich purple and glowing white morning glories crowded the flower beds in front of the deep porch. Shagbark and black hickory trees shaded the graveled front walk.

We pulled up in the circular driveway, parking behind Amen's Mustang.

"What a great place," Gabe said, climbing out of the car.

"Amen told me Uncle Boone offered to buy her a house anywhere she wanted, but she insisted on this place." I stooped down and picked a long-stemmed yellow and orange wildflower. "Look, Butter and Eggs," I said, holding it out to him.

Gabe's expression was confused. "What?"

Amen came out on the front porch and answered for me. "It's the name of the wildflower. Miss DeLora used to quiz us kids all the time. Benni *would* remember the one that pertained to food." She was dressed in cutoff jeans, a white cotton tank top, and rubber thongs, looking more like the girl I used to play with during those muggy Arkansas summer days.

"Come on in," she said. "Miss DeLora's made y'all some iced tea and ginger cookies."

The wishing well in front greeted us with a soft gurgling of water. It was actually a working fountain, most likely the creation of Uncle WW.

Inside, the cabin was pure Miss DeLora—family pictures, old fans, hand-embroidered samplers, and her breathtaking quilts. Her favorite colors were obvious in the quilts and window coverings—turkey red, black, grass green, pure sky blue, hot pink. A black and salmon-pink Snail Trail quilt lay across her black vinyl sofa.

"Oh," I said, picking up the sofa quilt. "Lord forgive me, I purely envy this quilt. Y'all'd better check my pocketbook when I leave."

Amen grinned up at Gabe. "She's soundin' more like us the longer she's here."

"So I've noticed," he replied.

Miss DeLora came out of the kitchen carrying a tray of glasses and a crystal plate of thin, star-shaped cookies.

"Grandma, let me help you," Amen said, rushing over to her.

"Now, get back, child," she scolded. "I'm perfectly capable of carrying a couple of glasses of iced tea and some cookies." She nodded toward the large, airy living room. "Take a seat, and I'll serve this up."

"May I help, ma'am?" Gabe asked, reaching for the tray. He gave her his most ingratiating smile.

She smiled back up at him, batted her eyes in a flirtatious manner, and allowed him to take the tray without protest. "Yes, you may, young man. Just set it there on the coffee table. You must be Benni Louise's new husband." She undid her lacy white apron and carefully folded it, setting it on a side table. "My, you're a nice-looking fellow."

Amen rolled her eyes at me and jerked her head in the direction of the kitchen. "Grandma, Benni and I will get the napkins."

"That's fine, Amen," she said, already sitting down next to Gabe on the sofa. "I'll just get better acquainted with Benni's young man. What did you say your Christian name was, boy?"

In the cheery yellow, red, and white kitchen, I couldn't help giggling at Amen's mock exasperated expression. "Now, c'mon, Amen, you know Miss DeLora's always been a flirt. Let her enjoy my husband."

She leaned against the white refrigerator, folded her

arms across her chest, and smiled. From the living room came a burst of male and female laughter. Amen opened a drawer and took out some red-and-white-checked napkins. "They sound like they're doing fine without us. Let's take a walk."

In the living room, Miss DeLora was pouring Gabe another glass of iced tea and urging more cookies on him.

"Here's the napkins, Grandma," Amen said. "Benni and I are going to take our tea and go down to the lake."

Miss DeLora waved her hand at us without taking her eyes off Gabe. "Take your time, girls."

Carrying our plastic glasses of iced tea, we walked down the narrow, mossy path toward the lake, about five hundred feet from Miss DeLora's front porch. There were only a few boats out this Wednesday afternoon. The weak October sunlight glinted off the dark surface of the water. In the distance I could hear a motor start, stop, then start again. One of the boats inched across the lake.

At the small dock, next to some river birches, we sat down on the edge and dangled our feet over the water. A flock of goldfinches darted in and out of the dark green elmlike leaves.

"It's been so long since I've been here," I said. "I can't believe how much it's changed."

She snorted softly. "Yeah, as they say, that's progress."

We sat silently for a moment, drinking our tea and watching ducks bob for food, their fat feathered tails pointing straight to heaven.

"Reckon that's where the term *a sitting duck* came from?" she commented.

"No doubt," I said.

"I know how they feel," she said, narrowing her eyes as if looking for something on the pine-jagged horizon.

"I imagine you do."

Another silent moment passed. Then she said, "Duck and me are in love. We want to get married."

I was stunned silent. Finally I managed to stutter, "Uh, gee, that's certainly a conversation stopper."

"You don't approve?" Her voice was sharp, accusing.

"No, that's not it at all. I'm just surprised."

"Because I'm black and he's white?"

I slammed my glass of tea on the dock, sloshing some on my jeans. "For cryin' out loud, I'm married to an Hispanic man! How could you say that?"

"So what's the big surprise? That someone like Duck could fall in love with someone like me?"

That really got my dander up. "Amen Harriet Tolliver, I oughta push you right into this lake. I'm *surprised* because I'm still back in the sixties when we were all kids playing in Emory's tree house, scheming ways to get ice-cream money and singing rounds of 'Greasy, Grimy Gopher Guts' at the tops of our lungs until Miss DeLora came after us with a flyswatter. Moving from that to you and Duck doing the horizontal mambo under satin sheets is a big leap, okay? Just give me time to comprehend it."

She fished a piece of ice from her glass and popped it in her mouth. "The horizontal mambo? You've been reading too much bad fiction." She crunched down hard on the ice cube.

"As for you marrying Duck, you'd better do it quick, or I'm gonna tell Miss DeLora you're feeding among the lilies without the benefit of wedding vows."

She laughed and laid back on the dock, cradling the back of her head in her arms. "Oh, Lord, the Song of Solomon. Remember reading that out loud to each other when we were thirteen? The things we imagined?"

I laughed with her, glad we'd sidled around another conflict about race. "Yeah, and it's way better than we ever dreamed, isn't it?"

"Way better." She sighed. "You know, Grandma loves Duck. She'd approve of us even though she'd have her say about the difficulties of a black woman marrying a white man. It just happened by accident. We were thrown together when he became involved in my campaign. He's been such a support, both financially and emotionally. I think maybe I've always been a little in love with him. Just never wanted to admit it."

"Does anyone else know?" I asked, lying back and joining her, staring up at the deepening blue sky. A flock of ducks flew over us, their wings flapping with that impossible triple-time frenzy that always made me mentally hold my breath, sure their heavy bodies would fall out of the sky like feathered bombs.

"Just Quinton and Emory."

I sat up abruptly. "Emory knew and didn't tell me! He's in for it now." I narrowed my eyes at her. "And you. Some friend."

Her deep, carefree laugh rolled over me, taking me back to our childhood when our biggest problem had been finagling enough money out of the adults to buy Goo Goo Clusters and RC colas at the Piggly Wiggly.

"Good, that tells me I can actually trust him to keep his trap shut when necessary." She rolled over and faced me, head propped up on her hand. "I was going to tell you, really I was. And if it makes you feel any better, the only reason Emory knows is 'cause he caught us kissing in Little Rock the first night he came back home. I should have realized that the first place he'd hit coming into town would be Varsity Burger out near the university. He and Duck always loved their chili cheeseburgers. They must have caught a cravin' at the same time."

I drew my knees up under my chin and stared out over the rippling, catfish-colored lake. "So, who else knows besides Quinton and Emory?"

"No one that we know of. We've only been dating about five months or so. We both agreed it wouldn't be the best time for it to come out. After I'm elected . . ." She corrected herself. "*If* I'm elected, then we'll go public. Shoot, that's assuming we're still together. Maybe this is just a fling."

"You don't really believe that."

She sighed and sat upright, crossing her legs and resting her elbows on her knees. "No, I don't. But there's lots of things . . . people to consider. We haven't even told our kids. Step-families are hard enough. A mixed race one in the South has to be every kid's nightmare."

"You could always move to California. San Celina has a great university. I could teach you to brand and castrate cattle."

She threw back her head and laughed. "Me, a cowgirl? No, thanks, Annie Oakley. I'll leave the cattle rustling to you."

I picked up a tiny hickory nut lying on the rough dock and pitched it at her. "Huh, do your homework, girlfriend. Cattle rustling is cattle *stealing*. I ain't no rustler. I have my *own* herd."

"Heavy on bulls, I'll just gander," she said, laughing.

We'd both stood up and were brushing off the backs of our jeans when Miss DeLora and Gabe stepped out on the porch.

"You baby girls get on back up here," she called. "I only got a little time to show you my quilts 'fore I have to be gettin' ready for the gospel singin' tonight. I'm makin' my peach cobbler for the pie social and I can't be makin' it with y'all hangin' around here."

Inside, Miss DeLora took us into her bedroom and opened the double doors of a huge, pine cupboard where at least fifty or so quilts were tightly packed. As she pulled one after the other out and laid them on her four-poster bed, cedar chest, and rocking chair, my exclamations turned to murmurs of appreciation at the intricacy of each pattern, the sheer originality of the design, and the stories she told about each one.

"This here's my own mama's last quilt." She spread out a double-size, wedding-ring quilt over her bed. Rather than the tiny pastel conversation prints often used in thirties' wedding-ring patterns, the fabrics were a joyous mixture of red and purple, green and azure prints with the backgrounds of the connecting rings being a solid orange, grass green, and brilliant blue fabric rather than the more common plain white muslin. "She made it for my brother, Remar. He married a Chicago girl by the name of Esther Rose. They was killed three months after their wedding in a train accident." She shook her head, her face not sad, just remembering. "Mama loved Remar special 'cause he was born with one leg shorter than the other. Had to wear shoes with a lift. He could talk a mockingbird into bein' a crow, that's a fact. He sold insurance." We all stared at Remar and Esther's wedding quilt, reminded of the fragility of life, the quirkiness of fate.

"This one," she said, pulling out what appeared to be a sampler quilt, "was made by me, my six sisters, and our spiritual sisters. We called it 'Almost Family.' " Again the colors were bold and bright with fabric-pattern combinations that delighted the eye with their sheer love of life—all sizes and colors of gingham, army green and shocking pink, mustard yellow and deep plum, pattern on pattern on pattern. Each square had a set of initials worked into the pattern.

"Whose initials are these?" I asked, running my fingers over the tiny stitches.

Miss DeLora gave a wicked smile. "It's the ones who got away," she said, glancing up at my husband. "Not the ones we caught."

Amen and I looked at each other and laughed.

"You never told me that story before," Amen said.

Miss DeLora shrugged a tiny shoulder in her granddaughter's direction. "Girl thinks she knows all there is to know about me."

"That's Amen," I said, smirking at my friend. "Thinks she knows everything about everyone."

"Huh, don't I know it?" Miss DeLora agreed.

"You shut your mouth, you skinny little white girl," Amen said, " 'fore I come over there and shut it for you."

"You and what army?" I retorted.

"Were they always like this, Miss DeLora?" Gabe asked.

"Honey, they was even worse as children. Always pick, pick, pick. Can't tell you the times I had to separate them two to keep them from scalping each other."

Amen turned to her grandmother. "Show her the special quilt."

"What special quilt?" I asked.

Miss DeLora held up a finger and turned back to her bed, groaning slightly as she bent over and pulled a pasteboard box from under her bed. She pulled out a quilt wrapped in a white sheet. "Let me lay it out here."

We watched silently as she unfolded a brilliant pine and deep green quilt. The eight-star pattern, made up of triangles of the two solid green fabrics and tiny white-and-green-flowered fabric, was repeated with forty-two stars— six by seven. Quilted in the squares between the stars was an intricate fern-leaf pattern. Taking a closer look at the incredible quilting, I saw that each fern leaf had been stuffed separately. As with many old quilts I'd studied, I was amazed at the care that had gone into their design and construction, at the vision and creativity of these artists who would have scoffed at the idea of calling themselves by that name. By the look of the fabrics, it appeared to be about fifty or sixty years old. I continued to study the quilt, something niggling at the back of my mind. Why did it appear so familiar to me?

"Pretty, isn't it?" Amen said, an amused look on her face.

"Yes," I said. "The hand-stuffed fern leaves especially . . ." Then it occurred to me. "Hey, this is like the one that won the Sears 1933 World's Fair quilt competition.

I thought I recognized the pattern. It's called Star of the Bluegrass."

Miss DeLora's old face beamed. "She recognized it."

"Well, almost," Amen said, still smirking.

"So it took me a few minutes," I said. "I'm gettin' old."

"No, that's not it. Remember the story about Miss DeLora cooking dinner for Mrs. Roosevelt and her escorts?"

I looked from Amen's smiling face to Miss DeLora's. "No way," I said, my voice low and unbelieving.

"What's going on?" Gabe asked, looking truly clueless.

"They was broke down by the side of the road," Miss DeLora said. "Guess they was on their way down to Warm Springs, Georgia, where the mister had them a house. It was pretty dark and cold, and they couldn't get the car started to beat the band. I was goin' by on Daddy's old wagon pulled by a couple of mules on my way home from town. I asked if she needed a ride and took them to my place where I sent your uncle Jayjay on one of the mules back into town to fetch a car repairman. Mrs. Roosevelt was lookin' a little peaked, so I offered her and the two men with her a little supper. Made some of my fried catfish, corn biscuits, put out some of my pickles and stewed tomatoes. Had a buttermilk pie made up that morning. She said it was the best meal she'd had in a year. Nice lady, that Mrs. Roosevelt. Told me to call her Eleanor, but I told her I reckon I couldn't do that, her bein' the wife of the president and all. We had ourselves a nice little chat. Sang a few songs. Didn't have a bad voice for a white woman. Then she sent one of her men out and brought back this package a'holdin' this quilt. Said she'd be honored if I'd take it. Gave me a letter with it, too, tellin' whoever would try to claim it that she'd givin' me that quilt free and square. Then she asked for my recipe for buttermilk pie. Gave it to her, too. Only person I ever did."

"The letter is in my safe-deposit box," Amen said.

"Did Mrs. Roosevelt make the quilt?" Gabe asked.

I turned to him and said, "No, it's . . ."

Amen interrupted my explanation. "We gotta go, Grandma, and let you get your peach cobbler made. I'll pick you up about five, okay?"

"That's fine," she said, running her hands over the quilt.

Amen kissed her grandma and motioned at us to follow her.

"Does she know how valuable that quilt is?" I asked when we were out in the front yard. A light afternoon breeze had picked up, causing the tops of the hickory trees to sway like hands waving.

"Not really, and I don't want her to know. I want her to enjoy that quilt while she's alive without feeling obligated to donate it to some museum. I've convinced her to not let many people see it, tellin' her they'd just be jealous. That's seemed to work so far."

"What's so special about that quilt?" Gabe asked.

"It's the actual winning quilt from the World's Fair contest I just mentioned," I said. "The quilt was presented to Mrs. Roosevelt when the fair was over, and it's been missing ever since. It's one of the great unsolved mysteries of the quilting world. In terms of historical value, it's priceless."

"I thought you'd get a big kick out of seeing it," Amen said. "Now you're in on the secret. Don't be spreading it around."

I crossed my chest and held up three fingers. "Ranch woman's honor. That is so cool. The quilt world's gonna flip when it's revealed."

"Hopefully not for a long time," she said.

"Absolutely," I agreed.

We were walking down the gravel pathway to our cars when a small blue pickup pulled up with a screech in the driveway. A young black girl in her twenties wearing cornrows, a pink T-shirt, and white jeans jumped out. Her sharp reddish-brown cheekbones were glossy with tears.

"Lavanda," Amen said when the girl ran up to her, breathing hard. "What's wrong, honey?" Amen looked panicked herself.

"They've arrested Quinton," she cried, collapsing into Amen's open arms.

10

$$\text{❈ ❈ ❈}$$

"TELL ME WHAT happened," Amen said after hugging the girl. As the girl gulped and tried to speak, Amen cradled her nail-bitten hand in both of hers.

"They . . . they . . . came over to the campaign office about an hour ago. There was two police cars, and when he told them he wouldn't answer their questions, they argued and he yelled at them and then they . . . they put handcuffs on him. Oh, Amen, they didn't even let him call anyone or lock the office. I had to just close the door and run down here. I didn't want to call 'cause Quinton always said you hate getting bad news over the phone. Oh, Amen!" She put her face in her hands. Loud, convulsive sobs rocked her thin body.

I glanced up at Gabe's face. No hint of emotion. Was he remembering last night? No doubt about it, this police force had more than a slight problem with eager handcuffs.

"Lavanda, take a hold of yourself," Amen said, patting the girl's back. "We can't be of any use to Quinton if we're hysterical." Her tone, though sympathetic, was just a tinge severe. In a spooky, peek-into-the-future moment, I heard

Miss DeLora in my friend's voice. She turned to Gabe. "What are our options here from a legal standpoint?"

"It depends on what they have on him," Gabe said. "First thing I'd suggest is get an attorney down there as quick as possible."

"I'll call Duck. He probably knows someone."

She ran to her car and in minutes had reached Duck on her cell phone. She turned away from us so we couldn't hear her words. Next to us, Lavanda made small choking sounds in the back of her throat, trying hard to obey Amen's command to stay in control.

"Are you working on the campaign?" I asked, trying to give the girl something to concentrate on until Amen finished talking to Duck.

"I'm Quinton's fiancée," she said. A trickle of mascara ran down her cheek. She wiped it away with the back of her hand.

"I'm Benni," I said, holding out my hand. "And this is Gabe, my husband."

She shook my hand, sniffing wetly. "I know. Quinton told me y'all were comin' from California. I'd like to live there, but Quinton says it's too dangerous out there, all the gangs and drive-by shootings and such. We plan on movin' to Atlanta when he's out of law school."

I didn't answer, knowing from experience that trying to defend California to the rest of the country was never successful. I had to bite my tongue to keep from pointing out that I'd seen a good amount of violence since landing in Arkansas three days ago.

Amen walked back over to us, gripping her cell phone tightly. Perspiration dotted her upper lip. "Duck's calling an attorney friend now. He should be at the police station soon. Said there probably wasn't any use of us going down there, that his friend would take care of things, but I'm going anyway." She glanced up at the cabin. "I guess I'd better tell Grandma before some old busybody starts yappin' at her on the phone."

I touched her arm. "Is there anything we can do?"

She shook her head no. "Thanks, not right now." She turned to Lavanda and said, "You'd best go on back to the office and lock up. Then go on home and wait. I'll call you when I hear something."

Lavanda gave a small whimper and nodded in understanding. After getting her the keys from her purse, Amen walked the trembling girl over to her pickup, talking low to her and rubbing the center of her back. Quinton's fiancée gave Amen a fierce hug before climbing into the truck.

"I'll wait for you in the car," Gabe said as Amen walked back toward us, her head bent, studying the ground. "Give her a moment of privacy with you."

I squeezed his hand in thanks. Amen waited until Gabe got into the Explorer before lifting her head and looking at me. Shiny tears streamed down her cheeks.

"Oh, shoot," I said, putting my arm around her shaking shoulders. Her bones felt sharp and fragile, her bare skin hot to the touch. "It'll be okay. Really, it will be."

"We don't know that," she said.

"What could they possibly have on him?" I said. "There is just no reason for this except pure racism. Mark my words, it's a cooked up thing, like they were trying to do to Gabe last night. A good attorney will have him out in ten minutes. Criminy, you're going to have to revamp the whole police department when you become mayor. They can't go on harassing innocent people left and right."

She was silent during my ranting, her eyes darting down at the gravel driveway. A sinking feeling occurred in my stomach, and I stopped talking.

"Amen?" I said. "They don't have anything on him, do they?"

She looked up at me, her ebony eyes still glossy with tears. "Oh, Benni, he's so young and hot-tempered. You remember how that is. When you do things without thinking about it, when justice is a word that sets your blood to churning like someone's turned the blender on puree. Wisdom and patience aren't even words in your dictionary."

"What did he do?" I whispered.

She put a hand up to her eyes as if even the pale light of the weak afternoon sun was too much for her. "The other night, after the incident at Emory's, Quinton went looking for Toby Hunter. I thought I'd talked him down, convinced him to let it go, to just work harder to get me elected. I tried to persuade him that political power was the best way in the long run to fight people like Toby. You don't sink to their levels, but gain real power and fight them that way. He *said* he understood. He said he agreed with me."

"But?"

"I guess after he'd gone home that night, he got to thinking about it, dwelling on the scene over and over of this little punk spittin' on Grandma, got to thinking how people like Toby had been spittin' on people his whole life and getting away with it, and Lavanda said, after he'd had a few beers, he decided to go out looking for Toby. Wanted to say his piece. She tried to talk him out of it, but . . ." She gave me a rueful half-smile. "He's part Tolliver. Isn't no way you talk us out of anything we want to do once we put our minds to it."

I nodded in agreement. That was the pure truth. It was what gave Amen the courage and strength to both run for mayor and head the group that was for the church merger.

"So, did he find him that night?" I asked.

"He went cruising the parking lots of the bars where Toby and his buddies were known to hang out and finally found his truck at Lester's Roadhouse out by the interstate."

Lester's had been around since I was a kid. It was one of those redneck country bars where a Confederate flag was proudly displayed over the bar and was rumored to be the meeting place for the local KKK chapter that no one would admit existed. As kids we'd always been cautioned by Dove, Aunt Garnet, and Uncle Boone to stay away from the square brick building set back in the woods, that it was an evil and wicked place, which, of course, made it irresistible to us. Emory and I had gone there when we were seventeen and eighteen, curious about its interior and its reputation. Once inside, we were disappointed to find only a small dark room that smelled rank of beer, sweat, and hate. The large cartoon caricature of an African-American man with bulgy eyes and exaggerated thick lips with a rope around his neck that hung next to the flag made us bolt out of there without a look back. It was the first time in our young lives it occurred to us that sometimes our elders did know what they were talking about.

"What was he planning on doing?" A black man going alone into a bar like that. I shuddered to think of the possibilities.

"Who knows?" she said, waving her hand impatiently. "He *had* no plans. That's the blessed stupidity of youth. He said he just sat there in his car in Lester's parking lot getting madder by the minute when he saw Toby walk out alone. And Quinton, fool boy, decided to follow him." She stopped for a moment and stared out at the lake. I followed her gaze. Small waves kicked up, empowered by the afternoon breeze, the white tips of them bright against the flat, steel-colored water. One boat lingered, manned by a single fisherman silhouetted by the sun. She turned back to me. "Thank goodness Toby was alone, or we might be visiting Quinton at the funeral home rather than the jail."

I nodded in agreement. "Did Quinton ever catch up with Toby?"

She sighed. "He says no. Says that he followed him a ways, out to about a half-mile of his daddy's place by the lake." She pointed across the lake where the tops of some fancy cabins peeked through the trees. "Then, just for the orneriness of it, he bumped the back of Toby's truck."

I gazed out to where she pointed. "That's crazy! I bet you dollars to doughnuts that Toby's had some kind of gun in his truck."

"That's exactly what I told Quinton, but you know menfolks of *any* age, nine to ninety. You can't tell them nothin'."

I kept looking out at the spot across the lake. If I remembered correctly, that was the same area Toby's body had been found. I glanced back at Amen. The sick expression on her face told me she was thinking the same thing.

"He said," she continued, "that after he bumped him, he took off over to the west side of Sugartree where he knew Toby wouldn't follow. At least not when he was alone."

The west side of Sugartree was a mostly black neighborhood though the lines of race were beginning to blur with developers buying up hunks of land and building retirement condos and motels. It was just such a development that had bought the land where Zion Baptist resided.

"Then what?" I asked.

"Then Quinton said he went home. He lives in the pink apartments near the church. He said he took a shower and was in bed by midnight."

"What time was Toby killed?"

She shrugged. "Don't know exactly, but it was early the next morning they found his body. Quinton never said anything to anyone about his encounter with Toby. He said he didn't think anyone saw him. Apparently he was wrong."

"Are you sure there isn't anything Gabe and I can do?" I asked.

"I'll let you know what's happening as soon as I find out. You're going to the gospel sing and pie social tonight, right?"

I nodded.

"Then say an extra-special prayer for Quinton."

I gave her a quick hug. "You got it."

"Thanks." She turned and walked toward the house to

tell the news to Miss DeLora, her normally proudly set
shoulders slightly slumped. Quinton was her favorite
nephew, the son of her beloved sister, Gladiola. Gladiola
had died of diabetes complications when Quinton was ten,
and though Quinton was raised up well and strong by his
father, a railroad conductor, Amen had been like a mother
to him. Seeing him in jail would break her heart.

Gabe rolled down the car window. "Are you sure she
doesn't need us to go down to the station with her?"

I walked around and climbed in the passenger side. "She
said she'd let us know when she hears something."

He shifted the car into drive and pulled slowly around
Amen's Mustang. "Does she know what they have on
him?"

I told him the story as we headed back toward town. "Is
that enough to arrest someone?"

"If that's all they have, they probably didn't arrest him,"
he replied. "They're probably just questioning him. He
should have been more cooperative at the campaign office."
Though I know Gabe was sympathetic to Quinton, he was
also a cop, so I knew to tread lightly with my comments.

"They probably would have found a reason to take him
in anyway, don't you think?" I watched his profile, trying
to discern from his facial expressions what he was thinking
and feeling.

"Maybe," he said, still not willing to speak against the
same police who so unfairly misjudged him last night. "But
him getting angry only worsens his situation."

I leaned back in the seat and stared out the side window.
Thick piney woods sped past in a green blur. Gabe touched
the brakes, slowing us down slightly, to avoid a squirrel
dashing across the highway.

BACK AT AUNT Garnet's house, the war of the sisters continued. The battleground had resumed in the kitchen. The

pie auction tonight was to raise money for the annual Lottie Moon foreign missionary offering. Lottie Moon and her work had been involved the first time I ruffled Southern Baptist feathers, though not the last.

"Why was it okay for a woman to be the pastor of a church in a foreign country and not in America?" I asked Brother Cooke one year during Vacation Bible School. I was twelve years old. I'd asked Dove, and she said it was a very good question and I should ask the pastor.

"She was not officially a pastor," Brother Cooke said patiently, though I could tell the question made him uncomfortable. He glanced over at Dove who just smiled at him. "God doesn't allow women to be pastors or to teach men. And you know we Baptists believe in doing what God says."

"She ran the mission," I pointed out. "We learned that in Training Union. She did all the stuff you do. She taught the men about Jesus in her church."

"Well, in a manner of speaking. Actually, it was a mission," he countered.

"Isn't a mission a church?" I persisted.

"Yes, but . . ." He gave me an annoyed look, replaced quickly by a forced smile. "It's in a foreign country." He said the last sentence as if that explained it all.

"But it's still a church," I said.

"A *mission*," he repeated. "In a *foreign country*."

"And she ran it and taught the men."

"Yes." He took a white handkerchief out and mopped his brow. "*Foreign* men."

"But they're men."

"Yes, but . . ." He faltered, unable to logically answer my question.

"So, how come she can teach the men there and not the men here? How come . . ."

He broke into my sentence. "Benni, I think that these questions are best discussed with your grandma in private at home. Don't you think?" He glanced over at Dove, appealing for rescue.

"Smart as a whip, my little Albenia," she said with a wide smile.

"Yes, indeedy," he said, his mouth a straight line. He clasped his soft hands together and said, "When did y'all say you'd be goin' back to California?"

I always had a soft spot for good ole Lottie Moon. She was one of the first Baptist feminists, whether she realized it or not.

"So, what's the scoop on the Bobbsey Twins?" I asked Isaac and Uncle WW. They were sitting on the doily-covered Early American sofa watching a documentary on polar bears.

"Meringue," Uncle WW said, his eyes never leaving the flickering screen.

Isaac just gave me a somewhat dazed smile. He held his favorite Nikon on his lap, caressing it like a talisman. We all have our individual ways of comfort. On TV, two polar bears swatted paws, fighting over a red-streaked seal carcass.

"What?" Gabe said, confused.

"They're competing for who can make the highest meringue," I interpreted. "At least the competition's back to food. That's always a plus."

From the kitchen we heard the sounds of harping, two voices sounding eerily alike as they picked at one another.

"Getting any good pictures?" I asked Isaac.

"You bet, though it's not turning out to be quite what I expected." His snowy eyebrows came together slightly. "I was there when the police came and arrested Quinton."

Across the room, Uncle WW shook his head and clamped his teeth tighter on his pipe. "Darn shame. He's a nice boy. They got no cause to trump something up on him."

"He asked me to take pictures of it," Isaac said, his voice

a tinge apologetic. "Said that this was as much a part of the story of Amen running for office as her giving speeches."

"Did you?" I asked.

He nodded. "I developed the film upstairs in the bathroom. There's some pretty powerful stuff there."

"I'm glad you were there," I said.

"When Quinton's young lady went to find Amen, I drove down to the station to see if I could do anything, but they wouldn't let me see him. So I came on back and figured I'd wait to hear."

I gave him a quick rundown on what Amen had said.

"That's not much," Isaac said, his gray eyes hard. "How long can they keep him in custody on that?"

"Long enough to cause him and his family some grief," Gabe said.

"We'll know more tonight at the prayer meeting," I said. "Amen said she'd drop by and let us know what happened."

A crash of pans caused our heads to jerk up. Dove came barreling out of the kitchen, a swipe of dusty flour across her left cheek.

"I swear, if I stay in there another minute, I'm gonna knock the wax right out of her ears," she declared and headed up the stairs. "I'll do *mine* when she is through."

From the kitchen, a radio came on. One of those prayer-cloth preachers was going on about the dearth of compassion among today's Christians. His accent made *dearth* sound like *dirt*.

"Are Emory and Elvia back from Little Rock?" I asked. "Does he know about Quinton?"

"They came in about fifteen minutes ago," Isaac said. "He headed down to the police station to see if he could help. Elvia's upstairs."

The bird's-eye maple grandfather clock struck five times. "The gospel sing starts at six. You two guys are going, aren't you?"

They nodded, their faces not overly excited.

I chuckled at their expressions. "The migraine story wouldn't work two days in a row, huh?"

They shook their heads, their faces long as a couple of basset hounds.

"You'll feel better for having gone," I said, heading toward the stairs. "Think of it as spiritual Metamucil."

"That's a less than appetizing picture," Isaac said.

"Okay, then think of all the great pie you're going to eat afterwards," I called from halfway up the stairs.

"Now there's something a man can meditate on," Uncle WW called back amidst hearty male laughter.

Upstairs in her room, Elvia was contemplating two outfits. Both were coordinated designer blouse and skirt combinations—one a deep grass green, the other off-white.

"The off-white," I said. "It looks great with your skin."

She glanced quickly over at me, then down. I caught a flash of uncertainty in her face. Was my comment about her skin color some kind of gaffe? I blew air out in irritation. Not at her, but at a world that created a racial climate where I had to worry about every little thing I said to my best friend.

"You *have* always looked good in off-white," I said softly but firmly.

She picked up the silky blouse and ran the fine fabric through her fingers. "Ecru," she corrected me, a small smile tugging at her lips.

It was a relief to see a little spark of the confident Elvia I loved so much prevail in her voice.

"How was Little Rock?" I asked.

She sat down on the bed and pulled off her strappy sandals. "It was interesting seeing Emory's life and history. The campus was beautiful. We stopped by and visited with some of his old professors."

"Did you hear about Quinton?"

She nodded and inspected her nails. "Emory rushed out

of here the minute Isaac and your uncle told him. I feel so sorry for Amen. Have you seen her?" She opened a red leather cosmetic case and started searching the contents.

I sat down on the other twin bed, folding my legs under me. "We were at Miss DeLora's house with her when Quinton's fiancée came by with the news."

"Isaac and WW didn't know much," she said, finding the bottle of icy white nail polish and repairing a chipped spot on her nails. "You don't really think Quinton had anything to do with it, do you?" Her face pulled tight as she concentrated on her nails. Outside, I could hear a neighbor using a Weedwacker, its sharp, hazy buzz forcing us to speak louder.

"Of course not," I said. "Why in the world would he risk his career, Amen's career . . . shoot, his whole future, on killing a lowlife like Toby, even though the world's a better place without him in it?"

She looked up at me, blowing on the freshly painted fingernail. "Because he's young and passionate and idealistic and doesn't think two seconds about the future. I know. I've had six brothers who've gone through that stage at various times."

"I guess you're right," I said, propping my chin in one hand. "Well, I'd better go slap together something to wear."

"That new little print sundress you bought at the Farm Supply would look great. I think the horseshoes in the print are exactly the same color as your brown sandals." She finished repairing an index finger. "I still can't believe you shop for clothes at the same place you buy chicken feed."

"Their boutique has really cute stuff," I protested. "The latest fashions."

"For livestock, maybe."

"Shut up," I said good-naturedly, "or I'll have a skirt made out of a saddle blanket and wear it to your wedding."

"In your dreams," she said. Though I wanted to, I didn't ask her which part of that sentence she was referring to.

Contemplating the saddle blanket skirt, which actually didn't seem all that weird to me, I put off getting dressed another few minutes and knocked on Dove's bedroom door.

"Is it anyone but my sister?" she called through the closed oak door.

"It's me, Gramma."

"Come on in, honeybun."

She was sitting in a padded rocking chair, reading her worn black Bible. Though everyone in the family at different times had offered to buy her a new one, she just kept repairing this one with electrical tape.

"This one's got my smell to it," she'd say. "A new one would be too fresh."

I sat down on the needlepoint footstool next to her. It showed a small pug dog sitting in the lap of a little girl in a bright blue dress. I could remember sitting on this same stool when I was four or five years old.

"You hear about Quinton?" I asked, avoiding the subject of her sister. I'd learned long ago to steer clear of their feuds, if at all possible. Deep inside, I knew they cared deeply for each other; they just didn't *like* each other. I'd often wondered what in the world these two could accomplish if they ever decided to vote the same ticket.

"WW got a phone call from Bud down at the feed store who heard it from his nephew whose girlfriend's the daytime dispatcher at the station."

"The Sugartree express," I commented wryly, resting my cheek on her knee. "I wish Quinton had just stayed home that night. Amen's got enough trouble."

"Young men, bless their hearts, are ruled more by feel than sense. And it's situations like this that prove that."

"Well, I don't believe Quinton killed Toby, but whoever did deserves a silver medal."

She smacked the top of my head gently with her worn Bible. "That's no attitude to be taking to a gospel sing. Toby was God's child just as much as anyone else."

I jerked my head up. "I can't believe you think the world's a better place for people like Toby being in it. He's the definition of original sin."

"Don't be getting on your high horse with me, young lady. I know well as you Toby Hunter was a bitter pill to swallow, but he was still a soul in need of God. While he was alive, there was hope he could turn around. Then someone took that hope from him, and that ain't right. Only God has that right."

Dove and I stared at each other for a moment. In the background the Weedwacker abruptly stopped, and we could hear the chittery tick of the mantel clock on the dresser. Capital punishment was something that Dove and I had disagreed on before, though we respected each other's opinions and didn't argue about it . . . much.

"I can't help it," I said, breaking away from the visual standoff and looking down at my feet. "I guess I'm a bad Christian, but to be truthful, I'm glad he's . . . He can't hurt anyone anymore."

She reached over and ran a gentle hand over my head, smoothing back my hair. "Honeybun, life is a mystery, that is the pure truth. Thanks be to God that He's in control and that He has a more forgiving heart than the likes of us." The certainty in her voice, as always, gave me comfort.

"So, what's going on with you and Garnet?" I asked, figuring that as volatile as that subject was, it was certainly easier to discuss than capital punishment, justice, and divine grace.

"That woman," she said. Her peach complexion turned rosy in indignation. "Why does *everything* have to be a competition with her? I swear, it's just 'cause she's jealous of me and Isaac. I do believe she might have a crush on him. Not that I'm surprised. She's been trying to steal my boyfriends all my life."

I held back the giggle tickling the back of my throat. The thought of Aunt Garnet flirting with Isaac, with having *intentions* toward him, was a hoot. I gave her what I hoped was a properly sympathetic expression and said, "In all fairness, think of how exciting your life must appear to her. You can't really blame her. Isaac *is* a hunk."

She narrowed her eyes and studied my face to see if I was poking fun at her. Satisfied I wasn't, she said, "Yes, but that's no call to try and embarrass me in front of him. Land's sakes, does she really think he's going to leave me and go to her 'cause her meringue is a half-inch higher?"

"Hard to imagine," I agreed, standing up. "What kind of pie is yours?"

"Bittersweet chocolate–coffee cream," she said.

I groaned in anticipation. "Oh, man, save me a piece. You hardly ever make that pie."

"You know your daddy's allergic to chocolate. I gave you the recipe, and as far as I can see, you ain't got two broken arms." She stood up and set her Bible down on the nightstand.

I hugged her and said, "But it never tastes like yours."

She kissed my cheek, then gave me a smack on the butt. "Oh, you are just runnin' off at the mouth to hear your head rattle. Go get ready for the singin' and wear a dress. They already figure we're a bunch of western heathens out there in California. No use adding more grease to the frying pan."

"Yes, ma'am," I said.

In our room downstairs, Gabe was slipping on a grayish blue tweed sports jacket over a dark gray shirt. "Elvia said to tell you she'd left with Emory already. Do I need a tie?" he asked, using a lint brush on his slacks.

"Nah. I'm not even going to wear nylons."

"Pagan," he said, grinning, then checked his watch and said, "You've only got about a half hour."

"Plenty of time," I said, pulling my dress out of the suitcase. I gave it a shake and eyed it critically. Could I get away without ironing it?

"No," Gabe answered my unspoken question.

"Then fetch me the iron," I said with a sigh.

Lucky for us the church was within walking distance, because the parking lot was full, and the streets near the brightly lit brick building were jammed with cars and trucks trying to maneuver into any spot available.

"Wow, looks like everyone's turned out for this," I said.

"Your uncle was saying this morning that it's the first attempt at joining the two churches," Gabe answered.

The contrast in the two congregations' mode of dress alone made an interesting sociological study. The white church members were dressed somewhat casually, with sundresses and even some pantsuits; the men eschewed ties for this loose midweek service. The black church members tended to dress more elaborately, the women in bright-colored, classy suits with matching shoes and purses; the men wearing neat, pinstriped suits and silk ties. There were many more hats in their group, both on the men and women. The only group dressed exactly the same were the teenagers, who favored baggy pants, pierced ears on both sexes, and the boisterous laughing common to that age group no matter what race. Children of both races darted around the parking lot screaming and playing, unconcerned about this possibly momentous day.

I couldn't help wondering when the division by race started to take place. When they stopped being teenagers? When they got married, had children of their own? Would Amen and I have gradually moved apart as friends if I'd lived here? I liked to think we wouldn't have. Elvia and I never had. Our friendship had always come before our backgrounds. We became friends long before we'd even understood that we had real cultural differences.

I nodded and said hey to people I knew as we walked toward the sanctuary's doors. The pews were packed, forcing Gabe and me to squeeze into the second to last pew.

Behind us, a row of teenagers giggled and whispered mock insults at each other.

"I guess some things never change. The back row was where *we all* used to sit when we were teenagers," I whispered to Gabe. "Brother Cooke used to get so mad because there'd be grease spots on the wall from the boys leaning their heads back."

"Brothers and sisters," a big-chested black man boomed into the microphone. He introduced himself as Brother Folkes, pastor of Zion Baptist. "Welcome to God's house. A house He built for all His children, no matter what their color. Praise His Holy Name."

Spirited shouts of "Amen" and "Tell the story, brother," came from the rustling audience. They seemed to all come from one side of the church. I realized then that the people, like a wedding between the Hatfield and McCoy clans, had segregated themselves, black on the bride's side, white on the groom's. There were a few sprinkled dissenters on each side. Gabe and I had sat on the black side without realizing it. I noticed that four rows ahead of us, Emory and Elvia were also on this side. Miss DeLora, who had been a member of Sugartree Baptist almost as long as Dove and Garnet, sat on the white side, second row, aisle seat, the same place she had sat since I was in the nursery. As one of the few black members of Sugartree Baptist, she was in a particular place of wisdom regarding this merger.

"Looks like this togetherness plan has a ways to go yet," I whispered to Gabe.

Gabe glanced behind us at the teenagers, still giggling and whispering, though at a much lower level now. They were intermixed, their common ground age not race. "Maybe it'll happen with their generation."

"I hope so," I said.

Brother Folkes called on us to open our hymnals to page forty-two and sing as the two choirs shuffled in. It was an appropriate choice of songs—"When We Get to Heaven,"

"Leaning on the Everlasting Arms," and "Just a Closer Walk with Thee." The two sides of the church did their best to sing together, the result being somewhat choppy in pacing and spirit. After the songs, when the two choirs were finally settled up onstage, one in sedate navy robes with white collars, the other in bright purple robes with shiny gold collars, Brother Folkes handed the podium over to a young redheaded man who was apparently the youth minister. He started reeling off the activities of the week involving the youth of both churches.

"Got any room there?" Duck whispered. I nudged Gabe, and we moved over.

"How's Quinton?" I whispered back.

"They let him go," he said. "But not until I brought in one of the toughest criminal lawyers in Little Rock and we threatened to sue the city, the police chief, and the mayor. They're really wanting to pin this on someone quick, and Quinton made himself a perfect target."

"But what do they have on him really?"

"Nothing except the fact he might have been the last person to see Toby before he was killed. Quinton says he just harassed him some and then, when Toby was getting close to home, took off and went back to his apartment. The problem is there's no one to verify his story he was home in bed by midnight. The estimate is Toby was killed around two A.M."

"What a mess," I said, sighing.

"No kidding," he agreed.

"Where's Amen?"

"She'll be here for the pie social afterwards. Hopefully not too many people know about this yet. Quinton's kicking himself like crazy, afraid he's messed up any chance Amen had of getting elected."

"I sure hope not," I said, but I wasn't optimistic. Innuendo and rumors could irreparably hurt a person's reputation, especially in a small town like this. If nothing else, there was a good chance Grady would win because of the sympathy vote. Fair or not, there were probably some people who would hesitate voting for Amen simply because of the slightest hint of criminal activity concerning her campaign manager nephew.

After the announcements from the youth minister, there were general announcements, and then Brother Woodward, Sugartree Baptist's current minister, said a few words and led us in prayer.

"We're doin' things a little different tonight, folks," he said, his flushed face nervous. His thin blond hair clung damply to his sweating face. His anxiety surfaced in his occasional pause for a deep breath. You had to admire him, though, for attempting a merger between these two churches. A lot of people on the Sugartree Baptist side of the church didn't look very happy or cooperative. "In the spirit of brother and sisterhood, we've decided to conduct this prayer meeting with a musical bent. The ushers will be passin' out programs that will tell you when it's a group sing, but feel free to sing whenever the spirit moves you. Tonight we just want to worship the Lord as one body."

We settled back and for the next forty-five minutes watched two disparate churches attempt to become one. The side we sat on was definitely more comfortable with the energy the choirs were displaying as they sang their many gospel favorites—"Nothing But the Blood," "What a Friend We Have in Jesus," "I Come to the Garden Alone," and "It Is Well with my Soul."

Sugartree Baptist choir was doing their best to get into the joy and enthusiasm that Zion Baptist exhibited, but it took all the spontaneity they possessed to just sway a little and occasionally nod their heads. I watched Dove up in the choir standing next to Garnet and I could tell she was itching to be over on the other, more active, side.

Then the pianist started the strains of "I'll Fly Away."

"Oh, Lordy, here it comes," I said, louder than I realized.

Gabe and a couple of people around me turned to stare at me with curious expressions. Next to me, Duck just laughed. He knew what I meant.

"I'll Fly Away" was Dove's all-time favorite gospel song. I've known the words to that song since I was three years old. I think it was the second song I ever learned, the first being my daddy's all-time inspirational favorite, "Singin' the Blues" by Marty Robbins.

As Dove liked to say, that song *moves* her. She cannot sit still when she hears that song. They won't even play it Sunday morning at First Baptist in San Celina anymore at the request of some of the more staid members. In the spirit of Christian harmony, Dove didn't protest . . . much. They play it at least once a year, at an evening service, and make room for Dove to be spiritually moved.

As the song began, I watched her start swaying. Then her hands started to clap. Then her head started to bob. Now, what she was doing, feeling the music, letting it take her away, wasn't unusual to the members of Zion Baptist. It just looked out of place on the side she was on.

Her hands flew up. So did Aunt Garnet's eyebrows.

Next to me, Gabe chuckled. I elbowed him and whispered, "Don't you be laughin' at my gramma."

"I'm not," he said, still laughing. "I think it's great."

By the time we were singing the third verse, she'd floated over to her purple-robed friends from Zion Baptist and had thrown herself totally into the music. Aunt Garnet's face looked stiff enough to iron canvas on. In the front row, I spotted Isaac, who was smiling, clapping, and watching Dove with pure love in his face. Dove didn't look anywhere but up, her eyes following her uplifted hands in making a pure and joyful noise to the Lord.

By the end of the forty-five minutes, almost the whole church, except for a few old fuddy-duddies, were up clapping, singing, and feeling as one.

"Maybe this will work!" I shouted to Duck over the noise.

"I hope so," he said. "But Wednesday evening's one thing. Sunday morning's another."

I nodded, knowing he was right. The old saying was true that Sunday morning was the most segregated hour of the week. But it was a start.

At the end, before both ministers closed in prayer, Brother Folkes mentioned Quinton's "troubles" and asked for guidance and deliverance without stating what his troubles were.

Afterwards, in the fellowship hall during the spirited pie auction, I caught up with Emory and Elvia.

"Have you seen Amen?" I asked. A cheer went up. Someone had bid fifty dollars for a strawberry rhubarb pie.

"She took Quinton home," Emory said. He slipped his arm around Elvia's shoulders. "Said she'd drop by here afterwards. Since she was the one who arranged this, she feels obligated."

"This has to be tough for her," I said, glancing around at the chattering crowd, still mostly broken up according to skin color. A skinny bald guy wearing a pinstriped suit bid thirty dollars for Dove's chocolate-coffee pie. "Darn, I wanted that. I hope she made one for us to eat." I glanced over at the kitchen.

"Amen really needs to be here," Emory said. "Her competition sure is." He nodded over at a group of black men in dark suits and colorful ties. Grady Hunter was telling them something, using his hands in broad, open gestures, attempting to persuade their skeptical faces.

"He sure seems able to keep going in spite of his tragedy," I remarked.

"A true politician," Emory said. "I just hope that Amen realizes what kind of world she's attempting to break into."

"If anyone has the backbone to bring honesty and integrity to politics, it's her," I said confidently. A last bid for a pie went up . . . thirty dollars for Aunt Garnet's lemon meringue. "Uh-oh, the competition is in a dead heat. Elvia, let's avoid the bloodshed and see if they need any help in the kitchen."

"Go with her, darlin'," Emory said. "Try and snag me a piece of Dove's chocolate-coffee pie before it's inhaled by the hungry masses. Pretty, pretty please?" He took her hand and made elaborate kissing noises over it.

Elvia pulled her hand away in mock irritation. "Your cousin is crazy," she said to me.

"Tell me a new story, sister Elvia," I said, looping my arm through hers and pulling her toward the kitchen. "Go outside and help with the ice cream," I said to my cousin. "Half those ice-cream makers have to be hand-cranked. They'll need your muscle."

Inside the warm, steamy kitchen, women were busy cutting every kind of pie you could imagine—lemon meringue, dozens of chocolate, pumpkin, apple, cherry pies with lattice crust, pineapple cream cheese, rhubarb, blackberry, butterscotch, peanut butter, and even a long rectangular blueberry pie baked in a commercial-sized cobbler pan.

"Wow," I said, picking up a pie in each hand. Both had brown-tipped meringue I knew would have a slight crunch when you bit into it. "Everyone must have made double pies, one for the auction and one to share. Grab those two berry pies," I said to Elvia. "We'll take them out to the table."

"Thanks, girls," Shirley Arnett said, giving us a grateful smile. "We've got more pies than hands, that's for sure, and that bunch is a'gettin' hungry out there after seein' the pies auctioned." She leaned over and called out the kitchen window. "How's the ice cream comin', boys?"

"Almost there," a male voice called back.

Out at the long tables covered with white tablecloths,

people were grabbing up the plates of pie faster than they could be laid down.

"Over here, sisters," a dark copper-colored lady in a cobalt blue dress called to us, pointing to an empty spot on the long table. She grabbed one of my pies and started sliding pieces onto paper plates. "This bunch may not be able to sing or worship in harmony," she said to me and Elvia, "but they sure can suck up the pie in a right similar manner."

I laughed and set down my other pie, licking a bit of meringue that had stuck to my thumb. "Guess you gotta start somewhere."

She winked at us, tucking the white tea towel she had stuck in the V neck of her dress deeper into her cleavage. "Stomachs haven't got no color."

"Amen," I said.

"Speaking of her, is she comin' tonight?" the lady asked, her face sobering quickly. "We heard about poor Quinton."

Elvia and I glanced at each other. I should have realized that something like that would never be a secret for long in a town this size.

"She said she was," I said. "He's free now. Duck Wakefield's got him a good lawyer."

"Praise Jesus," the woman said, sliding the last piece of lemon pie out of the pan and starting on a cherry. "That Dr. Wakefield's a good man, a real friend to Amen and her kin. You know, it's a setup. That boy would no more kill someone than I would."

I nodded in agreement. Not seeing Dove's pie, I chose a wedge of pecan pie. After offering Elvia a bite, which she turned down, I shoved a forkful of fresh pecans and gooey sweet filling in my mouth. Of course, right then my name was called out in a shrill Southern whine that brought back childhood memories of a less pleasant nature.

"Benni Ramsey, I swear, you haven't changed one little bit!"

The tone with which it was said made it clear it wasn't a compliment. I turned to face Duck's ex-wife, my ex-nemesis, Gwenette Johnston Wakefield who-knows-what now. The same sentiment could apply to her, and it wouldn't have necessarily been a compliment. Hadn't anyone told her that fluffy, platinum-streaked, Farrah Fawcett curls had gone out in the seventies? I had to admit, though, she was in good shape. Her skin-tight, white-as-powdered-sugar suit showed off a body that could not possibly have eaten a Moon Pie or Ho-Ho in twenty years. Maybe that explained the sour cream expression on her smooth face.

"Hey, Gwenette," I said, swallowing my huge bite of pie. I choked slightly on a pecan, causing Elvia to pound my back gently.

"Goodness, are you all right?" Gwenette asked, though her unnaturally bright blue eyes laughed at me. She looked at Elvia and trilled a high, grating giggle. "She always did like to bite off more than she could chew."

"Fine," I said with a gasp, gratefully accepting the glass of sugary red punch from Elvia, who had not smiled back at Gwenette. I gulped it down, trying not to spill any on the front of my dress. "How are you?" I said when the bulk of my pie had been washed down.

"Real fine," she said, giving a huge, pageant smile. All her teeth were exactly the same color and size. I wondered how much they had cost Duck.

"This is my best friend, Elvia Aragon," I said.

She gave Elvia a long, interested look, taking in her expensive outfit. "I've heard a lot about you. Our Emory's quite enamored." She turned her laughing eyes back to me. "Always so open-minded, our Emory."

Elvia's face stiffened. I gripped my empty paper cup, telling myself not to buy into her word games, reminding myself I was in church, to turn the other cheek.

"How's your mama?" I asked, turning to a safe, Southern topic that was always appropriate.

"Ornery as ever," she said, a pink manicured hand flying up and touching her big curly hair as if to make sure it was still there. She looked directly at Elvia. "That's a Dana Buchman suit, isn't it?"

"Yes," Elvia said, her face wary.

"It's simply precious. I swear, Emory always did have such lovely taste in women's clothes."

"Gwenette," I started, "why don't you take your chicken-fried comments and . . ."

Before I could finish the less than Christian comment I was about to make, two voices similar to hers in shrillness and sugary drawl called out, "Gwenette, honey, that suit is just to die for. *To die for.*"

She turned to smile at the two women wearing similar big hairdos and light, summery dresses.

"Who's that with Benni?" one stage-whispered. "Is *that* Emory's California girlfriend? The one he's been braggin' on all week?"

We could see the back of Gwenette's head bob up and down in assent.

"Why, she's real pretty," one of them said, sounding surprised.

Gwenette shrugged. "I suppose." Then she moved a step away, but not far enough so we couldn't hear the second part of her statement. "Though not hardly as white as the rest of us, is she?"

The two women giggled and looked guiltily over at us. I glanced over at my friend, whose face froze in shock. Heat started somewhere deep inside my chest, moving rapidly to my head until it felt like it was going to burst. I started toward the women, not sure what I would do or say when Elvia's fingers bit into my upper arm, her nails digging into my skin.

"Don't," she said. "Please."

I turned back, her stricken face causing me to want to cry out in despair. "We can't let them get away with a comment like that! Elvia, I have to do something."

"No, please," she said, her voice so low only I could hear it. "It will bring even more attention to me. I can't take that right now." Her eyes begged me. The humiliating place they put her in made me so angry at that moment I could understand why Quinton might kill someone for spitting on his grandma.

"What can I do?" I asked.

"Let me go back to the house. Tell Emory I wasn't feeling well."

Before I could argue, she walked away, out of the fellowship hall, out into the darkness. I was tempted to run after her, but I suspected she wanted to be alone now, to think about what just happened, to maybe call back home and talk to her mother or one of her brothers, hear their comforting Spanish words, reestablish her security and identity. I knew that was something I couldn't do for her.

I glared over at the three women, who watched Elvia walk out the door, satisfied expressions on their priggish faces.

"Don't worry, honey, they'll answer for that before the throne of judgment one day," the lady in the cobalt silk dress said behind me. I turned and faced her. It was obvious by the expression on her own angry face that she'd witnessed the whole scene and had probably experienced similar situations more than once in her life.

"Maybe that's not soon enough," I said, frowning.

She shook her head, and the glossy cherries in her tiny round hat trembled. " 'Revenge is mine, sayeth the Lord,' " she said. She held out a cup of red punch. "Have a drink and a slice of pie and don't let a sorry piece of work like her royal highness over there ruin your evening."

I took the cup of punch but passed on the pie, my appetite definitely gone. What I planned to do was wait a half-hour or so and then go see Elvia.

I walked by Gwenette and her two tittering cohorts, giv-

ing her white-suited back a dirty look. At the giggling of
her friends, she turned and smiled at me. That last self-
satisfied smile did it.

I stepped forward, faked a stumble and tossed my whole
glass of red punch across the front of her lily-white suit.

The scream that burst from her pink lips reminded me
of a pig being slaughtered.

"Oh, oh, oh!" she cried, doing a comical little dance and
brushing at the bright red watermelon-sized stain spreading
across her chest and lap. Her friends squealed in unison and
dabbed at her.

"I am *so, so* sorry," I exclaimed loud enough so everyone around us would think I was sincere. "Please, let me
help." I grabbed a napkin and joined the dabbing. When I
was close enough, I said in a low voice, "Gee, that dress
ain't hardly as *white* as it used to be, is it?"

She slapped my hand away, causing even her girlfriends
to gawk in surprise. "Get away from me, you little . . .
witch."

I don't think witch was actually the first word that came
to her mind.

People watched us curiously, waiting to see what would
happen.

I backed up, a beseeching smile on my face. "Oh, Gwenette, please forgive my clumsiness. You know how high
heels have always been difficult for me."

We both looked down at my flat sandals. I grinned at
her.

"Benni!" Dove called from the kitchen, a witness to the
whole incident.

"Coming," I answered, lifting my hand to Gwenette in
an apologetic gesture.

"What was that all about?" Dove said, pointing a pie
server out at the hall.

I whispered in her ear. "She made a racist remark to
Elvia."

Dove looked at me long and hard, her face severe. Finally she said, "And you only threw one cup of punch?"

I laughed, hugged her, and said, "I'm going to find Elvia. She said she was going back to Aunt Garnet's. Tell Emory and Gabe what happened, okay?"

"You go on," Dove said. "I'll tell them where you went and bring you both a piece of pie."

"Thanks, Gramma."

As I weaved through the cars in the crowded parking lot, I thought about what I would say to Elvia. I would definitely tell her about my punch spill all over Mount St. Gwenette and hoped it would cheer her up. But I knew this incident would only add one more reason to her growing list of why she and my cousin shouldn't make a life together.

Near the pastor's office, next to a huge magnolia bush planted in front of his small window, Detective Billy Brackman stood smoking a cigarette, holding it behind his back after every puff in a furtive way that told me he'd tried to quit more than once.

"Caught ya," I said, laughing.

He laughed in reply, took one last puff, and threw the cigarette down on the grass, grinding it out under the toe of his brown boots. "Yeah, guess you did. Awful habit. My wife's always after me to quit, but I just can't."

"Do you belong to Sugartree Baptist?" I asked.

He nodded. "Since I was a teenager. Me and Sandi—she's my wife—met in Sunday school. My parents moved here from Kentucky when I was fifteen."

I thought his twangy, hill country accent had sounded just slightly different from the soft, syrupy drawl of a native Arkansan.

"You like it here?" I asked.

He shrugged. "It's okay. Good as anyplace else, I guess." His eyebrows lifted in interest. "Where I'd really like to live is California. But I can't get my wife to move away from her mama."

"California's nice. At least the part where I live."

"I want to move to Los Angeles. Or San Francisco. I want to work for an agency who's got somethin' on the ball, someplace I can learn new things. Not like this place."

"Frustrated, huh?"

"You said it." He crossed his arms over his chest, resting his hands underneath his armpits.

"Because of the Hunter investigation?"

"If you want to call it an investigation."

"I know how it can be," I said, trying to loosen him up. "Gabe sometimes gets annoyed even where we live because he'd been used to having all the latest equipment and experts when he worked in L.A. In San Celina, we don't even have a morgue. They just take homicide victims to one of the local mortuaries who are contracted with the city."

That set him off. "I know what he means! I can't believe how backward they are here and how they're just content to stay that way. Really pisses me off sometimes. I mean, would it kill the chief to look through a catalog once in a while and order something new?"

I made a sympathetic noise in my throat.

He tilted his head, his eyes curious. "Your husband talk much to you about his cases?"

I nodded, not wanting to lie much more than that, though I added, "He doesn't actually investigate cases anymore, being chief and all, but we talk about what's going on."

"You like listenin' to him?"

"Sure. It's interesting."

"Wish my wife did. All she cares about is them dang pageants."

"Pageants? You mean, like beauty pageants?"

He pulled a pack of Marlboro cigarettes out of his front shirt pocket. "Yeah, but for little girls. It's our daughter she enters. Spends every spare penny we have on spangly outfits and dance lessons." His bottom lip grew tight when he stuck another cigarette in his mouth. It took three tries with his Zippo lighter to ignite it.

"You don't like them?" I asked, trying to figure out a way to get the conversation back to the investigation.

"Between you and me, it gives me the creeps seeing all those sweet baby girls dressed up and struttin' around like grown-up ladies."

"I know what you mean. So, do you have a partner you can talk to about your cases?"

He shook his head no. "Chief doesn't believe in partners. We rotate all the time, even from street to detective duty."

"So who's working on Toby Hunter's case besides you?"

"Me and a couple of other guys. Not that much to work on really. They've pretty much decided that Quinton Tolliver's their man."

Now we were getting somewhere.

"Isn't that a bit premature?" I asked, trying to keep my voice casual and easy. Sarcasm or anger wouldn't get me far right now.

He shrugged, drew deep on his cigarette. The orange circle glowed bright, then faded. "I don't think he did it, but what I think don't mean much."

I shifted from one foot to the other, trying not to lean toward him eagerly. "Why don't you think he did it?"

He flicked an ash into the bushes, then glanced around guiltily as if expecting someone to scold him. "Shoot, I may not be a city-trained detective, but it doesn't take Columbo to figure out all they've got is circumstantial evidence. His car was seen followin' Toby Hunter, and he bumped his truck, that's it. 'Course, thirty years ago, that was enough to hang a black man."

The stark reality of his statement turned my blood to ice. "Thank goodness it's the nineties."

"Well, he ain't out of the woods yet. The chief wants to clear this up quick. So does the mayor."

"I'm sure they do, but it's more important to find the right person."

"That's what I think. Like I said, what I think don't matter much in the scheme of Sugartree politics." He looked in disgust at his half-smoked cigarette.

"So, aren't there any other suspects?" I persisted.

The almost startled expression on his young face told me his training had kicked in, and he realized he shouldn't be discussing the case with me.

"I gotta go," he said, tossing his cigarette down. "Nice talkin' to you."

"Same here," I answered, watching him walk across the parking lot. Using the toe of my sandal, I ground out the still-glowing cigarette. What I'd found out troubled me and I wondered how much I should tell Amen. The police chief and mayor sounded determined to let Quinton take the fall for Toby's murder. Was it because they knew who really did it or because it would guarantee the winning of the election for Grady Hunter if Amen's campaign manager was charged with murder? Maybe both?

I turned and gave out a little yelp of surprise when I found myself face-to-face with Mr. Lovelis.

"You scared me," I said, bringing my hand up to my throat and laughing nervously.

His dark, creased face didn't smile. Instead he bent down and picked up the cigarette Billy Brackman had tossed on the ground. "Young man should know better," he grumbled.

"Yes, sir," I said meekly, feeling as embarrassed as if I'd done it.

He gave me a long, searching look, then said, "Quinton Tolliver didn't kill Toby Hunter."

"Yes, sir," I stuttered. "I agree."

"Others in this town toted a grudge against the Hunter boy."

"Yes." I didn't say more, hoping he'd elaborate. Did he know something? Or perhaps see something? I was willing to bet there wasn't anyone in town who knew more about people's comings and goings than Mr. Lovelis.

He looked down at the crushed butt in his hand. "Filthy habit." Then his hooded eyelids slowly closed and opened, like an old tortoise lazing in the sun. "Young miss, you'd just better watch out," he told me, then turned and walked across the parking lot toward his car.

"Yes, sir," I said softly, wondering what it was exactly I needed to watch out for.

11

BACK AT AUNT Garnet's house, I found Elvia upstairs, sitting on her bed brushing her black hair. Electricity crackled through the room with each deliberate stroke. I imagined flipping off the overhead light and seeing red and orange sparks shoot around the room like streak lightning.

"Are you all right?" I asked, instantly regretting my words. What did I expect her to say?

"Oh, sure. Never been better."

I sat down on the bed next to her. "I threw punch on her if it makes you feel any better."

She looked over at me, surprised. Her eyes were red-tinged and swollen from crying. "You did what?"

I told her about my "accidental" stumble and the full glass of red punch Gwenette was currently wearing. A tiny smile came to her face.

"Thanks," she said, setting the silver-backed brush down on the chenille bedspread. "But it doesn't change things long-term. I've been doing a lot of thinking and I've decided I don't ever want to be subjected to something like that, someone like *her*, ever again."

Panic for my cousin caused me to blurt, "Elvia, she's the exception, not the rule. Think of all the great people you've met in Arkansas. Emory loves you. He'd do anything for you."

"He can't change where he was raised. As optimistic as you are about love conquering all, the reality is a person's background has a tremendous amount of influence on the success or failure of their other relationships, especially married ones. When I get married, Benni, you know it's for life. That's what I believe, what I've always believed. I'm not sure Emory and I have the kind of love that can overcome our differences." Her dark eyes, glossy as chips of onyx, filled with tears.

"Life . . ." I started, then stopped. I wanted to tell her that life was not a textbook. That sometimes you just had to take a chance, jump in the river, and start kicking. But who was I to tell her what chances to take, to assume I could even comprehend the fears she held deep inside, for herself, for Emory, and for her future children?

"What can I do?" I whispered.

She shook her head sadly. "*Amiga,* there's not a thing you can do. I don't think I could survive a divorce, especially if we had children. And I'd most certainly end up in prison, because I'd kill anyone who did to my children what Gwenette did to me."

"And I reckon I don't get an ounce of say in any of this?" Emory said. His sudden appearance in the bedroom doorway startled both Elvia and me. His accent was exaggerated, which always happened when he was mad.

And he was very mad.

Two bright spots of color tinged his pale cheekbones. Sweat beaded his upper lip, and his breath was deep and measured. I'd only seen Emory this angry a few times in our lives. That was enough for me. I sensed it wasn't Elvia he was mad at, but at the situation, at the ignorant behavior of people like Gwenette, at his inability to protect someone he loved. Unfortunately I wasn't sure Elvia, as emotionally vulnerable as she was right now, would grasp that.

She refused to meet his eyes. "I don't want to talk about it now, Emory."

"You know," he said, coming into the room, his musky male scent overpowering the flowery female perfume of the air. "I don't give a tinker's—"

"Emory," I snapped, standing up and facing him. "Cool down."

We locked eyes. I tried to nonverbally communicate that right now wasn't the best time to discuss this.

"Benni," he said, his voice calm, his green eyes wide and glowing, "this is between me and Elvia. Please leave."

I held his gaze a moment longer, then gave in, knowing there was no use trying to reason with him when he was this emotional.

"Fine," I said. When I brushed past him I couldn't resist whispering, "Cut her some slack, cousin."

Without answering, he slammed the bedroom door behind me.

I paused outside the room, wanting to stay and listen, but even my snoopy nature had some scruples. Sitting downstairs on the porch, I could hear their angry voices rise and fall like ocean waves, their exact words as loud and indistinct as a stormy sea. Emory's voice started angry, then became softer, cajoling. Elvia's voice remained steady and low, raising only once in a high-pitched wail. I sat on the porch, chewed on a hangnail, and contemplated going back to the church to find Gabe.

About a half-hour later, the front porch screen door slammed open with a wooden thump, and Emory strode past me.

"Emory, wait!" I jumped up from the rocking chair and ran down the porch steps after him. "Is everything okay? Did you guys work things out?"

Hands jammed down in the pockets of his gray slacks,

he didn't stop walking. His bitter laugh rang harsh and metallic against my ears. "If you think okay is wasting a year
of my life . . . No, make that twenty-four years of my life,
on a stubborn, self-centered woman who doesn't love me
enough to even talk about what happened tonight, then yes,
everything's okay. It's just *dandy*."

I double-stepped, trying to keep up with his long strides.
"Maybe a little time . . ."

He stopped dead in the middle of the street. Shadows
from the leaves of the trees painted jagged dark shapes
across his face. His pale eyes seemed to glow like a cat's.
"I've given her all the time I can spare," he said, his voice
thick with pain. "I love her, but she doesn't love me . . . at
least not more than she fears people like Gwenette. There's
nothing I can do about that. It's time to move on."

He continued walking, and I didn't follow him, but stood
in the middle of the street, the heavy smells of autumn
swimming around me—sweet, burning hardwood and
damp, spongy soil, the slight scent of water in the cool dark
air—and wanted to cry for my two best friends. I toed a
place in the sidewalk where maple roots had lifted the concrete, trying to think of something I could say or do to
mend this rift between them.

Eventually I walked back to the house and waited for
Gabe. When he finally came home he sat next to me on the
swing, and I told him what had happened. His face was
sober and hard until I told him about the punch incident.

He gave a half-smile, took my chin in his hand, and gave
it a tiny shake. "You are a pistol, woman."

"I wish we could do something."

"*Querida,*" he said, pulling me close, resting his chin
on the top of my head. "You know this is something they
have to work out themselves."

"It's all that stupid Gwenette's fault. Someone should
have tied her in a gunny sack and thrown her in the creek
when she was born."

His quiet laugh soothed me. "Maybe you should keep that comment between you and me." Then his voice grew serious. "As disgusting as that woman's behavior was, the truth is, if it hadn't been Gwenette, it would have been someone else. Elvia knows that prejudice exists, and there's not a thing any of us can do about it except try to battle it in the ways we are given. I've had to deal with it every day of my life in one way or another. So has she. The trouble is she's managed to spin herself a safe little cocoon in her bookstore in San Celina where she's in total control. Emory cracked that comfortable cocoon, and now she's running scared."

"But wouldn't she still have to face prejudice if she married a Latino man? Who you marry doesn't change your skin color."

"No, but I don't have to tell you that people marrying out of their cultural backgrounds sets a lot of people's teeth and hidden prejudices on edge. Prejudices they would have sworn they didn't have manage to sneak in the back door. Look at some of the comments your ex-brother-in-law, Wade, made last year when he came back. He was deeply angry you remarried, but it was doubly bad because I have brown skin."

"He was being an ignorant jerk."

"And there are a lot of ignorant jerks out there."

"I know all this," I said, sighing. "But all I care about right this moment is helping Elvia and Emory not lose each other. She knows deep inside no man will ever love her like Emory does. Isn't that enough to overcome their different backgrounds?"

"Only they can make that decision. Our job as their friends is just to be there to listen."

"I'm afraid Elvia will want to leave tomorrow."

"Then you will drive her to the airport and assure her you still love her and will be her friend. She's probably terrified that she'll lose you, too."

"You know that would never happen. Maybe I'm being completely naive, but I still believe this will all work out. They're meant to be together, I just know it."

"Your cockeyed optimism is one of the reasons you stole my heart, Señora Harper. And you just might be right this time."

"Speaking of right," I said, feeling generous since he was being so nice, "you were, for once."

"What do you mean, for once?" He gently tickled my side.

"Stop that," I said, wiggling away. "I mean, about Amen. She was hiding something. In all the hullabaloo about Quinton getting arrested, I forgot to tell you."

"What was she hiding?"

I lowered my voice. "She and Duck are in love. They want to get married."

He whistled low under his breath. "Politically that's a bombshell, all right. It's pretty poor timing in her campaign for an announcement like that."

"Since when does timing have anything to do with falling in love?"

He pushed the swing with his foot and started us rocking. When a car slowly drove down the quiet street, his arm involuntarily tightened around my shoulders. "Do very many people know?"

I shook my head no. "Only Emory and Quinton and now us."

"Is that it?"

"What do you mean?"

"Is that all she told you?"

I sat up and looked at him, confused. "What else could there be to tell?"

He shrugged, continuing to push the swing with his foot.

"Are you implying there's something else she's hiding?"

"It's just a feeling."

"You know, if I said that, you'd chauvinistically dismiss it as feminine intuition."

"Don't get all hot and bothered. I may be wrong. This may be what she's hiding, but I'm guessing there's something more."

"Using what criteria?"

"My instincts."

I heaved a dramatic sigh. "I think you just don't like Amen, and for the life of me I don't know why."

"I like her fine. I just think she's not as up-front as you believe she is, which, of course, makes her the perfect politician."

"You are so cynical," I said, annoyed at him now. "I think I know her better than you. You're out of line on this one, buddy boy." I scooted over to the far end of the swing and glared at him.

"You're always wanting to know my feelings, and when I tell them to you, you get mad. How fair is that?"

He was right there, though I was not ready to admit it. I stood up and started down the porch steps. "I'm going to go see if Emory's okay."

He was up out of the swing and standing in front of me in two seconds. "Benni, let's not argue, okay? I'm sorry if I insulted your friend. I'll keep my thoughts to myself from now on. Let's not ruin a good vacation." He reached over and caressed my bottom lip with his calloused thumb. "*Lo siento, mi corazón.* Will you forgive me? *Por favor, mi alma, por favor?*"

I frowned at him for a minute, then felt myself melt as his thumb moved back and forth across my lip, his sea-colored eyes reaching deep into mine. "Geeze, Friday, wipe that pathetic look off your face. I'm not mad, even though I do think you're dead wrong about Amen."

He smiled and kissed me. "I'll walk you over to Emory's. Those punk friends of that Hunter boy make me nervous." He glanced up the empty street. "This is a nice little town, but I'll be glad to go home to San Celina."

"I don't need an escort." Before he could protest, I held up my hand. "Besides, I'm going the back way through the fountain forest. I won't be on any public street. There's no way I can get hurt."

"Okay," he said, glancing once more up the street. "Then I'll go to bed and read until you get back."

I heard Emory before I saw him when I walked through the back gate into his yard. His voice-cracking rendition of Hank Williams's "I'm So Lonesome I Could Cry" would not do much to bring Elvia back, though if they had a vegetable garden it would probably scare off the crows. The sound came from overhead. I stood on the flagstone patio and looked up at the tree house. If he was as ripped as he sounded, how would I get him down from there? I slipped off my sandals and climbed the rope ladder. It was wet with dew and hard to get a good grip.

Inside the tree house my cousin lay across the carpeted center of the floor, cradling a fifth of Blanton's bourbon whiskey, his head propped up on some books.

"Sweetcakes!" he said. "How nice of you to join the party. Have a drink." He took a long swig from the bottle and held it out to me. "It's Daddy's best. Fifty bucks a fifth." He put a finger in front of his lips and gave a lop-sided smile. "Don't tell him I stole it."

"Oh, Emory," I said with a sigh, sitting down next to him. "You know this won't accomplish a thing except give you one horrendous hangover tomorrow."

"If you're goin' to be lecturin' me, cousin-o-mine, then take a hike. And for your information, I plan on stayin' drunk for at least a week . . . or until that woman leaves, whichever comes first."

"You love *that woman*," I said, pulling the bottle out of his hand. "And things are going to work out, trust me."

He didn't protest when I took the bottle and put the pewter-horse stopper back on. "How can you say that?" He brought a trembling hand up to his face. "I'm sure you must have heard most of our conversation."

"Me and half the neighborhood," I said.

"Then you know we'll never see eye-to-eye." He hiccuped and groaned. "All I have to offer her is myself, and that's apparently not good enough for her royal self to even take a chance on." He sat up and faced me, crossing his long legs. He tilted precariously to the left. "There's no way it's goin' to happen for us. You'd best get used to that fact right now. I have."

I sat the bottle in the corner and stood up. "C'mon, you sorry piece of Southern manhood. We'd better get you out of this tree house while you can still climb down the ladder."

"I'll just sleep here tonight, thank you very much," he said, suddenly straightening, then swaying slightly over to the right.

I caught him and, with a bit of a struggle, pulled him up so he was standing. "No way am I leaving you up here to tumble out and break your neck. I think you're being a stubborn, crazy, irritating *man*, but you're still my favorite cousin, and I'm not going to let you get hurt."

He looked down at me, his green eyes hazy and miserable. "Too late, sweetcakes," he whispered.

After about a half-hour of coaxing, I managed to get him down from the tree house and upstairs to his room. On the way up the long staircase, though I tried to shush Emory's piercing diatribe on what was wrong with women today, he woke up Boone.

"Hey, Daddy," Emory said. "Better cancel the caterers 'cause there ain't never goin' to be no weddin' in this ole house."

"What's going on?" Boone said, standing at the top of the stairs in a brown velour bathrobe.

"You weren't at the gospel sing tonight?" I asked, not believing he hadn't heard the story five times over already.

He shook his head no as he came down the stairs and took Emory's other arm. "I had some paperwork to catch up on down at the office. Let's get my boy to bed, and then you can tell me what happened."

By the time we reached Emory's room, he was almost out cold. I pulled off his expensive leather loafers and covered him with a quilt.

"Things will look better in the morning, kiddo," I said, tucking the quilt around him. "I promise."

Outside Emory's room, I gave the highlights of the evening to Uncle Boone.

His rugged old face twisted in pain when I told him about what Gwenette said about Elvia. "The acorn doesn't fall short of the tree," he commented. "Her parents are 'bout as heartless as folks can be. Fired their maid one time when she left work because her son was hit by a car and was down to the emergency room in critical condition." He pulled his robe tie tighter. "I'll talk with Emory in the morning, see if we can't remedy this."

"I'll come by tomorrow sometime and see how he's doing," I said, leaning over and kissing my uncle's rough cheek. "You go on back to bed now."

I was out the front door and walking down the tree-shaded street before I realized that I'd broken my promise to Gabe. I hesitated and considered going back, but the familiar street was empty and quiet, so I kept going. Bright spots of moonlight filtered through the treetops and glinted on the concrete sidewalk. Memories of playing hide-and-seek on these same streets with Emory, Amen, Duck, and all the other kids until ten or eleven at night were as fresh as if they'd happened yesterday. I wasn't ready to concede to the fact that Sugartree was not the same town I once knew. I rounded the corner and glanced across the desolate courtyard square. The courthouse clock struck midnight. I stopped and automatically counted the strikes. A few neighborhood dogs commenced to barking, then in a few minutes fell silent. From where I stood I could see the side of Sugartree Baptist's sanctuary, bathed yellow in a weak security light. In a flash the security light went out, and my heart jumped. A memory came to me from an old TV show or something seen in a darkened movie theater—visions of a burning cross. I shook my head and laughed at myself. This wasn't a television show, for pete's sake. A lightbulb goes out, and I've got the Klan burning a cross in the church's front yard. My imagination sometimes amazed even me.

Still, I stood and watched the church for a few minutes, just in case. All I saw was a man walking around the corner, his face obscured by the shadows. He carried something in a paper bag under his arm, something small enough to be obscured by his biceps. He passed the church, and a flash of moonlight lit his face for a split second. I let out my held breath when I saw it was only John Luther. He was a head trustee of the church, the person in charge of the grounds and maintenance. He was checking the church one last time before going home and was probably in the process of replacing the burnt-out light. Again I laughed at myself, hurrying down the street toward Aunt Garnet's house. This was one flight of fancy I would certainly keep to myself, especially from my husband, who already had more than enough reason to doubt my sensibility.

Of course, I felt differently the next morning when the spray-painted swastikas were discovered on the sanctuary's front door.

12

❋ ❋ ❋

"QUINTON'S ARREST MADE the front page," Uncle WW said when Gabe and I came down to breakfast. He handed the *Sugartree Independent Gazette* across the table to Gabe.

"Surprise, surprise," I said, reaching for the blue bowl of scrambled eggs in front of me. "What did they say?"

"It's not very long," Gabe said, scanning it. "Probably because it was a trumped-up charge to begin with." He tossed the paper aside and reached for the glass pitcher of orange juice. "Journalists." He said the word with the same tone as he would say *cockroach.*

"Where's Isaac?" I asked.

"In the kitchen," Uncle WW said. He nodded over at the scrambled eggs, toast, and juice. "He's the cook this morning since the girls have moved on to other things."

"Oh, no," I said. "What other things?"

"Gathering flowers for the grave-cleaning tomorrow."

Gabe raised his eyebrows in question.

"We're spending the day at the old Sugartree cemetery cleaning up the graves," I explained. "Kind of like your Day of the Dead, only we don't actually have a set day for it. Most of the old-time cemeteries around here don't have perpetual care, so whenever there's any kind of a reunion, we always clean up the graves. It's an all-day thing with food and everything." I grabbed a piece of toast and said, "I'm going to say good morning to Isaac. I'll be right back."

In the kitchen Isaac was poking at sausage patties in an ancient iron frying pan. "Wow, Dove ought to rope you and drag you to the altar right away. A man who will cook is hard to find."

"No roping needed," he said, flipping the patties. "I'd marry her in a minute if she'd have me."

I stared at him, stunned. "Seriously?"

"Seriously. She's the holdout, not me."

I took another bite of my toast, chewing on that and his words for a moment. "What is it with all the women around me?" I finally exclaimed. To explain my remark, I gave him a quick summary of what had happened between Emory and Elvia.

He shook his head and drained the grease out of the pan. Sliding the sausages onto one of Aunt Garnet's orange Fiestaware platters, he said, "Guess everyone's afraid of commitment these days."

"My advice, Isaac, is to take the bull by the horns," I said. "Don't take no for an answer."

He huffed with amused derision at the thought of forcing Dove to do anything she didn't want to do.

I laughed and patted his arm sympathetically. "Well, I'll put in a good word for you whenever I can."

We were all sitting at the dining table enjoying our peaceful, noncompetitive breakfast when the phone rang. Uncle WW came back into the dining room, his old face ashen.

"There's trouble down at the church," he said. "We'd best get over there."

We threw our napkins down and rushed out of the front

door. On the walk through the square, Uncle WW told us what the pastor had said. "Somebody's spray-painted the church. Pastor saw it this morning when he went to open the sanctuary for some ladies who were going to straighten up from last night."

We joined the small crowd gathered in front of the church. The church's blue double doors were painted with two black, glossy swastikas.

"Who would do a thing like that?" Uncle WW said, his teeth clamping down tight on his pipe.

I glanced over the crowd, looking for John Luther. My mind flashed back to last night, to his prowling around the church, a small paper sack clutched under his arm. Was he the one who did this? Should I say anything to anyone? If it wasn't him, just the idea that I'd accuse him would hurt him deeply and probably harm our relationship permanently. On the other hand, he *was* suspiciously lurking around the church last night . . . or, my more open-minded self countered, he was checking the building, which was *his job*. John Luther wasn't a racist, I would have bet my savings on that. He and Amen were friends from childhood. Why in the world would he paint swastikas on his own church?

I slipped my hand into Gabe's, taking comfort in its warmth and strength. I couldn't even tell him. Not unless I had something more than the possibly innocent thing I saw last night.

"Want some coffee?" I asked Gabe. The police had arrived and were taking pictures of the damage.

"Sure, want me to come with you?"

"No, you stay here and watch what happens. I'm going to go over to the 3B."

I walked the short block to the cafe, trying to formulate how I could approach John Luther. Before I could confront him, I needed more than just what I saw last night. I needed physical proof.

Like an empty spray can.

On a hunch, I walked past the 3B Cafe and around the corner to the back of the old brick building. I was right; the four businesses that shared the building also shared a common trashbin. No one was around, so I lifted the lid and looked inside.

Garbage is a detective's best friend, I remember Gabe saying one time. The sweet, strong odor of rotting garbage wafted up and almost knocked me over. My heart beating double time, I pulled out a crate and used it for a step so I could see better, looking for something that resembled a spray can. I pushed aside a couple of flattened pasteboard boxes and thought I spotted a brown paper sack that looked like the shape I saw under John Luther's arm last night. I leaned farther in, reaching for it.

A hand pulled my shirt back, and I yelped in surprise.

"What are you doing?" John Luther demanded. In his other hand, he held a white plastic bag of garbage.

I turned, pulled out of his grasp, and stumbled down from the crate. "Nothing!" I said in childish denial. I could have kicked myself. What was I thinking looking through his garbage in the middle of the day? I should have come back at night.

Right, a little voice sarcastically said, and get arrested by one of those handcuff-happy cops.

John Luther's face went dark with anger. "I asked you what you were doing."

"And I told you nothing," I said with as much dignity as I could muster after being caught digging through someone's trash. Heat rose up in my cheeks. But, as Dove would say, my luck was running kinda muddy anyway, so I might as well jump in the swamp. "Actually I did see something in there that looked rather interesting."

He walked over to the trashbin and closed the lid. "Have you lost your mind? Why are you going through my trash?"

But there was something on his face, a slight expression of panic that confirmed what I suspected.

"John Luther, have you lost yours?" I asked.

His eyes shifted sideways, as if he were expecting some-one to come around the corner. "I don't know what you're talking about."

"Then let me take another look in that trashbin."

He clamped a hand down on the lid. "You need to mind your own business."

"I'd say painting disgusting symbols of hatred on God's house is everyone's business, wouldn't you?" There, I said it. I waited to see his reaction.

The area around his eyes went white. "You don't have proof of anything."

"I saw you walking around the church last night."

"I was checking the doors. I'm the head trustee."

"How could you do something that vile? What do you hope to accomplish? For cryin' out loud, John Luther, you and Amen have been friends forever. What is going on?" I was truly confused.

A minute went by before he answered. "I'll deny I had anything to do with it. By the time you get someone back here to check the trash, trust me, there won't be anything for them to find. No one will believe you over me. You know that."

He was right. I was an outsider, no matter how many years I'd visited, no matter who my family was. And I'd be accusing one of the town's—the church's—most loved and trusted leaders.

"But why?" I whispered. "Just tell me that. I don't un-derstand."

"Because I just don't want to share a church with blacks," he said. "They can be police. They can be politi-cians. Shoot, I don't care if they own businesses and teach my kids. I just don't want to change the way I worship God on Sunday, and if we merge the churches, that's going to happen. They'll take over 'cause that's the way it always goes. What happened didn't hurt anyone. It's just a little paint." He opened the bin and tossed in his sack of trash.

I stared at him, dumbfounded by his skewed reasoning. "But it does hurt people."

"Not physically," he said, folding his arms across his chest. "And maybe people will think twice about votin' for the merger."

I didn't know what else to say to him, so I turned and walked away. The few bites of toast and sausage I'd eaten this morning felt sour in my stomach. Tears pricked my eyes as I walked around the corner and back toward the even larger crowd gathered in front of the church. Old Brother Cooke was standing on the top step in front of the painted swastikas saying a prayer, asking for forgiveness for the perpetrator, for harmony among the races, for grace between all human beings. Flashbulbs from cameras punctured the pale morning sunlight.

"I have to talk to you," I whispered to Gabe. We broke away from the crowd, and I pointed toward the bench in the courtyard square we'd sat on the other day. "I need to sit down."

"What's wrong?" he asked, his face alarmed.

In halting sentences, I told him what had happened.

"First," he said when I was finished, "I'm not going to lecture you about sticking your nose where it doesn't belong, how it could hurt you and other people, too."

"Good, because I don't think I could stand it right now."

"Even though you shouldn't and it could."

I raised my eyebrows at him.

"Sorry, that just slipped out."

"What should I do? Should I go to the police?"

"Tell me again what he said."

After I repeated John Luther's words, Gabe shook his head. "He never actually confessed. Honestly, with the climate of this town being the way it is, I can't believe I'm telling you this, but I think you should keep what happened to yourself. For the time being, anyway."

"That doesn't seem right."

"It's not right, *querida*. Just prudent. This battle started long before we came to town and will continue long after we leave. I'm not certain that you getting involved will necessarily be the best thing for anyone."

I leaned back against the park bench. A slight October breeze kicked up some papers around our feet. "I just can't get over his weird reasoning. He thinks it's okay for Amen to be mayor or teach his kids, but he doesn't want to sit next to her in church. What's that all about?"

Gabe leaned forward, resting his elbows on his knees. "Like I told you, people have all sorts of hidden prejudices that surface when things start to change. I guess church is the racial boundary your friend found was his."

"I'm not sure *friend* is the proper term for John Luther," I said, trying not to sound bitter. "And frankly, it changes everything I thought about him. How do we know he didn't literally kill two birds with one stone?"

"What?"

I realized then that I hadn't told him what I'd learned from Crystal when I was getting my hair cut at Beulah's yesterday morning. So much had happened since then; it felt like it had been a week. I quickly told him about what Toby had done to Tara and about a possible new suspect: Ricky Don, Tara's old boyfriend. After the incident with the church, though, all my bets were on John Luther.

"It makes perfect sense now. If John Luther killed Toby Hunter, then not only would he be avenging his daughter, but with the ruckus it's been causing between the blacks and whites in Sugartree, chances are the two churches would never merge."

Gabe blew out a sharp, irritated breath. "Let me remind you once again I don't like you being involved in this."

Ignoring his comment, I sat upright and grabbed his forearm. "What if he's not working alone?"

"Now you're really reaching. Are you suggesting an organized group is involved with all this?"

"Is that so hard to believe? Have you looked at the Internet lately? I don't have to tell you how many hate groups there are. It's not unreasonable to consider that one is active here in Sugartree."

His face grew troubled. "All the more reason for you to stay out of it. If there is an organized hate group involved, then it's something bigger than you or I can deal with."

"What if Toby Hunter was supposed to be a martyr? I've heard of that. Someone being sacrificed for the good of the cause. Kill a guy like Toby, who's a loose cannon anyway, and make it appear blacks did it. Just the thing to get people riled up. I swear, I've heard of that happening."

"I think you read it in a John Grisham novel," he said, his mouth a straight line.

"Well, that doesn't mean it couldn't happen."

"Yes, but it's going to happen without us being involved. We leave on Monday, Benni. There's nothing we can do to change any of this in the time we're here."

I inhaled deeply and laid a hand on his thigh. "You're right. I'm just going off on a tangent. What I need to do is get back to figuring out what to do about Elvia and Emory."

"That's also pretty much a lost cause, I think," he said, reaching up and massaging the back of my neck. "Though that's never stopped you before."

My neck muscles relaxed under the kneading of his strong fingers. "They're not a lost cause. They're my best friends. They might have given up, but I haven't."

"Lord help them," he said.

"Lord help us all," I replied grimly.

13

"I'M GOING TO drop by and see Emory," Gabe said, standing up. "Then maybe we can go on that fishing trip today."

"I'll meet you at the house. I need to see what Elvia has planned."

He held out his hand and pulled me up off the bench. "Be easy on her, Benni."

I looked up at him and frowned.

He held up his hands in apology. "Okay, I'm sorry. That was a bit condescending of me. You two have been friends for most of your life, so who am I to tell you how to act?"

"Sergeant Friday, you just successfully avoided a belt in the stomach."

Back at the house I found Elvia clearing the kitchen table. "Hey, sorry to run out on you, but wait'll you hear what happened."

Her face tightened as I told her about the symbols painted on the church's doors. "No offense, *amiga,* but I'm counting the days until our flight leaves on Monday."

Her comment gave me hope for her and Emory. At least she wasn't demanding to be taken to the airport this morning.

She cradled the glass dish of cold scrambled eggs in her hands. "Wipe that scheming look off your face. I don't plan on making up with Emory, and the only reason I'm not leaving today is because the amount of money they want to change my ticket is outrageous."

I picked up a plate of biscuits and brushed past her on the way to the kitchen, trying to hide my relief. For once I was thankful for her frugal nature. In the kitchen I started running hot water in the sink. As I washed and she dried, I tried to keep the conversation away from anything controversial or race related.

"You should come tomorrow to the grave-cleaning day," I said. "I think you'd find it interesting. It's a sort of Day of the Dead Southern-style."

Her face looked wary.

"The men hardly ever go," I added, to assure her it wasn't a trick to get her back together with my cousin. "It's mostly a female thing."

"Maybe I will, then," she said, taking a glass from me and wiping it efficiently. She put it away in the cupboard above her, then turned around suddenly, her face twisted in pain. "Benni, I hope . . . this thing with me and Emory . . . the fact that we can't . . . I hope that you and I . . ."

I wiped my wet hands on my jeans and held them out to her. "Elvia, you are my very best friend in the whole world and have been since we were in second grade. Don't even think about it one more minute. I love you, and even if you and Emory never speak to each other again, that will not have one iota of bearing on our friendship."

She took my hands, her face softening in relief.

"Besides," I added. "Emory will most likely move back to Arkansas now, and the only time I'll see him is when I come back here. He won't even be a factor in our everyday lives."

I wanted to crow out loud when my words caused her mouth to turn down slightly. A tiny flickering in her eyes confirmed it. She still loved him, I thought. There's still hope in Sugartree.

"I think I'll go upstairs and read," she said after we finished. She carefully folded the embroidered tea towel and hung it over the back of a kitchen chair.

"Me and Gabe are going fishing out at the lake. You're more than welcome to join us."

She shook her head no. "I'd rather stay here."

"Okay, guess we'll see you for dinner."

"How's Emory?" I asked Gabe when he returned. We were out in the garage digging through my uncle's extensive collection of tackle.

"Barely conscious," Gabe said, picking up a rod and testing its feel. "I sure wouldn't want to be in his shoes when he is fully conscious." He had a small smile on his face.

"Well, that's what he deserves," I said. "He's being a stupid idiot."

Gabe just shook his head and didn't answer.

After he and I chose our tackle, we stopped by the Piggly Wiggly to pick up drinks and food. We ran into Duck in the soft drink aisle. He was wearing a blue dress shirt, dark slacks, and a gray diamond-patterned tie.

"It's Thursday, Dr. Duck," I said. "Why aren't you doing heart transplants or vein reamings or whatever it is you cardiologists do?"

"How's it goin', kids?" he said, making a face at me and shaking Gabe's hand. "Monday is heart transplant day. Today we're havin' a going-away potluck for my receptionist at the office, and I said I'd bring drinks."

"We're going fishing," I said.

"Wish I could join you." He put a twelve-pack of diet RC Cola, a six-pack of root beer, and a six-pack of 7UP in his basket.

"Did you hear what happened over at the church this morning?" I asked.

He shook his head no, so I told him the whole story. His face turned a dull angry red. "Dang it all, that's just what we need. Who would do something like that? What in the world is wrong with people?"

I bent over our cart and began rearranging the potato chips, Moon Pies, and bags of fruit, afraid my expression would give something away.

"That would take longer to discuss than any of us has," Gabe said.

Duck nodded, gripping the handle of his cart until his knuckles were white. "Does Amen know?"

"I have no idea," I said. "I didn't see her in the crowd." I turned to Gabe. "Did you?"

"She wasn't there."

I turned back to Duck. "I guess you saw the newspaper this morning. She's probably with Quinton."

"I talked with her about two hours ago," he said. "Quinton's staying with her and Lawrence for the time being, though he's not thrilled about it. They haven't charged him with anything yet, but the damage is already done. She got three threatening phone calls this morning. And now with this church incident . . ." If he gripped the cart any harder, he was going to sprain a finger.

I patted one of his hands. "Amen told me about you guys. I think it's great."

He let out a heavy sigh. "I'll just be happy when we don't have to sneak around anymore. I'm gettin' too old for this."

"What do you plan on doing?" I asked.

He shrugged and grabbed two liters of club soda. "Depends on what happens with the election. Truthfully, I'd like her to drop out now, before she or Quinton or Lawrence gets hurt. But you know Amen, stubborn as they come and brave as an eagle . . . no matter how impossible the cause."

"And that's one of the reasons you love her," I said.

He gave a weary smile. "You're right, Curly Top. I guess if we make it through this, we can make it through anything."

"Tell her to call me when you see her."

"You got it."

"Let's drop by the Dairy Queen on the way to the lake," I said, trying to sound casual. To satisfy my own curiosity, I wanted a good look at Tara's boyfriend, Ricky Don, though I wasn't sure what that would accomplish.

"Why?" Gabe asked.

"I want a Coke," I said, regretting my quick response the minute it was out of my mouth.

"We have Cokes in the back," he said, his voice suspicious.

"I want a Coke with ice."

He looked over at me, his mouth turned downward. "Okay, Ms. Harper, it's a little late in the game to be trying to pull something over on me. Why do you want to stop by the Dairy Queen?"

"Turn right here," I said, pleased when he obeyed. "I just want to take a quick peek at Ricky Don. You have to agree he's an excellent suspect."

"I agree . . ."

"See! I think . . ."

He reached over with one hand and laid it across my mouth. "I agree and I'm sure it's something the police have thought of and will look into."

I pushed his hand away. "Not according to Detective Brackman. *He* says they've practically decided that Quinton's the one. It sounds like to me they aren't even looking for other suspects."

"Benni, do you realize what . . . who you're dealing with here?" His expression turned from irritated to troubled.

"We have only four days left. You can't solve the problems of generations in four days."

"No," I said, motioning for him to pull into the Dairy Queen parking lot. "But I have to do what I can to deflect suspicion from Quinton."

He pulled up in front of the Dairy Queen, in the exact same spot we'd parked in the night he was handcuffed. When he turned to me, his blue eyes were hard. "Did it ever occur to you that Quinton might have done it?"

I gaped at him. "I can't believe you said that."

"I'm just trying to get some perspective here. Frankly I wouldn't have blamed him one bit and probably would vote for temporary insanity if I was a juror and given the chance, but the fact is, there's a lot about this case we don't know. Snooping around trying to second-guess the police is only going to get someone hurt." He took my hand and brought it up to his lips, running them across my palm. "And I don't want it to be you . . . or anyone else in your family."

I touched his cheek with my free hand. "Amen's my friend, Gabe. I have to do something. All I want to do is take a look at this guy. That's all."

"Fine, then I'll go with you," he said, opening his door.

I preferred that he didn't because I knew I'd be bolder in my questions if he wasn't standing next to me, but I wasn't about to argue with him here, where the memories of his humiliation the other night were still fresh.

Luckily Ricky Don was working the counter this morning. I glanced down at his nametag after I ordered two Cokes, heavy on the ice, and said, "I talked to a friend of yours the other day."

Gabe took my hand and squeezed it hard. I tried to pull away, but he kept a firm grip.

"Really, who?" Ricky Don asked. He was a plain-looking young man, clean and neat with blond hair and brown eyes. Nothing uniquely distinguishing about him . . . except for the large purple bruise on the side of his jaw.

His blond-lashed eyes widened slightly when he looked up at Gabe, obviously recognizing him from the other night.

"Crystal down at Beulah's Beauty Barn. She said you'd known each other since you were kids."

"Crystal's a nice girl," he said, scooping ice into two plastic cups. "Likes to move her mouth a little too much, but a nice girl."

"I guess she and your girlfriend, Tara, are friends. I met Tara, too. Her dad and I are old friends."

With his back to me, as he filled the two cups, he said, "Tara's not my girlfriend and if Crystal said she was, she was lyin'. *That's* what I mean 'bout her movin' her mouth too much."

Gabe squeezed my hand hard enough to elicit a small yelp.

Ricky Don turned back to face me. "You okay?"

I jerked my hand from Gabe's. "Fine. Sorry if I touched a sore spot," I said, flexing my own slightly throbbing hand.

He shrugged and slid the drinks across the gray Formica counter. "No problem. That'll be two dollars even."

As we walked away, he called out to Gabe. "Uh, sir . . . Mister . . . Uh, Chief Ortiz?"

Gabe turned around, his expression neutral. "Yes?"

"About the other night." His young tenor voice cracked and seemed to skip, like a scratched record. "I . . . the other night . . . I'm sure sorry. I was the one who called the police. If I'd known . . ."

"It's okay, son," Gabe said, smiling at the stuttering young man. "What happened wasn't your fault. You did the proper thing in calling the police."

"Okay, thanks," he said, his red face visibly relieved. "Really, thanks."

"No problem," Gabe said and gave him a small wave.

"That was nice of him," I said, climbing into the Explorer. "And of you."

"He really did do the right thing. Sugartree's police department certainly needs some overhauling, but when things get so bad that people are afraid to call the police, then a town really has problems."

"Absolutely," I agreed, giving him a big smile.

"Your winning smile is not going to get you out of my lecture about minding your own business," he said.

"Did you notice the bruise on his jaw? Don't you think that looks suspicious?"

"Benni . . . ," he started.

I stuck my tongue out at him. "Ah, consider it said. I've heard it all before." I held out his drink. "Sweeten up. Have a Coke."

"You know, your tongue spends more time outside of your mouth than in," he said, turning out onto the highway.

"Friday, I'm not touching that remark with *any* length of pole."

"And with a reply like that, you're lucky you're in public in broad daylight, or I'd have your clothes off in two minutes."

On the drive out to the lake, I told Gabe about Elvia's decision to fly back with us on Monday morning. "That's a good sign, don't you think? They could still make up. A lot can happen in four days."

He grunted as we turned left at the sign for Mayhaw Lake. "Don't you ever get tired of minding everyone else's business? Have you ever considered getting a hobby?"

I settled back in my seat and said, "You should talk. Let's forget all this for a while and find us a good fishing spot even if ten-thirty is a little late to be fishing."

"Catching fish is a mere ten percent of why one fishes," Gabe said. "It's a meditative thing."

"You have been reading way too much philosophy and not enough *Sports Afield*," I commented. "But whatever floats your boat."

We drove around Mayhaw Lake looking for a dirt road I remembered led to a secluded spot at the far end of the lake. While searching, we passed a road that was cordoned off with black-and-yellow crime-scene tape. I turned to stare as we passed it. "I bet that's where they found Toby's body."

"Probably," Gabe said.

"Do they really think that tape's going to keep anyone out?"

"They most likely don't care at this point. They've probably done all that can be done with the crime scene."

"Which was probably a whole lotta nothing."

Gabe didn't answer.

"Right here," I said, about a half-mile later. We drove slowly down the familiar dirt road and found my old fishing spot. In fifteen minutes we'd set up lawn chairs, our red Coleman cooler, stuck our fishing poles in the soft dirt, and settled down for a contemplative and calm afternoon. The shade from the hickory and oak trees was cool and soothing, causing both of us to mentally and physically slow down. With our sometimes too busy lives, moments like this were rare, and we both knew it. For the first two hours, we talked about everything except what had happened since we'd arrived in Arkansas.

"I think I'll take a walk," I said, stuffing my Moon Pie wrappers down into the Piggly Wiggly bag we were using for trash.

"You'll need to walk five miles to burn off those two Moon Pies," Gabe commented, his voice lazy. He'd moved from his chair to lying down on the old blanket I'd spread on the grassy bank. His eyes were starting to droop. "And stay away from that crime scene."

"Take a nap, grumpy," I said, nudging him with my foot as I walked by. "I'll be back in an hour or so."

He murmured his answer, already halfway asleep.

I headed up to the main road and walked along it for a while, looking at the expensive vacation homes going up and the ones already finished. Though the builders and architects were doing their best to keep the "country" feel to the area, I couldn't help but lament the number of hickory and pine trees that were felled to build these homes.

When I passed the crime-scene tape, I gave in to temptation and strode down to the lake. More crime-scene tape marked off a spot that, if it hadn't been cordoned off, would have looked like just a small clearing next to the lake similar to the one where Gabe and I were parked. If there had been any clues here, they were long gone.

Disappointed, I went back up to the main road and continued walking, finally turning off the paved road onto a well-maintained dirt road named Sugar Oak Way and walked deeper into the forest. The people who bought property out here were obviously more interested in privacy than in having a personal lakeside dock. The cabins, when I could see them through the dense, green foliage, were more like lodges than cabins. I picked up a handful of large white-oak acorns and tossed them one by one as I walked. The road narrowed, and soon glimpses of cabins became impossible. The only thing that told me that any humans inhabited this forest was the occasional mailbox.

After about a mile or so, the still-sultry October afternoon air caused me to take off my sweatshirt and tie it around my waist. The quiet green buzz of the woods set me slightly on edge. As a child, the thick, leafy Arkansas forests, so different from the oak-dotted, rolling hills of California's Central Coast, often frightened me. When I was allowed to tag along on camping trips with Emory, Uncle WW, and Uncle Boone, I was always a bit apprehensive when we veered off established pathways and forged through the woods using only walking sticks to clear our path through the veiny-leafed carpet of kudzu vine. Fearful of getting swallowed up in the primeval-feeling greenery, I'd focus my eyes on Uncle WW's plaid-flannel back. As I tripped after him, I occasionally grabbed a reddish purple kudzu flower, inhaling its strong grape odor and wishing I was back at Aunt Garnet's eating a pimento cheese sandwich.

I wiped the beads of sweat off my upper lip and chided myself for not bringing water with me. Moist air seemed to envelop me like a damp blanket, yet my mouth was dry as a day-old biscuit.

At the end of the dirt path stood a green metal mailbox and a gravel driveway going deep into the woods. I turned to go back and had only walked a few feet when a male voice called to me.

"Mrs. Harper, what brings you out to my neighborhood?"

I turned to face a smiling Grady Hunter. He was wearing a pale pink golf shirt, khakis, and burnished leather boots. He opened the mailbox and stuck his hand deep inside.

"Just taking a walk," I said, pulling my knotted sweatshirt tighter around my waist. I gestured back toward the lake. "Gabe's fishing. Or rather he's got a fishing pole stuck in the sand. When I left him, the only thing he was likely to catch was forty winks."

He gave a practiced, politician's laugh at my lame joke. "I was never much of a fisherman myself. It tends to do to me exactly what it's doing to your husband—puts me right to sleep. That's why I didn't bother buying one of the lakeside lots." He flipped through the handful of envelopes and magazines. "So, you decided while he slept to reacquaint yourself with the unsurpassed beauty of our natural woodlands."

I nodded, not voicing my opinion that if this area kept developing, the only thing natural left would be the wood cut to make the log cabins. Instead I said, "You get mail delivered all the way out here?"

He chuckled, his tanned face genial. "Our postal service is very accommodating."

Would it be as accommodating if the houses weren't worth half a million dollars? I wanted to ask.

"You look thirsty," he said. "Would you like to come up for a glass of iced tea, or is your husband expecting you back at a certain time?"

I glanced at my watch. There was something about this man that made me nervous, an instinct that said to watch my back. On the other hand, my curious nature wanted to see what the house of my friend's political rival looked like. "Some tea would be nice. I'm not on any certain schedule."

"Great, come on back, then."

I followed him down the long gravel drive, and we talked idly about the unseasonably hot day, the trouble he'd been having with ticks on his hunting dogs, the activities the church had planned for the weekend, and Arkansas forests compared to the rolling hills of the central California coast.

"You like to hike at home?" he asked.

I shrugged. "Sure, though I prefer riding. You can see where you're going and where you've been. Your forests are harder for me. They're denser. I'm always afraid I'll get lost."

"I'm a walker myself. Especially since I've gotten older. Insomnia, the middle-aged person's disease. I know what you mean about the forests here. They *are* dense. But I know them like the back of my hand, even at night. Love to walk at night. Relaxes me."

Our conversation moved on to the weekend's various activities. "What's this about a Ping-Pong ball drop?" I asked, figuring if anyone knew, he would.

He tucked his mail under his arm and said, "Actually it's my idea. It's part a fun thing for the visitors and part advertising gimmick for the downtown merchants. I've hired a Cessna to fly over the town around noon on Saturday and drop ten thousand Ping-Pong balls over the town square. They'll have Bible verses printed on them, invitations to come to the services on Sunday, discounts for different downtown businesses, and even some free prizes.

There's five Ping-Pong balls that are printed with free weekends at a bed-and-breakfast in Eureka Springs, ten with fifty-dollar savings bonds, and one for a free bass boat."

"Don't the balls hurt when they fall?"

He laughed. "Not at all. We did it last year to start our Christmas shopping season, and it was a hit. You will not believe the lengths people will go to get those balls."

"I'll make sure and be there to see it."

"Bring your catcher's mitt," he said.

We came around the corner, and I almost gasped at the gorgeous two-story lodge that lay before me. If I'd ever had a dream mountain cabin, I was looking at it now. Sitting in front of the cabin was a white Range Rover being carefully washed by Mr. Lovelis.

"Hello, Mr. Lovelis," I said.

He nodded. "Miss." He didn't look at Grady Hunter, but continued to wash the car with small, deliberate circles.

"He works for me when he isn't tending to church maintenance," Grady said, opening the stained oak front door for me. "There's a lot of upkeep on a place like this."

"I imagine so," I murmured.

Inside, the cabin was decorated like something out of an Adriondack lifestyle magazine. I lost count of how many Pendleton blankets were scattered about the huge living room. Leather, dark-stained oak furniture, and stuffed game dominated the decor. Grady Hunter obviously lived up to his name. The walls held two stuffed ten-point buck heads, a couger's head, a bobcat's head, a display cabinet with what looked like antique rifles, and a buffalo head over the huge stone fireplace. It was a house void of any feminine influence.

"I'll just go out to the kitchen and ask Melba to make us some tea. Are you up for a little snack, too?" He looked at me expectantly.

"Sure," I said, even though I wasn't a bit hungry.

When he was gone, I wandered around the room looking at the expensive, decorator-coordinated western and Ozark knickknacks and the framed black-and-white photographs on the wall. Most of them were of Arkansas in the early 1900s. I wandered through an open door into what looked like a library or study. A large leather-topped executive desk sat in the corner of the book-lined room, and across from it were two deep-brown leather high-backed chairs. A pipe stand sat on the sturdy magazine table between them. Out of habit and because I knew you could often tell a lot about a person by what they held in their bookshelves, I ran my fingers across the shelves at my eye level. Predictably he was fond of Ernest Hemingway, Jim Harrison, and James Ellroy, all macho-men writers, though he also liked biographies. He appeared to own the biography of every United States president.

I perused another shelf that held a bunch of leather photo albums. I pulled one out and flipped through a few pages. In many of the photographs, a freckle-faced, laughing boy and a delicate, sweet-faced woman mugged for the unseen photographer. It took me a second to realize the innocent-looking, Huck Finn–like boy was a young Toby Hunter. Did Grady Hunter see this boy in his dreams or the ugly, hate-filled person his son had become? And how much of that latter person had Grady been responsible for? Though I was not someone who automatically blamed the parents for a child's behavior, he'd picked up that hate somewhere.

Thinking about John Luther, I had to concede that Mr. Grady Hunter wouldn't be the first person whose public appearance and opinions didn't match his private ones. I slipped the album back into its place and pulled out another one. On the second-to-last page, as I was looking at pictures obviously taken at a cabin in some Ozark piney woods somewhere, I saw the edge of a photograph peeking out from behind one of Grady holding a large fish. Curious, I pulled it out. After staring at it for a long, shocked minute,

I shoved it back behind the fish trophy picture, slammed the album shut, and shoved it back onto the shelf.

By the time Grady came back, I was sitting on the living room sofa, flipping through a *Southern Living* magazine.

He set a tray on the square coffee table in front of me and poured a glass of iced tea into a heavy topaz-colored glass. I stared at the small crustless triangle sandwiches in front of me, my stomach churning.

"I hope you like egg salad," he said, handing me a glass.

"Love it," I replied, taking a quick gulp of tea.

He filled a matching topaz-colored plate with three sandwiches. I took it and murmured my thanks, thinking all the while about how I could get out of this house, away from this man, before I gave away with my transparent face the fact that I'd seen a picture I was sure he didn't want me to see.

"So, tell me about your job," he said, settling back on the sofa facing me. "I hear from the prayer requests from Garnet that you have quite the little sideline of solving murders."

I bit off half a sandwich and took another gulp of tea, taking my time answering. "You know how she likes to exaggerate."

That picture. Oh, Lord, that picture. If it was in this house and I found it, maybe Toby did, too. And maybe he wouldn't hesitate using it against his father.

"Yes," he agreed, chewing a sandwich. "Garnet does like to embellish her prayer requests. We all know that about her. But we love her anyway. A truer heart for God you'll never find."

I nodded and didn't answer. My mind was whirling a mile a minute. If what was in that picture was made public, it would be the end of Grady's career in Sugartree. Maybe in Southern politics altogether.

Not to mention Amen's.

Though I tried not to think of it, the blurred photograph

of them kissing on the cabin porch where he'd been holding the prize fish moments before burned in my mind.

Three things kept repeating themselves over and over.

What had she been thinking?

Would Grady . . . or Amen kill Toby Hunter to keep their affair quiet?

And, dang it, would I ever hear the end of the fact that Gabe was right again?

14

I FINISHED UP my sandwiches and tea as quickly as I politely could.

"Thanks for your hospitality," I said. "Don't bother to see me out. I know the way back."

"Okay, then," he said, a bit puzzled at my haste, but never losing his smile. "I guess we'll see each other at one of the festivities."

"I'm sure we will."

Outside, I heaved a sigh of relief and started down the gravel driveway toward the road. I sensed his scrutiny through the cabin's huge picture window, though I didn't turn around to verify what might just be my own paranoia.

Grady and Amen? If there were two people in this world I would have never connected romantically, it was them. Opposites in every way I could imagine—politically, socially, culturally. How did they go from nurse and mayor to lovers to political rivals?

Out at the road, Mr. Lovelis was trimming the grass around the mailbox with a Weedwacker.

"Hey, again, Mr. Lovelis," I said.

He gave a curt nod but didn't say anything.

I was a few steps past him when an idea hit me. I stopped and turned around. "Mr. Lovelis, how long have you worked for Grady?"

He turned the machine off and pushed back his cap with a grass-stained finger. Sweat shone on his brown forehead. " 'Bout ten years."

"So you worked for him when his wife was alive?"

He nodded, his old face neutral. His dark eyes watched me with the intensity of a wary dog who'd been punished too often.

"So I guess when she was in her worst time, before she passed away, she had nurses coming out regularly."

He nodded again. "Some."

"Would one of them have been Amen Tolliver?" I blurted out, regretting it the minute I did, but needing to know. Thank goodness the one thing I could count on with Mr. Lovelis was that my disloyalty to my friend wouldn't go any further than his ears.

He nodded slowly, then turned the Weedwacker back on and went back to work.

I worried that piece of information like a terrier with a sock the whole walk back to the lake. Gabe was awake when I strode up, reeling in a wiggling fish.

"I can't believe I actually caught something," he said, laughing. "I was sitting here reading when the line jerked. I've been fighting with this little guy for ten minutes. Did you have a nice walk?"

"Great," I said, digging for a Coke in the cooler, grateful for the cold, sweet burn as it trickled down my throat. I watched him reel in the fish—a good-sized bass that would impress even Uncle WW—shifting from foot to foot in anxiety. He was going to want to bite through steel when he heard what I'd done, but the fact that it proved his intuition right might mellow him some.

I waited until he had reeled in the fish, we'd packed up

the car, and were driving back toward Sugartree before I told him what had happened on my hike.

"You snooped through this guy's private photo albums!" he bellowed. "Woman, do you have any scruples whatsoever?"

"You're acting like I went through his underwear drawer," I said, irritated that he was focusing on what I *did* rather than what I *found out*. "The photo albums were right out there in plain sight."

His fingers squeezed the Explorer's black steering wheel. "On his shelf in his study is not exactly in plain sight."

"It's not like I read his checkbook register or opened his medicine cabinet," I argued.

He muttered irritably in Spanish.

"Now, stop that. Speak English or keep it to yourself. And, anyway, what I did is beside the point. The fact that he and Amen had a relationship that included kissing is a major break in this case."

"This isn't a case, Benni. At least, not for us."

"You can't deny we're involved. My only problem is how to approach Amen with what I know without losing her friendship."

We pulled out on the highway. I glanced at the weed-thick ditches lining the road and wondered where Mr. Lovelis had found Tara. I rolled the car window down and let the late-afternoon breeze cool my face. Tara's wide, frightened blue eyes hovered in the back of my mind. I hoped she was getting some kind of counseling to help her through her ordeal. Gabe and I didn't speak of my discovery again until we pulled into the driveway.

He turned off the ignition and twisted to face me. "It's a waste of breath for me to tell you this is none of your business."

"Yes," I said, thinking, well, we agree on something anyway.

"Keep me informed," he said, his voice crisp.

"I will."

A pained expression, almost sad, came over his face, then was gone. "And be careful."

I touched his chin with my fingertips. The roughness from his day-old whiskers caused a lurch in my stomach. I loved this man so much. "Gabe, all I'm going to do is ask Amen about it, I swear."

He caught my hand and held it to his cheek. "Let's unload the car and show my fish to your family."

After they made a fuss over his fish, someone mentioned supper. Dove and Garnet assured us they had it under control. Their frugal natures had decided, competition or not, leftovers had to be consumed. From the kitchen where they were preparing our leftover supper, arguments about who was decorating which family member's graves trickled out to the porch where we all sat waiting. Great-Great-Grandma Neeta's tombstone was obviously a coveted assignment.

"They shelled peas this afternoon," Isaac said. "Then we had to weigh them." His face was amazed.

"They're actually enjoying this," Elvia said, smiling.

Uncle WW and I just shared an amused look.

"Hey," I said, "just be glad they didn't make you *count* them." I stood up and stretched, making a point not to look at Elvia. "Tell the girls I'll eat later. I want to go on over to Emory's and see how he's doing."

It took all my resolve not to peek at her expression.

"Be careful," Gabe called after me.

Over at Emory's, I found him in the basement den lying on the leather sofa, an old Spencer Tracy movie flickering across the wide-screen TV. The sound was off and there was a cold pizza with one piece missing covering the square coffee table. His hair was uncombed and his face tinged a pale yellow. He wore a faded red Razorback sweatshirt and a pair of black sweatpants.

"You look like crap," I said, lifting his legs and sitting down on the sofa.

"Go away," he said, pushing at me with one bare foot.

"Oh, suck it up, you wuss. That's what you get for drinking too much bourbon, no matter how expensive it was."

He stared at Spencer Tracy and Katharine Hepburn arguing on the television screen. "I repeat, get lost."

"Are you going to let a little setback like yesterday throw you?"

He readjusted the three bed pillows behind him and poked at me again with his foot. "Yes." Then he reached for the remote control and changed the channel to a monster truck race.

"She really does love you," I said, slapping at his foot.

He looked at me with narrowed, bloodshot eyes. "Read my lips. I . . . don't . . . care."

"Yes, you do."

He grunted. "And *if I did*, what difference would it make? She's made it clear she doesn't want to have anything to do with me and my life."

I stood up and gave his messy hair a tug. "So, what you need to do is convince her you'd give up that life . . ." I gestured around the large, book-lined room. ". . . this whole world for her. Like Gabe staying in San Celina for me. Women can't resist a man who will give up everything." I looked down at him. "That's providing, of course, you actually would give it up for her. And for the record, cousin, I think you're being a big crybaby. Grow some *cojones*."

With that remark, I turned and left the room, not looking back. That was the most I could do. The rest was up to him. I was determined to have one more talk with Elvia, too, then leave it all to their hearts. I decided not to tell Emory of my discovery about Amen and Grady. Right now, he was too occupied with his own problems.

Back at the house, I took my plate of leftovers and shot

the breeze with the men on the porch for a while, then said a quick good night to Dove and Aunt Garnet in the kitchen. They were busy at opposite ends of the big country kitchen making cookies to take to the cemetery tomorrow. I didn't dare ask whether it was quantity or quality they were competing for so I took a butter cookie from each and headed up to Elvia's room.

I knocked softly on the door. "Cookie delivery," I called.

"Come on in, *amiga*." She was sitting on one of the beds, flipping through a *Better Homes and Gardens* magazine.

"Snagged two fresh cookies from the cookie competition going on downstairs," I said. "Want the dog or the cat?"

She shrugged, and I handed her the cat wrapped in a paper napkin. "Why are Dove and your aunt making cookies?"

"Since it's a little ways out to the old pioneer cemetery, we always take lunch. Better not eat breakfast tomorrow so we can partake of both ladies' feasts. You'll have a good time, I think." I bit the head off my dog.

She leaned against the headboard and nibbled on the cat's ears. "Only two more days after that until I go home."

With that comment, I decided to get down to brass tacks. "I just saw Emory."

She continued eating her cookie and didn't look at me. "So?"

"He looks and feels terrible. In his misery, he drank too much bourbon last night and is feeling the effects of it today."

"Why should I care about that?"

I flopped in front of her on the bed. "Because you are being a *cabeza dura*, not to mention self-righteous and just plain stupid."

Her dark eyes flashed in anger. "You think I'm a hardhead because I don't want to raise my children in a racist environment?"

I plunged right in, figuring even if she got mad at me, I had to at least give it a shot. "I think you're being stubborn and silly and will regret it the rest of your life if you throw away a chance to marry someone who loves you as much as Emory does. And as for raising your children in a racist environment, you two didn't even get far enough to talk about where you're going to live, for pete's sake. All I gotta say is life is hard, my dear friend, and no matter where you live you and your children will have to face prejudice, so you may as well face it with someone who loves you and would love and protect your children with every ounce of his heart and body." I jumped up and tossed the remainder of my cookie in the plastic trashcan. "And that's all I have to say on the subject. *Buenos noches*."

I left before she could get a word out. Chew on *that*, I thought.

"What have you been doing?" Gabe asked a half-hour later as we were settling down in bed. "You've got an entirely too satisfied look on your face."

"Shut up and kiss me," I replied.

THE NEXT DAY, Uncle WW and Gabe decided to go fishing instead of going to the cemetery. Isaac, of course, couldn't resist the photographic opportunity. I drove me, him, and Elvia and the load of flowers and gardening equipment while Dove and Aunt Garnet followed in her huge Buick.

"For the life of me I don't understand how they can fight like they do and still ride in the same vehicle," Isaac commented, glancing uneasily in the rearview mirror. "What do they talk about when no one else is around?"

"Probably us," I said, laughing.

The old Sugartree cemetery was about five miles past the turnoff for Mayhaw Lake down a narrow, hard-packed dirt road. Dappled sunlight shining through the oak and piney woods rippled across the hood of our cars and our faces as we drove carefully down the bumpy road. When we turned a corner and the rusty white wrought-iron gates appeared, we slowed to a crawl. A metal sign hung from the iron entrance arch: SUGARTREE FREE CEMETERY. Underneath it, another sign dangled. The weathered piece of plywood held the hand-painted admonition: THIS CEMETERY IS NOT A COUNTY-MAINTAINED FACILITY. PLEASE CLEAN UP AFTER YOURSELF.

Near the entrance, there were already a dozen or so haphazardly parked cars. I pulled in next to a shiny old yellow Cadillac where three elderly black women in flowery pantsuits and one elderly white man wearing a white straw cowboy hat were struggling to unload some folding tables from the trunk.

"Need any help?" Isaac asked after we'd parked.

"Why, yes, sir, we would 'preciate it," the man said.

As Isaac helped the man carry the tables to a wide smooth spot of grass under some shade trees that had obviously been designated the picnic spot, Elvia and I started unloading plastic gallon tubs filled with flowers.

"Put 'em over there with the others," Dove said, pointing over to a pickup truck loaded with every color and type of flower imaginable. The side of the truck was painted with the logo of a smiling hen wearing a sandwich sign stating, TIDWINKLE'S FRESH EGGS.

A small protesting sound came from Aunt Garnet's throat. Some of the flowers were Aunt Garnet's prize roses, saved especially for her ancestors' final resting spots.

"We're commingling our bounty," Dove said, ignoring her sister's glare, "in the spirit of Christian fellowship. Now, let's all get to work. There's a lot to be accomplished today."

Sharing a quick amused look with Elvia, we did as we were told and hauled the plastic buckets of flowers over to reside with the others. Then we carried two huge ice chests of food over to where Isaac was helping unfold and set up the tables.

"What should I do after this?" Isaac asked me.

"Just get your cameras and do your thing," I replied. "Elvia and I are going to get our assignments and start cleaning graves."

There were, according to the pastor's wife, over three hundred graves in this cemetery. Many were of families who didn't have relatives here to pretty them up, but it had always been tradition to beautify the whole cemetery, so visitors like Elvia and I would help out wherever needed.

"Grab some clippers," I told her after being assigned a section. I picked up a bucket of water and a wooden-handled scrub brush.

We were given a set of graves toward the back of the cemetery since our family plot had plenty of representation. Indeed, between Dove and Aunt Garnet and the various cousins, uncles, and aunts, the Mosely group of headstones would have more than enough primping. Hundred-foot-tall loblolly pines and chiquapin oak trees shaded the area where we clipped the long grasses around the moss-stained graves carrying the old-timey names of Charity Bennett, Essie Lue Smyth, Eldon Stryker, and Reddic Montgomery II.

Elvia and I worked without talking, me scrubbing the lichen-encrusted tombstones, she clipping the grass around the base, enjoying the a cappella singing of the wild finches, the rustling of the wind in the brilliant leafy tops of the sweet gum trees, and the low murmuring and occasional spirited burst of gospel singing. We stopped for a moment to stare with delight at an unbelievably bright carmine-colored cardinal who swooped down and landed on a headstone only a few feet away from us. It chattered at us in avian anger.

"There's so much color here," Elvia said, her voice a soft sigh.

I nodded in agreement. There was no doubt Arkansas had its natural beauty and that there was much to admire about this state, not only its God-given landscapes and rich animal life, but the resilience of its people and the goodness that ran through many of them, no matter what their status in life or color of skin. The type of people who would share their last crust with a stranger, help you if you were broken down on the side of the road, march side by side with you for your right to sit where you please on the bus or a vinyl-covered stool in a roadside cafe. I was tempted to say this to Elvia. But I didn't. I went back to scrubbing the top of Velta and John Whittaker's tombstone and prayed that hearts would soften—both hers and Emory's.

"Hey, how many y'all get done?" Amen said, walking up holding an old rake with a duct-taped handle.

"More'n you, I'll bet," I shot back.

"Ha, I've been here since seven A.M. Y'all hadn't even rolled out of the sack 'fore then." She grinned at me. "You two look like twins."

"Not my choice of clothing," Elvia said, standing up and rubbing the small of her back. We were wearing identical Wranglers and faded red Sugartree Hornets sweatshirts.

"The jeans are mine, the sweatshirts are my cousin Rita's," I said. "I had to convince Miss Fashion Plate over there that graveyard dirt was something she definitely didn't want to attempt to clean out of Ralph Lauren designer jeans."

"Did you tell her we always take a group picture after lunch?" Amen asked, chuckling.

"No!" Elvia exclaimed, answering both Amen's question and the question as to whether she'd be in the picture.

"Thank you very much, Miss Mayor-Elect," I said. "I was saving that surprise for after I'd fed her."

"I'm taking a break," Elvia said, giving me a small glare. "Even though you don't deserve it, would you like something to drink?"

"I'll come, too," I said, throwing my scrub brush in the bucket of dirty water. "I need to empty this and get new water anyway."

"Dump it here and we'll get some in the creek," Amen said, pointing over to a thick stand of willow trees. "It's closer."

"Okay," I said, then turned to Elvia. "I'll join you as soon as I get fresh water."

"Good," she said, "then we can discuss the picture you *forgot* to tell me about."

"Yes, ma'am," I said, smiling big at her. She shook her head and smiled back, not really mad.

"I envy your friendship," Amen said as we walked past a group of elderly ladies in almost identical dark stretch pants and flowered polyester blouses arranging mixed bouquets of red and pink roses, cultivated daisies, and stalks of wild tiny-flowered pinkweed. "The easiness of it."

One of the women started singing, "It Is Well with My Soul," in a deep, full-throated alto, and gradually, as I followed Amen down the narrow path toward the creek, one after another, the soft, high-pitched sopranos of the other ladies joined in, and we were serenaded all the way to the bubbling creek below.

"Well, being constantly in each other's presence since second grade helps," I said. "And we forgive each other a lot."

She nodded, her face thoughtful as we dipped our empty buckets into the deepest part of the creek. The agitation of our buckets caused tiny brown fish to dart behind a grouping of jagged rocks.

"Does the race issue ever come up?" she asked, not looking at me.

I waited a moment before answering, knowing we were on unsteady ground. "You probably aren't going to like my answer, Amen, but actually, no, it doesn't that often. Mostly we ignore it." I stopped, then said, "No, I take that back. We don't *ignore* it. It just isn't an issue in our every-day life."

"And you think that's okay?" she said, her voice bitter, her dark eyes appearing angry. "You think that's realistic?"

I jerked my bucket of water out of the creek, sloshing half of it against my jeans, flinching visibly when the cold wet denim stuck to my thigh. "No, it's not *okay*, it's just the way it is. I'd discuss it with her if she wanted. I'd discuss it with Gabe if he wanted, but mostly we just live our lives, you know? A lot of the stuff that happens to all of us every day doesn't have a thing to do with the color of our skin." I set my bucket down, irritated and apologetic at the same time. "Amen, what do you want me to say? I'm at a loss here about what you want. I'm your friend and I know you're black and I'm white and there's a million things about what you and Elvia and Gabe have gone through that I'll never, ever understand, but I truly don't know what you want me to do or say. I'm your friend. I love you. I'd give you the Sugartree Hornets sweatshirt off my back if you wanted it. That's all I know to say."

She stared at me a minute, her face unreadable. Then a small smile tugged at the corner of her mouth. "Keep your ratty old sweatshirt, you smart-mouthed cracker."

"That's Miz Cracker to you," I said, picking up a hand-ful of acorns and tossing them at her.

As we started back, though I didn't want to wreck our easy mood, I also knew that I might not find her alone again, so I casually said, "I had lunch with Grady Hunter the other day."

"Is that right? How'd that come about?"

I told her about my and Gabe's impromptu fishing trip and my accidental meeting with Grady on my hike. "He seems like a very nice man," I said.

"Told you he was," she said, moving ahead of me on the path.

"You never told me you worked for him," I said to her back.

She stopped and turned slowly around, her chest heaving slightly with the strain of our uphill climb from the creek. Her shaded eyes studied me without blinking. "I took care of his wife," she finally said. "For the last nine months of her life."

I hesitated, then blurted out, "I saw a picture of you and him."

By the stricken look on her face, there was no doubt what photograph we were talking about. She slipped a hand over her eyes, and her slender body trembled slightly in the warm dappled sunlight. "He kept . . . He showed you that picture?"

"No, it was in an album. He doesn't even know I saw it. I . . ." My face grew warm. "I'm sorry, Amen. I saw it sticking out from behind another photograph and I looked at it. He was obviously trying to hide it, and . . . I'm . . . sorry."

Her hand came down, and a tired expression seemed to lengthen her face. "It's not what you think. We didn't *do* anything. Not that he didn't try . . . and not that I didn't *want* to. But we didn't. That kiss was it. I told him to destroy that picture. He took it with a timer. We were just goofing around. We weren't thinking."

"Were you in love with him?" I asked.

"No!" Her answer came too quickly. "It was just a kiss. *That's all*. He was stressed, my William had just died, and we were both lonely and confused. We spent a lot of the time I was there talking. I learned a lot about politics from him, believe it or not. During his wife's last months, she slept a lot, and there wasn't much for me to do except wait with him. He loved his wife, and I loved William, but she was dying, and I missed William . . . Grady's wife died a month or so later, and my job was over. We never spoke about it again." Her fist came down hard on her thigh. "I can't believe he kept that picture. If that came out, it would look like . . . It would ruin . . ." She stopped. Above us, a squirrel chattered in agitation, scolding us for invading its domain.

"Both your chances of being elected mayor," I finished.

"Yes," she said softly.

A thought occurred to me. "Are you sure no one else knew about it?"

"Who could . . ." But the answer came to her before she finished her own sentence. "Toby," she whispered.

"If I found it so easily, what if he did, too?"

She leaned back against the thick trunk of a white oak tree, looking up through the gnarly branches. The squirrel continued to chitter at us. "But if he used it, it would hurt his father just as much as me, maybe more. Why would he do that?"

"Maybe that's what he wanted. And maybe Grady found out about it and stopped him."

Shock widened her eyes. "Are you suggesting that he killed his own son to save his career?" She shook her head vehemently. "No way. I know Grady. He'd resign first."

"Look, Amen, I know you like and admire Grady Hunter, but I'm telling you we've got to get the suspicion off Quinton. Frankly, I would think you'd be glad to find someone else for the police to point a finger at."

Her eyes flashed anger. "Benni, my nephew didn't kill Toby Hunter, and I'm going to prove that, but not by directing the blame toward an innocent man."

Who I wasn't sure was so innocent. But with how she was reacting, I wasn't about to say that. Obviously there were some complicated emotions running through her concerning Grady, and they were beyond my ability to decipher. "Okay, then let's look at who else wanted Toby dead."

"Half the town," she said sharply.

"Granted, but we need to narrow it down." I didn't want

to mention how much influence Grady had with the police, that possibly he could be directing the suspicion away from himself. Right now, I knew she wouldn't believe that. "There's also John Luther and Ricky Don, both of whom had means and motive."

"I can't imagine John Luther beating anyone to death, can you? He's just not that violent. My gosh, when we were kids, he was afraid to hold the frogs we caught down at the creek. Remember?"

I bit the inside of my cheek, wishing I didn't know what I did about John Luther. "No one completely knows another person. And we're not kids anymore."

"That's the truth," she said, sighing deeply. "Oh, Benni, I want Toby Hunter's killer caught, I truly do. I just wish it was someone I didn't know, and the chances of that are pretty slim." She picked up her bucket of water. "Are you going to tell the police about Grady and me?"

"Don't be ridiculous. It has no bearing at all on their case."

"That we know of," she said softly.

We didn't voice what I knew we both were thinking. What if Toby had found that picture and not told his father about it, but blurted it out to Quinton? Could Quinton have struck out in anger and killed Toby? Or . . . this suddenly occurred to me. What if he'd shown it to Duck? A sick feeling churned in my stomach.

"Oh, dear Lord in Heaven, what am I going to do?" she asked, looking up, her face crumpled in sorrow.

I watched her in silence, wishing I could take some of that pain on my own shoulders.

"Let me talk one more time to that young police officer, Billy Brackman," I suggested. "He seemed real irritated about how this investigation was being run, and I bet if I catch him at the right moment I can pry out of him what's being said. Then we'll see what we are up against."

She nodded. "Let's take this water back and get something to eat before the food's all gone."

We joined the crowd gathered around the tin-foiled-covered dishes and platters set out for the noon meal. After a quick blessing by one of the elders of Zion Baptist, we filled our plates with cold fried chicken, potato salad, baked beans, and slices of fresh watermelon. I glanced over the five different kinds of pie, planning for later.

"I'm going to join my aunties over yonder," Amen said, nodding at a group of ladies unfolding webbed lawn chairs under a large maple tree. From this distance, their high laughter and darting words reminded me of the birds who had serenaded our work earlier. "Get back to me when you find out something." She paused for a minute, then leaned over and kissed my cheek.

"You're okay, girlfriend."

I watched her go over to the women who welcomed her with a flurry of laughter and teasing. I took my plate of food and joined my family under an oak where Isaac had spread out a couple of blankets and set up our own webbed chairs. Elvia was sitting in a chair drinking a glass of iced tea and nibbling on a chicken leg.

"Where's the girls?" I asked Isaac who was sitting next to Elvia eating a piece of pecan pie. "And does Dove know you're eating your dessert first?"

He grinned at me. "At our age, you *always* eat your dessert first. And the lovely Mosely girls are still arranging flowers on their mama and grandmama's graves."

I flopped down on the blanket at his feet. "Getting some good pictures?"

"Wonderful," he said. "Took ten rolls already."

Eventually Dove and Aunt Garnet joined us, and after lunch we resumed our work, stopping occasionally for a glass of iced tea and a cookie or two. As we worked, I tried to figure out a way to talk to the young detective again, to question him in a way that wouldn't look planned.

Once during the afternoon, when we were arranging bouquets for each grave, Elvia asked, "Why are you being so quiet?"

I shrugged. "Just thinking."

We finished around four o'clock, and I hadn't come up with one single idea. The sun dipped toward the sharp points of the pine-tree horizon, and the animal rustlings and bird songs seemed to slow down and get muffled, growing longer like the shadows of the trees.

"What do you girls think?" Aunt Garnet asked as we stood in front of the Mosely plot and contemplated the decorated graves of my ancestors. There were double bouquets at every grave—each as different as its maker. Dove's mason jar vases held a combination of wild flowers, roses, and willow branches surrounded by pine cones and hickory sticks dotted with nuts that looked like tiny defiant fists. Aunt Garnet's were lovely, symmetrical arrangements of roses, white and lavender lilies, baby's breath, and deep green fern cuttings.

"I think that we should have Isaac take a picture of all these gorgeous flowers," I said, not about to take sides.

"I agree," Isaac said.

"Isaac added the stones," Dove said, pointing to the single stone that was placed on each tombstone. "He's half-Jewish."

"On my mother's side," he added. "We bring stones, not flowers."

"Why?" I asked.

"From what I've been told, in ancient times when a person died, stones would be piled over the body for two reasons—so people would know there was a dead body there and to keep animals from getting at the body. So, now, when a person puts stones on a grave, it symbolizes protecting the body and shows respect. Flowers die, but the stones don't change."

"A wonderful tradition," Amen said, walking up to catch

the last part of our conversation. "And much less work." She said to me in a low side comment, "Not to mention less competitive."

"Don't bet on it," I muttered back. "If we were Jewish, the sisters would be scouting for the biggest boulders, and we'd probably have to carry them."

She chuckled. "You're probably right."

Later that night at Aunt Garnet's house, after supper Dove and Garnet headed off to choir practice while the rest of us sat on the porch and greeted people as they walked by on their evening strolls, a small-town tradition that seemed to die a little more each year with cable television, e-mail, and computer chat rooms. I was still worrying about the problem of how to casually quiz Billy Brackman about Toby's murder when the phone rang.

"Stay still, I'll get it, Uncle WW," I said, jumping up from the porch swing I was sharing with Gabe, who was telling some long, involved fish tale that had us all laughing with its improbabilities.

It was Amen.

"I'm glad you answered," she said, sounding slightly out of breath. "You wanted a chance to talk to that young detective, right?"

"Yeah, why?"

"I just drove by the Dairy Queen, and he's there alone eating a sundae."

"How long ago?"

"I'm talkin' seconds. I'm on my cell phone. And he appeared to just be sittin' down."

"I'll get over there right now."

It was easier than I hoped getting away from the group on the porch. After everyone's long day grave-cleaning or fishing, everyone thought some Dairy Queen ice cream sounded good, but no one wanted to walk downtown to get it.

"I'm feeling energetic," I said. "I'll get it."

Gabe started to get up, groaning dramatically. "Sweetheart, I'll come and help you."

I pushed him back down. "Now, you just rest, old man. Besides, you have to finish your fish story. I'll drive so you don't have to worry."

He gave me a grateful look, which made me feel only a little guilty. "You sure?"

"I'm sure."

Down at the Dairy Queen, Detective Billy Brackman sat at one of the tables, finishing the last scoop of ice cream of what appeared to be a banana split. He'd left the bananas for last.

A large group of giggling, rowdy teenagers crowded both lines, on their way, it appeared, to a football game. A lucky break for me. "Can I join you until that group disperses?" I asked.

He nodded. "Sure."

I sat down across from him. "That's the healthy part," I said, pointing at the bananas.

He gave a weak smile. "I'll get to them."

There was a moment of silence.

Oh, well, I thought. Might as well plunge in since there was no casual way of bringing up the case. "So, how are things going with the Hunter murder?"

He shrugged, his face twitching slightly in annoyance.

"Is Quinton still their chief suspect?"

He gave me a long look, his clear, Kentucky-hill country eyes guarded. "You know I can't talk about this with you."

I gave a deep sigh. "I know, Detective Brackman." He visibly puffed up slightly when I used the title. "I'm just so concerned about Quinton getting railroaded, and you're the only person on that backwoods police force I think has a lick of sense." I knew I was taking a chance on completely alienating him, making a derogatory remark about Sugartree's police department, but I was hoping his youthful irritation at his colleagues would momentarily overcome his good sense.

"Look, I agree with you, okay?" he said, attacking the slices of ice-cream-soaked banana with his plastic spoon. "There are others in this town who had just as much reason to want Toby Hunter dead."

I decided to show my hand. "Like John Luther Billings and Ricky Don Stevens."

The flash of surprise on his face told me I was barking up the right tree. Then he frowned and shoved a spoonful of bananas in his mouth. "They were suspects, yes. That's no secret to them or anyone else. Most everyone in this town knows what Toby did to Tara."

"What about Frank Lovelis?"

His eyebrows moved toward each other in confusion. "What about him?"

I had to admit it just occurred to me. What did anyone really know about Frank Lovelis, where he came from, what his background was? In desperation to fatten the suspect pool, to draw suspicion away from Quinton, I said, "He was the one who found Tara. Maybe, after dwelling on it for a while, he was so upset by what Toby did, he killed him. Did anyone ever think of that?"

By the widening of his eyes, I could tell no one had. I felt bad directing suspicion toward Mr. Lovelis. On the other hand, the more suspects, the better. For Quinton, anyway.

Billy pushed the empty plastic sundae dish to the side. "He's pretty old. And that's pretty farfetched."

"I know," I said, resting my chin on the palm of my hand. "I admit it's stretching, but I'm just trying to make a point." A point, I thought, that will make you go back to your superiors and question their single-minded pursuit of Quinton. "It could be any number of people. I mean, it could even be his own father, for crying out loud." I threw that out, waiting for his reaction.

"Lordy, Mrs. Harper," he exclaimed. "That's about as big a crock of"—he paused, blushing slightly—"cow dung as I've ever heard. It's one thing to suspect John Luther and Ricky, but Mr. Hunter? Why in the . . ." The red in his face deepened. "Why in *heavens* would he kill his own boy?"

I reached over and patted the top of his hand. "As my dear husband always says, the why isn't our problem, but that of psychiatrists and God. The who is the only thing we're interested in, and my point is it could just as well be Grady Hunter as Quinton Tolliver. The spot where they found Toby's body isn't that far from Grady's house. I think it would take a lot of courage for someone to present that possibility, to give Quinton a fighting chance by pointing out that any number of people, including Toby's own father, had just as much means and opportunity as Quinton." Motive, too, I thought, though I wasn't ready to tell the detective why it was possible that Grady Hunter might possibly have had a reason to silence his own son.

He stood up abruptly, picking up his empty sundae bowl and tossing it in a trashcan. He paused in front of the metal trashcan for a long moment, his back to me, and I thought I'd pushed him too far. When he turned around, I expected an angry man. Instead, I saw a young, pale face full of apology.

"I don't know if I can be that person, Mrs. Harper," he said in a rough, boyish voice. "I have to live here. I need this job." He stuck his hands deep in the pockets of his jeans and walked down the street toward downtown.

"I understand," I said, though he was too far away to hear my words. In that moment, I felt with great shame like the know-it-all interloper I was. Who was I to challenge him to do something that would at best alienate him from his colleagues and at worst possibly cost him his job? I felt like I'd both failed Amen and made a fine, struggling young police officer feel bad about a situation that was beyond his ability to change. I bought two quarts of ice cream and drove back to Aunt Garnet's house, berating myself the whole way.

Later that night, when we were in bed, I told Gabe everything that happened today, everything I'd discovered. He listened without interrupting, my head on his chest, his warm arms surrounding me. When I finished, he was quiet for a minute or two.

"Okay," he finally said, his even baritone not betraying an ounce of his own feelings. "You're neck deep in this quicksand of human emotion. What are you going to do?"

I turned my head to look at him, my cheek still resting on his chest. "I was hoping you could advise me, Chief."

He scratched the center of my back gently. "You know what I'd advise you, and I know you'll ignore that, so what are you really asking?"

I sat up and looked down at his shadowy face. "I guess I'm not asking anything. I just wanted you to know."

"So, now I know." His voice still hadn't changed tone.

"Let me just ask you one thing. If it were you, if this were your investigation, what would you do?"

He sighed deeply and closed his eyes. "I'm not going to tell you that."

"I already know. You'd re-question everyone involved and look for holes in their stories."

He opened his eyes. In the gray darkness they looked black and menacing. His voice was soft. "Take me with you if you plan on doing anything dangerous. Just promise me that."

"I promise."

"ALL I'M GOING to do is talk to Quinton," I told Gabe the next day as I sat in front of the vanity braiding my hair. "So you don't have to worry about me today."

He kissed the top of my head and said, "Let me do that."

He undid my loose braid and started French-braiding my hair. The feel of his hands working my hair into the intricate braid felt familiar and comforting. "I always worry about you, but at least I know when you're talking to Quinton nothing will happen to you. Talk to me before you speak to anyone else."

"Where are you going to be today?" I asked his reflection.

"What's on the family agenda?"

"There's the carnival for the kids at the church with game booths and stuff. I imagine I'll be roped into helping in one of the booths. At noon, they're doing the Ping-Pong ball drop. Tonight is a progressive dinner sponsored by the deacons of both churches."

His hands still moving with a steady rhythm that always relaxed me, he said, "Okay, a carnival I know. But what is a Ping-Pong ball drop and a progressive dinner?"

"I asked Grady Hunter about the Ping-Pong ball drop yesterday. I guess it's something the town merchants and churches thought up. Grady is paying for the plane—a Cessna, I think he said. Anyway, at high noon the plane flies over the town square and drops ten thousand Ping-Pong balls, and people catch them."

Gabe laughed and reached for the rubber band I held up. "For what reason?"

"The Ping-Pong balls have discounts on them for local businesses and some free prizes, too, like free bed-and-breakfast weekends and fifty-dollar savings bonds. Oh, and some are printed with Bible verses and invitations to come to church services. The big prize is a bass boat."

"Sounds . . . interesting," he said, lifting my finished braid and kissing the back of my neck. "And a police officer's nightmare. You certainly have peculiar ways of having fun here in Arkansas."

"I think they're closing the square to car traffic that hour."

"A wise move. And the progressive dinner?"

"You eat each course at a different house. For example, appetizers here, salad at Emory's, main dish at whoever's. I don't actually have our map yet, so I don't know whose houses we're going to. I assume Dove or Aunt Garnet will give it to us. You never had progressive dinners in Kansas?"

"No, we prefer to do all our grazing in one pasture."

I turned and poked him in the stomach. "It's fun, Friday, and the whole point is socializing."

"That's why Kansans don't have them, I guess. Eating is serious business, and we don't want talking to interfere with it."

I picked up a hand mirror and inspected his braid work. "Perfect as always. I knew there was a reason why I married you."

In the kitchen, Isaac was loading film into a couple of cameras. Elvia was sitting across from him sipping a cup of tea. I poured a cup of coffee and looked around for something to eat. "Hey, y'all, did I miss breakfast?"

"Doughnuts again," he said, pointing over at two white bags. "The sisters were up early marking Ping-Pong balls with Miss DeLora."

"For who?"

Elvia said, "Your aunt said both churches decided this would be a good way to advertise their services. They're offering free homemade pies to each first-time visitor if they show their Ping-Pong ball to the usher."

"Bribing people with pies to come to church," I said. "That's . . . innovative."

"Soul food, so to speak," Isaac said with a smile.

I laughed and dug through the bag looking for a maple bar. "You do plan on getting pictures of this Ping-Pong ball thing, don't you?"

"Is Jimmy Carter a Democrat?" he asked.

"So, do we have our orders?" I asked them.

Elvia handed me a sheet of paper. "We're working the carnival, and here's the schedule for the progressive dinner."

I glanced down at Aunt Garnet's flowery script. "I work the fishing booth. Good, I always loved that game as a kid."

"I'm working the candy apple booth with Dove," Elvia said.

"Save me one, then. Hmmm. . . ." I said, looking over the progressive dinner map. "Appetizers at Emory's. Salad at Brother Johnson's. I don't know him. He must be with Zion Baptist." I didn't look up at Elvia, though I could imagine her expression, one of nonchalant indifference that I knew in my heart was a sham. "Soup and bread at the Watkins's house. Main dish at Miss DeLora's, and coffee and dessert at Grady Hunter's. It should be fun. I haven't done one of these in years."

Elvia said, "Dove says they're expecting about fifty at each house. Can Miss DeLora's cabin handle that many?"

"It's usually not too crowded except at the last house 'cause people arrive and leave at different times. Miss DeLora has that big backyard, too, and the evenings haven't been very cold. She'll probably have tables set up outside."

Gabe joined us a few minutes later. "What's for breakfast?"

I held up my maple bar. "The sisters are marking Ping-Pong balls, so this is it."

He poured a cup of coffee and said, "I'll go downtown and buy breakfast. Meet me in the square at noon?" The unspoken part of that request was so I could tell him what I'd found out.

"Wouldn't miss it for the world," I said. "If I'm not there, look for me in the fishing booth."

I went into the living room and called Amen.

"How's it going?" I asked.

"Okay, what's up?"

"How's Quinton doing?"

"Fine. As of last night, he's bunking with Emory. He was staying here, but we all agreed that he'd probably be safer at Boone and Emory's. Even Toby Hunter's trashy friends would think twice about messin' with Boone Littleton's house. We're also keepin' him away from the campaign office. Quinton's not too pleased about it, because the last month before an election is the most crucial time, and there's a lot of work to be done. He's certain this whole thing was instigated to keep me out of office."

"You mean Toby's murder? That seems a bit farfetched."

"Not the murder. Just the suspicions on him." Her sigh over the phone revealed her fatigue. "To be honest, I'm about ready to toss in the towel. Even if I do win, it'll be an uphill battle my whole two year term. I'm not sure I have any fight left in me."

I didn't jump in like I normally would have and insist that she did have the fight and that she would triumph. Who can know another person's thoughts and feelings, say when they should give up or when they should keep going?

"You're a strong, good person, Amen," I simply said. "I believe you'll do what is right and best for you and for what you believe in."

"Thanks," she said. "What did you find out from the detective? I'm assuming it wasn't much, or you would have called me last night."

"You're right, he didn't have much to say. I tried to convince him to talk to his bosses about spreading around the suspicions, but I don't think he went for it. I was kind of disappointed."

"Why? Did you really think he'd put his butt on the line for us? Why would he do that?"

"Oh, I don't know," I said, trying not to sound as sarcastic as I felt. "Perhaps justice. Truth. Integrity. Doing the right thing."

"Dream away, girlfriend."

"Look, I want to talk to Quinton. Would that be okay with you?"

Her voice went sharp. "Why do you want to talk to him?"

"I just want to hear from his mouth what happened that night."

"And find out if he knows about me and . . ." She left the sentence open, and I knew that Lawrence must be in the house.

"Have *you* asked him?"

A long silence. "No."

"Don't you think we should know if he knows? I mean, you don't want this . . . God forbid, if he should actually get charged and go to court . . . you don't want it to come out then and blindside his attorney."

Another long silence, then a whispered, "No . . . yes . . . no . . ." I heard a sob catch in her throat. "Oh, shoot, I don't *know*."

I didn't answer, waiting. If she really didn't want me to talk to Quinton, I wouldn't.

"Okay," she finally said, her voice still subdued but stronger. "Talk to him. Find out if he knows, if you can, but, promise me, do it without actually asking him. I don't want him . . . or anyone to know if we can keep it that way."

"Okay, I'll talk to him this morning and tell you what I find out at the carnival. Are you going to the progressive dinner tonight?"

"I'll probably just go to Grandma's part and Grady's. I promised Grandma I'd help her, so it looks like main dish and dessert is all I'll get."

"Hey, that would satisfy me. What's Miss DeLora making?"

"She wanted to do her famous barbecue ribs, but we talked her out of it. Too messy. So we decided on chicken and broccoli casserole and that old church potluck standby, lasagna." She was silent for a moment.

"Amen, are you going to be all right?"

She hesitated, then said, "Sure, fine. I'll see you later."

"Yeah, later."

I hung up and was staring at the phone deep in thought when Elvia came into the living room.

"Something wrong with the phone?" she asked.

I shook my head. "No, just thinking."

"About what?"

"Just all the . . . confusion going on the last few days. That was Amen. With everything that's happened, it sounds like she's ready to quit the race."

Elvia's face was sympathetic. "I don't blame her. Sometimes the price a person has to pay is too high."

I didn't ask her to elaborate. I didn't have to. Her sad brown eyes said it all.

"I'm going to talk to Quinton," I said.

"Why?"

I shrugged. "I don't know. See if the police forgot something."

"Or maybe find out if he didn't tell them everything."

I smiled and sat down on the arm of the sofa. She knew me too well. "Maybe that, too." I gave her a hopeful look. "He's over at Emory's. Want to come?"

She shook her head no, her mouth a thin line. "Nice try, *gringa loca*, but to quote your uncle WW, don't be poking in that fireplace and start messing around with my fire."

I gave a loud laugh. "Elvia Marisol Aragon, you *have* been here in Arkansas too long."

"*That's* what I've been trying to tell you," she said, laughing, too, in spite of herself. "See you at the carnival."

As I walked over to Emory's, my hopes for him and Elvia had already started climbing again. If she could joke about any of this, there was still a chance, right?

I met Uncle Boone as he was coming out of the front

door, and he sent me to the back patio where Emory and Quinton were having breakfast with Miss DeLora. Emory looked a lot better than the last time I saw him. He wore khaki cotton slacks and a dark brown cashmere sweater. His face was pale and drawn, which on him looked tragically handsome and appealing. I wished I'd managed to get Elvia over here somehow. One look at his vulnerable face, and I knew she'd take him back in a heartbeat.

"Hey, Benni," Quinton said, standing up when I walked up to the glass-topped patio table. "Want some coffee? And I think there's a croissant or two left." He looked very much his age this morning in his baggy jeans and Arkansas Razorback T-shirt. Twenty-two years old. Though it was only fourteen years since I was his age, it seemed an eternity.

"Such manners your great-grandson has," I teased Miss DeLora. "He's a sterling example to his more barbaric, older friend here." I jerked my head in my cousin's direction.

"Hey, I bought the croissants," Emory said. "And made the coffee."

Miss DeLora laughed and winked at me. "He called and had the croissants delivered, and he opened a new bag of coffee beans."

"He makes horrible coffee," Quinton said.

"I know," I said, "but we love him anyway." I leaned down and kissed Emory's cheek before sitting down on the padded patio chair. His skin was freshly shaven, smooth and cool under my lips. "You're looking much improved today, cousin."

He shrugged, his face neutral.

After a little small talk about the carnival and the progressive dinner tonight, I said, "I only dropped by for a few minutes because I'm due at the fishing booth by ten. Quinton, could I talk to you a minute?"

Miss DeLora stood up and started stacking plates. "I'll just take these inside and wash them up real quick."

"You will not," Emory said, jumping up to help her. "You aren't the housekeeper anymore, Miss DeLora. You're a guest. I'll help you carry them in, and we'll leave them for Rhonda."

"I don't think that girl's gettin' them clean enough," she nagged gently as he followed her through the open French doors. "Why, when I was here, you could see yourself in the plates. Maybe I need to speak with her, see what type soap she's usin'." Emory's voice murmured good-natured sympathy.

Quinton and I glanced at each other and laughed.

"Grandma's got a slight problem with letting go," he said.

"I don't envy Emory and Boone's new housekeeper."

Quinton leaned back and rested his big hands, fingers long enough to grip a basketball one-handed, on his stomach. "Emory says Rhonda handles Grandma just fine. Lets her give all her advice without interrupting, then goes right on doin' what she intended on doin' to begin with."

"Hmmm . . . kinda reminds me of Miss DeLora."

"That's for sure." He picked up a china cup of coffee and took a sip, making a face. "Cold. So, what do you want to talk to me about?"

I leaned forward, resting my elbows on the table. The hard glass felt damp on my thin cotton shirt. "I know you've been over this a million times with the police, but I want to hear myself what happened the night you followed Toby."

His young face froze with a stubborn look that told me this was not going to be easy.

"Quinton," I said, laying an open hand out on the table. "I'm just trying to help."

He gave a deep sigh, sat forward, resting his elbows on his knees, and said, "I'm so tired of talking about it."

"Just once more. Please."

With halting sentences, he told me what happened that

night. Nothing was any different from the versions I'd heard from Amen and Emory. After he finished, I waited a minute before responding, picking up a maple leaf that had fallen on the table, crumbling it into fine red dust on the glass table.

"Quinton, that's all the conversation that took place between you and Toby?"

His face contracted in disgusted irritation. "I told the police and Duck and his stupid attorney and everyone else on this planet that the only thing he said to me was 'Nigger, quit following me or you'll wish you hadn't,' and I said, 'You cracker-ass piece of shit, if you or any of your friends come near my family again, I'll kill you.' " He stood up, shoving the patio chair away with the backs of his knees. "But I *didn't kill him*. I rolled up my window and drove away. He stood there and watched me the whole way. I saw him in my rearview mirror."

I took a deep breath, taking in the woody smell of the October morning. Though I'd heard the story twice already, it took on a new seriousness hearing it from Quinton's angry mouth. No wonder the police suspected him. No wonder Amen was so worried.

But hearing his story wasn't my real goal here. I had to find out if Toby said anything to Quinton about his father and Amen.

"That's all he said?" I asked. "You're sure?"

"I'm *sure*."

"He didn't . . ." How could I say it? I looked up at his face, knowing I'd have to watch every piece of body language to see if I could detect a lie. "Did he say anything else about . . . anyone in your family? Did he . . . threaten . . . did he threaten Amen in any way?"

He tilted his head slightly, not sure what I was asking. "Threaten Aunt Amen? Like how?"

I lifted my shoulders and continued to study his face. He seemed to be genuinely confused.

"What I told you is all that we said to each other. Why are you asking about Aunt Amen being threatened? Did he say he was going to do something? Have his friends threatened her?" He clenched his large fists, his body tense, ready to fight.

I stood up and went over to him, touching him gently on the upper arm. I would have sworn in court that he didn't know about Grady and Amen. Not unless he was the best actor this side of Sidney Poitier. "No, Quinton, no one's threatened her. At least, not that I know of. It was just something I was considering. That maybe he had something on Amen and told you about it."

"Are you suggesting he was blackmailing us?" His young face was shocked, then angry. "Aunt Amen is the best, most honest person I know. There's *nothing* in her background for her to be blackmailed for. I can't believe you'd think that low of her. I thought you were her friend."

"I am her friend and I don't think low of her, Quinton," I said, wishing the look of disappointment in his eyes wasn't directed at me. "It was just something that had to be considered."

"Well, I hope she never finds out you thought that about her," he said, looking at me with hard eyes. "I gotta go upstairs and take a shower. See you later."

"Yeah, later," I said, watching him walk toward the house. I hated it that he was angry and disappointed in me . . . but better me than his aunt. I sighed and went into the house looking for Emory. I found him in the sitting room of his suite, looking over some legal papers.

"What're you doing?" I asked, flopping down beside him and laying my head on his shoulder.

"Just lookin' at some papers that Daddy's been after me to go over. What's up, sweetcakes? You look plumb defeated." He set the thick sheaf of papers on the dark wood coffee table in front of him.

I told him what just took place between me and Quinton, without telling him about Grady and Amen.

"I could have told you the kid didn't know about the relationship between Grady and Amen," he said, patting my knee. "You should've come to me first."

I sat up, my mouth open. "You know!"

"Of course I do. Amen might've been able to fool everyone else, but I know her too well. Granted, I wasn't sure of the depth of their relationship, but I sure as heck knew there was one."

"They never slept together," I said. "It was just . . . a friendship. Kind of like a mentorship, I think. He taught her a lot about politics, she said."

"Oh, Benni-girl, it was more than that, but I believe her when she said they never slept together. I've watched her through this campaign, even defended her to her own people a few times when she didn't go for his jugular vein as hard as I knew she was capable. I figured there was somethin' there keeping her from hanging him out to dry, even a few times when he deserved it. I think she fell in love with him during those months they were waiting for his wife to pass away, but could never admit it." He rubbed his chin and turned to me, his light green eyes curious. "How'd you become privy to this little secret, might I ask? Did Amen tell you?"

"No, I . . ." Again I was going to have to justify my snooping to someone. Why is it that it seemed so much worse when I told about it than when I did it? I explained about the photograph I not-so-accidentally saw.

He laughed, though it wasn't a pleasant sound. "Just like most criminals, he has to have some evidence of the deed. I wonder why that is?"

"So, do you really think that Quinton didn't know?" That would clear him for good, at least in my mind.

"I'm sure he didn't and I don't think he killed Toby. But the fact that you found that picture so easily does tend to make me agree with you that Grady's son could have found it, too."

That seemed a good time to tell him of my uneasy, even suspicious feelings about Grady. "Do you think I'm absolutely nuts?"

His face grew sober. "Unlike Amen, I don't see our esteemed mayor with such a glowing halo. He's unfortunately one of those Southern men who give us all a bad name. On the outside, all good manners and 'yes, ma'am.' Everyone's equal in the eyes of the law. And, 'yes, I believe in affirmative action,' but behind closed doors they're sayin' 'I'll work with 'em, but I don't want them livin' in my neighborhood or marryin' my pretty white daughter.' Talk about your mixed messages. In my opinion, that's how a lot of seemingly good people end up with sociopathic kids. I think his son was entirely capable of threatening to blackmail his own father and I believe that Grady Hunter is entirely capable of killing his own son."

I stared at Emory, surprised quiet for the second time in ten minutes. "Why didn't you tell me this before?"

He picked up the papers from the coffee table and stuffed them in the cordovan leather briefcase sitting under the table. "I've been just a tad occupied. And to be honest, I was hoping it wouldn't become an issue. I was hoping we could get this accusation aimed at Quinton taken care of without dragging his family into the quagmire."

I punched him lightly on the arm. "We tell each other everything, Emory Delano Littleton. How could you?"

He gave me a level look, then said, his voice a little sad, "Not everything, sweetcakes. We haven't told each other everything since we were kids."

I stared into his green eyes. This man I loved like my own brother. No, more than my own brother. Like my own heart.

"You're right," I said softly. "Look, forget Amen and Quinton for a minute. What about you and Elvia?"

He gave a small smile but didn't answer me.

I gave a little shriek and hugged him. "You've thought of something, haven't you? I knew you wouldn't give up! I just knew it. What are you going to do?"

"Never you mind. This is between me and Elvia. If it works, you'll be one of the first to know."

"*One* of the first?" I said, pushing him. "I should be the first."

"Get out of here, young Harper woman," he said, leaning down to close his briefcase. "Don't you have a carnival to work?"

I glanced over at the mantel clock over the fireplace. Ten after ten. "Oh, geeze! I gotta go. I was due at the fishing booth at ten."

"I'll just bet you got a line of anglers a'waitin.' "

THE CARNIVAL, SPONSORED by Zion Baptist and Sugartree Baptist was already in full swing by the time I walked the three blocks from Emory's house. The Ping-Pong ball drop at noon was a big incentive for people to be out and about this Saturday morning, but there was also the fact that everything at the carnival—games, food, and drinks, even chances at the beautiful cakes baked by the women of the church for the cakewalk—cost only a dime. The whole point of the carnival was not to make money, but to bring the community together—hopefully, to bring the two churches together. I waved at Dove and Elvia as I passed the candy apple booth and found the fishing booth at the far end of the church parking lot. Gangs of screaming, laughing children, black and white, raced from booth to booth, faces smeared with cotton candy and mustard from the hot dogs being barbecued by the church's youth group under a towering white oak in front of the church. Some quick work by members of both churches had made certain the swastikas were already erased with a fresh coat of paint.

I wondered if they'd asked John Luther to help.

"Where have you been, Benni Harper?" Mrs. Versie Pitts asked. She was frantically trying to take dimes and attach small prizes to the three strings dangling over the flowered sheet separating us from our customers.

Great, I thought, when I realized we'd be working together. Hopefully we'd stay busy enough that my uterus didn't become the central topic of conversation again.

"Sorry," I said, tossing my purse in the corner. "Here, let's just put a cup out front for the dimes, and we'll both tie on prizes."

I grabbed a large paper cup from our lemonade stand neighbors and scribbled with a felt pen across the front— DIMES HERE. I sat it in front of the Fishing Booth sign and freed up both our hands to attach the small plastic kazoos, horses, farm animals, sparkly rings, candy necklaces, yo-yo's, parachute men, whistles, compasses, miniature bottles of bubble water, and hair clips to the clothespin hooks. Someone who was obviously experienced at these carnivals had painted the skinny wood fishing poles pink, blue, or yellow so all we had to do was look up and see if we attached a girl, boy, or nongender prize.

After an hour and a half of attaching prizes and giving the jerky strings a tug so they knew they'd "caught" something, there was a lull in customers.

"Wow," I said, sitting down on a metal folding chair. "This must be one of the most popular games at the carnival."

Mrs. Pitts laughed and sat down next to me. "The little ones always have liked this game. And some of the older children play it, too, just for the memories, I think."

I laughed with her. "It was always *my* favorite game."

A head popped around the sheet. Mr. Lovelis asked, "Thirsty?" He held a tray of drinks.

"Sure," I said and handed a paper cup of lemonade to Mrs. Pitts, then took one for myself. "Thanks, Mr. Lovelis."

She gave him a warm smile. "Thank you, Frank. How lovely."

Without changing his perpetually sober expression, he nodded and moved down the line to the basketball toss game next to us.

Sipping my lemonade, I commented, "I don't think I've ever seen Mr. Lovelis smile."

Mrs. Pitts took a dainty sip, then slightly puckered her pink lips. "Frank Lovelis has had a sad life. Not a lot to smile about."

I didn't answer but widened my eyes in interest. Though I liked Mr. Lovelis, he *was* the one who found Tara that night and did have a mysterious past. At least mysterious to me. Right now I was sitting with the one woman who could clue me in. But getting information was a delicate thing when you were dealing with good Christian women like Mrs. Pitts who took seriously the Bible's admonitions against idle talk and unnecessary gossip.

When she didn't elaborate, I prompted, "That's too bad. Aunt Garnet told me about his story." That wasn't exactly a lie. She told me he had a story . . . just not what it was. "You've been very kind to him."

"He's been a real blessing to our church," she said. "And I hope we have been to him. Losing your family isn't easy."

I nodded, acting as if I knew exactly what she was talking about. "His wife and . . ." I paused and shook my head, as if trying to recall the details. I took a big chance and said, "The accident . . ."

"Daughter," she supplied. "Though I wouldn't call it an accident."

"No, no," I said hastily. "I mean . . . I just said that because I didn't know what else to call it. It was such a . . . tragedy."

"No, it was not an accident. That terrible man knew what he was doing when he broke into their house. Poor Frank. He's never forgiven himself."

"It really wasn't his fault," I faked. "Not actually . . ."

She sighed and sipped at her lemonade. "No, not really. If he hadn't stopped by that bar on the way home he would have been there, but it wasn't actually his fault."

"The man went to prison, right? Down in . . ." I was starting to feel guilty for my prying, but I had to find out the rest of the story now. Bless her heart, Versie Pitts was the only person in this town I could be this obvious with and get away with it.

"Georgia," she supplied. "He's still on death row from what I hear. Lord forgive me, but I hope he meets his judgment soon. What he did to Frank's wife and daughter before he killed them . . ." She stared down into her lemonade, her face sad and a bit puzzled.

"It's so sad," I agreed, not needing her to elaborate and hoping, like her, that this mysterious criminal would be standing before the Almighty God sooner than later.

"How old was his daughter?" I asked flat out.

"About fifteen or sixteen, I think," she said.

Though I hated it, I had to face the facts my prying had uncovered. It was entirely possible that Mr. Lovelis, after seeing Tara at the side of the road, could have, in a fit of rage—post-traumatic stress or something—confronted Toby and killed him. It was farfetched enough to almost seem credible. To me, anyway. The question was what should I do, if anything, with this information? As I contemplated my dilemma, the subject of my mental debate poked his head around the curtain again, startling me.

"Oh!" I said, jumping at the sight of his unsmiling face.

"Hot dog?" he asked, holding this time a tray of paper-wrapped buns.

Had he overheard my conversation with Mrs. Pitts? How long had he been gone? I looked over at her, wondering if she was worried. Her wrinkled face was benign and unconcerned. Then again, *she* didn't have anything to feel guilty about. Aunt Garnet's snippy voice admonishing me about the evils of gossip zipped along the electrical circuits of my conscience.

"Thanks," I said, taking one, sneaking a quick peek at his face. Still expressionless. No answer there.

Mrs. Pitts shook her head no. "Maybe later, Frank. Thank you."

Without another word, he was gone. I slowly unwrapped my hot dog and took a bite. I truly wanted to help Quinton and Amen, but was pointing a suspicious finger at an innocent man really the way to do it?

If he is innocent, a more cynical voice argued. Just because you feel sorry for someone, doesn't change the fact that he might possibly be a murderer. And if he was, he deserved to face the consequences of his crime.

But Mr. Lovelis was a good man, and Toby was a bad one. How was that fair?

True justice versus emotionally satisfying justice. Gabe and I had talked about those concepts often. Emotionally satisfying justice makes us happy someone like Toby was punished for his actions. Clean, simple, *done*. And what's most appealing is it didn't have to be done by *us*. True justice demands that even people like Toby get a fair hearing, a chance to give their side, their story. True justice would also demand that if Mr. Lovelis had killed Toby, that he be punished for his actions, too. Because Mr. Lovelis's actions, if he was the killer, not only affected Toby, but so many other people, including Quinton, who might end up taking the blame for a crime he didn't commit. Would Mr. Lovelis . . . or whoever killed Toby allow that?

I glanced at my watch. "It's a quarter to twelve. The Ping-Pong drop will be happening soon."

"That's probably why we got so slow," she said.

"I want to see it. Could we close up shop for a little while?"

"I can manage for a few minutes, dear. Go on and see if you can win something nice."

"I'll do my best."

The sight was something I'll never forget. Hundreds of people milling around the center of town clutching everything you could imagine to catch the Ping-Pong balls—leather baseball mitts, upside-down open umbrellas, cardboard boxes, plastic buckets, trashcans, laundry baskets. What was even funnier was the sight of that many people all staring up at the sky simultaneously every time someone thought they heard a plane. I scanned the crowds for Gabe or Elvia or Isaac—anyone I knew, but I couldn't find one of them. But like everyone else, when I thought I heard the plane, I looked up and scanned the skies. So *expectant* were we, so *ready*, I couldn't help but wonder if one of the ministers would take advantage of this ready-made metaphor and preach on the Second Coming at the Homecoming's Sunday service.

Finally the plane arrived, its chattering engine sounding like a large mechanical insect above us. A collective groan rose up from the crowd when it flew over and nothing fell from the sky.

"What's wrong?" I asked a large-bellied man wearing green army fatigue pants and a "Fish Tremble at the Sound of my Name" T-shirt. He held a huge black umbrella, open and ready. "Why didn't he drop any balls?"

"Testing the wind drift," he said. "Last year he was off about a quarter mile 'cause of the wind and about ten houses up yonder got their yards plumb trampled." He pointed to the other side of the courthouse, behind the 3B Cafe. "Guess Mayor Hunter told him to be more careful this year. Cost the mayor some pretty money to fix up them people's lawns. Gotta say this for him, though, Grady Hunter did it and didn't make anyone else chip in."

While we waited for the plane to return, I glanced around at the buildings surrounding the square. Two or three men were on the roofs of each, milling about, waiting.

"Why're they up there?" I asked the man who seemed to be an expert on this ritual.

"They's owners of the stores and such. Lots of the balls end up on the roofs so they toss 'em down to the people," he said.

We waited a few moments, and the sound of the plane started coming back toward us, a soft buzz in the air that was accompanied by a louder buzz from the excited people. Finally the plane was almost directly above us, and I heard someone yell, "They're a'comin'!"

Like everyone else, I gazed up at the sky, but I couldn't see anything except the clear blue air. Then, vaguely, against the sky, small white balls started to descend, hitting the streets with the *tick-tick-tick* of feet softly tap dancing, and then soon they were hitting the ground like a huge, artificial snowfall. Both kids and adults ran and screamed and lunged for the high-bouncing Ping-Pong balls. I stood where I was, unable to move because I was laughing so uncontrollably. I stooped down once to pick up the few that dropped in my vicinity.

As the balls continued to drop, I dodged people who chased the wildly bouncing balls like they contained gold nuggets and decided, free prizes or not, this was way too dangerous for me. I took my two balls and started back for the carnival fishing booth. I couldn't help wondering what kind of pictures Isaac took of this. It happened so fast that I couldn't imagine he got very many. As I walked, I read the two balls I'd picked up.

One was printed with "25% discount on shotgun ammunition—Big Buck's Guns & Ammo." The other said, "Free Christmas ornament from Dandy's Five & Dime."

I chuckled and stuck the balls in my purse. As a souvenir, they were much more amusing than the actual gift or discount they offered. Behind the curtain at the fishing booth, Mrs. Pitts had been replaced by Elvia who was busy attaching a plastic dinosaur to a blue fishing pole.

"Hey, thought you were pushing the candy apples," I said.

She gave the blue fishing pole a tug. "Mrs. Pitts needed to use the ladies' room. She put up a closed sign, but a few kids showed up, and I could hear them complaining, so Dove sent me over here." She nodded at a child's yellow plastic sand bucket sitting in the corner of the booth. "You look like you did all right with the Ping-Pong ball drop."

The bucket was full of marked Ping-Pong balls.

"Those aren't mine," I said, holding up my two white balls. "I captured these two babies then hightailed it out of the square. It was crazy out there."

Another fishing line appeared over the sheet. She glanced up at the pink stick, then picked up a pink sparkly necklace. "It has your name on it, so I assumed they were yours."

I went over to the bucket and picked it up. My name was written in felt pen in small, scrawling letters. The bucket looked like it held about twenty or thirty Ping-Pong balls.

"Maybe Gabe got them for me," I said. "You didn't see who put them here?"

"No, they were here when I got here. I just thought you were quick on your feet."

I gazed down at the bucket of balls. "Not *that* quick, *amiga*."

In the next half-hour, business picked back up, and Elvia stayed working with me, after assuring a returning Mrs. Pitts that she was indeed having fun.

"Oh, thank you, dear," she said, patting Elvia's shoulder. "I was thinking I'd like to take a lunch break."

We worked until two o'clock when two teenage girls sent by Mrs. Pitts took over for us.

"Cool prizes," one of them said, putting on a large, fake diamond ring. "I want this."

"Save a few for the paying customers," I said, laughing.

"We will," the girls said, giggling and digging through the baskets of toys.

I took my bucket of balls and walked with Elvia around the carnival. If togetherness and racial harmony were the goals, today Zion Baptist and Sugartree Baptist had achieved it. Hopefully the laughter and camaraderie of the carnival would spill over to the rest of church life.

After watching the cakewalk through a few songs, Elvia and I decided, since our official shifts were over, to go back to Aunt Garnet's house and take our time getting ready for the progressive dinner tonight.

"I'm glad you're going," I said, putting my arm through hers as we walked down the tree-canopied streets. "There'll be lots of people there. You won't have to say one word to Emory." Though I was hoping that whatever plan Emory had cooking in his devious mind would happen tonight.

"Benni, I'm going to talk to Emory and part on amicable terms. Just because we can't have a romantic relationship doesn't mean we can't be civil."

I sneaked a glance over at her face. She wore that stoic, no-one-can-touch-me look that I knew so well. Except I knew it for what it was, a mask hiding real fear.

"Sounds entirely sensible to me," I agreed, thinking, baby doll, you have no idea who you're dealing with. He's not going to let you go that easily.

At home she took charge of the shower first so I sat down at the kitchen table and started reading my Ping-Pong balls. There were two giving free donuts at Leon's Donut Shop, a free manicure at Beulah's, a free pie if I attended a Zion or Sugartree Baptist service, a roll of film from the drugstore, a six month's subscription to *Sugartree Today* magazine . . . I set that one aside to offer, in jest, to Elvia . . . a free fried pie from Boone's restaurant, three ten-percent discounts on my total purchases from the new Wal-Mart outside of town, one good for a free air freshener (my choice of ten scents!) with my next car wash at Bubba's

Car Washateria in nearby Frog Holler. I was having a great time and said a silent thank-you to whomever generously left me that bucket of balls.

Until I came to the second to the last one.

15

"I'VE BEEN KEEPING an eye on you all day," Gabe said, his voice exasperated. "And this happens." He stared down at the Ping-Pong ball I held out to him. With black felt marker someone had drawn a small swastika.

"Where were you? I never even saw you!"

"That's because I'm good at tracking people. I told you something like this was going to happen. When are you going to start listening to me?"

"It could have been anyone," I said, ignoring his lecture. "That booth was right out there in the open and was obviously unoccupied long enough for this to be planted. But if I was a betting woman, I'd put my money on John Luther."

He pulled me under his arm and rubbed his chin across the top of my head. "I hate this. I have no jurisdiction or power here. How can I protect you?"

I gave a hollow laugh. "At least we know I rattled *someone's* cage."

His face wasn't amused. "Did something happen today that I don't know about? Did you talk to anyone?"

"Only Mrs. Pitts, and I can't imagine she'd do this." I paused for a moment.

His eyes narrowed at the corners. "I know that look. *Something* happened. What?"

I told him of my conversation with Mrs. Pitts about Mr. Lovelis's past and the possibility he might have overheard. "But, honestly, Gabe, I can't see him doing something like this."

"Unless he felt threatened." He took the ball from my hands, studying it intensely as if the answer would slowly tap its way out like a chicken from an egg.

"If I suspected anyone, it would be John Luther. He's the one who painted the swastikas on the church."

"Allegedly," Gabe corrected.

"I *know* he did it. He's probably just being a jerk."

"You will stop asking questions now." It was a statement, not a question.

I sighed. "Yes, I probably will. What's the point? We go back in two days, and it's not doing any good anyway. You're right. There's too much history here, too many secrets. It would take someone a year to figure out who did what to who. I'll just have to trust in Duck's attorney. With his money, I'm sure he found Quinton a good one."

"No doubt," Gabe agreed.

As we got ready for the progressive dinner, we heard the rest of the household arrive and start their own preparations for the event. I slipped on a simple fitted skirt and a thin cashmere sweater in the same shade of mocha.

"You look real pretty," Dove said when I went into her room on the pretext of looking for some jewelry to wear. I really just wanted the comfort of her steady presence. "You oughta wear a skirt more often."

"Rancher calling the farmer a sheepman," I said. "You've worn a dress exactly twice since we've been here. Have you got a necklace or something for me to wear? My neck feels kinda bare."

She dug around in her luggage and found a delicate gold chain with a tiger's-eye cross attached. "This'll look good."

Standing in front of the dresser mirror, I put the necklace on. "This has been fun, but I'm sure ready to go home."

She contemplated me a moment, her blue eyes turning sad. "No wonder you're exhausted. You've been runnin' around tryin' to get this relationship with Emory and Elvia all sewed up and tryin' to help Amen and Quinton. Sometimes, honeybun, things just have to run their course. Most of life is like a river—the water's goin' to flow where it will. Sometimes we just have to stand far back on the bank and let it wash by."

I sat down on the pink chenille bedspread. "I know. I shouldn't have interfered in either situation, but I just like seeing everything, you know, fit."

She sat down next to me and hugged me to her. Her comforting touch, the familiar smell of her sweet talcum powder and almond-scented hair, was so calming. The balm of Gilead, my aunt Kate, Dove's oldest daughter, always called it.

"Don't forget," she said. "The Lord God is with you, and He is mighty to save."

"I've always loved the way that sounds."

"That old prophet Zephaniah knew what he was talkin' about. Don't forget it."

"No, ma'am," I said, kissing her soft, powdery cheek.

I went back to my room to fetch my purse. It was sitting on the nightstand. Next to it was the Ping-Pong ball with the swastika drawn on it. For some reason, I picked up the ball and stuck it in my purse. Downstairs Elvia was waiting for us on the porch. She was dressed in a turquoise-and-black sheath dress. She wore simple Native American silver and turquoise earrings and black leather sandals. Everything on her was perfect, except her eyes, which were smudged and sad.

"Hold still," I said, rubbing at an errant mascara spot under her left eye. "Now you look great."

She shrugged, uncaring for once.

"Ready to go?" Gabe said, appearing in the doorway.

"Our first stop is appetizers at Emory's," I said, reading the list of addresses and directions provided by Aunt Garnet. I glanced at Elvia in question. "We could always skip that and go on to salad at Brother Johnson's. He's one of Zion Baptist's deacons."

"I'm fine," Elvia said, standing up, her face empty of expression. "Let's not miss any of the dinner on my account."

"Okay, then it's soup and bread at the Watkins's, the main dish at Miss DeLora's, ending with coffee and dessert at Grady Hunter's."

At Emory's I stole glances at both him and Elvia, hoping something would happen. They were both seemingly relaxed and unaware of each other.

"They're crazy," I finally said, taking my plate of crab puffs and deviled eggs and sitting next to Gabe on the patio. "They're acting like they don't even know each other. Apparently my talk with both of them did no good whatsoever."

"Let it go, *chica*," he advised, taking one of my deviled eggs.

At Brother Johnson's house, a large wooden farmhouse with a garden full of hollyhocks, pansies, and a very pampered bird of paradise, I found myself in line next to John Luther. After nodding quickly at each other without speaking, we both acted incredibly interested in the large variety of salads—Caesar, garden variety green, potato, coleslaw, and Gabe's favorite, ambrosia.

We started to walk away from each other, then Dove's "forgive your neighbor" training kicked in. I turned and followed him out the front door.

"This is silly, John Luther," I said. "I don't want to leave Sugartree with us mad at each other."

"I'm not mad," he said, going out on the wide porch and sitting down on one of the steps.

Tugging at my skirt, I joined him, balancing my plate on my lap. "Then let's talk about what happened between us."

"What happened between us is you were snooping where you shouldn't have been, and that could get you in a lot of trouble."

I studied the untouched salad on my plate. "I agree that my snooping was despicable. But so was what I found, wouldn't you agree?"

He shoved a whole cracker in his mouth and chewed hard and fast, spewing bits of cracker back into his plate. "You're just like that gramma of yours, coming here tryin' to tell us folks who've lived here our whole life how we should act and be. Lady, you don't know all there is to know. There's a reason God made the races a different color, and they're just as happy to be apart from us as we are from them. You bleeding hearts from California who come pushin' your ideas on people who're perfectly happy with how things are make me sick."

I stood up, not willing to listen to any more of his rhetoric. Shock and disgust were just the tip of the iceberg of feelings pushing up through me just then. "You know," I said, keeping my voice cool, "it just occurred to me that perhaps the paint on the church and the paint that ruined so many of Amen's signs might have the same source."

He frowned up at me, his angry face looking so unlike the John Luther I'd seen the first day I came to Sugartree. Then again, a sudden memory of this same face going out to confront Toby was eerily similar to his expression now. Could he have killed Toby and somehow framed Quinton? Figuratively killing two birds with one stone—avenging his daughter and making sure that a white stayed in power in the mayor's office.

"And what about this?" I said, setting my plate down and opening my purse. I pulled out the Ping-Pong ball marked with the swastika and tossed it to him. He dropped his fork, trying to catch it. We watched it fall on the ground in front of him. Before anyone could see, he snatched it up and stuck it in his pocket. "What did you think this would accomplish? Pretty pathetic little act of cowardice, John Luther."

The high color in his temples told me I was accurate in my guess. He glanced around, then said in a low voice, "You'd best be gettin' home to California real quick before you regret comin' back to Sugartree."

I gripped my plate, tempted to throw my salad all over him, and looked him straight in the eye. "Your threats don't scare me."

"It's not you who'd get hurt," he said, his round face grim.

His words caused my heart to pound. What was I thinking, sparring with someone with his beliefs? My foolish interfering could put Aunt Garnet and Uncle WW in real danger. I started walking away, then turned back, determined not to let him have the last word.

I bent down so no one else on the porch could hear my words. "John Luther Billings, hear me good. If you or any of whatever lame-ass, red-necked, shotgun-toting goons you hang out with ever harms even one leaf on my aunt and uncle's property or one hair on their heads, I'll hunt you down and cut off your balls myself. And you know I can do it." I stood up and walked away without looking back.

"You okay?" Emory asked me when I went back into the house and put my still-full plate of salad on the table where dirty dishes were stacked. "You look a little flushed."

"I'm fine," I said, tightening my lips. "Just not very hungry."

He raised his eyebrows at me. "I'm the one who's lost the love of his life."

"So cry me the Mississippi River. That's your own dang fault."

He held up his hands in defense. "Hey, quit showing your canines. I'm working on it."

"Work harder," I snapped.

The next course, soup and bread, was at a large blue and white Victorian house three blocks from the Dairy Queen. We had to park across the street and down one block because some of the guests were swifter than we were.

"This is the Watkins's house," I read off Aunt Garnet's list. "He's apparently a lifelong member of Sugartree Baptist and owns the Dairy Queen. He should have asked to do dessert, don't you think?"

Inside the lavishly decorated country-style house, heavy on ruffled curtains and maple furniture, we lined up for a choice of tomato bisque soup, chili, chicken noodle, or twelve-bean. The choices for bread were, naturally, baking powder biscuits or corn bread. I passed on the soup and moved down the line to the bread. Behind the stacks of biscuits and yellow corn bread stood Ricky Don Stevens, Tara's jealous boyfriend. He wore a white full-length chef's apron and held silver tongs.

"Which would you like?" he asked, his tongs poised between the platters of bread.

I pointed to the biscuits, and he put two on a small stoneware plate.

"How'd they rope you into this?" I asked, giving him a friendly smile.

He nodded over at the host and hostess who wore matching western-style shirts in a bright aqua with white piping. "My mom and dad."

"Mr. and Mrs. Watkins are your parents?" I asked.

His young face grimaced just briefly. "Well, she is."

I nodded in understanding. Blended families. Even in a small town like Sugartree, they were probably more common than not.

From the kitchen door, a redheaded woman in a bright pink pantsuit called out, "Ricky Don, there's a fresh batch out of the oven here."

"Yes, ma'am," he called back and handed his tongs to a teenage girl standing next to him. "I'll be right back."

I watched him go into the kitchen and idly wondered again if this young, sweet-faced boy could possibly have worked up a temper enough to beat Toby Hunter to death. The detective said that it was obviously someone who was very angry. That was an understatement. Someone who hit Toby that many times, making mincemeat of the back of his head, was beyond very angry into crazy angry. Maybe an anger that had been simmering away, unrelieved, for a long time. My thoughts went back to my encounter with John Luther. He was still a top suspect in my book—not that my opinion mattered to anyone.

When Ricky Don came back in carrying a steaming platter of biscuits, I tried to think of a casual way to go back over and talk to him, but couldn't. And after my talk with John Luther and the threats he made about my family, it might be better if I didn't.

"He didn't do it," a voice behind me said. I turned to face Mr. Lovelis. He was holding a small, stoneware bowl of chili topped with cheddar cheese.

"What?" I said, caught by surprise.

"The young Stevens boy," he answered. "He didn't do it."

"How do you know that?" I couldn't help asking.

"I just know." He looked down at his chili. The grated cheese had melted in a thick, yellow blob. His gruff voice grew lower. "Best stay out of this ruckus, Miss Benni."

A bit late for that, I thought. Though it wouldn't be my

problem after Monday morning. There'd be two thousand miles between me and this mess. Considering that, I decided to press Mr. Lovelis for more information. "What makes you think Ricky Don didn't kill Toby Hunter?"

He set his bowl of chili down on an early-American maple end table. "He's a good boy. His parents are for the churches merging, and they brought him up to respect life."

"Even good boys can lose their tempers for a moment. Nobody would blame him one bit . . ." I paused and looked down at my biscuits. What I was about to say wasn't true to a certain degree. People would understand why he killed Toby, but the law would demand reparations. He could spend the rest of his life in prison. I glanced over at him as he was pouring soup into the bowls of two elderly black women wearing fancy hats and stockings with seams up the back of their trim legs. They were teasing him about his shaggy blond hair and his tiny gold hoop earring. He took their teasing in stride, smiling with respect and good humor.

Not knowing what else to say, I bit into a hot biscuit. The texture was perfect and the inside soaked with real butter. It almost melted in my mouth.

"Trust in the justice of the Lord," Mr Lovelis said, giving my shoulder a gentle pat before walking away.

I stared after him, not certain exactly what he was trying to say. Did he know who killed Toby? Was it him?

I finished up my biscuit, then went to find Gabe. He was outside on the front lawn, staring up at the night sky.

"See a good star we can wish on?" I asked, looking up with him.

"Just getting some fresh air," he said, putting an arm around my shoulders. I leaned into him, sighing deeply.

"Detecting's hard work," he said, his voice not entirely approving.

I bumped his chest with my shoulder. "Who said I'm detecting?"

"I've been watching you all evening. What have you found out?"

I told him about my encounter with John Luther and my conversation with Mr. Lovelis.

"Well, I've been doing a little detecting myself."

I looked up at him, shocked. "What! Tell me what you found out. Right now."

"While you and John Luther were shooting burning arrows at each other, me and your little Arkansas detective had a nice chat over potato salad and ambrosia."

"About what?"

"He's frustrated because his bosses have told him to back off investigating the Hunter boy's death. He thinks there's a coverup of some kind going on. . . ."

"I knew it!"

"And he wanted my advice about what he should do."

"What did you say?"

Gabe pulled me closer. The warmth of his body heat was more comforting at that moment than anything I could imagine. "To tread carefully. To keep his eyes and ears open and try to discern who he could trust and who he couldn't. I gave him the name of a buddy of mine in the FBI who might be able to help him. A coverup like that could have very serious repercussions. It could put his life in danger, not to mention his family's." He inhaled deeply. "I feel sorry for the kid. Corruption in a department is a hard thing to face when you're as young as he is. Hard to face at any age."

"Did he have any idea about what they're going to do with Quinton? They don't actually have anything but circumstantial evidence, right?"

He nodded. "Yes, but that's enough to screw things up for Amen until after the election, which Detective Brackman thinks is exactly what his bosses intend."

"So the most likely person involved in that is Grady Hunter," I said.

"That'd be my guess."

I shook my head and looked back up at the vast star-filled sky. "It's hard to believe he'd use his own son's death to further his political career. What kind of man does that?"

"An ambitious one."

"So, what can we do?"

"Nothing, *querida*. Absolutely nothing."

At the main meal at Miss DeLora's our choices of lasagna or chicken and broccoli casserole were serenaded by a youth band consisting of three singers, an electric guitar, a keyboard, and drums. They played selections spanning the decades from the twenties to the eighties.

Amen's son, Lawrence, stood behind the chicken casserole dish. A big, solid, shy-eyed young man, he was obviously a favorite with a lot of the church ladies. He took their compliments on his performance in last night's football game in modest stride.

"Hey, Lawrence, do you remember me? Benni Harper. I think you were seven or eight the last time we met. Me and your mama used to play together when we were girls." I held out my hand, and we shook. "I knew your mama when she was half your age."

He gave a shy grin. "Yeah, that's what she says. She says y'all used to really cut up together."

I leaned closer, holding out my plate. "All the really bad things we did were *her* idea. Trust me."

"I'll have to ask her about that," he said, grinning wider.

"Ask her about setting fire to the Winn-Dixie store."

His eyes widened. "You bet I will."

"She's going to kill you," Gabe said. "No parent likes people telling their kids about their wild escapades." He gave a half-smile. "You two set fire to the Winn-Dixie?"

"Only the pile of cardboard boxes in back," I said, laughing. "Firecrackers."

He nodded in understanding.

I stuck close to Gabe as we ate our main dish, staying

away from John Luther and Mr. Lovelis, trying to forget about what the detective had told Gabe. He was right; there was nothing we could do.

"Need any help?" I asked Amen when I took my empty plate back into the kitchen. She was washing dishes, and Miss DeLora was drying.

"Now she asks," Amen said, rolling her eyes at Miss DeLora. "After her stomach's been filled."

"Hey, I grew up in Baptist churches," I replied. "I know you have to get to the front of the feed line or you're SOL."

"What's SOL?" Miss DeLora asked, her face perplexed.

"Sure Outta Luck," Amen said, winking at me. Then she took the drying towel out of Miss DeLora's hands. "Grandma, you go on out and mingle with folks. Benni can help me dry."

"If you're sure," she said, untying her starched cotton apron. She handed it to me. "Here, let me tie you."

After she left, I asked Amen, "Where's Quinton tonight?"

"Told him to stay home, lie low for a while. He's really annoyed about it. Gets started on some big conspiracy theory he claims this is all about. Even Lavanda's getting sick of listening to him, and she thinks he walks on water." She swished a washrag through an iced tea glass, then dipped it in the hot rinse water. "You know, keeping him safe is turning out to be more of a job than running for this stupid office. Sometimes I think I've bit off way more than I can chew without choking to death."

I picked up the glass and started drying. "You know, Quinton might not be far off on his theory. Listen to what Gabe pried out of that young detective they have working on the case." I told her about Detective Brackman's belief about a coverup.

She quietly washed and rinsed glasses as I talked. After

I finished, she took a few moments to answer. "That means Grady would have to be involved."

"It certainly seems that way to me."

She turned to look at me, holding a dripping glass, her face tense. "I don't want that to be true. He's . . . he was my friend."

"I know," I said, taking the glass from her hands and dipping it in the rinse water.

DESSERT WAS NOT a long drive away. Grady Hunter's huge lodge house was lit up bright and inviting when we arrived. It was a house built for entertaining, and he was the consummate gracious host.

The desserts were a sight to behold. Every Southern specialty had been expertly prepared for our partaking— Lemon Chess pie, banana pudding with a perfectly golden brown meringue topping, pecan pie, a gorgeous Lady Baltimore cake, and peach cobbler with real whipped cream.

"I've died and gone to heaven," I said to Elvia, taking a crystal dessert plate and getting in line.

"A small bite of each will satisfy," she lectured behind me.

"Maybe for you," I countered, taking a big spoonful of peach cobbler.

After eating enough to feel justifiably guilty, I wandered around the woodsy living room where Grady and I had sipped tea a few days ago, casually listening to snatches of conversation, most of which revolved around how the Razorbacks were doing this year. I finally settled down on a corner sofa where I could observe the crowd without participating. After my depressing conversation with Gabe and seeing the agony this whole situation was causing Amen, all I truly felt like doing was cowardly flying back home tonight, leaving this whole mess for someone else to clean up. I picked up a *Sugartree Today* magazine and was flipping through the recipes when Grady Hunter's voice interrupted me.

"So, did you get enough to eat?" His smiling face looked down at me.

I set the magazine down. "Sure, everything was great."

"My cook's a truly gifted baker," he said.

"Yes, she is."

Without asking, he sat down next to me on the sofa. "Bet you'll be glad to get back home."

I murmured an affirmative answer.

"When do y'all leave?"

"Monday morning."

"Has your trip been fun?" His face was genial, his eyes steady as a mule's.

"Sure, but it's always good to go home."

"Yes, it is," he agreed. "You know what has become hardest for me now that I'm older? When visitin', I mean."

"What's that?"

"You just can't be yourself, and I find that immensely tiring."

I thought about his comment for a moment, then said, "But isn't that what being a politician is all about?" I felt my face grow warm. Geeze, what a rude thing to say. I basically just accused him and politicians in general of being phonies. Even though I believed it to be true, maybe I'd better buy that new Miss Manners book when I got back to San Celina and memorize it. "I'm sorry," I stammered. "I meant . . ."

He gave a tired, cynical chuckle. "It's all right, I know what you meant. And I agree with you. With this race between me and Amen, I've come to reconsider my desire to be in politics. There's a big part of me that would love to quit and just sit at home and read books on Southern history. That was my major in college, you know. History."

"Then why don't you?"

He shook his head sadly. "Too many favors owed. A lot

of people went to a great deal of trouble to get me here."
He smiled again, his politician's friendly smile. "And I'd
like to think I could make a difference in people's lives."

I crossed my legs and shifted in my seat, trying to think
of something else to say. Though he could provoke sympathy in me, there was something about this man I didn't
trust. Was his little emotional confession a ruse to gain my
sympathy, another politician's game? As cruel as it was, I
decided to hit a nerve.

"Why are you doing this tonight?" I asked.

His face was puzzled. "What do you mean?"

I looked him directly in the eyes. Their deep blue depths
reminded me of a lake I'd seen once in the High Sierras
when I was a girl. Daddy told me the lake had no known
bottom, and that thought fascinated me. We camped there
for three days, and each morning Daddy would find me at
the edge of the lake peering into the water, certain if I
stared down in it long enough, I could prove my dad wrong.

"Your son was killed—murdered—only a week ago.
How can you stand being out in public like this? Hosting
a party?" I watched his face, waiting for a reaction.

Like the practiced politician that he was, his expression
didn't reveal any emotion when confronted with a situation
he didn't control. Then a sadness flowed over his features.
Was is real or manufactured?

"People expect me to carry on," he said, standing up.
"That is what a good leader does. I bear my pain in private."

At that moment, one of Zion Baptist's members, a tall,
walnut-colored man, clapped his hands for our attention.

"Friends, I'm afraid we've some sorrowful news. Our
dear Quinton's been rearrested."

A collective sigh came from the crowd, followed by a
building, angry murmur.

He held up his large hands, and the murmuring softened.
"Please, join me in a prayer for his deliverance."

We bowed our heads, and the room was quiet as the man started praying.

"This is your servant's prayer," the man said, his voice starting soft and pleading, its bass tremor pouring out over us like thick molasses. "Hear us, oh, Lord of Hosts. Hear us and show us your mercy and grace. Your never ending mercy and amazing grace. We thank you. We thank you for your child, Quinton. We thank you for his courage and his heart. We trust your child to You, oh, Father, to You who knit him in his mother's womb. We thank you, Holy God of Israel."

Murmurs of "amen" and "yes, brother" echoed through the rustling crowd.

"We thank you," he continued, "for Quinton and for all who gather in your name tonight. Oh, Jesus, we thank you for our families because they need us; we thank you for our friends because they love us; we thank you for our brothers and sisters in You because they give us comfort, and, Sweet Jesus, we thank you for our enemies because they keep us on our knees looking up to You, looking up to the hills of glory, looking up to the hills from whence came our help. Because you are our help, oh, Holy Spirit . . ."

I sank back deeper into the sofa, knowing from experience that this would be a long prayer. Feeling more than a little guilty, I opened one eye a slit to see how Grady was taking the news.

He was gone. Curiosity prompted me to slip down the hallway and search for him. In his haste, the door to his study had been left open a crack. His angry voice was low but distinct.

"Why in heaven's name did you do that?" he said. He was quiet for a moment as someone on the line was obviously explaining themselves. "Of course he'd carry a gun, you idiot. I would, too, if I were him. Your men had no cause to pull him over except pure harassment. You should have called me first. It was supposed to be a diversionary tactic, not the ruination of some young man's life. Get this straightened out now." He slammed the phone down.

Propelled by some force I couldn't control, I pushed open the door.

His expression of surprise was genuine. I guess he thought no one would think to walk out during the prayer for Quinton. "What the . . . ? How much did you hear?"

"Diversionary tactic, huh? That's pretty low even for a politician. The fact that it's your own son's murder you're using is beyond my capacity to understand." I stared at him a moment. "Does being elected mayor mean that much to you?"

He stared back, his hand still in his pocket, his face hard and unyielding. "There was talk of me running for governor next term."

My eyes widened involuntarily. "Are you saying that since it was a higher office you aspired to, your son, not to mention Quinton Tolliver, were expendable?"

His back stiffened. "My son was a troubled boy. It's . . . better this way."

"For who?"

"There are people I owe. All this"—he swept his hand around the lavish office—"the high-class life Toby enjoyed, the new trucks, the hunting trips, the expensive bass boats, was all made possible by people who expect me to give back. Toby could never understand that."

"Does money mean that much to you?"

His face flashed hard with anger now. "You don't know what it was like growing up here. It hasn't been that easy for me."

My expression of disbelief set him off more than any words I could have said.

He pointed a finger at me. "I am so sick of everyone thinking I've had it easy. You don't know. *No one* knows what it was like."

"Oh, sure," I said, looking around the lavish office. "Poor Grady Hunter, he's really had to suffer. Try that story on one of the people in town who have to eat boxed macaroni and cheese four times a week."

"You don't know," he snapped.

I shrugged. "All I see is a pretty good life here and not much concern about anyone else."

His face grew red. "When my father died, he left my mother and I destitute. The great high and mighty business man, Grady Hunter Senior, so respected in Sugartree, died with five hundred dollars to his name. The shame of it drove my mother into a depression she never came out of. She died before I could . . ." He stopped and inhaled deeply. "Before I could earn it back. It was real touch and go when Toby was small, though we did our best to hide it. The *family name*." He spit out the words. "I promised my mother I would keep the shame of my father in the family. I did whatever it took to restore our family's pride and financial standing. And the people who helped me—well, without them, I'd just be some high school history teacher barely making ends meet."

"And your son would probably be alive."

"I'll make sure Quinton Tolliver is released. He won't suffer for this."

"Is that right?" Gabe said behind me. "That's certainly debatable. I think he's suffered already. But, without a doubt, this second arrest will guarantee your reelection."

We both turned to stare at Gabe. His dark face was a neutral mask. How much had he heard of Grady's diatribe?

"I never meant to hurt Amen," Grady said. "She's . . . she's a friend."

"Yes, Grady, we know all about your friendship," I said. "I saw the picture. I think you just took advantage of her when she was vulnerable."

He licked his lips nervously. "What picture?"

"Oh, for cryin' out loud . . ." I started, but Gabe interrupted me.

"Mayor Hunter," he said, moving in front of me smoothly so that I had to peer out from behind him. At that moment, it occurred to me that Gabe worried about Grady becoming violent. I glanced around. Was there a gun within reach? I didn't see one.

"Mayor Hunter," he said again, his voice easy, non-threatening. "What happened with your son?"

Grady's face turned pale. For a moment he couldn't speak. Then he stuttered, "I . . . he . . . Chief Ortiz, you know someone killed my son."

"Mayor Hunter," Gabe repeated yet again. "What happened with your son?"

He swallowed hard. "I told you, someone killed him."

Gabe moved a step closer, his voice still steady and insistent. "Mayor Hunter, *what happened with your son?*"

He didn't answer this time but stared over Gabe's shoulder at the painting on the study's wall. It was of the old mill down in Little Rock. The opening scene in *Gone With the Wind*.

"Mayor Hunter." Gabe's voice became softer. "What happened with your son?"

"My father used to take me to that old mill," Grady said, his voice jerky. He raised a trembling hand to his mouth. "He liked to stand and watch it. Sometimes we'd stand there for hours and watch it. He knew every stone and patch of moss. He loved that movie. Said Rhett Butler was a man's man."

"Mayor Hunter," Gabe said. "You need to tell me what happened with your son."

He continued staring at the painting. "My son was a troubled boy. Right from the beginning. He was a troubled boy."

"But you tried to help him." Gabe's voice was deceptively gentle.

Grady moved his eyes from the painting to Gabe's face. In that instant, his face seemed to drop, and the sharp, handsome features seemed to blur, as if we were seeing a picture shot through cheesecloth.

"Chief Ortiz," he said, "people depend on me. You know how that is."

Gabe nodded. "Yes, but sometimes, even though people depend on us, we have to do what is right."

He shook his head slowly. "Sometimes you start out right, and things . . . pile up. People come at you and ask and ask . . ." The words caught in his throat. "People depend on me," he repeated. "I can't let them down. It's important that I don't let them down."

"It's more important to do what is right," Gabe said.

Grady's jaw set stubbornly. From where I stood I could see his throat flex. "I have many important friends."

"You can't avoid this," Gabe said. "Now that you're a suspect, your whole life will be an open book. I've already given a name of an FBI contact to one of Sugartree's detectives. There will be an investigation."

"I didn't do anything," he insisted.

"What happened with your son?" Gabe asked again.

"I told you," Grady snapped. He was visibly breathing harder now. "*Someone* killed him. Someone killed my boy."

"What happened with your son?"

"I told you . . ."

"What happened with your son?"

Grady swore, his fist clenched involuntarily. "I've had just about enough of this, Mr. Ortiz."

I noticed that he took away Gabe's official title. That little change told me that Gabe's interrogation was wearing him down.

"Mayor Grady," Gabe said, "you killed your son."

I gasped softly, surprised Gabe would say it outright. Was he trying to shock Grady into confessing? Would it work?

Grady started rubbing his hands. His eyes darted behind Gabe's back to the door.

"Close the door, Benni," Gabe said.

I swiftly did what he said. The murmur from the crowded living room became muted.

"Mayor Hunter, the FBI will tear the Sugartree police department apart. Whatever it is you and the police chief have going will be exposed. It's over."

"He's an old friend," Grady said stiffly. "I asked him out of respect for my feelings not to investigate too deeply into my son's death, that it was too upsetting to me. He did nothing wrong. I assured him it was one of Toby's marginal friends, the result of an argument. I didn't want him to harass Quinton. I did everything I could to keep that from happening."

"Mayor Hunter," Gabe said, "aren't you tired of all this? Don't you want it to be over?" His voice sounded kind, understanding.

Grady wilted slightly. "Yes, I am tired."

"Tell me what happened with your son. I have a son, so I know how boys can be. Sometimes they can push you and push you until you can't take it anymore."

"He was trouble from the beginning," Grady said, his voice a whisper.

Gabe moved a step closer. He was within hand-shaking distance now. "Grady," he said, using the mayor's first name. "Grady, what happened with your son? If you killed your son, you have to confess. God can't forgive you if you don't confess."

I looked at my husband in surprise. God was not someone whose name he invoked thoughtlessly. And, I was sure, in most interrogations, an experienced criminal would scoff at such a blatantly manipulative statement.

And Grady Hunter was, without doubt, an experienced criminal, but he was also a grieving father and a man raised in the church, a man who'd wandered deeper into the abyss than he'd ever thought possible.

"It's all up to you," Gabe said. "No one can make that

decision but you. Your soul depends on it." He sounded for, all the world, like the revival preachers I'd grown up hearing every summer of my life.

"You find the suspect's weakness and play it," I remember him saying once about interrogating people. "Most people show their vulnerable spot five minutes after you meet them, if you know what to look for."

Grady choked back a deep-throated sob, but wouldn't answer.

"You need to decide right now," Gabe said, his voice insistent. "There's not much time left."

Grady stared at him and wouldn't answer.

"You need to decide," Gabe repeated, unrelenting. "You need to take responsibility. You *know* this, Grady. You know this. It's over. Just let other people take care of things now. It's over."

Grady's eyes welled up, and he looked straight at Gabe. "He was going to blackmail me with that picture. He was disgusted that I would kiss a black woman. It was that group he was in . . . He was a sweet boy, really he was. He used to love to help his mother make baskets for the poor. I don't know what happened to him . . . Those boys he hung around . . ."

"Grady." Gabe closed the distance between them and put a hand on his shoulder.

"God have mercy on me," Grady said, his voice wet and choked. He brought a hand to his face, covering it. "I killed my only son."

We were all silent for a moment. The air seemed thick and warm in the spacious study. In the background, we could hear talking, an occasional laugh, no one aware of the momentous act taking place a few feet away.

"How?" Gabe asked softly.

Grady kept his eyes focused on Gabe's expressionless face. "I didn't mean to kill him. I didn't mean to kill him, I just wanted him to shut up, to go along with the program.

He taunted me, called me a nigger-loving fool. He was drunk and he wouldn't shut up . . ." His hand fell away. "So I picked up a piece of wood and hit him once. Then I couldn't stop. I was out of my mind with anger. Oh, God help me, I couldn't stop. I loved my son, but he wouldn't shut up. He just wouldn't *shut up*." His head dropped, and he started sobbing. The horrible sound of his grief filled the beautiful room.

"You need to tell the police," Gabe said. "You need to put this to rest."

"Yes," Grady whispered. "Rest."

Then he looked back at Gabe. "Chief Ortiz, will you kindly escort me down to the police station?"

Gabe took a deep breath and nodded. "Yes, sir, I will."

Epilogue

THE NEXT DAY, at the Sunday morning church service, the story of Grady's confession was the talk of the church. More than a few people turned and stared when Gabe, Elvia, and I walked into the crowded sanctuary. It was obvious it had gotten around that Gabe was the one who'd convinced their beloved mayor to confess to murdering his son. From some of the people's openly hostile expressions, it wasn't something they'd be congratulating him for. I gripped his arm, squeezing it in support. I was proud of my husband and stared boldly back at the angry faces, daring them to say a thing.

But there were just as many smiles and looks of approval as we walked down the aisle to a middle pew where Amen, her son, Lawrence, and Quinton slid down so we could join them. After Gabe accompanied Mayor Hunter to the police station last night, I took Amen aside and told her what had just happened. For the first time in my life, I saw Amen Harriet Tolliver cry.

"What a fool I was," she said, wiping her streaming eyes with the sleeve of her pale yellow blouse.

"No, you were a vulnerable woman who was grieving for her husband. You were just being *human*."

She smiled through her tears. "Thank that handsome husband of yours for me."

"I will, but it would be better if you did."

"Oh, I will, don't you worry. And *thank you*. For not giving up."

I leaned over and hugged her. "No problem. Want my Sugartree Hornet sweatshirt, too?"

She laughed as she hugged me back. "I don't want any part of that ratty old sweatshirt, girl. I want a brand-new one."

"I'll send you one from the San Celina Police Department."

"And I'll wear it with pride."

When I sat down next to Amen in the pew, she reached over and grabbed my hand, squeezing it hard. Her palm was warm and damp. Her dark eyes were shiny with tears.

"Thank you," Quinton said, looking first at Gabe, then at me.

We both nodded our acknowledgement.

Before the sermon started, Brother Woodward, Sugartree Baptist's current pastor, took the pulpit and said, "Though this is unconventional, we've decided to hold the vote for the church merger this morning. We figured this was the time when the most members would be present. Considering the sensitive nature of this subject, we've also decided a written vote would be the most harmonious. A ballot is in your program. If you are a member of this church, please fill it out with your vote and put it in the collection plate. The results will be announced after the sermon."

The sermon, a joint effort by both Brother Woodward and Brother Folkes, was naturally about forgiveness, tolerance, and how Christians should be the first to be willing to change, to accept strangers in their midst, not the last. Glancing around at the faces of the people, I imagined I saw more expressions of agreement than dissent, but then, as Gabe so often accuses me, maybe I was just seeing what I wanted to see.

Emory was sitting up front with Miss DeLora and Uncle Boone. I watched the back of my cousin's blond head and wondered if he had anything planned for today. There was still the dinner-on-the-grounds this afternoon and the all-day singing. If he had a plan, it better be implemented soon since our plane left at nine A.M. tomorrow.

The choir sang one more medley of gospel songs, and then Brother Woodward returned to the pulpit.

"Our closing scripture will be read by Emory Littleton, after which the results of the vote will be announced. Then we will all partake with great joy of the feast the kind ladies of both churches have prepared for us and continue to praise the Lord for the rest of the day." He nodded at Emory.

Emory, looking like a picture from an Aramis cologne ad, stood and walked up the steps to the pulpit. His navy suit, white dress shirt, and deep maroon tie were absolutely perfect. He looked over the audience, spied us in the middle row, and trained his eyes directly on Elvia. Next to me, I sensed her tensing. I slipped my arm through Gabe's and waited to see what my cousin would read.

"My text this morning," he said in his smooth as caramel drawl, "is the book of Ruth, chapter 1, verses 16 and 17. May we all be blessed with the kind of loyalty and faith the widow Ruth felt toward her mother-in-law, Naomi, who was giving her permission to leave her and go back to her people." He opened the Bible in front of him.

Bible pages softly rustled in the congregation as people searched for the verse. He spoke without looking down at the Bible, having obviously memorized the words. His eyes never left Elvia's face.

" 'Entreat me not to leave you or to return from follow-ing you; for where you go, I will go, and where you lodge,

I will lodge; your people shall be my people, your God my God; where you die, I will die, and there I will be buried. May the Lord do so to me and more also if even death parts me from you.' "

He continued to stare at Elvia whose face was frozen. The room was as still and quiet as the center of a tornado.

He slowly closed the Bible and said, "Please, Elvia Marisol Aragon, marry me."

"*Muy cojones*," Gabe murmured.

There was a long, silent moment. Elvia took my hand. I squeezed it. Whatever she decided, I tried to tell her with my touch, would be okay. I would still love her and be her friend.

She slowly nodded yes, and Emory's face broke into a smile that I could see held relief as much as joy. The church broke out into loud applause, and Emory came down the aisle and took his place next to Elvia. Over her head, he caught my eye and winked.

"Well," Brother Woodward said when he returned to the pulpit, "that will certainly help make this a day to remember." His smile quickly turned to a sober expression. "Now, I have the results of the vote. There's no use draggin' it out, but apparently neither church is ready for this step. The decision to merge lost by twenty-three votes. Let us pray in the spirit of Christian fellowship and for a reconciliation. As the Lord himself says, 'Do not be discouraged. In this world you will have much tribulation, but fear not, I have overcome the world.' "

Before he could pray, a voice rang out of the audience. A very familiar grating voice that had spent more than its time on earth nagging at me and Emory.

"For heaven's blessed sakes, what is *wrong* with you people?"

We all turned to look at Aunt Garnet, who stood up, her pale, rice-powdered face indignant. Next to her, Dove's eyes widened with surprise.

"Muy cojones," I murmured this time.

"If we don't merge, both churches will die. And we'll deserve to. The most important thing is what God wants us to do. Can you imagine Him wanting any of his churches to fade away?"

"Garnet," a male voice behind her said, "the vote's done already been taken. You'd best let it go."

At that, my own dear gramma stood up, linked her arm through her younger sister's, and said, "Garnet's right as rain on this, and y'all better listen to her. I move we take another vote."

"I second that motion," Miss DeLora called out.

A round of voices called out their approval.

"Third it."

"Fourth it."

"Another vote! Let's take another vote!"

Now I didn't think that Emory's little drama could be upstaged, but if any two people could do it, it was the Mosely sisters. Next to me, Gabe chuckled. I jabbed my elbow into his side.

"Hey," he said, with a soft groan. "You have to admit, only in your family . . ."

The unexpected and unprecedented uniting of the Mosely girls on *any* subject was worthy of consideration, and with the congregation so worked up, the deacons and two pastors had a quick meeting up front and decided to let the people vote one more time. As pieces of paper were passed out, scribbled on and then collected, the choir sang another round of gospel songs.

After the votes were tallied, Brother Folkes stood in front of the congregation, clutching his large black Bible as if it were a shield. He glanced over at Dove and Aunt Garnet, gave them a nod and smile, then said, "The votes have been retaken. I'm sorry to say the motion to merge the churches still lost by eighteen votes." He cast Dove and Aunt Garnet an apologetic look.

"That's okay, baby sister," Dove said, her arm still linked with Garnet's. She patted the top of her sister's hand. "We convinced five of 'em. There's still hope."

"And on that note," the pastor replied, "let us bless the food and eat."

AFTER EMORY'S IMPASSIONED proposal in the church, he and Elvia started planning an early-spring wedding. I, of course, was asked to be matron of honor, a role in my best girlfriend's life I thought I would never play. She swore to me the bridesmaid dress would flatter me. She promised there'd be no chiffon or large hats. I told her I'd wear a gunny sack and dance down the aisle barefoot if that would assure me that she and Emory would become man and wife.

We settled on gray silk.

Amen dropped from the election shortly after Grady Hunter's arrest when her car was fire-bombed outside of a Burger King on the edge of town. Lawrence had just stepped out of it moments before.

"I'll try politics again when he's away at college," she said. No one could blame her. She worked on the campaign of a sociology professor who'd been one of her supporters on the city council. He ran against a conservative businessman who had many of the same ties to big business as Grady Hunter's. The sociology professor won by a very small margin of votes.

"It's a start," she said.

Amen and Duck were married by a justice of the peace a month after we returned to San Celina. That wasn't good enough for Miss DeLora. So they were married again by Brother Woodward and Brother Folkes in Sugartree's sanctuary.

"You're double-married," I told her when I called to give my congratulations. "Just like me and Gabe. And now you two can legally feed among the lilies."

"Thank God for good ole Solomon," she replied, laughing.

Dove and Aunt Garnet were in harmony for that one glorious moment in church, but peace with the Mosely girls was not meant to be. When they got home that night, they commenced to arguing about what their daddy's favorite vegetable was—corn or peas. Since there was no way possible to verify his preference, it is still being argued to this day. They hugged the next day before Dove and Isaac left for their drive home to California, but they weren't speaking.

"Ain't family grand?" Uncle WW said, grinning around his pipe.

The church merger never happened, though a group of people from both churches meet two Saturday nights a month in various houses, singing songs of praise and praying for healing among the races. Sugartree Baptist did co-sign a loan for Zion Baptist to buy a lot over by the Dairy Queen. Together the two congregations are planning to build Zion Baptist a church.

As Amen would say, it's a start.

Isaac published a photograph series in *Oxford American* magazine depicting Amen's short career in politics. The series brought a lot of attention to the causes Amen was concerned about, and a clearinghouse for charities in Little Rock offered her a job. She's in charge of hundreds of thousands of charity dollars, deciding where they should go, how they would best be used. She is, as they say, in Razorback heaven.

On the day they got back to San Celina, Isaac surprised Dove with a one-carat diamond ring. She called me in a panic, not knowing what to do.

"Marry him," I said in between bites of an apple.

"Well, I believe I will," she replied. So it looks like there'll be two weddings come springtime.

As for me and Gabe, we're still going strong. Working,

arguing, making up, still looking for the perfect house, being in love. As Uncle WW would say, just living this grand ole life as God intended.

And, I guess, in the end that's really what it's all about, isn't it?

Note from Author

THERE ACTUALLY WAS a quilt competition sponsored by Sears, Roebuck and Company during the 1933 Chicago World's Fair. The theme for the fair and the contest was "A Century of Progress," since Chicago was also celebrating its one hundredth birthday. The contest remains to this day the largest quilt competition ever held. Almost 25,000 women entered quilts, hoping to win the twelve-hundred dollar prize and bonus, a cash amount that was greater than the 1933 annual income of an average family.

The winning quilt was initially called "Unknown Star" and later "Star of the Bluegrass." It was entered by Margaret Rogers Caden of Lexington, Kentucky. The quilt was presented after the fair to Eleanor Roosevelt, and no records of the quilt exist after 1934. Because laws concerning presidential gifts had not yet been passed, Mrs. Roosevelt was free to give it away, something she was known to do with White House gifts. Its whereabouts remains one of the unsolved mysteries of the quilt world.

Grateful acknowledgment is given to the book *Patchwork Souvenirs of the 1933 World's Fair,* written by Mer-

ikay Waldvogel and Barbara Brackman. If you would like
to read more about the winning quilts and the stories behind
them, I highly recommend this excellent and fascinating
work.

FOR MORE INFORMATION about Earlene Fowler, her ap-
pearances, San Celina, quilts, and future Benni Harper ad-
ventures, please visit her website:

http://www.earlenefowler.com

And now
a preview of

Steps to the Altar

the next Benni Harper Mystery
by Earlene Fowler

I WAS AFRAID to move.

One unlucky stumble or shift in weight and it appeared to me that I could bring Miss Christine's whole knickknack-filled teahouse down around my mud-caked boots.

As much as I loved Miss Christine, a former Vegas show girl who was rumored to have once been a mobster's girl-friend, only one thing could entice me into this garden of girlish delight. Too many clichés flitted through my mind: fish out of water, square peg in a round hole, and the most appropriate, the infamous bull in a china shop.

But it was this or having my best friend, Elvia Aragon's, wedding shower, a shower I'd waited to give since we were both second graders trading my pimento-cheese sandwiches for her homemade burritos, in my own cramped Spanish-style bungalow. I wasn't the only one who'd waited a good many years for this momentous event. When the shower's guest list hit forty, I started panicking. After moaning about the problem to my friend, Amanda Landry, expert quilter and pro bono attorney for the Josiah Sinclair Folk Art Museum, where I was curator and head bottle washer, she suggested I rent Miss Christine's Tea and Sympathy Parlor for the whole afternoon and let someone else do most of the work.

Relieved, I jumped at her advice and called two weeks ago. Thanks to Miss Christine, most of the preparations were ready to go and we were in the final phase—selecting the menu. Amanda, a good ole Southern girl raised by a rich society mama in Alabama, was having the time of her life.

"I'd forgotten how fun showers are," she said, giving me her wide, white-as-new-cotton grin. Anticipation brightened her smooth-cheeked, ivory complexion as she peered toward the kitchen where Miss Christine and her chef, José, were working on sample trays of sandwiches, scones, and other teatime treats.

Trying to avoid what could be a small but very costly disaster, I carefully crossed my legs, resting my ankle on the knee of my slightly grimy Wranglers. I'd forgotten how crowded this place was with English china, silver, and Victorian geegaws. I'd come straight from the ranch, where I'd helped Daddy and Sam, my stepson, stack a ton of hay bales. My shoulders, unused these last few years to the manual labor, were already starting to ache. At that moment a couple of aspirin washed down with a Coke sounded more appetizing to me than chicken salad sandwiches.

"I still think A. J. Spurs Restaurant would have been better," I grumbled.

"Sure, if we were wanting steak sandwiches for you and a bunch of your ranch women friends at a Cattlewomen's luncheon," Amanda said, flipping back her thick, auburn hair. "But this is *Elvia* we're talking about. She's waited a good long while for this wedding shower. I'll bet she's attended a lakeful of them in her thirty-five years on this earth and it's payback time, babydoll."

I sighed and said, "You're right. If anyone deserves the best, it's Elvia. I'm just always afraid I'm going to trip and break a million dollars' worth of china in these places."

Amanda laughed. "This isn't Tiffany's and I promise I'll pay for whatever you break."

I was picking at a piece of oat hay stuck in my jeans when Miss Christine, wearing a dress that appeared to be made of a hundred black-and-red silk scarves, came floating out of the kitchen followed by a short, thick-chested Hispanic man in a spotless white chef's coat. He carried an ornate silver tray the size of a tractor seat.

"Ladies, thank you so much for being patient," Miss Christine said. "I can assure you, it will be worth the wait. My José is a genius with petit fours and his honey-walnut scones." She rolled kohl-lined green eyes and fanned herself with elegant fingers that seemed to be made to dangle an ivory cigarette holder between their crimson tips. "Paradise on your tongues."

The sober-faced, middle-aged man set the tray on the linen-covered table in front of us. Amanda and Miss Christine sighed simultaneously as they surveyed the tiny, crustless sandwiches and other colorful treats.

Turning my head slightly, I peeked at José's hand, trying to see if the rumors were true. Yep, there it was. SC 13 tattooed in dark green between his thumb and forefinger. Gabe had told me that the chef here was once quite high in one of our local gangs. He'd gone to prison for armed robbery, studied there in a special program under a San Francisco pastry chef, and recently emerged from incarceration with a skill much more in demand than driving a getaway car. Somehow, Miss Christine managed to snag him out from under the five other gourmet restaurants vying for his prestigious talents.

He saw where I was looking and gave me an amused wink. I felt my face grow warm and pretended intense interest in the food he'd prepared. My identity as the police chief's wife here in San Celina, a medium-sized college and retirement town on the Central Coast of California, was not much of a secret, even though I didn't look like the typical police chief's wife. I did my best, wearing dresses whenever appropriate and making small talk at political shindigs and charity events, but my heart just wasn't in it. I was a country girl, reluctantly moved to town by the death of my first husband and the loss of our ranch a few years back. I still managed to get out to my gramma Dove and Daddy's ranch a few times a week, but my life these days included more afternoons punching computer keys down at the folk art museum than punching cattle. Not to mention, as my beloved second husband would point out, getting way too involved in the criminal affairs of San Celina County.

Or how my cousin Emory, Elvia's fiancée and a journalist with the *San Celina Tribune*, would most likely say in his sexy, Arkansas drawl, sticking my snout where it shouldn't be sticking. It did me no good to insist that all the homicides I'd been involved with were only because I happened to be unlucky enough to be in the crime's vicinity.

"That's okay, sweetcakes," Emory had said a few days ago, his even-featured, handsome face giving me a loopy grin. These days, drunk on the idea of finally achieving his life's dream, marrying Elvia, every expression he wore looked a bit goofy and amazed. "Without you, the chief's life would be incredibly pedestrian."

I gave a decidedly unladylike snort. "I'll remember to mention that the next time I get involved in a murder. *Not* that there's going to be a next time."

"Pay attention, cowgirl," Amanda said, smacking my knee. A tiny puff of chaff dust exploded and she waved it away like unwanted cigarette smoke. "What do you think of watercress, chicken salad, cucumber, and this lovely nutty-tasting spread for the sandwiches?"

I popped one of the crustless, star-shaped sandwiches in my mouth. It tasted like walnuts, mayonnaise, grape, and some other flavors I couldn't put my finger on. "It's all okay with me, though I vote thumbs-down on the watercress."

"Why?" Miss Christine and José blurted out simultaneously. The hurt look on José's craggy face made me instantly explain.

"It's not the sandwiches. I'm sure they're wonderful. It's just that watercress and I have a tumultuous history." I didn't want to go into detail about the first homicide I'd become involved with, the incident where Gabe and I met. Right before I discovered the body, I'd eaten watercress sandwiches at one of Elvia's book-signing events at her store, Blind Harry's. Later that night, I'd retasted the watercress in a not-so-pleasant manner. "Really, the watercress is fine."

José's face softened in relief. Miss Christine straightened her spine and asked, "What about everything else?"

I glanced over the pastel-colored cakes and cookies and tiny scones and croissants. "It's all perfect. I think we should have a bit of everything you have here. Enough for forty, no make that forty-five people. What do you think, Amanda?"

She popped another strawberry-and-cream-filled minia-ture croissant in her mouth. "I agree. And we'll have Lady Grey tea and a lovely mint lemonade."

"Very good," Miss Christine said. "We'll see you all here this Sunday afternoon then."

"Wearing clean boots and underwear," I said.

Amanda kicked me under the table, grinning as she did. "I wish I could have inflicted you on my dear sweet mama before she passed on to that great tea party in the sky. She so loved a challenge."

José laughed out loud, a masculine rumble that was wonderfully at odds with the ultrafeminine decor. Miss Christine bestowed upon me a tentative, but brave smile, not quite certain if I was joking.

Outside the tea parlor, Amanda asked, "What about the cake?"

"Ordered it a week ago," I said. "I'm dropping by Stern's Bakery with the check this afternoon. I need to talk with Sally about Dove's shower cake. This is not the only shower meeting I had on my schedule today, you know. I'm due at the historical museum in"—I checked my dependable Daffy Duck watch—"an hour to discuss Dove's wedding shower."

My gramma, who had raised me since I was six years old when my mother died of cancer, had, after some thirty-odd years of widowhood, decided to get married. Her fiancée, the world-renowned photographer Isaac Lyons, had entered our lives a year and a half ago when he'd come to San Celina to investigate his granddaughter's mysterious death. He and I solved the case and in the process he fell head-over-bootheels in love with my gramma. A man of impeccable taste if you wanted my unbiased opinion.

"That is so great," Amanda said, leaning against one of San Celina's black wrought iron lampposts. They were decorated on this cool, February morning with emerald green, royal purple, and bright gold streamers advertising this week's Mardi Gras festivities. "Dove gettin' married at seventy-seven after all those years being a widow. How's your daddy takin' it? Is he feelin' threatened by Isaac becomin' his stepdaddy?"

"Are you kidding? He is so thrilled to have someone *else* getting all Dove's attention and nagging he's been telling his cronies down at the Farm Supply that he's got the shotgun loaded in case Isaac tries to back out."

Amanda gave a delighted laugh. "Not much chance of that, I'll just bet. Isaac is downright besotted, far as I can see."

"Yeah, he and Emory could be January and February for a Men Crazy in Love calendar."

"Where're Dove and Isaac plannin' on living?"

"Out at the ranch. It's got four bedrooms and three bathrooms. Daddy says one more place at the table sure doesn't bother him."

"Have they set a date?" Amanda asked.

"Tentatively. It's after Elvia's for sure. Dove's thinking three weeks."

"Are you involved in the planning?"

I shook my head no. "Trying not to be. She hasn't decided yet what kind of wedding she wants and she's been driving me crazy with her suggestions. She wants it to be memorable, she says. Since Isaac's been married five times, she wants this one to stand out."

As if on cue, my new cell phone rang. "Happy Trails" reverberated from deep inside my leather backpack, and it took a few minutes for me to find the phone and answer it.

"Yes? Hello?" I said in that loud tin-cans-tied-with-a-string voice that none of us seems to be able to stop using with cell phones.

"Medieval," Dove yelled back at me. She must have been using her new cell phone too. "I could wear one of them pointy hats like Maid Marian. Make Mac dress up like Friar Tuck. We could serve chicken and fruit and eat it with our hands."

"That would certainly save on dishwashing," I said noncommittedly. However this wedding of hers and Isaac's turned out, I was determined not to be the person blamed for any mishaps, so I was agreeing with everything.

"Think I could talk your daddy into wearing tights?"

I held back my laughter. "Uh . . . if anyone could, you could." Not unless he'd just drunk a gallon of moonshine, I was actually thinking.

"I don't know," she yelled. "I don't look that great in pointy hats. Call you later." The phone went dead.

"What's the news?" Amanda's face was curious. Being an only child, she envied the complications my extended family brought into my life.

"I think we just narrowly missed a Robin Hood wedding."

"I loved Kevin Costner in that movie no matter what anyone said."

"Well, Dove doesn't look good in pointy hats."

"Who does?"

We hugged, said our goodbyes, and agreed to meet at Miss Christine's this Sunday an hour before the shower to set out the party favors and do a little decorating. Amanda, bless her Martha Stewart heart, was planning all the shower games. All I had to do was buy the prizes and my own shower gift for Elvia. That meant a trip to Angelina's Attic, a local lingerie store.

February was one of my favorite months in San Celina. The air was cool and clean-tasting, like water from a deep, rock-lined well. Cal Poly students had lost the frenetic gotta-try-it-all edge they sported at the beginning of the school year and hadn't yet acquired the end-of-the-year hysteria that would come in a few months. Except for the tinge of excitement brought on by the coming Mardi Gras festival and parade that San Celina proudly touted as being the biggest ones west of the Mississippi, the town had a calm, peaceful air to its tree-lined streets. I walked down Lopez Street toward Stern's Bakery, my mind wandering, thinking about the blissful time a month from now when both Elvia and Dove's weddings were over and life was back to normal.

At Stern's Hometown Bakery, a jingle of sleigh bells announced my entry into the almond-scented place. Sally, a handsome, white-haired woman who'd owned the bakery since I was a kindergartner, sat at a round glass-topped table thumbing through a photograph album of cakes with two older ladies. She lifted up a finger to let me know she'd be with me in a moment. I poured a cup of their strong dark coffee, picked a cherry-topped cookie from the tray of freebies, and sat down in a white wicker chair.

After Sally had taken the ladies' order and pressed upon them a free half dozen of her famous poppy seed cookies, she poured herself a cup of coffee and joined me.

"Hello, Mrs. Chief-of-Police," she said. "How're the dual shower plans progressing?"

"Just came from Miss Christine's Tea and Sympathy," I said. "It was brilliant of Amanda to suggest letting someone else do all the work. All I have to do is buy the prizes, Elvia's shower present, and write a check. And speaking of checks, that's why I'm here." I pulled my checkbook and a copy of the bakery bill out of my backpack. "I want to settle up my accounts for both cakes so I can mark one more thing off my list."

"I'm always amenable to accepting money," she said, tucking a strand of loose hair back into her bun. "The cakes will be ready when you are. Sunday and Wednesday, right?"

"Right. I'll pick up Elvia's cake about ten A.M. Sunday and Dove's about noon on Wednesday." I handed her the check.

"So, are you about ready to go nuts?" she asked, taking the check and standing up. "Want some more coffee?"

"No, thanks, I'll just have to find a bathroom, and from what I hear, the one over at the historical museum has been on the blink."

"What's going on over at the museum?" she asked, walking behind the counter and punching the keys to the cash register.

"Final preparations for Dove's shower."

"She is one brave woman, getting married again after all these years. How's she holding up?"

I grinned. "*She's* doing fine. Now Isaac . . ."

Sally laughed. "He should be used to it. Hasn't he been married a few times?"

"Five, to be exact. But *never* to a Ramsey woman."

Sally nodded, her pink cheeks shiny under the bright fluorescent light. "He needs to consult with the chief."

"Not if we can help it," I said, laughing. "We want this marriage to take place."

"Well, I'm so happy for both Dove and Elvia. I'll be at both showers."

"See you then." I snagged one more cookie and headed toward the historical museum.

The San Celina County Historical Museum was located one street over from Lopez Street in the old brick Carnegie Library building. As a child, before they built the new library out by Laguna Lake, I'd spent many long, lazy afternoons here in the children's department reading Curious George and Big Red books. When I was fifteen years old, I received

my first kiss under the olive tree on the patio from Jack
Harper, my late first husband who'd died in a car wreck three
years ago this month. Walking under the stone archway into
the old library never ceased to fill me with a sweet, sad
longing for times past. When the building came to house the
historical remnants of San Celina County and its citizens, I'd
spent even more endless afternoons as an adult helping Dove
catalog and organize donated items. As a thirty-year member
of the historical society, she knew every piece of clothing,
jewelry, tools, and needlework by heart.

Inside the cool entry hall, I spotted June Rae Gates, one
of Dove's oldest friends, behind the gift shop counter.

"Hi, June Rae," I said. "Everyone present and accounted
for?"

"Yes, ma'am," she said, locking the cash register and slipping the key in the pocket of her wraparound denim skirt.
She taped a hand-printed sign to the register that stated if
anyone wanted to buy something, to come find her at the
back of the museum. "We need to make it quick because
Elmo's cat has an appointment for a CAT scan and my college helper canceled out on me. I think she has a new boyfriend."

"His cat is getting a CAT scan?" I couldn't stop the giggle
that fell from my lips.

She patted her peppery hair. "I know, it does sound funny.
The poor thing's got arthritis so bad it can barely walk. I
don't think a CAT scan will show much but that it's as old
as the rest of us, but Elmo'd sell his new Cadillac for Inkspot."

I nodded, feeling sympathy for Elmo. I'd probably be just
as insistent when it came to my dog, Scout, a chocolate Lab–
German shepherd mix. I followed her toward the circle of
folding chairs. The rest of the Dove Ramsey Wedding
Shower Committee was already in place, munching away on
some of Maria Ramirez's chocolate cinnamon cookies. I
grabbed one with pink icing and slid into an empty chair.
The air was a sugary mixture of lavender- and magnolia-
scented colognes, the bitter scent of store brand coffee, and
the dusty, comfortable smell of a building that had survived
two World Wars and more than a few broken hearts.

After a brief report by all the members, we agreed that everything was on schedule and ready to go. June Rae went back up to the counter and I was standing around the coffeepot listening to Elmo Ritter's diatribe about the sad state of veterinary medicine (he'd been through four vets looking for the one who could give him the impossible—the fountain of youth for Inkspot) when Edna McClun, another of Dove's friends, grabbed my forearm and exclaimed, "You're just the person I was looking for!"

Why is it those words never fail to fill me with trepidation?

My response was automatic. "I didn't do it and I didn't see a thing."

"Oh, you," she said, patting my shoulder lightly. "You're such a card. Seriously, I have something I think you'll really be interested in."

Another statement warning me there was work involved.

I contemplated my half-eaten cookie, then looked back at her cajoling smile and said, "Okay, I'll bite."

"You know I'm on the committee to restore the Sullivan house."

"No, I didn't," I said, popping the rest of the cookie in my mouth, figuring I'd need the carbohydrates for whatever task she was wanting me to take on.

"Have you been reading about it in the historical society newsletter?"

"Yes, and congratulations on finally getting it declared an historical landmark." The Sullivan house, a Queen Anne Victorian on the far edge of San Celina's city limits, had been in a state of decay as long as I could remember. I had vague memories of someone saying the Sullivan family had died out and the house was repossessed for back taxes. I also vaguely remembered buying raffle tickets for a quilt made to raise funds to buy the property. I assumed the historical society must have succeeded when I read a few months back about the house being declared an historical landmark. On the property there was also another unusual structure, an octagonal barn, one of only two in California.

"Acquiring it wasn't easy, but generations to come will be glad we did," she continued. "The Sullivans were a very prominent family in San Celina County during the early part of the century. Arthur Sullivan and his son, Garvey, owned many of the best grain fields and the largest beef cattle herd in the county. They were also smart enough to build huge grain storage silos in the thirties, which they rented out to other farmers during the war when the farmers had to switch from bags to bulk because the government needed the jute for the war effort. The Sullivans also owned a good bit of downtown and were very involved with the building of Camp Riley up near San Miguel."

I glanced at my watch. Though normally I enjoyed hearing oral history from someone who'd lived during that time, I had a lunch date with Gabe in fifteen minutes. "So, what are you trying to rope me into doing, Edna? You know I've got a pretty full plate these days so it can't take too much time."

"Oh, it's something you can do at your leisure. It's about Maple Bennett Sullivan."

The name sounded familiar but I couldn't put my finger on how. "Maple Bennett Sullivan?"

"I'm sure you must have heard about the tragedy with her and her husband, Garvey."

I shrugged. The history of this county was rife with nefarious shenanigans usually involving land ownership, cattle rustling, and water rights. Every old family had its share of misfortune and sad stories. "Can't recall anything offhand."

"I don't see how you can't remember this one, my dear. It's right up your alley." Her watery blue eyes twinkled behind her round plastic eyeglasses.

"Why's that?"

"She murdered her husband, my dear girl."

National bestselling author
EARLENE FOWLER

Sunshine
and Shadow

**Spirited ex-cowgirl, quilter, and folk-art expert
Benni Harper is investigating the connection
between her favorite author, the murder of a
family friend, and a crazy quilt.
When she starts receiving strange phone calls
and anonymous letters telling her she'll be the
next victim, Benni's interest in the case
becomes even more urgent.**

"BEGUILING...INGENIOUS."
—*PUBLISHERS WEEKLY* (STARRED REVIEW)

"WARMHEARTED." —*BOOKLIST*

**Available wherever books are sold or
to order call 1-800-788-6262**

PC002

A Benni Harper Mystery

EARLENE FOWLER

National Bestselling Author of *Sunshine and Shadow*

Dis Ranch

BROKEN DISHES

Agatha Award-Winning Series

0-425-19597-X

EARLENE FOWLER

The Agatha Award-winning series featuring
Benni Harper, curator of San Celina's folk art museum
and amateur sleuth